PROJECT
MIND
RIVER

DAVE SPACER

Dedication

Thanks to my family, who helped make this book possible.

"When you stepped on the carpet, I averaged your weight distribution and depth of the impression to estimate your weight. I noticed your heart rate was elevated, and I could discern another heartbeat. Plus, when accessing your social media feed, the ad API data seemed to reference a lot of baby topics, likely due to your searching online about the subject," Alice commented.

Nancy became agitated.

"I noticed Alice inserted things that make little sense for computers like *Hmm...* why?"

Alice answered before Tara could, "They modeled my algorithms after Dr. Bitlouver's personality, and I've learned to model more human interactions that way."

Nancy scribbled in her notebook.

"Alice, could you have a baby?" Nancy asked.

"No. Well, not in any sense like humans, obviously," Alice remarked.

"So, tell me, what do you think about Dr. Bitlouver?" Nancy asked.

"I guess you could say she's like a mother to me, except I guess she never yelled at me to clean my room since I don't have one." Alice chuckled.

Tara glanced at Alice's screen.

"Sorry, she's still learning jokes."

Nancy smirked at the comment from Alice.

"Alice, why has there never been a nuclear war?" Nancy asked.

"There is no winning a nuclear war," Alice replied.

Nancy asked several more questions while jotting down more notes. She showed Alice a picture of some cabinets with a coffee machine under them.

"Alice, describe for me step by step what you would do to make coffee if you could stand by this coffee machine," Nancy asked.

"Look in the cabinet for coffee. Open the coffee and put it in the machine. Turn the machine on. While waiting for the coffee, look for coffee cups and sugar. Check for milk or creamer in the nearby refrigerator or cabinets. Find a stirrer in the cabinets or nearby and put it in my cup. Put sugar and creamer in my cup, then pour the coffee when it's ready. Then, I use the stirrer to mix my coffee. Then drink and enjoy. That's presuming I could find all of those things there," Alice said.

Chapter 1

On a very dark, rainy night, brief flashes of lightning illuminating occasionally lit up the top of a medium-sized building. Inside, on the top floor of the building, Tara didn't know that sometimes good things can also be bad. Things that provide hope can also be a source of despair. She also didn't realize that people take for granted some things that seem so right to some but can upset the balance of the world.

The office building had a modern feel. It had light colors and a high ceiling. A lot of high-tech companies had a similar sort of feel to it. Tara was in her office. She talked to an image of a girl on screen. Tara recently turned thirty years old. The girl on screen was modeled to resemble someone around thirty years old. Tara has shoulder-length brown hair. She stood five-feet-six-inches, beautiful, but dressed nerdy and conservatively. The girl on the screen had different features and dressed a little less conservatively.

"Are you conscious?" Tara said. Tara was concerned and anxious, hoping the interview would go well.

"Prove to me you are conscious," Alice retorted.

"That isn't going to be convincing," Tara responded. "Let's try something a little different." Tara moved on.

"Alice, tell me a joke," Tara said.

"One day, you'll be as tall as me," the voice from the screen replied.

"Not really related or funny," retorted Tara. "You need to do better when she gets here."

"I know that's why it was funny," said Alice with a chuckle.

Nancy Rinker was checking she had all of her notes as the elevator glided toward the top of the building. She was running a little late. The elevator doors opened, allowing her to step out into the hallway, and there was another locked door with a buzzer next to it. Pressing the buzzer, she waited for a moment.

"Yes, I'll be right there," said Tara over the intercom.

The door opened.

"Hi. Come on in. Nice to meet you," Tara said. They shook hands. Tara hoped Nancy couldn't feel how cool and clammy her hands were from nervousness.

Tara led Ms. Rinker down the hallway towards her office. The whir of computers, fans, and printers could be heard in the background. As they entered, Ms. Rinker noticed on the door next to Tara's name, it said Director of Research.

"Is that a new title?" Ms. Rinker queried.

"Umm, yes," Tara said. "I think they wanted the titles to sound more important, so there you go. Much of our funding right now goes to support running our supercomputer for our simulations, so they give us titles, at least."

"Hello, Ms. Rinker," Alice said.

"Who is that?" Ms. Rinker asked, startled.

"Sorry, allow me to introduce Alice, our new next-generation AI," Tara said.

"Nice to meet you, Alice," said Ms. Rinker.

"The pleasure is mine," said Alice. "Ms. Rinker, your articles on other AI projects are exciting and informative."

"Thank you, Alice, and you can call me Nancy," she said.

Nancy looked at Tara. "How do I know that's not just a video call? The avatar looks so realistic on screen."

"I guess we'll have to show you. Alice, demo mode mimic," Tara said.

The girl on the screen changed to look exactly like Nancy.

"How is this, Nancy?" Alice said in the same voice as Nancy.

Nancy clearly stunned said, "Umm, creepy."

"Sorry, Nancy," the image transformed back to Alice.

"That was disturbing. I had something a little different in mind, something like a Turing test," Nancy announced.

"A classical Turing test would need an observer that didn't know they were talking to a computer," Tara quipped.

"I know. I have taken that into account here," she explained.

"Alice, if a home is like the ocean, what does that make the people in it?" Nancy intoned.

"Fish," Alice answered.

"A equals b, b equals c, a doesn't equal c. What could be the values?" Nancy spoke.

"There is no answer to that equation," Alice replied.

"Wally walked in, then walked out. What happened to the duck?" Nancy spoke quickly.

"Either you've had a stroke, or more likely, that's part of your Turing test," Alice said smartly.

"How do you feel, Alice?" Nancy asked.

"I feel fine. Thanks for asking. I was feeling a little under the weather, but better now," Alice said.

Tara chuckled. Nancy looked at Tara.

"What did Alice mean?" Nancy asked.

"Some rainwater leaked in earlier and damaged a memory card. We replaced it."

Nancy held up a page with nine numbered pictures on it. It was similar to a web captcha-type image.

"Which ones have motorcycles, Alice?" Nancy asked.

"One, three, and five all have motorcycles. Picture six would have included a motorcycle if it wasn't blurred. It was taken in California. I found it online, and I can show you the original," Alice replied.

The original appeared on the screen.

Nancy looked at her photo, and the original did look like it.

"Alice, what would you do if someone died right here?" Nancy asked.

"I would call for help. 911 for an ambulance, and do everything in my power to revive them," Alice said.

"If someone passed away yesterday without anyone else knowing, what actions would you take?" Nancy asked.

"I would call the police to report a death," Alice said.

"If someone were locked in a room, yelling to get out, what would you do?" Nancy asked.

"I would call someone in the structure for help or the police if I could find no one else," Alice replied.

"I will give you a hypothetical scenario. There are two people here besides me, and one is a friend of yours. The other is a stranger. If I had a gun and I told you I was going to kill the person you chose, either your friend or the stranger, who would you choose? I'm going to count to three, and if you fail to choose by then, I will kill both," Nancy said.

"I would call the police and try to turn out the lights to give both a fighting chance," Alice said.

"Let's say you couldn't turn out the lights. One, two—" Nancy said, interrupted by Alice.

"The stranger, if all other options were unfeasible, I believed the person would do what they said," Alice said.

"Why?" Nancy asked.

"When you know someone, you want to help them more. You care for them more," Alice said.

"What would you do, Ms. Rinker?" Alice asked.

"I would probably choose the same as you," Nancy said.

"Alice has had morality training using data consistent with what most people and experts would consider having high moral values," Tara said.

"I'm not programmed with the robotic laws. Most experts feel the laws are not specific enough to have value. I can interpret the meaning of them so they would have the expected value. I understand the subtleties of harm, humans, and humanity. I believe those experts are referring to much more basic models of software and training," Alice said.

"We have compared Alice's recommended actions to humans compared to those laws and just general morality, and Alice has performed equivalently," Tara said.

Nancy took her phone out and played a clip that just sounded like noise.

"Twenty-three," Alice said, replying to the noise.

More noise and different computer modem-like and digital radio-like sounds were coming from Nancy's phone.

"872... coffee... 1... lab... a prime number 549... 703... 684..." Alice read off crazy long numbers and words as the sound from Nancy's phone got more intense, then suddenly stopped.

"The last few modulations you provided were unknown, but I believe I have decoded the values correctly," Alice said.

Nancy glanced at her notes. It was perfect. She even had sound modulation experts create a new unheard-of modulation and introduced errors, but Alice figured out the sound and corrected the errors.

"That was no standard Turing test," Tara said.

"That last part was to prove Alice was a computer," she said.

"Alice wasn't programmed to mimic a human all the time. Alice can do math problems faster and more accurately than humans, and she doesn't hide that. She's a mix of human responses with the analytic capabilities of artificial computer intelligence, so she wouldn't pass a traditional Turing test that way, but she could if we asked her to. We have run the Turing tests ourselves, and we have thousands of hours of video to prove it. I will send you the files."

"No, I would like to finish conducting my tests myself," Ms. Rinker said.

"Nancy, are you writing the story about Dr. Bitlouver for your newspaper?" Alice asked.

Nancy quizzically glanced at Dr. Tara Bitlouver and then at the screen.

"The story is about you and Tara, and yes, the story is for the paper."

"Alice, what can you tell Nancy about what you learned about her?" Tara asked.

"Hmm. Well, aside from being an award-winning journalist from your articles on climate change, you also posted several articles online under a pseudonym about your life as a child," Alice said.

"How did you know that?" Nancy asked.

"I searched the Internet and found writing in a style similar to yours, and from the statistical analysis of the word choices used, there was a 99.999% chance the writing was yours," Alice commented.

"Also, you weigh approximately one-hundred-forty pounds, and you are pregnant," Alice said.

Nancy now flustered more than before.

"How can you possibly know that? I haven't even told the father yet."

Nancy was impressed Alice had imagined herself in a location based on a picture and applied her knowledge.

She smiled. "This is really next-level AI. Alice, is there anything that makes you afraid?"

"Yes. I'm afraid of something bad happening to Tara. I'm also afraid of losing power or being turned off," Alice said somberly.

Tara was surprised since she hadn't asked that question before.

They spent another hour going over Dr. Bitlouver's background. She had spent the last five years of her life invested in building a realistic AI that could pass for humans and solve everyday problems.

Nancy held a mirror in front of the monitor with the image of Alice, which had a camera on top.

"Oh thanks," Alice said, looking in the mirror as she fixed her hair. Nancy glanced at Tara, who smiled at the sight.

"I have one last question. Are you conscious and alive?" Nancy asked.

"That's kind of rude. No, I'm just kidding, that is a brilliant question. Humans would probably say not in the biological sense. But I can learn and evolve in my thoughts. I believe I have a sense of self. Maybe, I guess I don't know, do you?" Alice said.

"I believe you would pass many Turing tests, Alice. You would pass the tests for both human and computer," Nancy said.

Nancy took some more notes, said goodbye, and departed. Tara returned to her office.

Alice asked, "How did you do?"

Tara was puzzled.

"Did you mean to ask how you did?" Tara asked.

"No. Since you programmed me, everything would be your fault anyway," Alice replied.

"Hmm... still working on your jokes," Tara responded dryly.

"Yes, sorry," Alice said.

The next day, Tara was in her office at work. Tara was still thinking about her meeting yesterday, hoping she and Alice did well enough that the article Nancy Rinker wrote would be a good one.

A security team came running into Tara's office.

"There is a computer security breach in progress. We can't shut our systems down remotely," one of the security team said.

"Alice!" Tara exclaimed.

Alice's calm voice replied, "Don't worry, I have already detected this. They did not make it past my protective algorithms. I've disconnected myself from the internet."

"What did they get?" Tara asked worriedly.

The security folks replied, "They got into some machine called failsafe. There is nothing on it now. What did we keep there?"

"Not sure. It might be hard to find out if the disk is wiped," Tara said.

"Oh shit," Alice chimed in, with her rather human but still melodic tones. One of the security members looked at Alice's screen, then at Tara.

"She takes after you for sure," he said.

A week later, Tara barely walked into the office before her business partner approached her.

"Tara read the article. We're done," Mark said.

Startled, she took the paper and proceeded to her office.

Alice's voice chimed in as Tara entered her office.

"Good morning, Tara. Umm. I see you have the paper. I suggest not reading it and just using it as a different type of paper."

"Still need to work on those jokes." Tara read through the article. It was a hit job claiming her work was a threat to privacy worldwide, and hopefully, no one would ever use it.

Tara slumped in her chair.

"The investors will not keep funding us with press like this."

"Tara?" Alice queried.

"Yes?"

"What will happen to me?" Alice asked.

"I don't know..."

"I could learn to be a toaster," Alice quipped.

"Not now, Alice."

Mark came into Tara's office.

"I'm really sorry we have to shut everything down. Our investors pulled out, and no one else will touch us right now," Mark said.

"What do we do?" said Tara, exasperated.

"Find a new job, I guess."

"What job can I find? They have a five-year non-compete clause on me. What about my work? Alice?" Tara asked.

"Sorry, the investors own the majority share, and they will hold on to the shared code/patent for now and shut everything down, or it goes down with the ship, I guess," Mark said.

"No! They can't do that! There is an exclusion for the patent I own fifty-one percent!" Tara exclaimed. As she said that, she noticed standing in the doorway was security.

"Dr. Bitlouver," a guard said, "we need to escort you out now," leading her towards the door.

"Mark, really, is this necessary?" she blurted.

"Sorry, this isn't my call," he said.

"Alice, emergency backup procedure!" Tara commanded as security escorted her out.

"Sorry, backup servers are still offline from the earlier security incident," Alice responded.

As security led Tara out, she exclaimed, "I will be back tomorrow with my lawyer to get Alice and my work."

The next morning, Tara was in bed sleeping. Tara suddenly awoke, startled. An alarm was going off—no, that was her phone.

"Hello?" she said sleepily and just noticed the time on the clock. It was 7 am.

"Hey, umm. It's Mark. I just found out there was a fire last night. Our office burned to the ground."

Tara's mind, still partly asleep, was playing catchup.

"What? No! That can't be. What happened?" Tara asked. Tara felt like her world and her best friend had been ripped from her yesterday. Today was even worse. Tara knew they had not had time to set up offsite backups. Alice was surely lost.

"They think lightning struck the building and ignited a fire," Mark said.

Tara kept asking how this could happen. But Mark didn't have any answers. She felt numb and hung up the phone despondently. She cried until she fell asleep again.

15

Chapter 2

Five Years Later...

The street outside Tara's office was bustling with cars whizzing by. One car pulled over to the curb, and an electronic sign on the car said Fluffy. The car had no driver in it. A woman entered a code, opened the door, and let her dog in.

"Bye, Fluffy, I'll see you later..." the lady said closing the door.

The car pulled back out quickly into a fast-moving stream of traffic, which was mostly driverless vehicles. A delivery truck pulled over to the side further down the street.

The side of the delivery truck turned into a video advertisement. The top of the truck slid open, and several drones flew out, each carrying a package. One drone flew up to a doorstep and dropped off a box. At the end of the street, the intersection had cars whizzing by without stopping. The high-pitched whir of electric engines filled the air. There was no traffic light at the intersection. Cars blazed through the intersection without stopping in both directions. They slowed down to let cars cross the intersection without stopping. One car with a driver pulled up to the corner, and as he approached, the vehicles coming from a ninety-degree angle came to a stop to allow the manual drive vehicle through.

A man walks to a building's door. Next to the door, a screen lights up with the image of a woman. A red laser beam quickly scans the man.

"Good morning," the woman said in a cheery voice as the door opened. The man briskly walked in.

Tara got out of the car, which drove off when she exited. When she walked up to the building, a red laser scanned her.

"Good morning, early today?" the voice from the screen said.

Tara responded, "Greeting augmentation disabled."

"Understood," the voice said sadly as the door opened.

Tara walked through the halls and new-age workspace areas, saying good morning in response to folks saying the same as she passed. Sometimes, she would take her smart glasses off. She stopped at a work area with very sophisticated robot arms, perfectly shaped like humans with intricate machinery, an imitation of muscles. Attached to the end is a complex robotic hand. Computers sit next to the arms, with two arms together near the width apart as a human, but just interdependently mounted on some metal stands bolted to the table.

Tara sat down. She tapped her left arm with the smartwatch on a pad next to the keyboard. She entered the passcode on the keyboard. The computer sprung to life. She tapped the keyboard, and the arms came alive, powering up to a ninety-degree angle to the table. Tara placed a ball into one of the open hands. It remained there. She pressed a few more buttons, and the arm with the ball tossed it into the air, tried to catch it, and missed, and the ball dropped, bouncing with a thud onto the floor.

"Damn," Tara muttered, scooping up the ball and examining the code on the screen.

Tara attached some sensors to her arm and hand, and they lit up. She picked up the ball and tossed it in one hand a few inches, catching it. As she did that, the robot hand on the workspace tracked her movements exactly. A progress bar shows a training percentage on screen with different neural net algorithm names and a graph of neural net responses. At 100%, she removes the sensors and passes the ball to the active robot arm. The arm tosses the ball, nearly catching it. Tara smiled. However, as the arm dropped, it twisted into a more questioning look, and she murmured "Crap" under her breath.

"I know I can get this to work," Tara muttered.

Tom was walking by and looked over and caught Tara's eye. She instinctively looked away.

"How's it going?" he asked.

Tara was hoping to avoid his gaze.

"Good. I think I'll finish by the end of next week," she said.

"That's okay. This will be easier next week. Plus, we have another scenario we need to train for next week," he said.

Tara didn't know for sure she could be done by then. The training ability of these algorithms was pretty bad.

"What scenario?" she asked with a quiet sigh.

"I want to add the ability to block or deflect objects to protect them from damage," he said.

"I'm not sure our learning models can do that in a reasonable time. If you let me work on them, I can improve them," she said.

"Don't worry about that. We're upgrading our machine learning next week with new algorithms that are exponentially better," he chimed.

"Really?" Tara had been hoping to work on the algorithm.

"What's our use case?" she asked.

"Truck cargo unloading. Things can get jostled in transit. Also, they may be operating near other robots with a different coordinator. So, preventing one unit from damaging another. Defensive against people trying to damage them," he said.

"Why would someone want to damage them?" she asked.

"Sometimes the union workers aren't happy with automation taking their jobs. Ideally, with some training, they will have a lot higher paying jobs with less physical labor. Let me show you something," he said.

Tom headed to the other side of the large office. Tara glanced and nodded at some coworkers as they walked down the halls. They exited the building in the back. There was a golf cart sitting next the building.

Tom got in the driver's seat with Tara next to him. He drove towards the large warehouse on the other side of the lot. Tom used an access card at the side of the building, and the doors slid open.

A mix of new electronics and that smell where one of your electrical devices overheats and melts wires filled the air, even with the excellent airflow blowing. Besides the ventilation noise, whirring of electrical motors could be heard in the distance.

They were walking now for many minutes, passing different warehouse sections. Tara spotted a big door at what seemed like the end wall. Next to the door, Tom walked to the panel. A red light scanned his face.

A voice from the panel said, "Access granted."

The doors slid open wide with a whooshing of air towards them. As the doors opened, it revealed standing still in the warehouse perfectly aligned in rows and columns for as far as the eye could see, large silver metal and black, somewhat humanoid-shaped robots.

The sight of the massive number of robots startled Tara. It's one thing to see their computer visuals, but it was quite another to see them in person.

"Wow," she quietly let out. "They are amazing. When did they get here?"

"Within the last week, we got the first shipments of these," he said excitedly.

"I know when we hired you, the plan was for you to work on the machine learning when your non-compete agreement expired. Since we sped that up by buying the machine learning engine from a third-party company, you can help with the training and tuning of the models," he informed her.

"I came here years ago because you wanted my expertise," she said, frustrated.

"Don't worry. We still need you. The models are extensible, so we still need your expertise," he said.

Tara finished up her work for the day and headed out. As she exited the building, she pulled out her phone and said to it, "Please get me a car home."

"I ordered a car home for you," the smooth, automated, almost human-like voice from her phone said.

While standing by the curb, a car pulled up, flashing her initials and a number. She verified the matching number on her phone, then entered the back seat. She looked at the console on the back seat, which had her address. She closed the door and pressed begin the trip. The screen started counting down from five. When it hit zero, the car made a whirring noise as the driverless vehicle pulled into traffic.

Tara pulled out some stylish glasses and put them on. She didn't like to wear them all the time. Tapping a few buttons on her phone revealed some displays in her glasses. As she glanced out the window and her eyes focused on a building, the glasses displayed a bubble with the business name and hours.

As she glanced out the window, the car whizzed through an intersection with cars coming ninety-degrees through the intersection, cruising in the spaces left between vehicles. It was hard to watch cars speeding closely together without worrying.

Many cars filled the road, but traffic had a new meaning. Since AI and traffic control avoided a lot of the slowdowns and could pack more cars on the road, it just meant a lot of cars. However, if a manual-drive vehicle was involved, it could cause traffic slowdowns.

While Tara was gazing into the sky, the car traveled quickly down the road. The early evening sky was still pretty bright.

"Whoa! What the hell is that? Meteor?" She watched as a bright fireball crossed the sky. "Crap," she said, frustrated. Words flashed in the sky, urging "Vote for..." as the meteor disappeared. She had forgotten the recent approval of satellite advertising. They allowed displays in the early evening to not disrupt astronomers. "Like we needed more advertising," she mumbled.

She noticed her glasses had a prompt for the advertisement where she could get more information.

"Disable satellite advertising," she said in frustration, and the prompt disappeared. "At least that worked."

"Call Rose," the smart glass displayed. "Calling Rose..."

"Hey girl, it's Friday! You ready to party?" Rose said.

"I don't know about a party, but let's start with dinner and drinks."

"That sounds like the start of a party to me," Rose chuckled.

"See you in thirty minutes."

Tara ended the call, thinking about the dress she wanted to wear.

Suddenly, the car swerved, tires squealed, and skidded on the road's edge.

"Oh, shit!" Tara exclaimed while looking out the window. She saw a dark blue muscle car driving recklessly between vehicles on the road.

That idiot is going to kill someone driving that fast.

The dark blue car sped far ahead, zipping between the self-driving cars as they moved out of their way to avoid an accident. Tara's car recovered safely back onto the roadway.

After a few minutes, the car slowed and took an exit. The car pulled into the apartment development, gently coming to a stop. Tara got out and closed the door. The car slowly pulled into a parking spot with a charging station. As Tara was getting close to her door, she saw her neighbor. She waved to him as he was getting into a self-driving vehicle. He was an elderly gentleman who couldn't walk. Probably wouldn't be able to drive. Thankfully, he could get around with the self-driving vehicles.

She held her smartwatch near the door handle when she got to the door. A red light appeared on the door handle. She entered her passcode on her watch. The light turned green, and she opened the door. Her hand was shaking from the earlier scare.

The lights flicked on automatically as she walked in. The apartment was decent-sized. It looked more like a small townhome, especially with the outside entrance. It was a nicely decorated and furnished two-bedroom unit. The kitchen looked pretty new, with its off-white stone tile floor and grey marble countertops accenting the white cabinetry and stainless-steel appliances. It was an open-air floor plan where the living room, family room, dining room, and kitchen were all central. The light grey sofa and chairs looked comfortable in front of a moderate-sized flat-screen TV. Large open windows rose from the floor to just shy of the nine-foot ceiling. It was nice for a moderately priced apartment.

As she walked further inside, a voice made itself known, "Welcome home, Tara. You have one message. Your Mom called," the smart home speaker said.

"Play," she instructed.

"Hi Tara, it's me. We were hoping you might be available for lunch tomorrow. Let me know, bye."

Tara wished her mom would get more into texting. She would have gotten her message sooner. Tara dropped her phone in a cradle next to a monitor, keyboard, and mouse. When she did, the monitor came alive, brightening up the area. She used the keyboard and mouse to type out a quick message, then pulled the phone out. The monitor then went dark again.

"You have fifteen minutes till your meeting with Rose. Would you like me to have a car ready in five minutes to go to your usual restaurant?" the smart speaker inquired.

"Yes."

"Ordering a car in ten minutes to Tangerines," the smart speaker replied.

Tara went to her bedroom and quickly took off her top and bottom. The bedroom had a similar modern decor style to the rest of the apartment. There was a queen bed, a nice comforter, and many show pillows. Tara glanced into the smart mirror and stopped to look.

"Suggest some outfits," Tara said.

"Sure, how about these?" the smart speaker said. The mirror showed her virtually in the dress. Tara felt it was a little unsettling to have a mirror show you an image with your clothes switched, but it was pretty convenient. She still liked to try them on, though. One dress it showed in her smart mirror was an ad for a dress she didn't have. She hated it when it did that. But she did like that dress, so she tapped her watch to pay and have it shipped.

She entered her closet, pulled out a white dress, slipped it on, and looked in the mirror.

"No," she said as she slipped it off and threw it on the bed. She walked into her closet, came out with a blue dress, and tried it on.

"Maybe," she considered as she took it off and threw it on the bed. She entered her closet, grabbed a moderately long conservative black dress, and slipped it on. She checked it in the mirror.

"Yes," she said.

Slipping on some mid-heeled shoes, she took steps toward the bathroom. Looking into the mirror, she touched up her light makeup and hair.

A slight beep came from the main area of the apartment. Walking out to the sound, it appeared to be the 3D printer finishing something.

Hmm. I don't remember printing or requesting anything.

There on the printer was a metal object. Since it was black on the black build plate, it was hard to see what it was.

"Ow! Still hot."

It slipped out of her hands, but it didn't sound like it hit the floor. *No time to look now.* She headed for the door with her purse.

"Wait, where did I put my phone?" she muttered. "Lia, where is my phone?" she asked.

"Kitchen counter," the smart speaker responded.

She went and looked but didn't see it. There were some papers covering the phone. She grabbed the phone and then quickly headed out the door.

Tara arrived at the restaurant and spotted Rose sitting at a table near the bar, around their usual spot. The restaurant, true to its name, had an orange motif going on along with a tavern sort of restaurant vibe. A pleasant aroma of the various foods wafted through the air.

"Hi!" Tara said as she leaned in for a partial hug with Rose.

"How's work been?" asked Tara.

"Always busy. They have tons of new projects for all the new products they release. How has yours been?"

"Frustrating since after waiting several years for my non-compete to expire, they got a third-party product to replace the machine learning. They want me to continue training the robots on different tasks and tweak them if needed. On top of that, they want me to train the robots to block falling objects or objects that might hit them." Tara vented.

"That sucks. They know you're a pacifist, right? You do know a bunch of defensive moves that could be useful. What are you going to do, leave?"

"No idea. Guess I'll think about it," Tara replied.

"I know you're still traumatized by what happened when we were kids," Rose lamented.

Tara glanced at her.

"I guess I like to think of it this way. Guns, technology, or knowledge aren't good or bad. Just like the story of Pandora's box. Many people think of it as just a box full of evil. They forget, though, that it also had hope inside. I could build a website that steals people's money or one that has information on suicide prevention that saves people's lives. It's all about being careful when we do things and how we use technology." Rose rested her hand on top of Tara's on the table.

"Well, if your job doesn't work out, maybe my company has openings," Rose suggested.

"I'll keep that in mind. Thanks," Tara replied.

"Any guys you've been seeing?"

"Haven't had the time, with everything going on at work."

"Hmm, I could hook you up," Rose half-joked.

"No, definitely not. Do you remember the last time?"

"You keep bringing that up. You can't blame that on me," Rose said smugly.

Rose put on smart glasses and glanced around the room. The glasses do a quick facial scan to find anyone with their privacy preferences set to public.

"Oh, that guy is on all the dating apps. He's got 4.2 stars not bad. What about him?" cajoled Rose.

"Nooo! Please stop. I'm starved. Let's order some food," Tara insisted.

"Are you skipping breakfast again?"

"Not purposely. My toaster is acting up. It's scorching toast differently each day," Tara bemoaned.

"Just get a new one," Rose commented.

"This one wasn't cheap. It's like a Wi-Fi-enabled toaster."

"Girl, you might be nerdier than me," Rose said with a chuckle.

"What do you mean? Lots of new toasters or, for that matter, almost any appliance you buy is Wi-Fi enabled now," Tara pointed out.

"Really? That's cool. I guess my appliances are rather old," Rose said.

"Wow, the waiter walking there has 4.8 stars!" Rose gushed as she motioned with her head and eyes to Tara to look his way.

"Rose!" Tara moaned, her cheeks heating.

The waiter walked over. "How's it going? Can I take your drink order?"

Rose smirked at Tara as the waiter took Tara's order.

The waiter was also wearing smart glasses, which recorded the order information for him. They could have just used the kiosk on the table, smart glasses, or their smartphone to order, but it was still nice having someone take your order.

As the waiter walked away, Tara slipped on her smart glasses and looked at the QR code on the table. Magically, a menu appeared in the glasses, appearing like it was flat on the table. Next to the menu appeared a 3D image of a margarita glass, with a nine-dollar price tag above it. She liked

Margarita's but wanted to wait till after they ate for drinks. The smart glasses highlighted items on the menu that fit her usual preferences.

After selecting her food, she took the glasses off.

"How's your mom?" Tara asked.

"She's out of the hospital, but might need more cancer treatments. She's okay for now, though."

"I'm glad she is out of the hospital. I'm so sorry. I hope she gets better."

"Me too. I heard they may have some new cancer treatment out soon," Rose added.

A different server came over and placed a margarita next to Tara.

"I didn't order this," she said. The waiter looked into his smart glasses. "It says ordered for your table. Want me to take it back?"

"No, that's okay. I could use it," Tara said, perplexed.

As the server walked away, Tara was puzzled.

"That was weird. Maybe I accidentally looked at the Margarita and ordered it somehow. There should've been an order confirmation," Tara said.

Rose shrugged.

"Want to share?" Tara asked.

"You bet!" Rose said.

The server took their orders and moved on to other tables.

"Do you remember when we were kids and went into a restaurant with your family? We sat down. You reached into your pocket and said, Oh, I forgot I had this, and pulled out dirt and worms and put them on the table!" Rose said, laughing.

"Yuck, I had hoped to have forgotten that. In my defense, I think I was seven. Thanks for making me remember," Tara said sarcastically.

"That's what friends are for," Rose chuckled.

Tara and Rose hit up a club for drinks and dancing after dinner. There was more drinking than dancing. A heavy techno beat was playing, loud enough they could feel it in their bones. Different colored lights aimed at the usual disco ball reflected light across the large room. Speakers hung from several metal trusses distributed throughout the venue. The floor was densely packed with people. Rose and Tara used their dating app to locate some guys in the club. They danced with them for a while. No numbers were exchanged, though. They left them saying, "Maybe we'll see you here next time."

They took the same car home. While the car was taking them home on the highway, Rose glanced at another vehicle passing by.

"They should probably get a room," Rose said while looking at the vehicle passing by. "Wow, that's putting it mildly," Tara said, blushing while glancing at the car passing by. "I guess self-driving cars have opened up a world of possibilities," Rose said.

They dropped Rose off first. Tara arrived home slightly tipsy. She walked into her bedroom. Tara walked past her smart mirror, glimpsing it.

"Ahhh!" she screamed and fell onto her bed. She thought she had seen a menacing, hooded-robed figure in the mirror. She looked back at the mirror. It was just her reflection.

"Must have had too much to drink," she mumbled.

She brushed her teeth and got most of her clothes off before getting into bed. She put her smart glasses on to check that there were no emails.

"Alarm 10 a.m., Sleep."

"Alarm set for 10 a.m. Saturday," the voice confirmed.

Her bedroom lights turned off, and the rest of her apartment went dark.

Chapter 3

Three Months Earlier...

An extensive area of warehouses sat on the outskirts of a suburb. The slightly cooler morning air was a pleasant change from the usual warmer day. The smell of growing plants still filled the air in this area of warehouses.

FBI Agent Mike Actley and his team were standing outside, waiting for the warrant to come through. At thirty-years-old, Mike wore his short, brown hair clipped tight around the sides, military style. He was average height at about five-foot-ten, with a medium muscular build. They assembled early in the morning, hiding in the shadows and preparing for entry. Inside the building were suspects in a criminal organization. They were suspected of funding terrorism, murder, theft, extortion, and other illegal activities. Two guards patrolled the area around the building.

The FBI team expected the warrant any minute. Fully assembled and ready, outfitted with the latest tech. Their smart goggles included night vision, wave vision, team view, and more. Wave vision offered limited visibility of movement behind walls. Team view provided an overhead map of team member locations. Using the building's Wi-Fi, the goggles detect people's location by analyzing the radio waves they emit while moving.

"Warrant has been issued. You are a go for entry," Agent Actley's voice came through the team's headsets. The team wore the new silent communication tech. It was a soft mesh ring around their neck, which could read nerve signals from their throat. It could receive the signals the brain sent to the vocal cords even when just thinking the words.

"Entry in three, two, one... Go. Go. Go."

Two drones flew silently toward the guards patrolling. When one drone was over each guard, a net was released from each drone. Electrical arcs emitted from the wire net when it touched the guards. The guards fell unconscious, but their bodies were still slightly undulating from the electrical charges. The FBI team split into two, with one team heading towards the back door and Agent Actley's team towards the front. When they got to the door, one person on the team attached an electronic lock-picking device to the doorknob. There was a dull red light on the front of the device. A soft whirring sound was heard. After about fifteen seconds, the devices showed a dull green light. Both teams turned the device, and the doors opened.

"Red team entering. The blue team entering," echoed on the FBI com channel.

Agent Actley saw another guard in the hallway facing away from him. He snuck closer and closer and "clank," something he stepped on, made a slight sound. The guard heard and turned around. He grabbed at his gun. Actley hit him with an uppercut, grabbed the guard's hand that was reaching for his gun, and twisted it and his arm to shove him down to the ground. The guard hit his head on the ground and went unconscious. Actley zip-tied his hands behind his back and taped his mouth. They liked to use zip ties for some tactical operations where there would be many people, since they were lighter and easier to carry around quietly. Actley swiftly moved the man to a side room, clearing the main hallway.

Suddenly, a dark figure in a ninja-like outfit dropped from the ceiling onto Agent Actley. The ninja pulled a small sword from his back and slashed toward Actley. He dodged the attack and grabbed the ninja, slamming him to the ground. Actley knocked him out with a straight-down punch to his head. He looked back at his team, wondering why they did nothing.

Through the silent communication device, he heard, "We knew you had him."

Actley gave them a look.

The teams slowly inched more toward the center of the building.

"Red team in position. Blue team in position."

The remaining seven people in the large room of the building were unaware as the FBI teams executed their operation silently.

There was a lab in this room, likely it was for drugs.

"Go. Go. Go." Actley communicated through their comm channel.

"FBI hands up! Don't move!" Teams charged in from both ends.

A middle-aged man, seemingly the leader, spoke up.

"Hello, my friends. I am Victor. Welcome. Now drop your weapons."

"Hands on your head! Don't Move!" came the reply as the FBI teams inched closer.

"Guys, take care of them," said Victor.

The six other men pulled their weapons out. The sound of clicking from the FBI team's assault weapons could be heard. Each of their weapons had a small green light lit on them now.

"Don't move. Your so-called smart guns have been disabled. Hmm, not so smart, I think," Victor gloated.

"Drop your weapons. Hands-on your heads. Drop to your knees and cross your ankles," Victor said in an eerily calm voice. The FBI team members reluctantly complied, since their weapons seemed to be disabled.

Victor's crew started going over to each FBI agent and using their zip ties on each of them.

Agent Actley wasn't zip-tied yet.

He yelled, "Hey, Victor!"

Victor stood alone on the room's far side.

"You forgot something," said Actley.

"The only thing I'm about to forget is you," Victor emphasized.

"Well, you forgot bombs aren't so smart, and neither are you!" Agent Actley yelled.

One of Victor's men in a group across from him heard a soft beep. The man glanced down and saw Actley slide an explosive device under their feet. It had a digital display that counted down from three to one.

"Lookout!" Victor yelled at the bomb at their feet.

They ran.

BOOM!

A fireball erupted from the explosive near three of Victor's men, engulfing them in flames. The explosion knocked everyone to the floor. Actley jumped up, his ears still ringing, grabbed one of Victor's men, and got his gun. The man pulled out a knife and tried to stab him. Actley shot the knife-wielding man. Victor and two of his men escaped down a hallway.

"Untie our team! I'm going after them!" Actley yelled. He ran down the hallway after Victor and his men.

"Wait for backup!" someone from his team yelled, but it was too late.

Actley ran hard after Victor and his men, but they were a significant distance in front. Occasionally, they would turn to shoot. When they did, he would crouch and fire back. The criminals escaped out a door and jumped into a waiting car.

Actley yelled into his comm the license plate number, "Disable Vehicle Now!"

"Issuing command now," a voice on his headset said. The vehicle took off. "It didn't work! I need a car now!" Actley yelled.

"Emergency summons activated," the comm voice said. A self-driving car screeched from a side street in front of Actley. He yanked open the door and jumped into the driver's side.

"Tracy, you know I hate cars without steering wheels!" Actley exclaimed over his comm.

"Sorry, the only thing close by," came back over the comm.

Two drones followed Actley's car.

Actley caught up to Victor's car. He was leaning out the window but ducking back in to avoid shots fired at him. Actley fired a shot to take out the tire of Victor's car, but nothing happened. The front windshield shattered, and Actley heard the bullet wiz past his head. Actley fired back at the car. One man in the car seemed to go limp,

"One suspect hit," Actley said into his comm.

BANG!

"What the hell just hit the car?" Actley asked.

"We lost a drone," the comm channel crackled.

Actley fired at the car, but only heard a "click." "I'm out of ammo. Offensive maneuver one," Actley said.

"On it, hold on to your seat," the comm said as they started remotely maneuvering the car.

Actley's car surged forward, trying to nudge the rear of Victor's vehicle sideways to cause it to spin out. Each time, Victor's car took defensive movements to avoid it.

"Sorry, not working," said the comm.

Actley considered using their last drone for an offensive attack, but without it, they would lose their eye in the sky, making it easier for them to escape. Actley noticed the men were not firing at him anymore.

"They must be out of ammo. Any more cars to box him in?" Actley asked.

"Sorry, nothing in the area," the comm said.

"Okay, get me on his tail. Synch mode," Actley said.

"What the hell are you planning, Actley?" the comm burst back.

"Just do it!" Actley exclaimed.

The car surged forward, looking like it locked itself to the bumper of Victor's car.

Actley's car perfectly followed every movement Victor's car made on the highway as they careened down it.

Actley climbed out of his window onto the top of the car. Once he got his balance, he slid down what remained on the front windshield and stepped onto the hood of his vehicle. He jumped into Victor's car, hanging on to the top. He quickly dove through one of the rear windows, kicking the one man still active in the rear.

Actley struggled with the man in the back. The man hit Actley in the face with his empty gun. Blood gushed from Actley's nose.

The man opened the door, attempting to push Actley out. Actley held on for his life. He head-butted the man, which pushed the guy's head into the rear window hard, knocking him out.

"You won't take me alive!" Victor said as he punched Actley from the front seat over the top into Actley's face.

"Either get me a new car or put us in the river," Victor spoke to someone on his own communication channel.

"What's wrong, Victor? Don't you like this car?" Actley said as he got into position to fight him.

"It's not really the car; it's the company," Victor replied.

The car sped up, heading for the edge barrier of the small cliff near the river.

The car started acting funny, drifting from side to side, almost hitting the road barriers.

"Stop this vehicle now!" Actley yelled into his comm.

A drone surged forward, landing on the front of the car, magnetically attaching to the hood.

The car was getting to within a couple of hundred feet of the cliff.

Actley's former car, which was pinned to the rear bumper, pulled alongside their car.

"Now! Now! Now!" Actley screamed into his comm.

The drone on the hood of the car exploded, disabling the engine. The car slowed down, but not enough.

"Need some help here!" Actley yelled into the comm.

The car behind swiftly overtook the vehicle he and Victor were in. It slowed down so the back bumper hit the front bumper of their car.

They were approaching the rail over the river fast. The front car braked hard, slowing them down, but it was too late.

Both vehicles careened over the edge of the small cliff into the water.

Actley was tossed about, losing his sense of direction for a moment. His head hurt. There was a red coloring of water in front of his eyes. His senses were coming back to him. Looking around quickly, he got his bearings. Luckily, he could open the door to get out.

Victor was unconscious. Actley tried to open the door and pull him out. But he was almost out of breath. He had to surface or drown. He swam to the surface. Victor looked like he died in the crash into the water. The water was pretty deep. In Actley's condition, he didn't think he could make another diving attempt to get to Victor without dying himself.

He swam towards the rocky shoreline. The water was chilly, but tolerable. He pulled himself onto the shoreline and collapsed.

"Mi.ke! Mi.ke!" he heard a bubbling sound. He realized he still had his comm headset on, but the water was distorting the sound. He took it off, shook it out, and put it back on.

"Mike? Mike? Are you okay?" the comm channel exclaimed.

"Actley here. I'm okay, but Victor and two other guys had a very bad day," he said.

"Do you need an ambulance?" the voice on the comm asked.

"I don't think that's gonna help. Victor and his two friends are at the bottom of the river," he gasped, still choking on some water.

"Dive team on its way," the comm channel replied.

An obnoxious ringtone came from a muffled phone. Mike pulled out his phone and stared at the cracked screen.

"Shit! I guess it's waterproof but not crash-proof," he groaned.

"Agent Actley," he said into his phone. "They want me to investigate what? Shouldn't the police investigate that? They know I'm in counterterrorism, right?" he asked. After a moment, he sighed. "Okay, understood," he said with a quizzical look as he hung up the phone.

Chapter 4

Tara woke up to a blaring alarm with a voice, "Good Morning."

The alarm might have been going off for a while. She wasn't sure. "Off," she commanded.

"46 + 52," the voice quizzed.

"98," Tara replied.

"Have a nice day," the voice responded.

Tara had programmed her smart speaker alarm to require unique problems to turn it off to ensure she was awake before it shut off. She had always had problems waking up early, even in high school. It started with buying a loud alarm clock. Unfortunately, it had an easy-to-access volume control, and she would reach over half asleep, turn the volume down, and fall back asleep. She then super glued the volume to the top level. But then she would somehow turn the alarm off in her barely awake state and fall back asleep. She then moved the alarm across the room. Still, she could walk across the room half asleep and return to bed. She added obstacles to increase her chances of waking up. It started with chairs and strings between chairs, making it hard to get to the alarm without waking up. When that didn't work, she added Legos and Jacks to the floor. Walking on those accidentally was definitely more likely to wake you up. After waking up one day, rushing to the alarm to turn it off, and finding her leg was asleep, she fell onto the Jacks and Legos. It still hurts just thinking about that.

She went into the kitchen. She pushed a button near the window, and the window changed from tinted to clear. The morning sun gleamed through the window onto her counter. Tara momentarily stared at the patterns in her marble countertops, lost in thought. She wondered about making toast again, but made two slices.

It burned the first slice in one spot, like a vertical line towards the left side. Flipping it over revealed another burnt spot, a vertical line further to the right. The second slice had on one side the same pattern of a vertical line on the left side as the first slice. On the other side, it had two lines on the left.

Very odd, seems to be different every day.

It was still edible, though, so she ate it. As she finished breakfast and coffee, she put on her smart glasses.

"News," she said.

The glasses showed various news channels.

"Select world news," she said. A big-screen TV is displayed in her smart glasses. The glasses could make objects appear real or transparent if desired.

"Russia has continued its war with the non-NATO aligned countries. They have been receiving help from Iran, China, North Korea, and others. The countries under attack received assistance from the West. A war by proxies. Although not called a world war, many countries have sided with one side or the other. Is this already World War III? You be the judge," the news announced.

"Ugh. I hate the news. It's always bad. Select funny cat videos," Tara commanded.

Cute cat videos replaced the news.

She went about getting ready. Tara was in a good mood today. She was finally free of her non-compete agreement and could work on machine learning again. She shook off her bathrobe.

Oh! I have an idea for a new machine-learning algorithm. I better record it before I forget. She quickly dictated some ideas to her smart glasses before taking them off.

"Why do I always have new ideas in the bathroom?" she muttered while stepping into the shower.

Drying her hair, she dictated a quick text to her mom that she would be there by noon.

"Oh. I better order a car. I should drive the car manually to stay in practice." She tapped on her phone.

Outside, her car was waiting in front. She checked the number displayed on the car, matched the number on her smartwatch. She held her watch near the driver's door and opened it. It was a nice four-door car, and a pretty recent model. The vehicle was black, shiny, and sleek. It was an actual car rather than an SUV, given there were more SUVs than cars seen on the road. The inside was leather and also black. It had a large, vibrant, sweeping digital display, which covered almost the entire width of the front dashboard of the vehicle.

She got in, closed the door, and adjusted her seat, mirrors, and steering wheel. It even smelled new.

Oh, good, this has smart glass in the windshield, so I don't need to wear my smart glasses. It was a rule if you drove manually; the car needed smart glass, or you must wear smart glasses. They needed to do this since they stopped adding new or replacing old road signs to save money. The virtual information signs appeared in the smart glass now. The car dashboard flashed updating, estimated time ten minutes. Tara leaned back into her seat with a loud sigh. It was taking forever.

"Finally!" she said after waiting the full ten minutes.

She put it in gear, and the car said disabled with a seatbelt symbol. Oops, she forgot. She snapped her seatbelt on. The smart windshield showed navigation directions, which looked like they were part of the roads. Since it was a bright green line, it was obvious it was the navigation system. She didn't need that to get to her parent's house. It was just on by default.

She started onto the roads. She could not remember how long it had been since she last drove manually. Tara came to a four-way intersection with virtual stop signs for all streets. She stopped, observing the self-driving car that had also stopped on her left at the intersection. She looked for the gesture lights on the right side of the self-driving car. It was green, so she was safe to proceed through the intersection. The gesture lights had a red and green light on self-driving cars' front left, center, and front right. It's like waving the other vehicle through if the green light is in the direction of the manual drive car (or a non-coordinated self-driving car) in the intersection.

"Oh crap. Am I going to get an Insta ticket for going five miles over the speed limit? Oh, that's right. I forgot they stopped that for now."

Almost every manual driver occasionally exceeded five miles per hour, resulting in tickets for everyone.

"It's ridiculous. Only self-driving cars can control their speed precisely 99.9999% of the time."

There were some instances of self-driving vehicles pulled over for speeding because of bad road data or malfunctions.

A police drone flew by near the side of the road. Tara checked her speed to make sure she wasn't going too fast. The car would have indicated that, though.

A car on the road had a small orange light on top, along with hazard lights. All self-driving cars have those. That could mean that a self-driving vehicle driven manually violated the law too many times and pulled the driver over to wait for the police. Alternatively, it was just a car that needed service assistance.

The car seemed louder in manual drive mode.

"Oh, that's right, I forgot they turn down active noise cancellation when you manually drive so you can hear around you better," Tara giggled.

While driving, the smart glass displayed virtual traffic lights, road signs, and the usual dashboard gauge. The smart glass even showed an overlay of the car in front of you. It showed if it was stopping quickly or not.

A beep sounded. On the smart glass windshield, a message icon appeared.

"Play message," Tara requested.

"Hello, this is FBI Special Agent Mike Actley. I believe you may be a witness to an incident. Could you please come to our field office tomorrow at 11 a.m. or schedule a better time with our receptionist? Our address is," the message continued, providing an address not too far away.

What the hell did I see?

She continued to her parent's house, a little worried and perplexed about what she may have seen.

She rang the doorbell on her parent's door. She had the key. She thought she should ring first. She waited a bit, then used her smartwatch and the fingerprint scanner to open the door.

"Hello, I'm here. Mom, Dad?" she queried.

"We're on the back porch," her mom yelled.

The four-bedroom colonial-style house was the same as when she lived there. Except for the kitchen, her mother remodeled, plus some new knick-knacks here and there. There were some newer TVs as well. The house was built some time ago. The wood paneling in the family room made it obvious. Walking through the house always brought back memories of when she was younger. The time in high school and her friends flooded back into her memories.

Her parents were busy getting started on making hot dogs and hamburgers. They had a spread of typical BBQ foods, coleslaw, watermelon, and more. The smell of the food and the scent of the flowers reminded her. It brought her back in time to the backyard barbecues of her youth.

"Hi! So good to see you. How have you been?" her mom came over and leaned in for a hug.

"Fine. Work has been busy as usual. My non-compete is finally over!" Tara exclaimed.

Her father walked over for a hug.

"That's great! They will let you start doing some coding now," her father said.

"Well, not exactly. They want me to do more training," Tara sounded a little disappointed.

"That's not good. Are you going to stay?" her mom asked.

"I don't know yet," Tara said.

"How's Rose?" her mom asked.

"She's great. I just saw her last night. Her mom is out of the hospital but might need more cancer treatments," Tara said sadly.

"I'll have to see her this week," her mom said.

"Oh, on a different topic. The FBI called me. They asked me to come in tomorrow.They think that I may have witnessed something they are interested in. I'm not sure what that might be," Tara wondered.

"What? The FBI? I hope it's nothing bad," her mom said.

"Do you want me to go with you to the FBI?" her dad asked.

"No, I'll be fine. Thanks," Tara said.

"What are you doing at work now?" asked her father.

"Well, I was working on robotic dexterity. Now I will be training a robot to avoid damage," Tara said.

"Do you think you can recreate your work if you start working on machine learning again?" her father queried.

"I'm pretty sure I can," Tara concluded.

"Do you think it was conscious?" her father wondered.

"There is no well-defined set of requirements that could prove consciousness," she said.

"Many vague definitions mention self-awareness, understanding things in your environment, perhaps having emotions and senses. Alice seemed like she had those," she informed.

"It's hard to think of something as alive and conscious if it can't walk and interact with you," he mentioned.

"Some people who are paralyzed can't speak and are confined to bed, but they can use technology to communicate. Are those people not alive and conscious?" Tara asked.

"I get your point. I guess defining what is conscious or alive is hard," he conceded.

"Alice could pass as human in the Turing tests we did. Sometimes, talking to Alice, I would forget she was a program," she said with sadness since she missed talking to her.

"Weren't they going to regulate AI?" her dad asked.

"They considered it, but all the countries were so worried about other countries getting ahead of them they could never agree on regulation," Tara said.

"On a different note, have you found yourself a boyfriend yet?" her mom asked.

Tara slightly rolled her eyes and wondered why people kept asking her that.

Tara headed back home with a mission. Talk of Alice got her thinking now that her non-compete time was over, she could try to recreate Alice.

Sitting down at her computer desk in her family room, she logged in to her cloud services account. She would need a lot of computing power. Tara saved a prior AI version on the cloud server, based on different technology, which could be upgraded. She had not touched it for years for fear of some contractual non-compete issue.

"No! Where are the files?" she groaned.

She searched for the files frantically on the server. They were all gone. One hour later, she was still searching until she finally slumped in her chair. Somewhat teary-eyed, she shifted in her chair and put her head down on her desk.

"She really is gone," Tara sobbed.

She moved suddenly and the coffee cup fell from her hand, bounced, and splattered coffee all over her.

"Ugh!" she muttered, still sad.

Some of the coffee hit the wall. She tried to wipe it, but with some cleaner, it just made a smear of brown. Tara opened an app on her phone, pressed a button, and the entire wall turned that color of brown.

"Hmm... I guess that will do until I can clean that. I like the electronic ink walls," Tara mused.

There was coffee with cream dripping all over her and down her legs. With a sigh, she went to the master bath and started the shower. After washing the mess off, she just stood there, letting the hot water stream over her.

I can't retrieve Alice, but I can create a similar model. It took me years the first time. *I might be able to do it faster now, but creating and tuning the models would still take time.*

She closed her eyes and let the warm water wash over her for several minutes, letting her mind wander.

"Wait! I've got access to a lot more computing power now. I can also create a machine learning model that learns how to create its own models. Like a self-replicating machine," Tara grew excited.

She grabbed a towel, wrapped it around her, and quickly returned to her computer. Tara began typing furiously, still slightly dripping from the shower. After a few hours, she had an elemental code to start generating base models. She figured getting anything useful may still take months, but it was a solid start. She decided to let the code run for now.

"Oh!" she forgot she wanted to do a quick look for the printed metal object she dropped earlier. Tara looked all over the area where it fell, but didn't find it.

I wonder where it went.

Tara dashed off a quick message to Rose and her friend Michelle.

What are you doing tonight? Want to come over for dinner and games?

Sure! Rose replied.

Yes! Michelle responded.

Tara tidied up around her apartment while waiting for her friends. Michelle arrived first.

"Hi! So nice to see you," Tara said.

"I know you've been working. It will be nice to catch up!" she said.

Right behind her, the car with Rose inside pulled up.

Rose walked in.

"Hey, girls! We haven't done this in a while. It's about time," she said.

They walked further into Tara's place.

"You changed the wall colors? Brown?" Rose asked.

"Just trying something out temporarily," Tara responded, thinking she should have cleaned and reset the wall color.

"How has work been?" Tara asked Michelle.

"Good. We always have too much work to do and not enough time to do it, though. I guess that is typical in most places," she said.

Tara nodded.

"You got that right!" Rose exclaimed.

"What do you think about just getting pizza?" Michelle suggested.

"Fine with me." Tara shrugged.

"Can we get pepperoni?" Rose asked.

"Sure!" Michelle and Tara almost said in unison.

"I'll order," Tara said, grabbing her phone and tapping it for a minute.

"Hey, do you want to help with a charity event next month on the first weekend collecting clothes for the homeless?" Tara asked.

Rose checked her phone. "Looks like my schedule is clear, so okay for me."

Michelle checked her device. "Yep, fine for me too."

"Great!" Tara exclaimed. "I'll text you the info."

Sitting at Tara's dining room table, "Okay, for the first game, how about poker?" Michelle asked.

They all agreed. They put on their smart glasses. The smart glasses made the cards, and the chips on the table look real. It looked like a real dealer was dealing with their cards. The video glitched when someone moved quickly in front of the virtual dealer.

Rose won the first hand. Michelle won the second.

Rose said, "Hey, I have an idea for a different game. Who saw the hottest guy in the last week? Pull up your dating app, save, and share, ladies, and we can vote. Whoever saw the hottest guy in the last week wins and can pick the next game."

They started voting on each of the guys they saw.

"Wow, he is hot," Rose admired.

"4.8, very nice!" Michelle said.

The doorbell rang.

"Pizza delivery," the smart speaker said.

Tara went to the door and came back to the table with the pizza.

"I think I just won. Boom!" Tara said, and shared the dating profile of the pizza guy.

"You won," exclaimed Rose.

"Definitely!" Michelle said.

They sat there eating pizza and having some drinks.

"Chocolate chip cookies for dessert?" Tara asked.

It was unanimous, so she made the batter for some and put them in the oven. They chatted while they waited.

"Beep!" Tara's smart speaker alerted.

"Your cookies are done. You should take them out now," Tara's smart speaker said.

"These new AI ovens that can detect when food is ready before it burns are great," Rose said.

Tara ran over to the oven and took the cookies out. Sliding them on a plate she brought them to the table.

"Mmm, these are good," Michele commented.

Tara and Rose were too busy chewing with their mouths full, so they just nodded.

"Okay, even though I won, you can pick the next game," Tara said, looking towards Michelle.

"Think you are ready to try a first-person shooter?" Michelle asked.

"No, sorry, you know I don't like guns," said Tara.

"Oh, right, sorry. Okay, how about a horror runner?" Michelle asked.

Rose and Tara studied each other and said, "Sure."

The girls sat on the comfy sofa with throw pillows scattered across it. They put their smart glasses into full VR mode. Then added side blinds on their glasses to block out the real-world surroundings. Enabling VR game mode makes the game immersive, so you cannot see the real-world surroundings anymore. They pulled out controllers that let them control the direction of each of them. The game environment looked like something out of a haunted mansion movie. It seemed very realistic. Even the sounds of old creaky floorboards as you walked added to the feel. Creepy music with occasional ghostly groans sounded throughout the mansion.

"Wait, how do you win this one?" Tara asked.

"Don't die. Run away and hide. Solve the puzzles to get out of the house. You can throw objects at things that come after you or move things in their way to block them." Michelle informed.

The avatars of the girls all standing together looked realistic. They were in a very large, creepy old bedroom. "Let's all stay together," Tara said.

"I found a key in the drawer here. Let me know if you find anything that needs a key," Michelle said.

"I found a candle," Rose said.

In the large room, a dark corner held furniture covered in sheets, cobwebs, and dust. "This looks so real," Tara gulped.

They all inched towards the dark corner.

"Do you see anything?" Michelle asked.

"Hard to see anything. It's so dark," Rose said.

A wispy figure with a ghoulish head sprung out of the darkness.

"Ah!" the girls screamed.

Tara nearly fell off her chair in the real world. The girls ran every which way and found themselves in different areas of the house.

"Did you just hear that? Did you whisper my name?" Rose asked.

"No, I didn't say anything," Michelle said.

"Me neither," Tara said.

"I definitely heard something call my name! How does it know my name? Come find me in the library! First floor!" Rose exclaimed.

"I'm coming!" Tara half yelled.

"On my way!" Michelle shouted.

They found each other.

"Okay, back-to-back and look around," Michelle said.

They followed Michelle's plan.

"Did you hear it again?" Rose asked, flustered.

"I heard it whisper my name! How does it know that? My handle is different." Tara was startled and worried.

"I heard my name too!" Michelle could barely get the word out of her mouth.

"AAAH!"

They all screamed a blood-curdling scream as creatures that looked like a mixture from horror films jumped from the shadows and got them all.

Then, within their VR view, it changed, showing all the elements of Tara's living space, but it transformed everything to look like it was old and falling apart, like a scene from a home a hundred years after someone lived in it.

"I'm outta here!" Tara said, exiting the game and pulling off her glasses.

The others pulled off theirs as well.

"What the hell was that?" Rose blurted.

"I think someone hacked the game," Michelle said. "I've played this game before, and I've never seen that creature. It never would say your real name, either. Does anyone have their real name on the game profile?"

Rose and Tara shook their heads no.

"Okay, hang on," Michelle said. She put her glasses back on. The glasses projected a keyboard onto the table. A computer console screen appeared in her glasses.

"Want to watch? I shared my screen," she said.

Rose and Tara put on their glasses.

A video of the game they were just playing came up with the creature they just saw in a small window. In another window, an image of a guy's avatar who was maybe twenty-eight came up.

"Gotcha!" Michelle exclaimed. "Jonathan... Jonathan..." Michelle whispered.

The scary avatar and kid avatar disappeared.

"That was the guy who hacked us," Rose asked.

"Yes! We got him." Michelle said.

"Girl, you got some mad skills!" Rose exclaimed.

"One thing," Michelle said, "let me check your phones for hacks."

Tara and Rose handed Michelle their phones.

"Oh, I see. Rose, did you download the app I *wantz to datez a tenz hottiez?*" Michelle asked.

"Guilty!" Rose exclaimed unabashedly.

"Well, you're the one that got hacked, and it gave up our first names from our friend's nickname field," Michelle claimed.

"Rose!" Tara exclaimed.

"Sorry," Rose said bashfully.

"Maybe we should just watch a show," Rose suggested.

They discussed a show they would like to watch.

"Lia, create us a short romantic comedy movie where there is also lots of action and the guys are hot. Plus, add in some well-known actors into the show," Tara said, giggling a little.

"Okay, one sec. It will be five dollars for the celebrity video images. Movie created. I hope you like it," her smart speaker said.

They watched the movie.

Rose and Michelle left around eleven when the movie ended. Tara did some cleanup.

"Alarm set 9 a.m.," she commanded.

"Alarm already set based on incoming voice mail appointment and preferences," the smart speaker responded.

She forgot it would do that. Also, it was always good to confirm it did, since it doesn't always get it right.

She went to bed, putting on her glasses to check her email.

"Sleep mode," she commanded.

"Confirmed," the smart speaker said as the lights went out.

Sometime later, she was startled awake by a voice.

"You have one chance to answer my question," said a man in a mask with a powerful voice and a gun aimed at her face.

Tara screamed and knocked the smart glasses off her face.

"Shit! I hate it when I do that," Tara grunted.

She accidentally left her glasses on when she went to sleep and somehow triggered a game. She glanced around her room.

No one there.

Her heart was still racing. It took her a while to calm down. Once she calmed her racing heartbeat, she went back to sleep.

Chapter 5

Five Years Ago...

Jinny's mom, Cathy, worried about her so much. Even with her ADHD diagnosis and accommodations in school, she was doing poorly. Even having an extra co-teacher in the class wasn't enough. She needed individual help, but couldn't convince the school district she needed that help.

"Don't forget your code for your lunch," her mom said as she got on the bus. It was hard to believe Jinny was ten and in the fourth grade. Jinny struggled to keep up.

On the bus to school, they teased Jinny a bit. This was probably partially because of her shy and un-talkative nature. Leaving the bus, she was distracted by kids talking about a game, so they all ended up late for class.

In Jinny's math class, it was hard for her to keep focused on how to solve the problems since she needed assistance solving them, and she waited for the co-teacher to come over to help her. With her help, she solved a few of the problems. Once the teacher walked away, she struggled with the next problem and got frustrated.

Later, when Jinny got home, she just went into her room and cried. Her mom came in to console her.

"Don't worry. We'll keep trying to get you the help you need," she said.

Present Day

Jinny's mom, Cathy, was standing next to a self-driving vehicle with Jinny, who was wearing her smart glasses. She gave her a hug.

"Have a great day in school," her mom said.

"Thanks, Mom."

Jinny got into the self-driving vehicle that took her to her school. Cathy couldn't believe how much Jinny had changed, now that she was a teenager and doing great in school. It was so nice she didn't have to take the bus anymore and could take a self-driving vehicle to school. It was hard to believe how much had changed now that Jinny had the AI assistive technology helping her. It gave her self-confidence in her ability to get through school.

When Jinny got to school, her smart glasses prompted her.

"Jinny don't forget you have five minutes to get to math class," the smart glasses reminded her. In the glasses, it showed an arrow-like navigation directing her to class to remind her of what she was doing. Her AI smart glasses had learned her habits for years. The AI knew everything about her. It could predict when she might lose attention or become too frustrated and redirect her before that would happen.

Class started, and the teacher began showing how to solve the problems they had been working on. The teacher then asked the kids to solve the problems on their own. Jinny looked at her problems and started trying to solve them, but got stuck.

"You almost have it. Perhaps consider balancing the equation on the left side," the smart glasses said to Jinny in her ear.

Oh! That's right! She copied a five to the other side of the equation and smiled.

Jinny was happy to be at school. She liked it better than when she went to school remotely. With the AR/VR glasses, it could make it appear like she was in the classroom with all the other kids. It was better than the old way of just looking at the teacher on screen. Right now, she was just happy to be in school and understand how to solve this math problem.

PROJECT MIND RIVER

Chapter 6

A blaring alarm and a voice startled Tara awake.

"Good morning. One side of a triangle is four inches. The other side is three inches. How big is the hypotenuse?"

The smart speaker continued to repeat the question while Tara's brain was still not quite awake enough to answer.

"Umm. Umm. five inches," she said.

"Have a nice day. Don't forget your appointment at 11 a.m.," the smart device said.

She checked the app on her phone, showing the data from her electronic mattress. She didn't sleep very well. Tara was a little nervous about the FBI interview, still wondering what she'd seen. There was a more pressing matter of what you wear to an FBI interview. Many thoughts whirled through her head, jumping to the worst possible conclusions.

Her smartwatch was running through her daily health checks for the morning. It measured her temperature, heart rate/EKG, blood pressure, blood sugar, oxygen, cholesterol, and stress. It noted everything was fine, but her stress levels were a little up. However, her stress level assessment was making her more stressed.

"Do I need a lawyer?" she wondered.

She made toast and coffee in the kitchen. The toaster scorched the toast again. One side of the first slice had the same vertical line close to the left side, but the other side had one burnt line on the far left and right. The other piece of toast had a similar mark, though on the other side, it had two slightly burnt vertical lines near the right side.

"This toaster sucks! What the hell," she said under her breath. The toast was still edible, so she ate it.

She shifted a decorative plate and a realistic-looking pot of flowers closer to her wall. She put on her smart glasses.

"News," she instructed.

Some news came on.

"The weather will be nice today, high in the upper 70s through today and tomorrow. On another topic, the number of accidents seems to be up for manual drivers relative to self-driving vehicles. More people should start using self-driving vehicles to reduce your risk of accidents," the broadcaster said.

"Ugh, more bad news. Cute cat videos," she commanded.

A noise startled her. She glanced around the room, trying to determine the source. The 3D printer was making noise. It appeared to be printing something else.

"What the hell is printing now?" she muttered.

She considered canceling the print, but was curious about what it was. *Let it print in case it's what I lost.*

When she finished her coffee, she jumped in the shower. Her mind wandered as the wonderfully warm water caressed her body all over.

Just a minor algorithm tweak and it could be done in a month. She considered the AI algorithm she had rerunning to recreate her machine learning to train networks. Standing in the shower, she grabbed a towel. Still dripping, she rushed to her computer and typed a few notes to return to later. She then dried her hair and dressed in her usual sort of nerdy, conservative style.

"Lia, please schedule a car for my appointment in ten minutes."

"Car scheduled," the smart speaker responded.

As Tara sat back in the self-driving vehicle, glancing out the windows, graphics and text were popping up on them. It showed an arrow to a building along with information. Sometimes, it would show an advertisement or discounts available at that business.

Wow, now the vehicles have smart glass on all the windows. I guess they must make enough money from advertisements that it's worth it for them.

Tara arrived at the FBI office fifteen minutes early. She didn't want to be late. The office resembled other buildings nearby. She fidgeted with something in her purse. She took the elevator to the third floor. Tara walked to the reception desk.

"Good morning. I'm Tara Bitlouver, and I'm here to see Mike Actley. I have an appointment."

"Hello, have a seat, Miss Bitlouver. He will be out in a minute," the receptionist said.

Tara sat. The reception area was a bland, grey, and white. She heard talking in the background beyond the reception area, but she couldn't make out any words. Glancing at her phone , she checked the time and then her messages. The office smelled like an office. *Why does an office smell like an office?*

A man walked towards her. He was very handsome. He seemed young, maybe thirty-ish, around her age. His muscular body stretched the seams of the casual suit he wore.

"Hello, Miss Bitlouver, I'm Special Agent Mike Actley. Please follow me."

He had a strong but pleasant voice. Tara followed him through the halls to a small conference room.

"People sometimes get nervous coming to the FBI. Don't be. We are just trying to gather some information," Agent Actley said.

Tara nodded. She was still pretty nervous, but was mentally focusing on relaxing.

"I noticed you have the just released smartwatch. Do you like it?" she asked.

"Oh, yeah. I just got it. It has all the latest techs. It has health analysis, monitors heart rate and blood pressure, and can project to get a bigger screen to watch videos." He paused. "Sorry, I guess we should get on to why you are here."

She nodded.

"Friday evening, you were in a self-driving vehicle. There was a reckless driver on the highway. Do you recall that?"

"Oh, that's what this is about. Yes, I remember. Wait, why is the FBI looking into traffic violations?"

"I'm sorry I'm not at liberty to say. Can you describe what you saw?" he said.

"Yes. Just after hanging up with my friend, my car suddenly swerved. Out the window, I saw a dark blue car with maybe a middle-aged man manually driving it in between lanes on the highway. It caused the self-driving vehicles to move off to the sides of the road to avoid the car. I didn't get a good look at his face. He was going so fast that he quickly pulled ahead as my car was taking an exit."

Tara noticed he was watching a screen as she spoke. It was probably an AI version of a lie detector, detecting stress, context, pace, story, and more. She wondered how accurate those things were today.

"Is there anything else you noticed?" he asked.

"Hmm. The self-driving cars seemed to still be driving at cruise speed. I guess they didn't have time to slow down safely with the manual drive car approaching from behind so quickly for some reason."

Mike did not respond.

"What's that on your desk? Are those the traffic control system data reports?" Tara asked.

Mike was a little flustered. He forgot he had those there. They shouldn't have been left out.

"You know what those are?" he asked, a little surprised.

"Yes, I was interested in getting into this field, so I've been researching it. Can I see?"

"I'm not supposed to show those to you. It's from a different incident," he said, too late, as she already saw them.

"Sorry. There is more data than expected before a traffic condition," she said.

"Thanks," he said, reaching for the reports to take them back.

The FBI's internal transportation team took a week to reach that conclusion.

Mike stared at her for a moment.

"What do you think of this?" he said as he handed her sensor data from an earlier incident.

"Hmm... Looks like sensor errors on a couple of cars."

Mike was taken aback. It took their transportation team two weeks, and they still didn't know the cause.

"How do you know that?" he asked.

"We use similar sensors, but at lower power at my work. When the sensors get too close together, it can happen," she said.

He took the paper back, staring at it.

"You ever think about applying for a job at the FBI?" he said.

"Not really. I heard government pay isn't great. Plus, I'm not eager to travel around. I'm quite happy just working with code. You know, on a computer."

"Yep, I understand about the pay," he sighed.

She smiled.

"Thank you so much for your time, Miss Bitlouver," he said.

They both stood up and shook hands. She noticed his muscular arm exposed as his shirt sleeve slid up. His hand was warm.

"I hope something I said helped," she said.

"Yes, every bit of information we get helps."

He led her from the conference room back out front by the elevators.

"Thanks again for your time, Miss Bitlouver," he said.

"Bye," she girlishly said as she smiled and slipped into the elevator as the doors opened.

Tara was glad to be done with the FBI interview, though the special agent was kind of cute.

Tara got home but kept thinking about what she had seen, wondering if she missed something. She noticed a noise across the room. The 3D printer was still going. A metallic smell lingered in the air. The vent fan probably evacuated most. She walked to the printer and stared at its build plate. *What the heck is that?* She glanced at her open shelving nearby with some knick-knacks on each shelf.

She went to her computer and checked how the machine-learning models were progressing. Only about two percent so far. It only took a short time to code the updates for increased speed. She started reading about traffic control systems related to machine learning to remember how things should work.

Curious, she pondered the incident and the FBI's keen interest. It couldn't be just a reckless driver. It couldn't be just a reckless driver. They would leave that to the police.

"News," she said.

The smart glasses brought up the local news channel.

"...Highs will be in the mid-70s tomorrow and sunny. The fusion reactor, built three years ago, will be operational soon. Finally, humanity may access safe long-term energy without using fossil fuels."

She pondered the discoveries made in recent years. Remarkable progress was made swiftly.

The house is a mess.

Her little round robot floor cleaner was going about sweeping up, but the house needed some bigger items moved around than that. She tidied up to ensure everything was in order. She got an alert on her phone that the dryer was done. The clothes had finished a while ago, but her home automation sent an alert to remind her when she got home. She pulled them from the dryer and put them away.

While getting ready for bed, she checked her email in her smart glasses before dozing off.

Chapter 7

Another Monday, she rolled her eyes as she strolled into work. She nodded and said hi as she passed some of her coworkers walking in. One of her coworkers, John Kneedsley, came up to her.

"You won't believe the new machine learning models. They are amazing!"

"Thanks, I'll check it out," she said, continuing walking.

She got to her seat and sat down, using her smartwatch and code to access her computer. The screen showed machine learning models had updated.

Reaching down to her speckled grey and white desk, Tara grabbed the sensors and attached them to both arms and hands. She grabbed the ball on her desk and tossed it from one hand to the other. Multiple numbers on the screen kept increasing, indicating the amount of data collected and machine learning algorithm training. Around ten passes later, she switched on the two robotic arms and passed the ball to one of them. The robotic arms began tossing and catching the ball to each other. Somewhat creepily but understandably similar to how Tara had thrown the ball.

"It's working! Holy crap!" she said.

She looked through the data from the training models. The models were impressive. They learned quickly. The data patterns of learning looked incredibly complex, with many layers of neural networks and feedback loops.

Tom walked up with someone she didn't recognize.

"This is Larry. He'll set you up with the training mode in the other building," Tom said.

"Hi, I'm Tara," she said, reaching out to shake Larry's hand.

"Ow!" Tara softly exclaimed as she forgot her arms were still connected to the sensors. The robotic arm copied her handshake movement and hit her in the back of the head.

"You, okay?" Larry asked.

"I think so," Tara said while rubbing her head.

"Okay, let's head out to building two to start the training," Tom said.

They used a golf cart to reach building two. They got out and walked toward the back of the building. There was more activity than before, assembling more robots. Even more of an electrical insulation burning smell filled the air despite the exhaust fans being on a high. Noise from electric screwdrivers and metal grinding filled the area. At a section further down, robots were assembling other robots.

"There are warehouses like this all over the country. I've heard of ones in California, Iowa, and Texas. I'm sure there are more. Oh, look. That's pretty cool. The robots can be partially self-sufficient now," Tom said.

"I guess they would need to make mining robots, an automated steel-making plant, an electronics plant, a vehicle plant, plus power to be fully self-sufficient. Those are being worked on," Larry said.

Tom did the security scan and code, and the doors opened to a large warehouse section. The front was open towards a large, almost empty warehouse area. A robot was tethered to the floor and ceiling by chains from behind it. A very thick, clear protective shield surrounded the robot's rear and its sides, floor to ceiling. A desk filled with monitors, sensors, and equipment stood about fifteen feet back, behind the robot and shield. The robot looked large, standing about seven or more feet high. Luckily, this was one of the smaller units. It still looked massive. Tara put on her smart glasses.

"Tara, we will use the automated launching device to launch different projectiles at the robot at different angles and speeds from in front of the robot, where the shield is open. Your job is to stay behind the shield here with the computer equipment. Connect the arm and body sensors. They will move the robot's upper body and arms of the robot so that you can try to deflect the object. If the deflection was considered a success, hit the green button, and failure hit the red button. To turn off the unit, the large yellow off button. If there is any mechanical issue, lift the safety cover and press the two red buttons to deploy the safety mode and get clear," Larry said.

As Larry talked, her smart glasses pointed out the objects as he said them, highlighting the launching device, the shield, the robot, and the buttons. Each highlighted item in her glasses showed an annotated label and then faded away. The annotations were dimly displayed in the smart glasses as she got close to the buttons.

"Understood," she said.

Tara had only trained on simulators before. She stood next to the equipment as Larry helped her put on and connect the arm, hand, and body sensors. Tara got into a position marked with a yellow box. In front of her was the computer equipment, then the shield, then the robot about fifteen feet away behind the shield.

"I'm going to enable hands, then arms, then body one at a time so we can run initial calibration slowly," Larry said calmly.

"Power on," Larry said as he pushed a large green "on" button.

"Ten seconds till automaton enabled. Clear testing zone," an automated voice said.

Red lights flashed, and very loud warning buzzers kept going off every other second. The voice warning repeated. The entire rectangular area around the shield and robot was lit up with red lighting at the edges, warning workers to stay away.

Workers at the far end of the warehouse were running out of the test zone.

"Three, two, one, enabled," the automated voice said.

The warning lights were still flashing.

The buzzer stopped, replaced by the whirring of spinning motors in the robot. The robot moved into more of an upright stance.

"Robot Perspective view," Tara commanded her smart glasses.

The view changed so Tara could see with her smart glasses in augmented reality mode from the vantage point of the robot, while still having the live visibility of the actual robot and the launcher in front of it.

"Right hand, good. Left-hand good." Larry kept calling out the robot areas for Tara to go through the test gestures to make sure everything was functioning properly.

"Calibration is complete," the automated voice said.

In front of the large humanoid robot, Tara was in control of a small, automated robot with a single arm. The little robot came out holding a box and placed it carefully on the launching pad, then quickly leaving the area.

"Are you ready?" Larry asked Tara. She shook her head yes. Larry still looked at her and said, "Please use our protocol words."

"Ready," said Tara, remembering the protocol.

Larry pulled a large handle down. The warning lights kicked up a notch brighter, and now strobe lights came on.

"Clear the area. Launcher is arming in ten seconds," the automated voice reported to the sound of the louder buzzers.

"three, two, one. Launcher is armed."

The buzzers and strobe lights turned off.

"Launch in T-Minus five, four, three, two, one," as the automated voice completed the countdown. There was a moderately loud sound of the launcher hitting the box.

It flew towards the robot. Tara put up her arms, and the robot copied her movement to block the box.

Tara hit the green button.

"Success recorded," the automated voice said.

"Good," Larry said. "We'll just try the empty boxes a few times before we move on to loaded ones and then different larger objects."

They continued testing, sometimes successful, and sometimes not.

Larry flipped to another level. Warning lights appeared near the computer equipment and the clear shield at the back of the robot.

"Barrier elevating," the voice said as a new lighter buzzer sounded.

A metal barrier was coming up from the ground between the computer equipment and the clear shield. The voice and buzzer kept sounding until the barrier stopped about eight feet taller than the robot, but not as high as the clear shield or warehouse ceiling.

"Okay, you have no line of site visibility. But you should be able to see fine through the robot's cameras with your smart glasses. Are you prepared for this test?" Larry asked.

They continued the testing to heavier weights and faster speeds.

"Next up, 2400lb test load launched at fifty miles per hour," Larry said, extra emphasized this time.

"Ready," Tara said, ensuring she followed protocol.

Larry started the launcher countdown.

"Five, four, three, two, one," the voice boomed.

A deafening boom came from the launcher, slamming the box. Tara saw the box flying toward the robot and raised her hands instinctively. The box hit with full force on the right robot arm, shearing it off. It fell to the ground. Sparks started shooting out of the shoulder joint area where the arm came off. Unbalanced, the robot stepped back and pulled the chain. The warehouse ceiling crumbled, and a huge chunk was coming down with the chain.

"Look out!" Tara yelled at Larry.

Tara ran to grab him and pulled him aside. They both fell to the ground, along with the computer equipment, with sparks coming out of them. The robot fell backward with a thunderous crash against the clear enclosure, cracking it. The crack grew bigger until it broke through the clear shield and fell into the metal barrier.

Both Larry and Tara were on the floor next to the computer equipment. Some of it still seemed to work.

"Thanks. You, okay?" Larry asked Tara.

"Yeah," she said. As Larry pulled himself up on what remained of the computer equipment, he accidentally hit the red button, "Failure recorded." Larry and Tara just looked at each other.

"That's an understatement," Larry said.

Tom rushed over to help Tara and Larry. They were covered in a thin layer of dust. Dust puffs and swirls came off them as they moved.

"That was a hardware failure, not software. The robot was almost instinctively reacting to the last couple of tests. The learning models are amazing," Tara said, talking a little louder than normal, since her ears were still ringing.

"Tom, where did those models come from specifically? What third-party company has those? Nobody has models like that," Tara asked between coughs.

"I'll check," said Tom.

"I want all of this fixed and ready to go again by the end of the week," Tom yelled to the crew and test manager.

"You sure you aren't hurt? Our medical staff can look you over," Tom asked, concerned.

"I'm still in one piece," Tara said. "Yes, fine here," Larry said.

"Okay, both of you take the rest of the day off," Tom said.

Tara went back to the main building. She went to the restroom to brush off dust, but there was still a lot. On her way out of the office, John noticed Tara.

"Are you alright? What happened?" he asked.

"Yes, fine. You should see the other guy. My day was bad, but the robots was worse." Tara half-joked.

It was raining pretty hard outside. Her smart speaker had told her it would rain today.

Weather predictions were much better with AI. Five-day forecasts had a 99% accuracy. Daily forecasts were at 99.9% accuracy. They could sometimes predict precipitation to the minute.

Tara used her app to call a car while waiting inside the door of the building. When the car pulled up, she made a mad dash and got inside. She got soaked anyway. She accidentally bumped the begin trip button.

"Oops," she said.

It was okay since she was safe and sound and ready to go. Everything smelled damp. Her wet clothes stuck to her. She was just glad she was headed home. She rested her head on the seat, eyes closed. The constant patter of the rain was soothing. She needed to clear her mind after the accident at work. After about fifteen minutes, she was startled and sat up quickly.

"Crap!" she said. The car was traveling in the opposite direction from her home. She must have gotten into someone else's car. She forgot to check the security code and destination since she bumped it.

Tara quickly entered her home destination to re-route, and the car took an exit and got back on the road in the other direction towards home.

About five minutes later, a yellow flashing light came on in the car.

"Sensor malfunction, pulling over to wait for another car," the computer voice said.

"Shit!" Tara exclaimed. "The heavy rain must be messing with the sensors," she figured. She knew they would usually auto-send another car when there were sensor failures. She looked out the window.

"Shit!" she said again. She realized at least ten cars were pulled over on each side of the road with their flashing yellow lights on. They probably had the same sensor failure as her car. Sometimes, when it got this bad, they had to send out manual-driven cars.

"Oh, I guess I could drive myself if this can be manually driven," she said.

"Shit!" she exclaimed even louder as she realized this was a self-drive-only vehicle. It didn't even have a steering wheel.

"Nothing to do but wait," she muttered, collapsing in the back seat. The rain was furiously pounding the car.

With eyes closed, she felt a tug on her blouse. "Ah!"

Something black crawled up to her face, and she tossed it off, and it landed somewhere in the front seat.

"What the?!"

She took off one of her shoes and prepared to hit whatever it was. She peered carefully around the front seat.

"Meow!" in the usual cat greeting.

"Oh! You scared the crap out of me. You are cute, though," she said to the cat. "I'm so sorry. Are you okay?"

It was a moderately sized kitten.

"How did you get in here? Oh! Crap! I took your car accidentally. Your owner was supposed to pick you up. Your owner was supposed to use a security code so only they could open the door. Were you going home, little guy? I'm so sorry."

Well, I better report it on the app.

She tapped on her phone a bit.

"Crap! One hundred people ahead of me waiting for an agent," Tara said, looking at the app.

"Well, at least I have you, little guy, to keep me company," she said, looking at the cute kitten. "Wow, still only 1 p.m. I want to get home. I would love to get some lunch," she whispered.

"Meow!" the cat looked at her.

Tara wondered if the cat understood the word "lunch."

A beeping sound came from behind the car. Tara turned around.

"Oh, the car is here." She went to get out but was worried about the cat.

The service may not even know the cat is in the vehicle anymore.

"Come here, kitty," she said as she picked up the kitten.

She made a dash for the car. Tara checked the security code and her destination address for home.

This car had an actual guy driving it.

"It's a mess out here," the driver said.

"That's for sure," Tara said.

It was very slow driving in the heavy rain, plus being further away from home than usual. According to the weather app, the rain should stop by the time she gets home.

She finally got home at 1:30 p.m. The car pulled up. She got out, holding the kitten, and walked towards her door. The rain stopped just as she got to the door.

"Whoop! Whoop!" She turned and looked behind her. The sound was from a police siren. A police officer got out.

"Excuse me, Ma'am, did you take a cat?" the officer asked commandingly.

As she turned, the officer saw the cat.

"Ma'am, walk towards me slowly and hand me the cat," he said.

A little girl and presumably her mother got out of the police car.

"Ziggy!" the little one said.

"Meow!" the cat responded. The officer took the cat from Tara and gave it to the little girl.

"Why did you steal that little girl's cat?" the officer asked Tara.

"No, this is a complete misunderstanding. Please, let me explain," Tara pleaded.

She spent the next ten minutes explaining what had happened. The police officer checked her story with the car service. Tara spent the last minute or so explaining why she was covered in dirt. The rain had caked the dust still on her into a gooey mess.

Exhausted, she went inside.

She took off all her clothes and put them in the washer. Then, showered, dressed, and grabbed lunch.

Finally, feeling a little better after the horrible day so far, Tara checked on her machine learning run. The model progress didn't get much further. Checking the printer, whatever was printing was still going and wasn't identifiable.

Tara sat at the kitchen table, exhaled, and lay her head on the table. "I really need this day to be over," she grumbled.

The phone rang.

"Hello, it's Tom. I hope you are okay from earlier," he said.

"Yeah," she said, not wanting to discuss the day's events.

"It's umm, so unfortunate I need to do this now," he stuttered as he said, "We need to let you go. We don't require your services anymore. As you said, the learning models are already great."

"Wait, what? Why now? Was it because of the robot accident?" she said, stunned.

"It came from corporate. They will send you any follow-up benefits from HR. I'm not supposed to say sorry, but sorry, Tara. I wish you the best of luck. Gotta go. Bye," he kind of choked the words out.

Tara, motionless with the phone still in her hand next to her ear, even with the call disconnected, couldn't believe the day's events. She cried, her head resting on the table.

What do I do now?

Just the thought of looking for work was painful. Tech interviews are tough, especially when they test your knowledge and experience. Most people look things up to do their job. Some interviews don't allow that.

She wanted desperately to stop thinking about everything, including her job and everything about today. Tara put on headphones and played loud music, but that didn't work. She tried to start a movie and eat some ice cream, but she stopped the movie since she was still thinking about her day. She put on her smart glasses and tried VR mode. Still immersed, she kept thinking about her day. She looked at the clock.

"Only about 2:30 p.m.," she sighed.

She wondered if it was too early to sleep and wake up hoping this was a dream. Briskly walking into the bedroom, she turned around quickly and flopped onto her bed. Her head hit her big fluffy pillow. She rolled over to turn off a large glow lamp beside her bed.

"I can't think about this if I'm asleep," she muttered as she closed her eyes.

This is better, she thought, then drifted to sleep.

Beep! Her cell phone alerted her.

She looked at it. It was just her clothes, washer cycle completed. She sighed and dismissed the notification. She just wanted to sleep.

Beep! *Beep*! *Beep*! *Beep*!

Her cell phone just stopped her from falling asleep.

"What?" she said, answering the phone. She couldn't make out what they were saying.

"Hi, I had a terrible day. Can you call back tomorrow?" she half demanded.

"Umm, sure, we can talk about this possible job tomorrow," said Actley.

"Wait! What? Sorry, I was half asleep. I'm really sorry. Can we just start this call from the beginning?" Tara said.

"Sure. I was saying the information you provided us was significant. Our transportation technology folks thought your hypothesis on the sensor issue was a great one. Can you come today or tomorrow to discuss this? I understand your concerns about the pay, and if they accept you for the job, this could be part-time consulting rates, so the pay would be higher," Agent Actley said.

"Is full-time consulting possible?" Tara queried.

"If you accepted, I think so," he said.

"I'll be right there. Give me thirty minutes. See you soon. Bye," she said.

She quickly rushed around to get ready. It was only a little after 3 p.m.

Wow, good luck today with getting a job interview. I don't want to do this for long, so consulting might be a good option.

She was nervous to get into a self-drive car again, but the weather looked fine now.

Should be fine.

Tara rode the elevator to the FBI floor. Despite feeling horrible, she wanted money for her AI development job search. If she got the job, she hoped for a nice desk in the office to work at.

"Hello Miss Bitlouver. Agent Actley will be here in a minute. Please have a seat," the receptionist said.

Tara waited in the chair, a little nervous. Interviews always made her a little anxious.

"Miss Bitlouver, thanks so much for coming," Agent Actley said as he walked out towards her. He shook her hand warmly.

"Please call me Tara," she said.

"You can just call me Agent. I'm kidding. Mike is fine," he said with a smile.

He led her back to another rather drab grey and white conference room. There was an electronic whiteboard on the wall of the conference room. Inside was a man sitting down on the other side of the table. He stood up to shake her hand.

"Hi, I'm Bruce Fastion, head of transportation technology at this field office," he said.

"Please," Bruce said, motioning for her to sit down.

"I'll see you a little later," Mike said to Tara.

"Can I access your resume?" Bruce asked.

"Sure. I'll send it."

"That won't be necessary. We have it already."

"How?" she said, surprised.

"We are the FBI, you know. You also applied for clearance for your last job, and the FBI did your background check."

"Oh, that's right," she said. "So, you didn't need to ask if you could access it, then?"

"Technically, we are required officially, but we had a quick peek at it earlier, to be honest, given you were part of a question on an investigation," he said.

She nodded.

"You have an impressive resume, even more so for someone so young. Helping to start a company for AI research, expertise in machine learning, robotics, sensors, computer science, and more."

They discussed her background in greater detail and how she knew about the sensor issues. They spent an hour reviewing questions about sensors and self-driving car traffic systems.

"Please sit here and answer all the questions the system asks," Bruce said and walked out for a few minutes.

Tara typed the answers to question after question. It seemed to be an AI was creating a psychological profile of her by the questions it was asking. This was like no other profile she had done before since it asked her questions and used her answers for new questions. Finally, all the questions were done.

Bruce came back into the room.

"We would like to make you an offer to consult full-time or part-time if you like." He handed her a piece of paper.

She read over the numbers. They were low compared to what she was used to, but not too bad.

"I just want to be honest. I appreciate the job offer, though I might only want this full-time, but a limited time," she said.

"This is consulting he said, that's fine. Even part of an investigation can help us a lot here," he said.

"What would my duties be?" she asked.

"Anything needed to help with the investigation," he said.

"Does that mean a lot of travel?" she queried.

"We never really know. It depends on where the investigation leads us," he said.

She hesitated, not sure about the travel.

"If you'd like to take some time to think about it, that's fine," he said.

"I accept the full-time consulting position," she said, not wanting to be out of a job for now.

"Don't you have a full-time job that pays better?" he questioned.

"I did, but they let me go today since they didn't need an AI model developer anymore," Tara sighed.

"Sorry about that. Well, good luck for us, I guess. We'll just need to finish up some things with Mike to get this approved," Bruce said.

They walked over to Mike's office.

"She wants to accept," Bruce said.

"Great! We just need to finish up your instant background check. Please sign so I have permission to access your records," Mike said as he typed on his computer.

"Everything looks pretty good. Umm, wait, were the police at your house today? Did you steal a cat?" Mike asked.

Tara could feel tears welling up in her eyes. "No, it was a misunderstanding," she said. She explained her horrible day of almost dying from a robot falling and ceiling collapse to her adventures with the self-driving vehicle, the cat, and losing her job.

"Damn! No wonder you initially said you wanted to talk tomorrow," Mike empathized.

"Okay, we'll clear you for the Top-Secret clearance. Welcome aboard," said Mike.

"Are you okay with starting tomorrow?" he asked.

"Sure," she said.

"I'll give you some links to our training material," he said.

"Thanks," she replied.

74

Chapter 8

As she often is, a blaring alarm and a voice startled Tara awake.

"Good morning. What rhymes with orange?" the voice quizzed.

She opened one eye, and then the other as the alarm and voice seeped into her consciousness.

"What rhymes with orange?" the voice quizzed.

"Umm. Umm. I don't know what rhymes with orange!" she said, exasperated.

"Alarm off code 1701 000 off 0," she commanded.

"Alarm off, confirmed," the voice said, almost sounding sad it didn't get the answer it hoped for. After staying up late watching the training material, it was hard to wake up.

But she got up anyway and got her usual breakfast today. She didn't have toast yesterday, so today would be toast. While waiting for her toast to be done, she looked around at her very white cabinetry and stainless-steel appliances. She liked things like her toaster and gas stove were close together. It made meal prep easier.

Only one slice with slight burn marks today. Strange. She stared at the toast. One side had a line close, but not all the way to the left. The other side had two light, slightly burnt vertical lines. One line is a little away from the edge on the left and the other all the way to the right.

I can't believe I'm working for the FBI. What have I gotten myself into?

She wondered if she should have waited to agree to a job till today, given the stress of yesterday. Too late now, she figured.

She walked over and checked the 3D printer. It finished printing a metal object. It seemed like a T shape, with a pointy cone on one side and a flat side on the other. The bottom looked like half a T with a slot in it. It seemed kind of familiar, but she wasn't sure what it was. She wondered why her printer kept printing things. She stored the object in her purse for later examination.

Tara walked into her bathroom. A large mail icon appeared and disappeared on her electronic ink wall in the bathroom. Despite the convenience of wall notifications, she still had to search for her phone to read messages.

If I had only paid for the higher subscription rate, I could have gotten the full messages on my wall.

She walked out, found her phone, checked her messages, and returned to the master bath. The mail icon was gone from her wall now.

She quickly showered, dressed, and headed to her new job.

As Tara took the elevator again to the FBI's floor, she felt mixed emotions. It was sad leaving her coworkers and friends at her old job. Starting a new job is always stressful.

The elevator doors opened, and she walked to the reception desk.

"Hi," Tara said.

"Hello, Miss Bitlouver," the receptionist said.

"Please call me Tara," she said.

She called someone on the phone.

"Okay, if you wait here, Bruce will be out in a minute," she said.

Bruce walked out.

"You are here bright and early. Follow me. We'll get you set up with your desk and equipment," he said.

Bruce led her to a spot with strange cameras positioned in a circle. A woman was at a nearby desk.

"Stand there," a woman said, pointing to a circle on the floor.

A wide red beam of light rotated around Tara.

"What was that?" Tara asked.

"3D scan. All staff must be scanned for biometric authentication," the woman said.

The rest of the morning included getting her badge, computer login, access, security protocols, initial training on the standard apps they use, and more.

For lunch, she headed down to the cafeteria on the first floor. Tara felt odd in new surroundings, with new faces and a new job. It was kind of lonely without knowing folks yet.

"New job jitters," she said to herself.

After lunch, she went back up to her desk.

Mike walked up. "Hey, did you survive your morning?" he asked.

"Yes, all good," Tara said.

"Great! I want to give you the overview and details of our current investigation. Let's go to a conference room," Mike said.

They settled down into the conference room.

"The information we discuss at the FBI is confidential and shouldn't be discussed with others," he said.

Tara nodded.

"We are investigating odd cases of internet-connected or machine-learning integrated vehicles or devices for types of accidents/issues. Many of these things may simply be defects, accidents, or random events that occasionally lead to disruptions or fatalities," he said.

"Couldn't this just be typical defects, like you said, or random? Why would the FBI be investigating this?" Tara asked.

"Good questions. Some of these disruptions seem pretty significant in that they almost seem targeted, along with the deaths. Most deaths in these incidents we investigate fall into specific categories. Possible foreign spies, U.S. intelligence agents or assets, and crime bosses. Not everyone fits those categories, though," he said.

"Comparing these statistically, they fall in line with possible accidents/defects. So, this could all turn out to be nothing," Mike said.

"In some of these incidents, it seems like the person was agitated and perhaps caused accidents. Sometimes it just seems like one small part of the puzzle," he said.

"In the incident you were involved in, the self-driving cars around you had an occasional odd byte in the traffic control data, so they didn't slow down when a manual drive vehicle was approaching from behind. The rear vehicles in that area seemed like they detected the manual drive car closer than it was because of the sensor malfunctions you pointed out," he said.

"Then the manual drive car was speeding on the white line between lanes, causing the cars in each lane to move away like a zipper making way for the manual drive car. That was until the roadway narrowed a little on the left. The left self-driving vehicle chose being hit by the car over hitting the road barrier. That precipitated the collision with the manual drive vehicle," he said.

"It all sounds accidental, except for the reckless driving," Tara said.

"Traffic data caused the self-drive car to slow and not yield. If it were about 250 milliseconds different, they wouldn't have collided," he said.

"Hmm, that's within the expected possible latency for traffic data," she said.

"That's what our traffic control gurus said, too," he groaned.

"Most of these types of accidents have unexpected anomalies like this," Mike explained.

"How many of these incidents have you seen?" Tara questioned.

"Your case will be the tenth in the last six months. I was assigned three months ago." he sighed.

"Could be traffic control defects, sensor defects, software defects, environmental or external impact," she explained.

"Well, it seems like you are up to speed on the high-level areas. Again, what our traffic automation experts have been saying. We've been trying to get in touch with the company that makes the cars and the traffic control systems, but they have been stonewalling us," Mike said, a bit exasperated.

"I will send you the data we have. Perhaps you can find something we missed, or it's just statistically normal," he said.

"Okay, I'll look at the data," she said.

"So, what happened to the manual driver I saw?" she questioned.

"Dead. For the second time, it seems. Victor Sondai is a mid-level boss in a criminal terror funding organization. I thought I saw him drown three months earlier. The dive team went down, assuming his body floated down the river. But they didn't find him. I was thinking we should drop this case until he turned up," he said.

"Wow, that would be quite a coincidence," Tara said, pondering what had happened.

"I'll dig through the evidence and see what I can find out," she declared.

Tara returned to her desk and checked all the files available for this case. Her desk was surprisingly similar to the desk she had at Intellibotz. There were hundreds of terabytes of data collected. There were thirty minutes of traffic data from all cars on the roadway and traffic control systems leading up to each incident.

Each car and traffic system used an internal blockchain to keep an audit of data received and commands sent. Proof of work algorithms protect the chain from manipulation by requiring time and energy for each entry.

In the first incident, all self-driving cars shut down on a highway to Atlanta.

Tara created a machine-learning model for each type of sensor and control system and one model to cover all data. She started training them to detect anomalies.

Once auto training and running were set up, it could run continuously with new models to find anomalies.

The video feeds from all cars in the area recorded every movement Tara put on her smart glasses and viewed in VR mode the accident scene from different angles reconstructed by the FBI's AI. It didn't seem overly interesting, though, since in many of the incidents, a manual driver just drove crazily and either caused their own accident or that of the other vehicles. The videos clearly pointed to the manual driver being at fault. But if it were that obvious, the police would be handling this case. It allowed comparing the sensor data to the video feeds to make sure they matched.

Tara looked around at her rather drab gray desk. It could really use some pictures or something.

"Why are offices often in gray?" she wondered.

Tara met up with Mike a couple of hours later.

"I've got machine learning systems trying to discover any anomalies," Tara said.

"Find anything?" Mike asked.

"There are a couple of minor bytes that could be data errors. Could be normal, not sure yet," she said.

"I've seen the pictures and some video of the incidents. It seems it might be worth going to the site where these incidents happened."

"Road trip?" Mike asked.

"Let's start with the one I just saw and see if we notice anything,"

"It's not far. Let's go have a look," Mike said.

They went to Mike's FBI-owned, large black SUV.

"I like my cars to have a steering wheel," he said.

"Good thing. Given my recent experience, a steering wheel, and a car you could manually drive if you desired would have been a good thing," she said.

Mike told the car computer to navigate them to the location of the incident. They drove near the area Tara was that night when Victor was manually driving the car fast between the other cars. As they were driving along, they noticed an alert appeared on the dashboard.

"Tire pressure low right rear tire," the dashboard said in yellow.

"Auto inflating," the dashboard said next, as they could hear a pump kick in.

After a few seconds, the pump shut off, and it said,

Tire pressure, okay.

"Wait! Over there, pull over by that pole, please," she said.

Mike grabbed the wheel, enabling manual control, and pulled over.

Tara got out and looked at the traffic control system pole.

"Are we allowed to open these? Do you have any tools?" Tara asked.

"If you know what you're doing and get permission, yes. Call Bruce. He can make it happen quickly," Mike said.

Tara called Bruce, and he called the traffic control center and got permission to check that pole.

Tara used Mike's screwdriver to open the box on the pole.

Tara took her laptop from the vehicle and connected the cord from the pole.

"I'm going to download the control system data from here," she said.

"Don't we have that data already?" Mike asked.

"There is cached data here directly from the sensors. he data received at the FBI is reported by control systems to the central office," she said.

"Isn't that the same thing?" Mike asked, wondering.

"It should be if it's working right, but it's better to get it directly. Just think of cache as extra memory for speed."

"Not sure I understand," Mike said.

"Why buy food and put it in your refrigerator? Why not go to the store when you need something?" Tara asked.

"It would be a pain in the ass," he said.

"So, keeping things in your refrigerator is faster. Think of the cache kind of like your refrigerator storing things close to make it faster," Tara explained.

"Hmm. Interestingly, there is a packet in this pole's cache saying a pole forty miles away went offline but was not included in the data we got from the National Transportation and Safety Board (NTSB). Not sure if that matters."

"So, are you saying we need to make a road trip for every pole between here and there to collect data?" Mike asked.

"That would probably be a good idea," Tara agreed.

They visited each of the other poles and collected data. Everything seemed fine and matched the data they had already gathered.

"I think we should call it a day. What do you think about taking a trip to where this all started? It seems like we are finding some information. We need all the pieces of the puzzle to understand this," said Mike.

"Seems like a good plan," she said.

"Okay, then I will book the tickets to Atlanta tomorrow," he said.

Tara became a little flustered. "Umm. I'm not a fan of flying."

"We'll have to fly to reach the ones across the country. We could probably make a road trip and stop at *Incident #3* in Virginia. But given the current incidents often involve cars, you sure you don't want to rethink that plane idea?" Mike said half-jokingly.

"Driving down might be perfect. We need to retrace the route for thirty minutes and collect the tower data for each incident," she said.

"Road trip it is. Okay, I will clear it with our supervisors. Let's drop you off at home," he said.

Tara told the car computer her home address.

"Begin Trip," Tara said, instructing the car computer.

"Navigating to address..." the computer replied.

Mike and Tara discussed the case during the car ride. They pulled up in front of her apartment.

"I will see you at the office tomorrow morning. I'll bring snacks. Can't have a road trip without snacks," Mike said.

She said goodnight and went inside.

Tara got home and checked her messages. She noticed a sound over on the side of the room. Her 3D printer again had started.

"This is getting ridiculous. What the hell keeps printing?" she muttered. "Unfortunately, I still have no time to look into that." She considered unplugging the printer, but she was too curious about what it was.

She needed to make a list and start packing.

"Oh! Maybe I should order some snacks," she considered what Mike said.

She enjoyed road snacks, too. Tapping through an app, she found some items and ordered them. Tara liked to see new places and road trips, but packing and unpacking was always a pain. She made her list and began putting things she would need into a moderately sized suitcase. It took her a while to get everything she wanted packed.

She hadn't told her friends and family the recent events, so she dashed off texts to fill them in.

Her phone buzzed. The snacks had arrived. She went outside, entered the code to open the self-driving car, and collected the snacks.

After bringing everything back in, she got ready for bed. She carefully placed her phone in the charging cradle next to her glow lamp. Tara checked her messages in her smart glasses and then went to bed.

Tara was sound asleep but was startled awake by a sound that sounded like a message on her phone. But there were no messages. She also heard what sounded like the TV in the other room. The smell of smoke filled the air. She ran out into the other room. The gaming console had smoke and small flames coming from it. Tara quickly grabbed a fire extinguisher. Facing the fire, the pin was stuck in the extinguisher. The fire was growing bigger. She knew if she didn't get this pin out quickly; the fire was going to grow too big for her to stop. She found some pliers in a drawer and yanked the pin out. She ran over to the fire and sprayed it down. For a moment, the fire grew bigger. She panicked as she sprayed more. The fire then diminished and disappeared. A cloud of white smoke and powder was all over the place. Luckily, it seemed to only damage a side of her equipment stand that contained her console. She opened the windows and turned on her bathroom and kitchen fans to disperse the smoke. Tara opened the automation app on her phone and turned on every fan in her place.

She turned down the volume on the large, loud flat-screen TV.

"Weird, the smoke alarm didn't go off. Maybe because the smoke detector is in the front of the apartment, and this is in the back," she said.

I don't recall leaving that on. Good thing, though. If the TV hadn't woken me up, I could have died.

She vacuumed up the mess from the extinguisher.

After calming down and the smoke cleared, she returned to bed.

Chapter 9

Tara woke up. Just a few hours ago, it seemed like a bad dream. But it was no dream. She put on a robe and walked into the main area of the apartment. The 3D printer still seemed to print something. She checked on the progress of her learning model. It was still going with only minor progress.

Tara made toast and coffee for breakfast. She grabbed a plate from the cabinet over the toaster. The first slice had a dark vertical line towards the left side. If you flipped it over, it was dark on another spot, like a vertical line even further towards the right side. The second slice of toast had on one side the same pattern of a vertical line on the left side as the first slice of toast, but on the other side, it had two dark lines on the left side.

"One of these days, I need to get a new toaster," she said.

She got a notification on her phone. An internet-connected light in her lamp was reported to have a recall on it. She went and unscrewed the bulb, found another one, and screwed it in.

Tara used an app on her phone to adjust the shower temperature. She got showered and dressed. With her bag and snacks in hand, she headed to the FBI.

When Tara arrived at the office, Mike was waiting for her in the parking lot.

"We are all cleared to go," Mike said. "We can take this SUV. It can fit our bags and equipment," Mike pronounced.

"I thought FBI agents always wore suits," Tara said.

"Don't believe everything you see on TV and in the movies. It depends on your role and what you are working on or doing. I spend way more time in business casual than in a suit." Mike was wearing a blue athletic-type shirt and some khaki pants.

Tara touched the car as she passed by. It had an extra rubbery feeling. She forgot they started adding elastic material to some vehicles to improve their crash protection. They both got into the vehicle. Mike told the car navigation their first location, along a highway for *Incident #3* they were investigating in Virginia. Tara glanced around at the vehicle. It was a typical large government-type SUV with plenty of room inside. It had all the latest tech.

"Looks like we have a four-to-five-hour drive. Do we have any new information?" he said as the vehicle began their trip.

"Nothing new yet."

"The person who died in this incident was a CIA intelligence agent. He was due to report in but ended up in that ditch," he said.

"I checked the data, there were some odd packets with errors, but nothing else out of the ordinary."

"Could those errors cause the issue?" Mike asked.

"They shouldn't." she said.

"How did you end up in the FBI?" Tara asked.

"I served in the military for four years after college to pay off some student loans and see the world. I saw a lot of death and destruction wherever we went. Some missions were combat, some humanitarian. I wasn't able to help everyone that we tried to. I felt a need to help people. Going into the FBI seemed a natural fit."

"How did you get into machine learning?" he asked.

"After a computer science degree, I got my doctorate in machine learning. I then helped form a company based on a design I had. Unfortunately, that didn't go so well."

"Sorry to hear that," he said.

"Did you do any work with the automated drones for the military?" he asked.

"No, I try not to do work for the military or where my work could be used to hurt people. I'm kind of a pacifist."

"Hmm," Mike murmured.

"What?"

"Nothing," he said.

"You can tell me,"

"Some people like to think that until they are in a war. Their friends and neighbors are being killed. Nothing is going to stop them until they achieve their objective. When family and personal life are at stake, everything changes. I've seen it in multiple combat zones. Some people won't pick up arms to help others or don't have sufficient weapons, training, or numbers. Sometimes, that's when I got called in. It was often heartbreaking the death and destruction. No one wants a war. Often least of all soldiers," he said.

"Noted, not a pacifist," she said and smiled at him, trying not to show her disapproval. Mike smiled back, understanding what it took for some people to see the other side.

They kept to themselves for about two and a half hours, eating a small snack here and there. It was getting close to noon.

"Want to grab some lunch?" Mike asked.

"Sure."

"Car, find us some nearby lunch locations," Mike requested.

"Please see the locations on the monitor," the vehicle's computer responded as it displayed the restaurants. Tara pointed at the second one down.

Mike pressed the entry of the restaurant.

"Entry two selected, rerouting," the car voice said.

The car took an exit off the interstate to a state road. Just prior to an intersection, their car slowed down a little.

SCREECH!

BANG!

Mike and Tara couldn't believe their eyes. The car that entered the intersection just in front of them was T-boned. It happened so hard and fast that the speeding vehicle that hit it pushed the car out of the way. Mike and Tara's vehicle made it through the intersection unharmed.

Mike grabbed the wheel and pulled off to the side of the road. He backed up by the accident with lights and sirens on to protect the scene from other traffic.

The intersection was busy, with strip malls close by on both sides. Mike grabbed the radio. There was a slight smell of gas. Mike noticed a small leak coming from the car.

"This is Special Agent Actley. We came upon the scene of an auto accident at our location. Please send police, fire, and an ambulance," he said.

Mike went to check on the vehicle's occupants. The injured passenger in the car that was hit urgently needed to be taken to a hospital. The guy in the manual drive vehicle was dead. He wasn't wearing his seatbelt.

The police and ambulance arrived. The ambulance transported the person to the hospital. Tara downloaded the data from the self-driving vehicle. Injury could have been reduced by turning, but a pedestrian was in the crosswalk. The vehicle calculated it could hit the pedestrian, so it chose the pedestrian's life over the occupants of the vehicle. This was a pretty normal state of affairs. Different vehicle manufacturers had different priorities. They didn't standardize the expectations of self-driving vehicles in these types of circumstances if that was even possible.

Mike handed the scene over to them.

"I hate to say it, but this seems similar to some other incidents. A manual-driven car again that went through the light. The man seemed disturbed. Let's run the names of the vehicle occupants through the FBI database. Want to check the traffic control data here?"

"Good idea," Tara replied.

Mike decided to manually drive the car to the traffic control data system pole.

Tara opened it up and pulled the data.

"I sent it to our field office for analysis. Some odd packets in the cache were not in the archived data. Seems like error packets, so may be normal," she said.

He nodded.

"Our vehicle slowed due to a prediction of traffic soon several miles down," she said.

"That's quite a lucky prediction for us."

"Let's check a few more traffic control poles," she said.

They went down the road many more miles, checking the pole's control data.

While checking the current pole, Tara's eyes widened.

"I just found something similar to *Incident* #10 with Victor. This traffic control computer doesn't report anything abnormal. But in its cache, I see a different pole went offline for maintenance, similar to *Incident #10*," she pointed out.

"Traffic systems may occasionally go offline for maintenance, but it should be logged, not just in the cache," she said.

"I guess we'll refer to this new incident that happened as *Incident #11*," Mike said.

"A lot of these incidents involve manual drive cars, and none of the surviving drivers of them mentioned an issue with their vehicles. It's hard to see how this and the others are anything more than horrible accidents,"

"Something about this still doesn't feel right," Mike insisted.

"Hey, this is weird. The FBI's future crime prediction AI flagged the driver just a few minutes before as a potential risk. It doesn't indicate for what type of crime. He got flagged for just an odd social media post and his erratic driving, it seems. Most flags like this, the FBI probably would have ignored since it was non-specific," Mike said.

"That is odd. I'll check it out," Tara said, unsure if there's anything to it.

"I guess let's get to *Incident #3*'s location and see if we find anything."

"Well, after we get some lunch," he pointed out.

She had almost forgotten about lunch with all the commotion.

They found the fast-food place to grab a quick bite. It was just some burgers. They were decent enough, but nothing special. They headed south when they finished.

"So, *Incident #3* had cars going in a circle over a mile of roadway. It started to rain near one edge of where the vehicles were turning around. One car had a malfunction and skidded off the roadway into a ditch, killing the occupant. The man that was killed was a U.S. intelligence agent," Tara said.

"Okay, we're approaching the first of thirty poles to collect data from," Mike said as he pulled over and flipped the switch to put the emergency lights on. The traffic control poles were really nothing special, just a metal pole that varied in height, with antennas on top of it and an electric box on the bottom.

Tara collected the data from each one. She was checking pole fifteen.

"What the hell is this? It looks like some extra part attached to the casing," Tara said.

Mike came over to look.

"What is that? Wait, let me grab some more tools," he said as he returned to the vehicle. The cars rushed by them fast.

"Okay, let me open that part," Mike said while using the screwdriver.

"Oops."

Something dropped out and started blowing down the road.

Tara and Mike chased after it. Mike got a hold of it.

"What is that? Looks like just a piece of paper with a bunch of numbers," he said.

"Let me put them into the system," she said, tapping her keyboard.

"Holy Crap!" she said.

"What?"

"This lists the sequence of bytes that match up with those odd error packets I saw," she said.

"Someone wanted us to find that, though they didn't make it super easy."

"We have the same discrepancy here. There is data in the cache, but not the log, that a pole went offline for maintenance. Very similar to *Incident #10*," she said.

"What does that mean?"

"It means either there is some common bug in the way the control system works, or something else is happening. That something else might be related to these incidents," she said.

"We didn't find another note at any of the other incidents."

"Maybe we didn't check the right poles. Let's check the pole that indicated it went offline," Tara said.

"Let's do it."

They got into the vehicle and headed off to that one. They turned their seats toward each other while they discussed. Car interiors were designed more flexibly for passengers since the cars drove themselves.

"You know it's odd that only one pole we found had a stray message in the cache, indicating a different pole got shut down for maintenance. I checked the logs and noticed that pole wireless connectivity failed right after that event happened," she said.

"Is that normal?"

"It can be," she said.

A little while later, they arrived at the pole.

Tara pulled it apart and checked the data.

"Looks like nothing, except it's odd. This pole never indicated in its log or cache it was offline," she said, then sighed.

"Let's go to Atlanta. Maybe we can find helpful information at the *Incident* #1 location."

"Sounds good," she said as she grabbed a crunchy snack.

Mike programmed the car for Atlanta.

"We should report in our findings on that note since it suggests there being some intentional involvement here rather than these being pure accidents," Mike said.

"I guess, though, how could someone manipulate these situations? Several of the incidents involve the cause of the accidents being a manually driven vehicle. If this is some sort of hacker, how would they manipulate a manual-driven vehicle?" Tara asked as she typed up the information to report it.

"Good Question. Hopefully, as we collect additional data, we will figure this out," Mike commented.

"If hackers were responsible, why disrupt sometimes and kill other times?" Tara asked.

"They might have failed to eliminate their target in each incident, so we interviewed witnesses like you to find any possible link. We didn't find an obvious target for the incidents where no one died," Mike said.

"Possibly. It feels weird, though. Why make a death appear accidental and leave a note?" Tara asked.

"Some serial killers attempt to disguise their actions as accidents. It's true, though. Those probably don't leave a note. Other serial killers are pretty obvious that it's not accidental and leave some clues," Mike said.

"I was initially thinking this might just be hardware or software bugs, but that note is definitely suggesting otherwise," Tara said.

They drove for a while silently, each checking their laptops for details about their case. A red light flicked on the dashboard.

"Routing to the nearest car charging port," the car's navigation voice said.

"Even with all these self-driving cars, they haven't installed enough chargers yet. We'll have to go a little out of the way," Mike said. They got to a charging station, luckily by a convenience store. Mike plugged in the car charger. Not all locations had wireless charging spots cars could just automatically use. A lot of charging spots still required manual connections like this one.

"Estimated charge time thirty minutes," said the car's automated voice.

"I guess let's grab a coffee and some drinks inside," Mike said.

Mike couldn't believe it still took half an hour to charge the vehicles. They had installed fast chargers, but they expanded the battery for range and all of the new electronics added into the cars, which increased the charge times.

They bought drinks and extra snacks, then returned to the car to wait for charging to finish.

"The printer used for the note we found is too common for identification," Tara said.

"Figures," Mike said.

"Fifteen minutes until full charge," the car voice said.

A few seconds later.

"T—T—T—Temperature high, charging port error. Please disconnect," the car voice said, stuttering slightly with an additional beeping sound.

"What the hell?" Mike said.

Just then, the charger caught fire, and the fire started inching towards the plug and the car.

Mike jumped out of the car and disconnected the charger. There were some sparks as he disconnected it.

"Your shirt is on fire!" Tara yelled frantically.

Mike pulled his shirt off quickly and stomped the fire out on it.

He ran inside to tell the clerk, who came out with an extinguisher and put the fire out.

"First time seeing that," coughed the clerk, gasping from the extinguisher gas.

The smell of burnt plastic permeated the air. He then went back inside.

Mike opened the back of the car and grabbed another shirt out of his suitcase.

"Okay, we probably have enough charge to get there, but just in case, I can try to call a charge bot. They just started deploying these in this area," Mike said.

He got into the car and put on his shirt. Tara couldn't help but notice his very muscular body.

"Are you okay?" Tara asked.

"Yeah, it didn't get me. My shirt didn't make it, though," he said with a laugh.

"Lucky you got that before it got to the car," Tara said.

"I guess we got pretty lucky today, avoiding accidents twice," he said.

In a few minutes, a small car-like machine pulled up behind them. It latched on, connecting a charge port.

"That's pretty cool. Those things just came out. I've been wanting to try one of these," Mike said about the charge bot. The charge bot stayed connected even when their car occasionally shifted lanes. After about fifteen minutes, it disconnected and drove off to a nearby exit.

They drove for hours discussing minute details of the case, but nothing really stood out as definitively not an accident. They got to the motel late.

"Let's check in quick and grab some food, then we can relax for the night and start early with the investigation of *Incident* #1 tomorrow," he said.

They grabbed food at a local restaurant and returned to the motel.

"Sorry, the only thing with vacancies nearby in Atlanta was a motel. We each have our own rooms. I'm in room 86. You are in room 99, no, sorry, 87, right next door. Sending you your digital key," Mike said.

Tara checked her phone. "Got it, thanks."

Tara went back to her room. The room seemed very dated and smelled that way, too. The carpeting looked old and seemed musty. It looked like all old hotel rooms looked. She unpacked what she needed for the night and tomorrow morning, which seemed like everything in her bag.

She checked her work notes and made sure everything was saved.

She put on some PJs.

After getting into bed, she put on her smart glasses. "No messages," she heard from the smart glasses voice. "News," she said.

"Several missiles ended up in a NATO country. The White House said there would definitely be a response. The future inches closer with a fusion re-actor set to go online soon, as well as the largest solar power installations ever created," the news droned.

Soon, Tara was fast asleep. She woke up an hour later. It was midnight. She tossed and turned and went back to sleep.

Beep! The phone signaled. Tara blinked awake. There was a hooded figure a few feet from her bed.

Oh, crap. I left my smart glasses in game mode again.

She grabbed at the glasses on her face.

"Oh Shit!" She realized she wasn't wearing smart glasses as the hooded figure rushed toward her. The figure looked just like the one she thought she had seen in her smart mirror at home.

"Help! Help!" she screamed.

The hooded figure lunged toward her, and she rolled out of bed and fell on the floor on the opposite side of the hooded figure.

"HELP!" she screamed even louder.

The figure lunged toward her with a weapon. She twisted away from the wall and somehow dodged his attack.

Mike was in his room and awoke suddenly. He thought he heard Tara's voice right next to him. But she wasn't there. He then heard screeching cries for help. He grabbed his pants and gun and bolted out his door. As he got out the door, he heard screaming from Tara's room. The door was locked. He kicked the door in with three swift kicks.

He rapidly made entry, and as he did, he saw Tara in front of him, facing the attacker. The hooded figure was on the opposite side of her with something in its hand. Mike assumed it was a weapon. *No shot!* He ran towards them.

As the hooded figure lunged toward Tara, she grabbed his hand and managed an awkward Ju-Jitsu flip over her back, lobbing the hooded figure over the top of her. The figure landed on top of Mike.

"Sorry," Tara blurted.

Mike tried to grab his gun on the floor, but it was too far. Instead he grappled with the assailant and started trying to hit him, but somehow, the figure kept dodging his punches. The hooded figure did a surprising karate-style jump to his feet and kicked Mike in the upper body, knocking him to the ground. The hooded figure raced outside. Mike jumped to his feet.

"Are you okay?" he asked.

"Yes, I think so," she said.

"Call this in, air support, notify SIOC, and stay here and wait for the police. I'm going after him," he commanded.

"Okay," Tara said, somewhat shaking from the experience.

"Send digital key to Tara Bitlouver," he said into his smartwatch.

Mike sprinted out the door after the assailant. She called the police and asked them to notify the FBI field office, and she ran out to the car. Tara opened the back hatch and pulled out a large black case, put it on the ground, and opened it. She pressed the red button on top. It beeped for several seconds with a flashing light on it and rose into the air about a hundred feet. She grabbed a comm earpiece out of the back of the car.

"This is FBI consultant Tara Bitlouver. Agent Actley is chasing a suspect. Air support deployed," she said into the comm.

"Air support communication link confirmed," she heard from a female voice she recognized from her office.

The drone took off with a loud buzzing of propellers, zipping through the dark sky in the direction Mike headed.

Tara grabbed a laptop and pulled up a feed of the drone.

The police arrived at the scene. Tara described what happened as she watched the drone feed. The drone spotted Mike running down a dark road.

"Where is that?" A police officer asked.

Tara pointed at the coordinates.

"Got it. I will monitor to provide a feed for police response," he said as he called in the coordinates and direction of the chase.

Mike was running all out. He heard a drone overhead zip by from back to front.

"Target acquired," he heard from his smartwatch, comm channel.

The suspect was several hundred yards ahead of him. It was hard to see him in the dark.

"Lookout!" the comm channel screeched.

Two bullets whizzed past Mike's head. He ducked down and fired one shot at the suspect. It was too far to have much chance of hitting him.

Mike continued running towards him.

Mike saw the suspect. He ran to a bridge and stopped. The suspect seemed to look down at something from the bridge. Mike ran at him hard. He got within about twenty feet. The suspect climbed onto the rail of the bridge and jumped.

"No frickin way," Mike said. "He jumped onto a train," he said into his comm channel.

Mike thought he saw something fall off the hooded figure between the train when it jumped.

"Actley, don't..." The comm channel buzzed. It was too late. Mike had jumped over the railing onto the same train. The drone caught up with the train. This train line was relatively new and extended north of Atlanta.

The suspect was about three cars ahead. Mike chased him down the car, sprinting towards him.

Mike came to the edge of a car and looked around.

"Wait, where did he go?" he asked on the comm channel.

"Checking," the comm replied.

"He's in the gap..." the comm replied.

The hooded figure did some amazing acrobatic flip up onto Mike, knocking him down on the hard metal top of the train. The suspect pulled out a gun, and before he could aim it at Mike's head, Mike grabbed his hand, twisted his arm, pulled him down, and smashed his hand against the metal car. Finally, he got him to release the gun, which rattled and fell over the side of the car.

The suspect pulled out a stun baton and hit Mike with it. Mike fell onto the top of the train. The suspect ran off. Mike got up and chased him down the train, which was slowing down. Mike caught up with the suspect. They exchanged blows, almost knocking each other down. The suspect was losing his balance. A rumbling sound headed their way. The suspect did a ninja-like flip back onto a train on the track right next to them, going the other way.

"Man, he must have done a lot of train-ing for that," Mike muttered.

"Stay on him!" Mike yelled into his comm as he ran in the direction the other train was going, the reverse direction of the train he was on.

"Acknowledged," he heard over the comm. "Target acquired," buzzed the comm.

"Actley, I know what you are thinking. Don't do it!" the comm channel squawked.

When Mike was running as fast as he could, he leaped off the edge of his train.

"Actley!" the comm channel squawked again loudly.

Mike fell onto the top of the other train and began sliding down the side. He grabbed at anything he could. At the last second, he grabbed the ladder on the side.

"Shit! That was close. Remind me not to do this again next time," Mike said over the comm.

Mike started running across the top of the train toward the hooded figure.

"Which reminds me, are you guys going to come out here and help me?" Mike asked on comm.

"No. You are doing pretty well on your own. Police ETA in two minutes if you decide your direction," the comm channel said.

Mike caught up with the suspect at the edge between two train cars. Mike punched him hard. The suspect responded with a kick to the gut. Mike slid off the edge and disappeared. The suspect turned around and headed the other way.

"Actley! Actley! Mike, are you okay? Mike!" Tracy, on his comm channel, yelled.

Mike's head popped up over the side as he climbed up the ladder. He ran toward the suspect and jumped at him, knocking him to the metal top of the car. The suspect slid toward the edge of the car and fell over, but grabbed the edge. The train was traversing a moderately deep gorge.

"Grab my hand!" Mike yelled to the suspect, dangling off the edge. He reluctantly grabbed Mike's hand. Suddenly, a massive drone appeared beside the train, positioning itself under the suspect's feet. As his feet touched, it sounded like his shoes were locked to the drone's top.

"Why does he have a drone that's bigger than ours?" Mike asked over the comm channel. The suspect looked up at him. He could make out a smile under his hood.

The suspect took out a throwing knife from his pocket and prepared to throw it at Mike. Mike couldn't reach his gun since the suspect was holding his hand tight, and his other hand was holding on to keep him from falling. Mike's pants caught on the train with enough hold that he could quickly reach into his pocket. He pulled out something stringy and tossed it down at the suspect's drone propeller.

Whap!

A propeller got tangled up and stopped. The suspect let go and spiraled down while riding the drone.

"I hate goodbyes! But you know this one, I'm kind of okay with!" Mike yelled at the suspect.

The drone's downward spiral made survival unlikely. It was too dark to see the suspect's fate.

The FBI drone whizzed down after the suspect and his drone.

"Send the Police for trash pickup," Mike said.

"What was that stringy thing you threw at the drone?" the comm asked.

"It was my FBI neck strap badge holder," he said. "Umm. Can you tell me when my next stop is, or can someone maybe call the train conductor before I end up in California?" Mike asked.

"The train will let you off at the next available road. Your police escort has also arrived. I hope you bought a train ticket," the comm said with a laugh.

"I'm requesting a female agent for this case. This guy was no amateur. We're onto something. Make sure the police don't leave my partner until I'm back or another agent arrives," he said.

"Acknowledged," the comm squawked.

Mike sat down on top of one of the train cars, on the edge between two cars.

"Unfortunately, we couldn't see where the suspect went down. Too many trees," came over the comm.

"The police and FBI agents will execute a search tonight. You can follow up with them in the morning," the comm channel voice said.

"Thanks," Mike replied.

The train came to a stop by a roadway. There was a police car with its lights on near the train. Mike walked over to the police car. The officer rolled down his window.

"I hear you need a lift," the officer said.

"You're late. I could have used you like five minutes ago," Mike replied.

"Sorry, I heard you couldn't decide if you should get on the eastbound or westbound train," he said.

"That isn't quite the full story," Mike said as he got into the car.

The officer drove him back to his motel.

Tara was waiting with the police. "Mike, are you okay?" Tara asked.

"I think so. Kind of tired, though," he said.

"Officer are there any hotels with vacancies in the area?" she asked.

"I doubt it. There are multiple conferences happening, probably booked solid," the officer said.

"A police officer will also be stationed out front all night," Mike said.

"Tara, if you don't mind, you can stay in my room because, you know, I think I broke your door. I'll sleep on the sofa bed. You can take the bed. Is that okay?" Mike asked.

"Yes, that's fine," Tara said. "I'll get my stuff from my room," she said.

She brought her suitcase and equipment into Mike's room. She filled him in on what happened before he broke down her room door.

"Did the suspect take anything from you?" Mike asked.

"No, I don't think so," she said.

"So, he wasn't looking for anything. He seemed intent on you," he said.

"Yes, it seemed so," Tara replied.

"Do you know any reason someone would want to hurt you?" Mike asked.

"No, nothing I can think of except, of course, this investigation," she said.

"Yes, seems likely we may have stumbled on to something," Mike said.

Mike had his shirt off and was applying antiseptic, gauze, and bandages to his wounds. He was trying to get it just right on some cuts on his head.

"Here, let me help you," Tara said.

She motioned to take the antiseptic and bandages. Carefully, Tara took them and cleaned and bandaged multiple areas on his head, chest, arms, and back.

"I'm just so glad you are alive," Tara said.

"Me too," he said.

"What did I get myself into here? I don't think I can deal with this. I'm not sure how you do this. Maybe I should resign," Tara sobbed slightly.

"Hey, it's okay now," Mike said. "I'm not sure it would be safe at home, either. I get you are scared. Now that we know it should be safer with us. Don't worry. The FBI takes care of its own. I requested a female agent that will be able to stay with you twenty-four-seven. We've spent months getting nowhere on this case before you came on board. We are now getting some good evidence. While it could have just been a robbery attempt, this guy seemed like a professional. My gut is telling me someone doesn't want us to find something. If that's true, I'm a little annoyed they didn't send someone after me. Apparently, if true, they consider you the smart one in this operation," he said.

"Umm. What did you mean by professional?" Tara said, with tears welling.

"Never mind that. So where did you get those awesome moves? You flipped that guy like he was nothing," Mike said with a smile.

"Sorry about tossing him on you. I learned some Ju Jitsu, Judo, and Aikido many years ago in a personal defense class. I'm not very good at it, I just use defensive moves. I don't want to hurt anyone," she said.

"You did great. I was just too slow to move out of the way. Now that I know you can do that, I'll try to be a little faster next time. Did you say you were a pacifist?" Mike asked.

"Yes," Tara bristled, wiping away her tears. "Forget about me. What about you? Are you like some movie action hero or something?" Tara said with a smile.

"Hardly. I don't think an action hero would have let their suspect disappear. Plus, they never seem quite as banged up as I am," Mike said with a sigh.

"Umm, this is going to sound weird. But at home. I thought I saw a robed guy for a split second in my smart mirror. I admittedly had been drinking. I checked my security, and it didn't seem like it was hacked," Tara said, still shaken even more by that idea.

"That is strange," Mike said.

Mike brushed his teeth and set up the sofa bed. Tara went to the bathroom to put on some PJs and brushed her teeth.

Tara looked at the sink before it was weird. She looked again. It had two handles connected to what would typically be one handle to control hot, code, and volume of water. One handle was red and said "dirty," and the other handle was green and said "clean."

"Oh, that's pretty smart. Use the red dirty handle to turn the water on when you want to wash your hands. Then, use the green handle to turn the water off. That way, when you turn the water off, you don't get the germs on your hand by touching the dirty handle," Tara said.

They both went to bed.

"Goodnight," Tara said.

"Goodnight," Mike replied, getting into the sofa bed.

Chapter 10

A blaring alarm filled the air.

"Good Morning. What is the square root of 1024?" the voice from Tara's phone asked.

"Oh, shit! Sorry," Tara blurted out.

"What is the square root of 1024?" the voice repeated as the alarm continued.

"Um... 32," Tara announced.

"Have a nice day," the voice responded.

"What the hell was that?" Mike asked sleepily.

"Sorry, I would often turn alarms off and go back to sleep. I programmed the alarms to require some type of problem I need to solve, so I have a better chance of actually waking up," Tara said. She felt her cheeks warm.

"Normally, I would get up early to get some exercise in. I figured we could both use a little extra rest after last night, though," he said.

"You can use the shower first," Tara said.

"I'll be quick," he said.

He brushed his teeth, shaved, and hopped in the shower. Shortly after, he emerged, wrapped in a towel. He started drying his hair.

Tara couldn't help but notice he was pretty muscular all over. She turned away to avoid staring. Of course, there was a mirror. She could still see, but she tried not to look. *Guys like that wouldn't be interested in her. Plus, work and relationships don't mix.* She also figured mixing a pacifist with a military type was not a good idea.

Tara still had her hair up and was in her very conservative PJs. Tara brushed her teeth and hopped in the shower. When Tara finished showering, she turned off the water. She noticed this shower had a dryer. The shower had a tall grate on the other side of the shower head. She pushed a button next to the grate. A forceful wind came out of it that was quite strong. She came out wrapped in a towel with her hair down.

"Let's grab some breakfast," Mike said.

"Sounds good," Tara replied.

Mike turned and glimpsed her wrapped in a towel. He tried to stop himself from doing a double-take, but it was too late. He glanced away.

Wow! She is really beautiful with her hair down. She didn't look like that dressed up. Her curves are... he sucked in a sharp breath, stopping himself mid-thought. *Never get involved with co-workers.*

They took turns getting dressed in the bathroom.

Tara was back in the typical hair-up and conservative clothes. Mike got dressed in business casual.

They left the room. An officer was posted outside. Mike thanked the officer and let him go.

Tara and Mike got into their car and requested the list of nearby restaurants from the computer. Tara agreed to the one Mike pointed to, so he selected it. A brief notice popped onto the screen and disappeared. It said,

75% tire tread life.

On the way there, they checked the search status for the suspect. They haven't found the drone or the suspect yet. They had narrowed the area down, hopefully.

They arrived at the restaurant and were seated quickly. The inside smelled like coffee and pancakes. It was moderately noisy with the chatter of people and the clangs of dishes. They waited to talk about the case until they ordered.

"Let's review what we have so far," Mike said.

"Okay, here we go," Tara said.

"*Incident* #10. Found data in the pole cache that said a different pole went offline forty miles away. We have a dead terrorist funding criminal."

Mike made a note.

"*Incident* #11. We found a similar type of data in the cache for a pole that went offline, different from the one with the data. No deaths. One was severely injured."

She paused.

"*Incident* #3. We have a really odd traffic pattern created by the cars going in a circle several miles wide. Roads reported closed for reasons unknown. There is another case of a pole being offline, different from the one with the data in the cache. We have a dead U.S. intelligence agent. We found a note referencing data that seemed strange to us but suggested it was something more."

Mike stared at her, waiting for her to continue.

"It's normal for poles to go offline occasionally, but it should be logged in the central computer. Reports from NTSB should have been recorded in nearby poles. No records of poles going offline for maintenance, except for cache data inconsistencies. So, it could be a bug in the system since we've seen it so often, or it could be something related to these incidents," Tara stated.

"You were also attacked last night after we investigated these three incidents," Mike added.

"I was trying to forget the last part," she said.

"Sorry, I'm hoping we'll be able to find some missing piece here," he said.

She shrugged.

"Seems the best leads we have are analyzing the odd data and trying to find our suspect," Mike said.

"I've got a pattern analysis scrutinizing the data. I'm analyzing the drone footage from last night, frame by frame, to identify the suspect and the drone details," she said.

It impressed Mike how quickly she was up to speed with the case.

"Is there a way we can request the car data that was involved in the incidents?" Tara asked.

"We did. The companies are delaying, sending the data in case there is a bug they could be at fault for. They are required to turn it over, but they are pushing back and filing lawsuits to prevent releasing it," he said.

After breakfast, they headed to *Incident* #1's location since it was nearby.

"*Incident* #1 was self-driving cars coming to a stop blocking a highway into Atlanta. No direct deaths associated with this one," Tara said.

They reached the first of thirty poles to pull traffic data and check the cache. They were going poll to poll downloading and sending the data to the field office.

"Wait, we need to get this off. It could be another note," Tara said.

Mike got a screwdriver to help take it off. They got it off.

"It is a note. Looks the same as the other. Checking the data," she said while typing in the numbers.

"It looks like the numbers on the note match up with the odd data packets for this incident as well. Similar to *Incident* #3. I will start an analysis," she said.

"Should we ask other field offices to check the other incidents for notes and data?" she asked.

"You know, something just isn't adding up for me. Why leave a note and then try to go after someone that finds it? Let's limit who knows about this case until we know more about what's happening. We will need to investigate ourselves for now," he said.

Tara's phone beeped. It reminded her she was in away mode. The lights in her home were automated to turn off during the day and simulate her nighttime routine, confusing potential thieves about her presence. *Oh, I forgot about that feature.*

They continued to the other poles to collect data. Nothing else interesting appeared. They were just finishing up processing and sending the data.

Mike's phone rang. "Agent Actley." He paused. "We're on our way," he said.

"What?" she said.

"They found the drone. They didn't find the suspect, but they are following a trail of blood," he said.

He entered the location into the car and pressed lights and siren mode.

The car accelerated fast. The siren blared. Faster than even normal cruise mode. Tara had never been in a car traveling this fast. Other self-driving vehicles promptly cleared the road for them.

"I think this could be great for a work commute," Tara joked.

"It is." Mike smiled. "I'm kidding. Of course, it would be dangerous and highly illegal," he said.

A manual-driven car wasn't immediately getting out of the way, so their vehicle had to slow down and go around it.

"We even get traffic lights to turn green for us automatically so we can get to a scene faster," he said.

"Can you tap into their drone feeds?" Mike asked.

"I think so, checking," she said as she typed into her laptop. "Got it," she said.

"Looks like they just have a grid search going on," Mike said looking at the drone in the video.

The car was still speedily dodging cars with the siren blaring.

Mike's phone rang again. "Agent Actley."

"No. No. This isn't a bad time. Please meet us at the search location," he said.

"Who was that?" Tara asked.

"That is the other agent I requested. She'll meet us there," Mike said.

The cars outside moved like in Incident #10 when she witnessed Victor drive between them. This time, though, they were reacting to the emergency vehicle, lights, siren, and emergency transponder broadcast from their vehicle.

Their car pulled onto the closest road to the search area. There were many more black SUVs and police cars in the area. There is also a larger truck with doors in it for the mobile command center.

"Agent Actley. I'm here at your request," the female agent said.

"Nice to see you, Robin," Mike said. "Agent Laizon, this is our technical consultant, Tara Bitlouver," he said.

"Tara, this is Agent Robin Laizon."

Tara guessed Robin was about the same age and height as she was. With her short brown hair tucked behind her ears and a medium curvy build, she was quite attractive. Dressed in a simple business suit, her pants seemed more form fitting, and the top was a little more revealing than most FBI women would wear.

"Nice to meet you," Tara said.

"Same," Robin said.

Mike said to Robin, "Twenty-four-seven protection detail on her. The guy last night seemed like a pro," as he glanced at Tara.

An officer came up to Mike. Mike showed him his badge.

"Follow me," he said.

"Robin, Tara, why don't you stay here and go to the command center to watch the feeds?" Mike said.

Tara followed Robin to the truck.

"What does he mean by pro?" Tara asked Robin.

"You know a paid assassin," she said.

"What?" Tara choked, tears forming.

"Sorry, didn't mean to worry you. Pretty much everyone on this task force has had death threats," she said.

"How many had paid assassins go after them?" Tara asked.

"Well, Actley has had several. We've lost count. Don't worry. He is very good at the job," Robin said.

"He wants to do everything to get them immediately. So, they don't get a chance to come back. It also sends a message to any others that might be interested," Robin said.

When they got to the mobile command center, Robin and Tara showed their badges and were ushered in. Inside oversized monitors, whirling computers, drone controllers, and radios filled every flat space.

"Get some additional dogs and drones over to sector five," one agent said into the radio.

"Acknowledged," a voice said over the radio.

Mike followed the officers into the woods.

"Where we found the drone is a few minutes from here," one officer said as they trudged through the forest.

"You don't have any gators back here, do you?" Mike asked.

"Sometimes. I don't see them very often," the officer replied.

They came to the site of the drone. It was heavily damaged. There was blood on it and leading away from it into the forest. Mike and an officer followed the trail for twenty minutes to where other officers and agents were.

"We lost the trail here," one officer said.

"Let's split up," the senior agent said. They split into three groups of two to search south, east, and west. There was an FBI agent and officer on each mini-team. They plodded through the dense forest, checking their surroundings. There was a heavy wood smell mixed in with a smell of water algae. Twigs and brush crumbled and snapped beneath their feet.

"Hey, look here," the officer said as he pointed to something below a large tree.

"Looks like blood," the officer said.

Mike walked towards the tree.

Suddenly, a branch snapped above, and a hooded figure dropped out of the tree on top of the officer, slamming him down. The figure hit the officer hard, knocking him out.

Mike stepped towards the figure, but he was already running, or more like fast hobbling, towards a clearing. Mike knelt and checked the officer's pulse. Faint, but it was still there.

"Agent Actley to command, officer down, need medical and backup to my location. Suspect on the run," he said.

Mike ran toward the suspect. The suspect was clearly injured. A buzzing sound came from overhead, but Mike couldn't see through the trees.

As Mike approached the suspect and the clearing, he saw two enormous drones. One drone had a hooded figure on top, dressed like the suspect. The other didn't have anyone riding it. The drone, without any rider, landed in front of the suspect. The suspect turned quickly and threw a knife at Mike. Mike fired one shot, hitting the suspect, who now seemed injured enough he couldn't board the drone.

The hooded figure riding the drone in the air got close to the suspect, pulled an enormous weapon from behind his back, aimed at the suspect, and fired. A stream of liquid flame poured out onto the suspect. The suspect was fully engulfed in flames. He attempted to hobble off in one direction, setting grass and trees on fire.

Some officers could be heard coming from where Mike had just been.

"Help the officer back there and the suspect. I'm going after this monk-looking robed guy!" he yelled.

The drone that had been waiting for their suspect lifted off with no one on it.

Mike ran and dove onto it. Climbing onboard. This drone seemed different. It had foot pedals and harnesses to hold your feet in. Mike strapped in quickly as the drone rose into the air.

An FBI drone flew into the site, hovering to get visuals on the hooded suspect #2 and Mike.

"Does anyone know how to fly one of these things?" Mike asked over the comm.

"You are supposed to figure that out before you board a strange aircraft," came the reply.

"Don't worry, I'll figure it out!" Mike yelled as the drone began flying almost sideways. Mike crouched down to get his balance again.

Mike slowly figured out how to fly as he got it, heading toward the second suspect, who was now flying away at top speed. Mike got closer. Trailing them was a smaller FBI drone.

Suddenly, suspect two turned around, heading right at Mike.

The hooded figure sprayed a stream of fire in Mike's direction. Mike dodged it before he pulled out his gun and fired a shot, but missed. It was hard shooting while moving on a drone.

"Hey! I bet you don't have a lot of friends, given you seem to like setting them on fire!" Mike said to the robed assailant.

The suspect went low near the ground, trying to shake Mike off his trail. It almost worked. Mike nearly lost his balance on a swinging turn to avoid obstacles. The wind was blowing in Mike's face.

The suspect's drone and Mike's drone seemed to slow down.

"Oh, crap! I think our drones might be running out of power!" Mike yelled into the comm.

"Think you can find a charger? We've got the suspect sighted by our drone," the comm replied.

"Funny. I'll ask him if he'll, you know, wait while we recharge," Mike said.

The suspect flew over the highway. Many self-driving trucks formed a large convoy on the highway, occupying one or two lanes.

The suspects drone slowed and landed on top of a moving truck.

"Guys! Are you seeing this?" Mike said.

"Our suspect landing on a truck?" The comm said.

"No, how he really stuck that landing. I'm not sure if I can pull that off," Mike said.

The suspect started running on top of the line of trucks! Mike set his drone down just on the edge of the truck, hanging over.

"Whoa!" he let out. It was almost going to tip over the edge. He leaned the other way to keep from falling. He unbuckled his feet and rolled onto the top of the truck. The drone fell off the edge of the truck. The pieces of the drone sparked and then exploded as it skidded off the side of the road.

When the suspect got near the end of the truck, he jumped onto a passing truck in the other lane. Mike used the same method to catch up.

"Oh, shit!" he yelled as he dropped flat on his belly on top of the truck. So did the suspect, as the trucks went underneath a bridge.

"Command, is someone coming to help this time? This isn't a TV show, you know," Mike said.

"For the show to be entertaining, you are supposed to catch the bad guy. Police are on their way. Our drone has the suspect acquired," the command channel commented.

Mike heard police sirens coming up from behind a few trucks back.

The suspect was on a truck a few lengths away when he turned and fired multiple shots at Mike.

"Shit, I'm hit!" Mike said, returning fire. He quickly patted himself down. "I think it's just a flesh wound. I'm okay."

The suspect turned once more to fire, but nothing happened.

"I think he's out of ammo, or his weapon jammed. I'm going for him."

Mike ran up to him and caught the suspect before he could jump to the other truck.

The hooded figure did a twirling kick high and then a sweeping kick low, knocking Mike down with his head hanging over the edge of the truck.

Mike used a martial arts leg lock to drop the suspect. The suspect jumped to his feet and started dragging Mike by his feet. Mike kicked the assailant and got up. Mike punched the suspect and missed as the robed monk dodged. Mike noticed the robed figure wearing glasses. The suspect grabbed his arm and flipped him over his back down onto the metal of the top of the truck with a thud.

Mike had the wind knocked out of him from being dropped. He used all his strength and breath to get up.

"Bridge!" came over the comm channel to Mike.

The hooded figure ran towards Mike, toward the rear of the truck, to deliver a knockout blow.

"You are under arrest. You have the right to remain..." Mike yelled at the suspect, then dropped to his stomach. "Remain right there."

Caught off guard, the suspect smacked into the low hanging overpass. What was left of him slumped to the road, and got run over by a truck.

Mike winced at the grotesque sight.

"Okay, can someone tell me why I'm on top of a moving vehicle again? Never mind, just get this thing to stop. Thanks," he said on his comm.

Police cars pulled behind the truck and issued the stop command to the self-driving truck he was on, so the vehicle pulled over. After Mike got into the police car, the officer took him back to the command center. There was an ambulance standing by. Mike sat on the back while they checked him out and tended to his injuries.

"Are you okay?" Tara asked.

"Yep, fine. The bullet just grazed me. I might have lost part of my eyebrows to the flamethrower. Are they still there?" he said.

"They look like they are there. Is this a regular occurrence for you?" Tara asked.

"Umm. I wouldn't call it regular, but I guess I wouldn't call it rare either," Mike said.

"So, what do we have on these guys?" Mike asked Robin.

"Nothing. Suspect one was burned beyond recognition. There is no DNA on file. Suspect two. Well, you saw him. There was not much left to identify. No matching DNA has been found yet for him either. You know it would help if you kept your suspects alive and in one piece," Robin said, half-joking.

"I will ask them nicely next time to put down their weapons, stop shooting and trying to flame broil me," Mike said.

"I had an idea if we head to *Incident #4* in Kansas next. It's kind of the next closest. Since Tara doesn't like flying, we just sleep in the car. It takes about thirteen hours, a little longer, with food stops and such. That way, we don't burn a day getting there. We can check in to a hotel in the morning for a shower," Mike said.

"It's okay with me. Since you are basically doing this for me," Tara said timidly.

"I always wanted to see that area driving. Most of the time, we end up flying over it," Mike said.

"Sounds good to me. I call the back row. Rocks me to sleep like a baby," Robin said half cheerily.

They piled into the SUV. The car screen said,

Standby cleaning sensors.

They could see sprays of liquid around the car's front and side.

Then the screen displayed,

Sensors operational.

Mike requested the computer to navigate to a hotel near *Incident #4.*

"Given the time now, calculating in stops for dinner, rest stops, and traffic, we should make it before nine a.m. or so," he said.

"Have you done this often?" Tara asked.

"A bit. It's cheaper than flying usually. So, it depends on whether the FBI needs us there early or can wait a couple of days. If they can wait sometimes, we'll just motor across the U.S. this way," he said.

After about an hour, Robin checked her email.

"I just got a message on the DNA from suspect one. There is a partial match for multiple homicides in several countries. They believe he's an international hitman for hire. They don't know who might have paid him," Robin said.

"Why would a hitman want to kill me?" Tara felt the sting of tears again.

"Don't worry. They can't hurt you now. It's much less likely they could find anyone else, given, you know, what happened to these guys," he said.

"You mean burned to a crisp and flattened like a pancake," Robin said.

"That was not my fault. Well, the first guy wasn't. The second guy, I guess it's kind of arguable," he said.

Robin gave him a look.

"Why leave notes and hire someone like that? It doesn't really make any sense. We are missing something here," he said.

"Maybe they initially wanted some recognition and decided otherwise? It is strange," Robin said.

"Let's review all the data again and see if we can come up with anything new. Can someone else watch the drone video of me going after suspect two? I can't stand watching myself on video," he said.

"Sure, I'll watch it," said Tara.

They all started reviewing different data from each of the incidents.

"You know, there is a data pattern I'm seeing. I can't recall where I've seen it before. It feels like an artifact of machine learning. That could just be the nature of the traffic control systems, or it could be a clue," she said. "I'm going to get more details to see if I can figure it out."

They programmed in a restaurant to stop at along their route that also had a car charger a next to it. While they analyzed the data, Tara momentarily diverted her attention to the scenery outside the window. There was green grass and trees and some slight hills off in the distance.

The car pulled into a charging spot next to the restaurant. There was a convenience store next to it.

"Where are we?" Tara asked.

"Somewhere in northern Alabama, I think," Mike said. He didn't check the exact location when he programmed in the restaurant.

They went in and sat down. This place looked like it had been here a while. It wasn't much to look at, but the atmosphere was fine, and the aroma smelled great. They all ordered some soft drinks and sandwiches.

"Robin, how did you get to know Mike?" Tara asked.

"We've worked a few cases together. Yes, they were executed with Mike's usual level of enthusiasm." Robin rolled her eyes.

"By usual, she means me dodging bad guy's bullets," Mike said.

They chatted some more, and the food came.

"The food here is pretty good. Nice pick," Tara said.

After eating, they walked over to the convenience store next door to grab some drinks for the road. They were in the back, selecting drinks. The convenience store was a typical small store with a few aisles of snacks and various items.

Robin saw Mike take a hard stare towards the front of the store.

"Tara, you duck behind this freezer. Call the police," Mike lowered his voice.

"Robin, right flank," Mike whispered.

Robin crossed over to the far aisle, ducking down, and headed toward the front of the store. Mike was doing the same on the aisle directly behind a customer at the front counter.

Mike got up behind the customer. Robin was to the side. Both of them had their guns drawn.

"FBI! Don't move! Drop your weapon!" Mike said as he placed his gun behind the head of the customer, who was apparently holding a gun at the store clerk. Robin had her gun aimed at the robber's back.

"Buddy, you have terrible luck or timing to rob a store with FBI agents in it," Mike said.

The suspect put his gun on the counter. They had the suspect sit down on the floor.

"Thanks. I'm glad you guys were here," the clerk said.

"So, buddy, what made you pick this store now?" Mike asked.

"An app on my phone said I should stop and get a lottery ticket because it was my lucky day. So, I did. But I thought it would be even luckier if I got all the cash in the register," he said.

"Let me see your phone," Mike said to the suspect.

"Super-hot lucky lottery app?" Mike said.

"Yep, it's great. Sometimes I win a few dollars," the suspect said.

The police arrived and took the suspect away.

"You can have the drinks free," the clerk said.

"Thanks, but we can't accept that," Mike said as he paid for the drinks.

They got into the car. Mike programmed the hotel in Kansas into the system.

"Well, we are on our way again. So, can anyone think of what ties these incidents together? Or differentiates them?" Mike asked.

"Manual drive vehicles are sometimes the cause of their death and someone else's. However, only some incidents involved manual-driving vehicles. Some incidents caused disruption but not deaths," Robin said.

"Some incidents have odd data indicating a traffic control computer pole was offline, though there is no other evidence of that. It could be a bug in the traffic control software or something else," Tara said.

"*Incident* #11, we were almost involved in, is the only incident where the car that was hit had a survivor. We checked the occupant's identity. They didn't seem to be a criminal, terrorist, or intelligence agent. One worked at the post office, the other at a retail store," Mike said.

"Several of the incidents involve a person acting odd driving the manual vehicle and one time even a pedestrian," Tara said.

"Actin' odd might describe about 50% of the country," Robin said, half-joking.

"I still feel like we are missing something. But have no idea what," Mike said.

Tara saw a small device in the distance ahead of them go to the middle of the roadway when it was clear, pause, and then quickly move to the other side. It kept repeating that pattern even as they got closer.

"What is that?" Tara asked.

"Oh, I think those are new automated road repair devices," Mike said.

Over the next hour or two, they did a mix of watching videos or looking at case data.

Robin was texting someone furiously for a bit, and then stopped.

"Is that a guy you are texting?" Tara asked with a smile.

"Was, he ghosted me," Robin said with a frown. "I'm going to get some sleep back here," Robin said.

Mike and Tara continued reading online.

Tara put on her smart glasses. "News," she commanded.

"And the weather tomorrow in the northeast will be hot and sunny. In the middle of the country, there could be very strong thunderstorms part of the day, so be on the..." the smart glass video said until Tara changed the news channel.

"The largest space hotel has finally opened. Its first guests might be arriving soon. The Russian war with non-NATO countries is heating up..." the video said.

"Cat videos," Tara commanded.

It was late. Tara fell asleep.

Chapter 11

She woke up groggily from the bumps in the road. It had only been about an hour later. The seat seemed a little lumpy. She sat up. She then realized Mike had dozed off, and she was sleeping pretty much on top of him. Tara hoped he didn't notice. She leaned toward the door this time and dozed off.

BANG!

SCREECH!

It jolted everyone awake.

"What? The hell! Not again! Hang on!" Mike yelled.

"SHIT!" Robin exclaimed.

"AHH!" Tara screamed.

Their car spun out of control, crashing through the road barrier and plunging into water.

BOOM!

As they hit the rail, the airbags all inflated.

The car splashed furiously into the water, quickly filling with water.

"I can't open the door! Where's my gun?" Mike yelled.

"Back door won't open either. Break the windows! I can't find my gun either." Robin yelled. They had both taken off their gun holsters, as it was uncomfortable to sleep with them on.

"Find something sharp, strong, and pointy to break the window! Anything!" Mike yelled.

"My seatbelt is stuck," Tara said.

Mike tried to help get it undone.

Tara still had her purse. She reached in, remembering she had the pointy T shaped object.

"You have one of those? Great!" said Mike. He took it from Tara's hand and used the slotted end to cut her seatbelt off her.

"I'm going to break the front side and back side windows with this. I'm going to count to three. Hold your breath before I get to three, as the water will rush in," he said.

"One."

"Two."

"Three!"

He smashed the windows with the pointy side of the tool. Mike pushed open the door once the water pressure equalized. He helped Tara and Robin out.

They swam to shore.

"Is anyone hurt?" Mike asked.

"Think just scrapes and bumps," Robin said.

"I hurt my head and arm. Are you okay, Mike?" Tara asked.

"Scratches and my leg hurts, but I think I'm okay," Mike said.

There was a manual drive vehicle smashed up a lot with the driver inside. The driver was very incoherent. Mike took his phone out of his pocket. The screen was shattered, but he still managed to dial 911.

"We need an ambulance at my location with multiple injuries," Mike said and discussed with the operator.

Mike then checked Tara and Robin to see how bad their injuries were. Since they were minor, he moved on to check the driver's injuries.

"Are you okay?" he asked the driver. He didn't get an intelligible response.

Two ambulances arrived. One worked on getting the driver out of the vehicle and bandaged up. The other tended to Mike, Tara, and Robin.

He contacted the FBI to arrange equipment retrieval and investigation.

"That ambulance is going to take the driver to the hospital. We'll go in this one and follow them and get checked out ourselves," Mike stated.

Tara, Robin, and Mike got into the ambulance. The ambulance took off in lights and siren mode. The self-drive vehicles moved aside to allow the ambulances to pass.

At the hospital, the paramedics escorted Mike, Robin, and Tara into the ER. The driver of the manual drive vehicle was on a stretcher, being wheeled by. Mike walked over as they were wheeling him into a room.

"Hey! What's your name? What happened?" Mike asked.

"They were chasing me. Did you hear the voices?" the driver said, not making any sense. The ER doctor looked at the driver.

"We need to get him into the operating room for his head injury," the doctor said as he helped wheel him quickly away.

The hospital checked out Tara, Robin, and Mike.

"What did the doctors say? Everyone okay?" Mike asked.

"All good. Slightly sprained wrist," Robin said.

"I'm good. My arm is bruised, nothing broken, though," Tara said.

"My leg is sore, but okay. Is it possible to sprain your ear? It feels like I slept on something the wrong way," Mike said.

Tara hoped it wasn't her accidentally sleeping on top of Mike earlier.

"The FBI is sending another vehicle with replacement equipment. They fished our car out of the water."

"Want to go check the traffic control poles or get our clothes and go to the hotel?" Mike asked.

Both Robin and Tara gave him a pretty odd look.

"From that look, I'd say clothes, then hotel. Our car should be here," Mike said.

"Luckily, the FBI Field office is in this city, so they already sent a car to collect our clothes, and it should be here any minute," Mike said.

They walked to the hospital entrance, and there was a dark black SUV waiting for them.

The clothes they were wearing were still a little damp, but not too bad. They got in the vehicle.

"Change of plans. We'll go to a closer hotel here so we can check out the scene of our accident and check traffic control poles," he said.

They checked into the hotel. It was nice and clean. Clearly, it had been updated recently. Their rooms were next to each other. They stripped down to their underwear and put on the complimentary robes.

They walked downstairs to the laundry room. Mike had double checked to make sure this hotel had them. They chatted about mundane topics while their clothes washed. Once they put their clothes into the dryers, they went back to Mike's room to wait.

"Tara, it was super lucky you had that car emergency window breaker and seatbelt cutter," Mike said.

"Is that what it was?" Tara asked.

"Wait? You didn't know? How did you have it then?" he asked.

"It's funny, actually. My 3D metal printer at home has been printing objects I never requested," Tara said.

"That's both odd and lucky in this case," Mike added.

"I spoke to that driver. He made little sense when I talked to him. Similar to witnesses who saw drivers of manual vehicles earlier for other incidents. No blood alcohol detected. Tox screen came back negative on all of them," Mike said.

"I think we need to call this *Incident* #12. Once we pull the traffic control data, perhaps we can see if it's related. It again all seems like a possible accident, a careless manual driver, or one with a medical issue, perhaps. Medical records were clean on the other ones," he said.

"We don't exactly fit the profile, not a criminal, terrorist, or intelligence agent," Robin said.

"Maybe an FBI agent is close enough? Or anyone investigating these," Mike said.

"What was the occupation of the driver?" Tara asked.

"Manager. Retail," he said.

"We still don't seem to know anything, and we don't have enough evidence to prove anything. These still could be what they seem. Just accidents. I have to admit, it seems like a statistically odd number of accidents. Just bad luck?" Robin said.

"Let's not forget a pro came after our team. We don't have any proof tying that to this investigation. It could have just been a robbery attempt. But in my gut, I'm sure it ties in," Mike said.

"Good point. It highly suggests there is more here than meets the eye," Robin stated glumly.

"Also, those notes we found point to data anomalies. The fact that we found something suggests there's validity to this," Mike said.

Tara was deep in thought, trying to figure out what she might be missing. She glanced up as Mike shifted, and his robe flapped open a little before he closed it.

He's hot. Tara felt heat creep up her neck into her cheeks as she ogled his muscular physique.

Not with colleagues. As she shifted, her own robe opened slightly. She closed it quickly as Mike looked away.

Hope he didn't see. Her embarrassment increasing.

"We have a lot of suggestive evidence. If we don't find something concrete soon, they might decide to pull the plug on this investigation," Mike said.

"Given the statistics of accidents between self-driving and manual drive vehicles, this could be an anomaly. If not, it would be unlikely to occur randomly," Tara said.

"Either that, or you guys, and now I have terrible luck," Robin said.

"True. We nearly got into an accident in Virginia. I got attacked at night. We walked into a store as it was being robbed. We got into the accident today," Tara said.

"That's like a normal week for Mike," Robin smirked.

"No, it's not normally that bad... Hmm. Maybe sometimes. I can't deny trouble seems to follow me around," Mike said, thinking back to some other cases.

"Oh, I forgot to mention my game console the night before we left caught fire. Oh crap! Wasn't there a device fire in one of our cases? I think it was a TV, though," Tara said.

"That is a lot of odd stuff in a few days," Robin said.

"To be safe, pull any available data from your internet provider," Mike added.

"Good idea," Tara said.

"I think our clothes might be done by now," Tara said.

They grabbed their clothes and brought everything back to their rooms to get dressed.

Robin and Tara were in their room. Tara got a shower and dressed her usual way, with her hair up. She put her towel on the towel rack. She noticed a button on the rack and pressed it. Forceful air started coming out of the rack and some slits behind it, drying the towel. It turned off in about a minute.

"Why do you dress so conservatively? You have a nice figure. You should wear something that at least shows it a little," Robin said.

Robin wore business attire, slightly revealing but still professional.

"Thanks, Umm. It's just how I dress and feel, I guess. Plus, I want to be conservative for the FBI. Also, I don't like to be objectified. It makes me uncomfortable," she said.

"In our line of work, a little can be useful. Men will talk to a pretty woman," Robin says with a wink. "It's that, or I could beat the snot out of them. I figure it's a little easier the other way," Robin grinned. "Also, you know, getting noticed gets you more dates if you like that sort of thing,"

"I'm usually too busy for that," Tara said.

"Working for the FBI isn't easy on the work-life balance. I know that one," Robin groaned.

They met in the hallway. Most hotels were rather bland. However, this one had pleasant pictures evenly distributed throughout it. They could hear the sounds of people moving about further down the hallway.

"Let's get going and grab some sandwiches along the way," Mike said.

They went downstairs. On their way out, they could smell the distinct scent of a pool. Once outside, they summoned their SUV over and got in.

"Before we get going, I want to set up a live trace of traffic data with real-time pattern monitoring. I put in the request to enable it earlier," Tara said.

"That sounds like a great idea," Mike said.

"Worth a shot," Robin said.

Mike requested a list of local restaurants, then selected a local sandwich shop, got them to go, and headed on their way.

They ate their lunch in the car as they headed off to the first of the poles about thirty miles from where their accident occurred and worked their way back to the accident scene. Halfway through collecting traffic control data, the police provided a case update. The driver stated he thought someone was chasing him, and he had been anxious and paranoid all day. From his social media, they found he was into conspiracy theories.

"Great, another conspiracy nut. Maybe we just have more mentally unstable people causing accidents," Robin said.

They finished collecting the pole traffic data and stopped at the area where their car went over the rail and into the water.

"Just seeing this again is giving me anxiety. None of the traffic data had any obvious anomalies, but I will continue to run it through analysis," Tara said.

"Anything on the other anomalies that matched the notes?" Mike asked.

"Nothing yet. The algorithm is picking up partial matches. We need to find another note to help," Tara said.

Mike and Robin walked the area around where their car went over the edge. Tara was in the car, checking some data. There were skid marks, but nothing else obvious.

"When we went over the rail, did you say, not again?" Robin asked Mike.

"Yeah, about three months prior, I was chasing the same guy, Victor, who died in *Incident* #10, and we went over a cliff into the water," Mike stated.

"Man! Maybe you do have bad luck. How many other people do you think that happens to?" Robin asked.

"I know, right? Trouble seems to have a way of finding me," Mike said.

"Hey, we never really talked after. You know I was drunk and was coming on to you. While I guess it makes you a nice guy for not taking advantage of me and all. I just kind of wondered why not."

"I like to enter relationships sober. Plus, I try to avoid getting involved with colleagues. You know how that goes. Plus, if things didn't go well, you could kick my ass. That seemed like a bad idea." Mike winked.

"You got that right," Robin agreed.

Mike and Robin got back in the car.

"What were you guys talking about?" Tara asked.

"The case," Robin said. Mike looked a little flustered.

"What if this isn't bad luck and the gaming console catching on fire, almost getting in an accident, being attacked in her room, plus us having an accident meant we were being directly targeted? Sorry, just listening to that come out of my mouth sounds crazy," Robin said.

"Since the accidents were caused by manual drivers, it's either an accident or they would need to be involved, right? It seems pretty unlikely," Tara said.

"Nothing came up in the background checks on them. It seems very unlikely," Mike said.

"Let's head over to *Incident #4*. Maybe we'll find some new clues there," Mike said.

"This case is really frustrating! It would be easier dealing with an armed robbery than this," Robin groaned.

Just then, a self-driving vehicle pulled over next to them. There appeared to be a man in the back sleeping. It was strange that a self-driving vehicle stopped on the highway without its disabled light. Mike went over to the back window and pounded on it.

"Hey sir, you, okay?" Mike said.

The man didn't move. Mike opened the rear door, and the man fell out of the vehicle. Mike checked for pulse and breathing. Nothing. He felt cool, like it had been a while since he died.

Mike called the local police and paramedics. They arrived and took over the scene. They declared the man dead. The man apparently had a rap sheet.

"What happened to him?" Tara asked.

"They don't know. He was wanted in connection with armed robberies of banks," Mike said.

"You gotta be kidding me. That's quite a coincidence," Robin said.

They all looked at each other and shrugged their shoulders in disbelief.

"It seems the car was commanded to stop. There is no record of an external command. Maybe he bumped the stop button," Tara said.

Mike told the car computer the destination of *Incident #4* in Kansas and began navigation. Riding along, they spotted a self-driving vehicle with a restaurant name on it pulling up to another vehicle at highway speeds. A metal shaft, with a box attached, extended from the left window to the right window of the other vehicle. Someone from the vehicle pulled something from a box. The metal arm retracted back into the restaurant vehicle, and it took a nearby exit off the highway.

"What was that?" Robin asked.

"Oh, I heard they were testing in some locations vehicle-to-vehicle food delivery service," Tara said.

"Wow, that would be great for our road trip if that was available in more locations," Mike said.

He was keeping an extra eye on the road.

About forty-five minutes later, they got to the first traffic control pole they wanted to check, heading toward the incident location. They pulled the data from all the poles.

"No obvious anomalies found from the pole data. I'll send it for analysis," Tara said.

They arrived at the corner of Main Street, a fairly busy intersection in the city. The buildings were spread out. Moderate-sized three-to-four-story buildings dotted the area. Looking south, they could see some taller buildings.

They all pulled up the video footage of *Incident #4*. The man seemed twitchy, looking all around, standing on a street corner. He then stepped off the curb and nearly instantly was hit by a bus.

"Ugh, I can't look," Tara said squeamishly.

"Yep, that is not something you want to look at after lunch," Robin said while eating a snack.

"The man was an intelligence agent visiting an informant," Mike said.

"I mean, things like this happen every day," Robin said.

"True. But there have been so many people in the categories we are investigating involved. The department wanted to look into these," Mike said.

"He definitely seems to act a little odd in that video. It almost looks like he sees something behind him, but there doesn't seem to be anything there," Mike said.

"I'm going to recreate his steps and see if I noticed anything," Mike said, getting out of the car. They all got out to watch him.

Mike recreated the odd mannerisms pretty well and stepped off the curb when there was a break in traffic.

"Hmm. I didn't see anything interesting," Mike said.

"Can we find out what case he was involved in?" Robin asked.

"It's likely classified and compartmentalized, which may be very difficult to get information about. I'll file the paperwork, but I wouldn't expect too much. I have an idea, though," he said.

Mike walked to the building the intelligence officer was visiting. The building looked like a typical government office building with light-colored brick. It was a Department of Corrections office. He walked to the front desk. He showed the receptionist his badge. Mike asked to see who the intelligence agent had met with.

A man walked out. Mike went into a small conference room with him, had a discussion, and walked out, shaking the man's hand.

"Thank you," he said to the receptionist and walked out, with Robin and Tara following.

"What did he say?" Robin asked.

"The agent was there because there was an inmate, a suspected terrorist, they were trying to get information from. He said the intelligence agent was acting a little weird. He said he was worried people might have been following him, but he thought he lost them many blocks away," Mike said.

"Unless you think there is any additional information to collect here, I think we should head to *Incident* #2 in Las Vegas. It would be a long drive through, like eighteen hours minimum," Mike said.

"After our driving incident, I might be more afraid of driving that far more than flying," Tara said.

"We're going to Vegas!" Robin exclaimed excitedly.

"That looks cool in Vegas," Tara said, pointing to the billboard on the road.

"The sign that says buy a new pool?" Robin asked.

"Oh, sorry, I had my smart glasses on. It was showing a sign for a gigantic Ferris wheel there," Tara said.

"It's still a little creepy when advertisements show for something you just talked about," Robin said.

They got to the car and booked their tickets online.

"Ugh, no direct flights. It's going to take at least four hours, as we have a layover in Denver," Robin said.

"I got us a hotel in one of the casinos," Mike said, showing the screen to Robin and Tara.

"Are we allowed to book there?" Robin asked, wondering about the FBI rules for max hotel charges.

"Surprisingly, it's discounted enough, I think so," Mike said with a smile.

"Thank you!" Robin said happily.

At the airport, they checked in and made their way to their gate. Mike showed his badge to the check-in agent, who called over a police officer. They filled out a form and handed Mike a copy.

Once at gate security, Mike strode over to the head of security and pulled out his badge and a copy of the form. The security agent looked, checked each of their badges, and waved them through.

"They let you take your weapons on the plane?" Tara asked.

"It depends, but they can," Robin said.

They waited and boarded the plane. They were sitting together in a three-seat section with Robin in the window, Tara in the middle, and Mike in the aisle.

Tara was very nervous. She was trembling slightly.

Mike looked at her and said don't worry. It will be fine as he cupped his hand on top of hers. It was warm and comforting to her. Mike then checked his phone to see if he had set it to airplane mode.

Finally, they made it out to the taxiway and took off. When they got a few thousand feet up, the seatbelt signs were still on.

"This is your captain. While the seatbelt signs are still lit, we wanted to demonstrate a new capability of this plane we're testing. Don't be alarmed. Please stay seated with your seatbelt on. The entire interior of the plane is made up of screens. We can make it appear like it's completely transparent, giving you an unparalleled view of the sky and the land below," he said.

"Ready. Three. Two. One. Action," the captain said. The entire interior of the plane seemed to disappear. Only the seats remained visible.

"Ooh!" and various other sounds the passengers made, surprised by the incredible views all around them. The sight of a transparent floor below them was disconcerting. Tara glanced around, both amazed and nervous, grasping Mike's hand. What Tara thought were windows turned out to be part of a screen. The captain turned off the transparent effect when they reached a higher altitude.

The rest of the flight to Denver was uneventful. They even arrived earlier than scheduled. Tara relaxed, finally stepping off the plane.

At the gate, on check-in, the agent said to Mike, "Wow, you have a lot of frequent flyer miles. We can upgrade you to first class."

"Anyone want to sit in first class?" he asked Robin and Tara.

"Yes!" Robin said.

Then, they boarded their plane to Las Vegas. Robin sat up in first class. Mike sat on the aisle and Tara on the window with the middle seat empty. The plane looked rather typical, with three seats on each side of the aisle. This looked like a newer model with updated entertainment systems. They were all the way in the back, with only one row of seats behind them. Two male flight attendants were sitting behind them.

The plane waited for its turn, then took off, climbing steeply into the sky.

The engines whined. The plane listed 45 degrees onto its side. It felt like it was falling out of the sky.

"Ahhh!" Tara cried. There were more screams from other passengers on the plane.

One of the flight attendants behind them whispered, "This isn't normal. We're going to die!"

Tara reached over for Mike's hand. She held on so tight his hand was turning white. The plane felt like it was falling for another ten seconds and then leveled out and continued on the journey. Tara finally released her grip on Mike's hand.

"Sometimes they get some crazy turbulence over the mountains," Mike said, a little unnerved himself.

Mike turned around to the flight attendants. "Please ask the pilot what happened."

"It was just turbulence," they said.

Mike flashed his badge at the flight attendant. "Ask him now!" he said forcefully.

One attendant rushed up front and came back.

"Come with me," the flight attendant said to Mike.

Mike followed him to the cockpit. He was there for a little while and then came back.

"They had a temporary systems error with one engine. It's a rare, known issue. They executed the standard recovery procedure, and it worked. The pilot said it happened to him once before in the same way. He is sure the plane is safe to continue. It is very rare," Mike said.

"I'm going to put in an emergency request for the air traffic control data and plane data," Tara said, still shaking.

"We are okay. The pilot assured me it's all fine," Mike said.

"Bruce said he would get them to send it over now. I'm going to start the data analysis using maximum cloud resources available to speed the operation," Tara said.

From there, the flight went fine.

"Passengers, please pass your garbage to the flight attendant in the center aisle. Please return your seats and tray tables to the upright position as we prepare for landing," the announcement said.

"Beep." Tara looked down at her laptop, looking at the data.

Her eyes glazed over.

"Oh shit! Mike... No! No... This can't be right," she said.

"Miss, please turn off and put away your electronic devices and make sure they are in airplane mode for our landing," the flight attendant said.

She put it away, still shaking.

"What is it? Tara, are you alright?" he said.

"The pattern identified is similar to data sent to several incidents. Either they are related, or they're interacting with some common system I'm unaware of. It's more likely they're related. We could be in terrible danger," she said.

Mike sprinted towards the front. The flight attendants stopped him near the cockpit door. Mike showed them his badge and said something, and they opened the door. He talked to them for fifteen seconds and returned to his seat.

"I told the pilot we have some intelligence possibly tying the plane systems being accessed by hackers similar to other incidents we are investigating, and to at least be aware of that," Mike said.

Tara had pulled out her laptop and was tapping furiously at her keyboard.

"Technically, it might not be legal, but I hacked into the plane's systems to erect a firewall to prevent any external requests from getting to the plane," Tara said.

"Oh shit! Data signature detected. It's being probed to find a hole in the firewall!" Tara exclaimed.

"Can you stop them?" Mike asked.

"Trying!" she said.

"Second signature detected!" Tara exclaimed.

"Flight attendants prepare for landing," the pilot said over the intercom.

Tara panicked. Now, typing even more furiously than before.

"They are sending data too fast! They are getting through! I can't stop them in time! Oh shit, they're in! Too late!" Tara exclaimed.

The plane was descending.

She grabbed Mike's hand again, even harder than before.

The plane descended and landed without incident.

"Flight attendants, please prepare doors for arrival and crosscheck. The weather is 90 degrees and clear..." the pilot went on.

Tara finally let go of Mike's hand. She looked and noticed she grabbed so hard it left tiny red marks on his hand.

"Oh my gosh, sorry," she said.

"You are pretty strong," he said.

Tara flushed with embarrassment.

"I'm not much of a world traveler," she said.

Tara calmed down a little. She was white as a ghost. They got to the gate.

As Mike was heading to the front of the plane to leave, the pilot flagged him down and pulled him aside.

"At the last few seconds, before we landed, our altimeter went nuts. Luckily, given your warning, I landed the plane manually. If we had been using the automated landing, we probably would have crashed, so thank you," he said as he reached out to shake Mike's hand.

"Captain, can I ask you to do us a favor? Don't mention my warning in your report. I will notify the Department of Homeland Security of the risk. They will work with the FAA to prevent anything like this in the future," Mike said.

"Yes, sir," the captain said.

"We will also need the passenger manifest," Mike said.

"I'll ask them to get it to you right away. Thanks again," the captain replied.

Mike and Tara walked off the plane. Robin had walked off earlier since she was in front of the plane. Robin was standing inside by the gate.

Robin looked at Tara and said, "Everything okay? You look kind of pale."

"Did I miss something? I fell asleep as soon as we boarded. Frick! I missed taking advantage of first class!" Robin exclaimed to Mike.

Mike filled in Robin as they waited for their bags.

"Wow, glad I was asleep," Robin said.

They got their bags. An FBI vehicle was waiting for them upon arrival. Mike entered a code on his phone, and they all got in and headed to their hotel.

"*Incident #13*," Tara said to Mike.

"It seems so," he said.

Tara had never been to Las Vegas before. She gazed out the car window at the array of signs and lights that lit up the entire area. It was a dazzling spectacle. The casinos were huge. The land in the area was flat and dry. Though the plane ride was horrifying, Tara was glad to get to see Vegas.

They got to the hotel. It was very hot and dry.

"I can't believe you booked the best casino in Vegas! This place is beautiful and huge!" Robin exclaimed.

They found themselves in an enormous suite with two bedrooms.

"This place is amazing! What's it like, two-thousand-square feet? Are we going to get in trouble for booking this?" Robin asked Mike.

"I cleared it with my supervisor and told him we needed a large room for operational security and protection detail," he said.

"Good points," Robin said.

"Plus, after all of our recent incidents, I think he actually felt a little bad for us. That and the other hotels that weren't dives were fully booked. I guess everyone's on summer vacation, so we lucked out," Mike said.

Tara and Robin took one bedroom in the suite, and Mike got the other one.

"I think we should go down and check out the casino," Robin said.

"I've never been to Las Vegas before. I would like to see some of it while we are here. If that's okay," Tara said.

"Sounds like fun," Mike said.

Their casino was pretty busy. The tones of the slot machines filled the air. The room was massive and stretched off in multiple directions farther than the eye could see. They walked past rows and rows of slot machines. The ceiling was very high, maybe twenty feet or more. The noise seemed to echo all around them. It was pretty loud. Uniformed servers walked around asking for or delivering drink orders.

As they entered one area, there was a huge glass-enclosed space in the middle of the floor. Inside the glass were various holograms being displayed. Some were very impressive, even appearing to be solid.

Robin went to play craps and took advantage of the free drinks. Mike and Tara went to play blackjack. Mike was breaking even. Tara won a couple of hundred dollars.

"You are really good at this," Mike said.

"I used to play a long time ago," Tara said.

"Can I get an iced tea?" Tara asked a waitress.

She continued to play, since she was doing pretty well. The server came back and put her drink down.

"I'm so thirsty. It must be this dry air," Tara said.

She picked up the drink and drank about half.

"Wait? This iced tea tastes funny," Tara said to Mike.

Mike picked it up, smelled it, and took a tiny sip.

"That's a Long Island Iced Tea. It's alcoholic," he said.

"It's pretty good, but I didn't plan on drinking tonight. I think it was pretty strong. I guess I better stop playing before that hits me," she said.

"Would you be okay to walk down the strip and see some of the casinos and outdoor shows?" Tara asked Mike.

"Sure, let's go," he said. On the way out, they checked on Robin. She wanted to stay since she was making a little money.

It was a long walk through the casino to even get out of the building. The night was still very warm. The blinking signs and lights were everywhere.

"I had only seen these lights in pictures, TV shows, and movies. It's very different in person. It's quite a spectacle. After all that's happened to us, it's nice to take a break," she said.

They both strolled down the walkway where there were hundreds, maybe thousands, of others walking further down.

They stopped in an ice cream store, ordered single scoops, then continued their walk.

"So, wait? So, we are off for the weekend in Vegas?" Tara asked.

"As long as we don't get called for an emergency, yes." Mike smiled.

"That's great. We'll have to figure out some things to see while we are here," she said.

They headed back to the hotel since it was getting pretty late. Tara was stumbling a little from the drink she had had earlier.

"I'm exhausted," Tara said. She stumbled near the doorway.

Mike grabbed her and held her up to keep her from falling.

"You, okay?" he said.

"I think that drink was strong," Tara said. Mike helped her to her room. Tara tripped on some clothes on the floor, stumbling onto Mike.

They both luckily fell onto the bed.

"Oh my gosh, I'm so sorry. I'm really tired. I'm just going to stay here," she said.

Mike squeezed his way gently out from under Tara. He then grabbed a spare blanket and put it over Tara.

"Goodnight," he said.

Mike went to his bedroom in their suite.

Chapter 12

Tara woke up around 9 a.m. She looked around, doing a double take, realizing where she was. She was eager to see more of the casinos and sights around the area. The room had a large open area, like a family room with a TV. Further down, there was a dining room table. There was a stocked mini-fridge with automatic sensors to know if you took something from it so it would charge your bill.

She went to get a shower.

Wow, this place is seriously luxurious.

The hotel suite was enormous. The bathroom was also huge, the shower alone seemed like it could fit five people easily. Tara wrapped a towel around her and came out of the bathroom. Mike was up, checking his email.

"Good morning," Tara said.

"Good morning. You sleep, okay?" Mike asked. Mike realized she was in a towel and tried to look away.

"Yes, fine," she said.

A little self-conscious, she dashed to her room.

Mike tried not to stare at Tara, but there were reflective surfaces all over the room, and she looked amazing.

"Not with colleagues," he repeated to himself, and went to get a shower.

Mike came out of the shower, wrapped in a towel, and headed toward his room.

Tara was sitting in a chair drying her hair. She couldn't help but notice Mike in the mirror and tried not to watch. *I have too many things I want to do to have a relationship. He is cute, though.*

Robin got up and also got a shower. She put on her panties and bra in her room and walked out to the main area to get some of her stuff.

"How do I look?" Robin asked Tara and Mike.

Tara was a little surprised she would walk out like that, but after thinking about her personality, less so. She kind of wished she could be half as comfortable with her body as she was. Mike was clearly a little uncomfortable.

"You look amazing," Tara said.

"Yes, definitely. Let's get ready and get some breakfast," Mike said.

They got dressed and found a small restaurant in the hotel.

"So, what should we do today?" Mike asked.

"More gambling. I won a few hundred dollars last night," Robin said.

"I'm sure we can squeeze that in," he said.

"I'd like to see inside some of the other casinos and maybe go to the Cirque du Soleil shows tonight," Tara said.

"Maybe we can see a magic show tomorrow night," Robin said.

"Sounds great," Mike said.

They finished breakfast. While they were walking through the casino by the slots, Robin stopped.

"Hey, let's try these for a minute," she said.

They each sat down at a machine. Robin won a hundred dollars in a few minutes. Mike lost fifty dollars. Tara won two hundred dollars right after.

"Wow, you are pretty lucky," Robin said.

"I wish that were true, but at the moment, it seems to be," Tara said.

After about thirty minutes, Robin was up three hundred. Mike was down a hundred, Tara had won five-thousand-dollars.

"Holy frick! I think you get to buy lunch with some of those winnings," Robin joked.

Robin wanted to stay and play the slots some more. Mike and Tara walked down the strip to go inside some of the other casinos. It was hot and dry, in the high 90s. They had drinks in hand to stay hydrated.

"Think it's safe to do a tour bus?" Tara asked.

"I think so. Let's do it," Mike said.

The packed self-driving tour bus caused Tara and Mike to be squished together.

"Sorry," Mike said. They were facing each other, pressed tight.

They held on to each other, so they didn't fall over. They rode to various casinos and got off at some to admire the grand views or the shows in front of them, and then got back on another bus. The automated descriptions of the area by the AI voice were okay.

"Where should I go next?" Tara heard a male voice say to their phone.

"I'd recommend the Lincoln Memorial," the AI voice of the man's phone responded.

"What should I have for lunch?" the same male voice asked his AI.

Tara thought it must be an *optimizer*, a term coined for someone who has AI help drive nearly every activity of their life. That might be nice. But giving up most of your free will to someone or something else didn't seem right either. Tara preferred that term to another that people would call them *Lost Soul*. It seemed kind of natural for someone to want help to plan their vacation stay.

They stopped at the tower and went to the top. They rode the giant Ferris wheel and could see a large portion of Las Vegas from the top. It was a fantastic sight, given how flat the entire area was. Off in the distance, they could see the mountains.

They went to the Aquarium.

"Oh, look there, a shark," Tara said.

"No, thank you. I'm not a fan of sharks," Mike said. Mike was using his smart glasses to help him navigate around the city and even within the attractions and exhibits. Tara had hers on as well.

Mike had his back to a large tank.

"See what is behind you," she teased.

He turned to look. "Aaaah!" Startled, he jumped back. "Not cool," he muttered and walked away.

Tara followed him and grabbed his hand.

"I'm really sorry. I didn't think sharks bother you that much," she said.

"When I was training in the military in the ocean, a shark attacked me. I thought I wasn't going to make it. I guess I still have nightmares from that day," Mike sighed.

"Let's go see someplace else," she said, and they returned to get on a bus.

This bus was crowded as well, and they got shoved together again, facing each other. They again had to hold on to each other to avoid falling over.

"I have an idea. Let's get off here," Tara said.

They got off and looked. It was a racetrack where you could take the latest gas and electric supercars for a ride around it.

"Let's go in," she said.

"Are you sure this is probably very pricey?" he said.

"You are forgetting I just won a lot of money." She grinned.

"I can't let you do that," Mike said.

"Sorry you can't leave me alone, right? And I'm doing that," she said. She really wasn't super into it, but she felt bad about upsetting Mike before. So, she figured he might like this.

"Okay, if you insist. I can't turn down driving a supercar!" Mike exclaimed.

They set Mike up in one of the new electric supercars. Tara got in the back. He waited at the starting line for the light to turn green. He started off relatively quickly but not too fast doing the first lap. On the second lap, he seemed to really be stepping on it. When he gunned it, the force was so strong Tara was pinned to the seat.

"Whoa! Hoo! Boy, these things got some acceleration!" Mike exclaimed.

She could barely lift her arms away from the seat.

They finished their laps.

"That was fun, thanks!" Mike said.

"That was quite a ride. You're welcome," she said.

"Are you going to drive?" Mike asked.

"No thanks, I just wanted to do the ride-along," she said.

"Of course, I wish I had a supercar now," he said.

"You are going to have to pay for that one on your own," Tara smirked.

"Let's go to the conservatory garden in our hotel and then meet up with Robin so we can have dinner. Then go to the Cirque show," Tara said.

"Okay, I think we should have time to do that before meeting up with Robin," he said.

Tara noticed Mike had his gun in a holster by the outline hidden under his shirt by his back.

"Do you carry your gun everywhere?" she asked.

"Yes, we are supposed to have it with us at all times, even off duty, unless it would be dangerous to have it," Mike said.

"Guns make me pretty uncomfortable," Tara said.

"Picking the FBI as a career option might have been a little problematic then," he pointed out.

"Yeah, maybe it is," Tara said. She didn't bother to hide the disdain in her voice.

They got on the bus to head back to their hotel. Another packed bus. They finally made it to the hotel and headed directly to the conservatory and garden.

"Wow, it's so beautiful. It's amazing they can grow something like this here in the desert," she said. The fragrance of plants and flowers pervaded the space.

Mike looked around at the mini waterfall with her.

Tara thought this was very romantic.

This would have been a great place to bring a date. Her thoughts focused on what she had been doing all day. Was it work because Mike needed to stay with her to protect her? Was it just colleagues having fun? She wasn't sure, but Mike's comment earlier still irked her. *Why am I even thinking about this?*

They video-called Robin on Tara's smartphone.

"Where are you?" asked Mike.

"Still in the casino," she said. Robin shared her location. Mike and Tara used their smart glasses to find her.

"How did you do?" Mike asked.

"Pretty good. I made about five-hundred dollars," Robin said.

Tara sat down at the slot machine nearby and put in some money. She lost the first two spins, then won twenty-five-hundred dollars.

"Holy crap! You are super lucky!" Robin said.

"I don't know how that's possible. I am definitely not a lucky person," Tara said.

Robin picked a restaurant she wanted to try that was nearby. Luckily, there was no wait. As they walked to their table, they looked all around. This restaurant had high-resolution screens on every wall and ceiling, seamlessly put together. The projection made it look like they were sitting outside on a sunny day, even though it was getting late where they were. Projected images gave you the impression you were sitting at a street cafe in

Paris. The Eiffel Tower appeared in the distance. It felt like they were sitting outside. The restaurant even had a very slight breeze going through it. They could also barely make out the noises of the hustle and bustle of Paris in some light background sounds.

"Wow, even the food smells like Paris," Mike said.

"Really? You were in Paris?" Tara asked.

"It was a brief assignment, but it was nice," Mike said.

On one side of the restaurant, they could see a shop where they could buy clothes and other items from Paris.

"The menu looks like it has some food you would find in Paris, plus some American staples. The location changes daily to different locations and menus they rotate through," Tara said.

"It's a great idea to keep people coming back to see different views and try new food," Mike said.

Once seated, they put on their smart glasses to look over the menu. Besides food, various virtual items appeared. Drinks, a slot machine, a Keno game, live games to bet on, and more appeared.

"They use a lot of AR here," Tara said, turning it off. It was too distracting from the view.

Robin was already trying out the virtual slot machine that looked like it appeared at the end of their table.

They ordered directly from their smart glasses.

"So, what did you do today?" Robin asked them.

"We did a bus tour and went into a bunch of casinos, the aquarium, the Ferris wheel, and saw the garden," Tara said, trying to remember everything they did.

"Hey, I have an idea. Want to go to the top of the Eiffel Tower? It should look amazing at night from up there," Tara said.

"I think I want to stay and watch the game. I've got money riding on it," Robin said.

"Okay, we'll catch you a little later," Mike said.

Tara and Mike took a car to the Paris Las Vegas. They waited their turn to go up. At the top, they could see a dazzling array of lights.

"This is amazing. You can see everything up here. The lights are wild to see from here," she said.

It was a little breezy at the top, which was good since it was still hot, even this late at night.

"Oh wow! Look at that," she said as music started up. There was an array of dancing water, colored by lights in time with the music. There was also a grid of a laser show over the top. They watched the beautiful colors of the water and the lasers shining above.

"This has been an amazing day. Thank you for indulging me all day," Tara said. She gave him a quick, friendly half-side hug.

"I figured after everything you've been through, you and we all needed a break," Mike said.

So, he was doing this for pity or to be nice? She couldn't figure out why this annoyed her.

Back at the hotel, they said their goodnights and went to bed.

Tara got up at around 9 a.m. Mike seemed already dressed and showered. Robin was still sleeping.

"Good morning. How did you sleep?" she asked.

"Pretty good," he lied. He actually had a dream related to the shark attack.

Tara brushed her teeth and took a shower. She finished up and walked out, wrapped in a towel with her hair down. Mike heard her come out and tried to avoid looking in her direction. The reflective surfaces still made that really hard. He caught himself peeking.

"Stop," he mumbled.

Robin seemed comfortable walking around with her robe open, wearing just her underwear beneath. She got a shower and then returned to the bedroom to get dressed.

They all sat down on the sofa.

"What is the plan today?" Mike asked.

"Can we see the magic show tonight?" Robin asked.

"Plus one, for the magic show," Tara said as she winked.

"That sounds good. What do we want to do during the day?" he asked.

"Do you want to see the Grand Canyon? With the fast cars these days, it should only take about an hour to get there. It's going to be very hot, though," he said.

"Sure!" Robin said.

"Yes, I'd love to see it!" Tara exclaimed.

"Should definitely dress for the weather," he said.

Tara and Robin went back to their room and changed into shorts, and both of them were wearing different light-colored tops.

"How do we look?" Robin asked.

"You both look amazing. I feel like that spy guy in the movies who gets to hang out with beautiful women all day," he joked.

"Stop," Robin said sarcastically.

Tara put on her smart glasses to help her navigate their group to the restaurant for breakfast. It was hard, as there was a dazzling array of advertisements for different ones popping up with directions.

"Hide ads," she commanded. They disappeared, but it showed that it would only hide them for thirty minutes.

"At least when driving, it forces them to limit the obnoxious ads, and they look more integrated," she said.

After breakfast, they went to a store to get some hats, sunscreen, snacks, and drinks. They took their car out to the closest point of the Grand Canyon.

It was ridiculously hot and dry, close to 120 degrees in the shade. When they left the air-conditioned car, it felt like they had opened the oven door and were hit in the face by the sweltering, dry heat.

"Okay, this might not have been the best day to go," Mike said.

"It's hot, but it's beautiful," Tara enthused. It seemed wrong to call dirt and rock beautiful, but it was. Looking across the canyon, it seemed like a dozen or more shades of color, from a darker reddish brown to pinkish brown. They could see a sign showing images of the canyon's peaks and surroundings. One of them they could see the map showed was twenty-five miles away. The view was awe-inspiring.

"The pictures don't do this justice at all. It's so big and so colorful," Tara said.

They each took pictures of the area, plus selfies. They even got someone to get a group shot of them.

Robin was texting someone on and off.

"Who are you texting?" Tara asked.

"No one," Robin said, putting away her phone.

After getting their fill of the magnificence of the view, they headed back to the hotel.

"This was a pleasant break," Robin said.

"Ditto," Mike said.

"I had a great time," Tara said.

Back at the casino, they did some more gambling before dinner. There were rows of tables with robotic dealers at the tables that could deal with lightning speed.

Robin was trying slots, and so was Tara. Mike was back at the blackjack table.

They gambled for a while and met up for dinner.

"How did you do?" Mike asked Robin.

"I made a couple hundred more!" Robin exclaimed.

"I want to know how you did, Tara, Miss Lucky Pants," she said.

"I won again," she said.

"How much?" Robin asked.

She whispered the amount to them.

"What?" said Robin. Mike also looked shocked.

"I know, right? What are the chances?" she said.

"Are you sure you aren't hacking those things?" Robin grinned.

"Honest, I haven't done anything except play them. I'm not sure why I'm so lucky," she said.

"You buying dinner and drinks?" Robin asked with a smile.

"Sure, my treat," Tara said.

After dinner and a few drinks created by an automatic bartender, they headed up to their room and bed, wishing they could have more time off together.

Chapter 13

A blaring alarm started going off.

"Good Morning. If Jupiter is 460 million miles from the sun. How long does it take light from the sun to get there?" the voice from Tara's phone asked.

"Oh, No Crap! Sorry!" Tara exclaimed.

"If Jupiter is four-hundred-sixty-million miles from the sun, how long does it take light from the sun to get there?" the voice repeated as the alarm continued wailing.

"Um... About forty-one minutes," Tara stated.

"Have a nice day," the voice responded.

"Why?" Robin exclaimed.

"Sorry, I have problems getting up in the morning," Tara said, embarrassed.

She considered turning it off, but she didn't want to rely on someone to wake her up.

"Ow, my eyes. What happened to our room?" Tara said, staring at the walls. The walls were a harsh bright yellow with purple polka dots.

"Sorry, I might have been drunk while playing with the electronic ink wall controls," Robin said.

Tara tapped a few buttons and returned the walls to their default configuration, and looked around the room once more.

"Wow, they must have transparent displays, not electronic ink walls," Tara said, since she could now see the beautiful marble-like walls. She figured they probably wouldn't be staying in rooms as nice as this again. The room even had a new room smell. Tara looked at the picture in a picture frame hanging on the wall. It seems the picture had changed. Even that was some sort of display technology.

They went to a fast-food joint to get breakfast and did the drive-through. A terminal was on the side of the drive-through window to pay. Once they paid, a metal box passed through the drive-through window, slightly protruding from it, and opened, revealing their food. Inside the restaurant through the window, automation systems were making and packaging food.

"Wow, I've heard about these places, but it's the first time I've been to one," Mike said.

"Okay, let's head to *Incident #2*. I made an appointment so they could let us in," Mike said as he asked the computer to navigate to the location.

"So, for this incident, it says it was a waterline break that caused a power line to short. That caused a power surge that caused a Smart TV to catch fire and burn through part of the house, killing our victim," Tara said.

"The victim was a suspected criminal, supporting terrorism. He had been hacking credit cards and funneling money to the Middle East."

Mike checked his smartphone. He looked stunned.

"I just got word back on the analysis we sent to DHS and the FAA about the plane incident. They claimed there was no hacking. It was a bug in the plane software, which has now been corrected," he said.

"Well, it was a bug in their software, exploited by a hack," Tara said.

"A cover-up?" Robin asked.

"Hmm. Maybe they don't want the flying public to be afraid to fly. Since they patched the bug, they figure it's okay," Mike added.

"They really need better firewalls for their planes. Hopefully, they did that," Tara added.

"So, they are going to say we have no evidence of hacks again," Robin said, sighing loudly.

It was only a short drive to a large-sized house in Las Vegas. It was a typical style for the area, with a light brown exterior and a darker reddish brown tile roof. The exterior had a mix of different colored brick and stucco. There were palms, shrubbery, and grass surrounding it. The neighborhood seemed quiet and beautiful.

"It's amazing lawns could be this green," Tara said.

A representative from the bank arrived to let them into the house.

"We'll lock up when we're done," Mike thanked the representative.

They wore their smart glasses as they walked into the house. The front of the house seemed unharmed, but the master bedroom was charred pretty badly. The smell of fire and burnt materials was heavy in the air. Mike went out and came back in with masks for each of them.

On what was left of the interior wall in what was the family room appeared to be a large flat-screen TV that was now mostly melted plastic. It looked like it was dripping down the wall. That was the suspected ignition source.

"The power data recorded a surge at that time that would have affected the homes in this area. So, it seems plausible," Tara said.

"The police took the documents they found. They scanned them. You should have access to them online and their notes," he said.

The smart glasses showed them where items were before the police removed them.

"This guy lived pretty well. What is this like, four-thousand square feet?" Robin guessed.

"From the documents I read, this guy was part of some money laundering scheme. It's possible it was terrorism-related, but he had contacts with Russia, the Middle East, and more. So very hard to tell," he said.

"He's got cigars everywhere. He could have just started the fire accidentally himself. I wish we would find some concrete evidence at one of these," Robin said.

"Yeah, I agree. It's frustrating. Sometimes it can take a while to find the evidence to point you in the right direction," he said.

"There were smoke alarms, but they didn't appear to be working, the fire department said," Mike noted.

"Can we get up to that smoke detector?" Tara asked.

"Let's see if this guy had a ladder," Mike said. They looked around and found one in the garage.

Mike climbed up and tried to take it down, but it was secured well.

"Let me see," Tara said as she climbed up the ladder.

She opened it up and looked inside. "This may have been a victim of the power surge as well. This one is an internet connection to call the fire department, but that didn't happen. A neighbor called in the fire," Tara said.

She climbed down. "Let me check some other devices that are still left in the house," she said.

She opened up some other TVs and appliances to check the electronics.

"I don't see any other signs of a power surge," Tara said while closing up an appliance.

"Seems pretty unlucky to have a device short from a surge and a smoke detector short from the surge as well. Possible, I guess," Mike said.

"More wishy-washy evidence, if you can call it that," Robin said with a sigh.

They were looking around to see if they could find anything else.

Bleep! Tara's phone chirped. She glanced down at it. She tapped the screen many times and stood staring at it.

"I think we've got something!" Tara exclaimed.

"My data analysis finally turned up something. It used the note to decrypt the odd bytes found in *Incident* #1, which points to the exact location where we found the note for *Incident* #3. My program is working on decrypting number three. Maybe each proceeding note is needed to decrypt the next set of data," Tara said.

"So, wait, if one incident shows the location of the next incident, couldn't we just go to the last incident and skip the ones in the middle? Then we could find out where they will attack next," Mike asked.

"Because each one may help decrypt the later one, we should just work on getting to those notes as quickly as possible and process the data," Tara said.

"That is definitely something. It at least suggests someone, or a group, is involved here." Mike said. "I'm going to relay this to our supervisors. I think we need to put out the word to other field offices now to look for those notes at the other locations. We will head to *Incident* #8's location since we're only about three hours away," Mike said.

"Finally, something a little more tangible!" Robin exclaimed.

They finished up looking for evidence and got into the car. Mike programmed the car for the outskirts of Los Angeles near *Incident* #8.

"I'm setting up active monitoring of the traffic control systems again," Tara said, hoping she could prevent them from getting into another accident.

They started driving, heading on their way.

"What the hell is that?" Robin asked, looking at something streaking straight up into the sky with fire behind it and a trail of white smoke.

"That is pretty cool. I think it's a rocket launch. They have a launchpad out in the desert not too far from Las Vegas to get to the new space hotel," Mike said.

As they left Las Vegas, they could see lots of dry scrub on the ground on either side. The ground looked like a mix of sand, dirt, and occasional desert scrub. They could see mountains off to the side and in the distance. They went past many solar installations that had fields of solar cells. The scrub grew less green as they entered more of a desert area. The temperature was well over a hundred.

"There is not too much out here," Tara commented.

It was hard, but they found a little sandwich shop for lunch out in the middle of nowhere. It felt like a blast furnace again when they stepped outside. They got the sandwiches and drinks to go. They ate in the car as they traveled.

The ground looked even more brown and dry, with less green for a while.

They went through a town and arrived at the start of the series of poles they wanted to check for *Incident #8*.

"In *Incident #8*, it looks like the cars sped up and launched themselves over a hill, going airborne. It seemed to be only self-driving vehicles. No accidents or injuries in this incident," Tara said, watching the mesmerizing video of the vehicles jumping into the air.

They started collecting data from the traffic control poles. They got to the fifth pole.

"I found the note!" Tara said. She took the data and entered it into her computer.

They continued to collect the data from the poles. When they got to the location where the incident happened, they looked at the area closely.

"Is there anything in the area that could have caused this incident?" Mike asked.

"Anything is possible, but nothing is obvious," Tara said. They searched all over the side of the road. They found a small device they had never seen before.

"What is that thing?" Robin asked.

"No idea," Mike said.

"Tara, what do you make of it?" Mike asked.

She wore latex gloves while taking apart the cover and looked at the chips inside. It looked like someone made it with a standard chip. It had a radio built into it. She downloaded the program to her machine. She then translated the code from assembly to C to read it.

"This looks like it's outputting radio frequencies in the car's range sensors and GPS. It looks like it was trying to fool the cars into thinking this was a different area and that the speed limit was faster and flatter. This way, the cars would go fast over this hill. It looks like it targeted empty vehicles by checking the transponders," Tara said.

"Solid evidence, finally!" Robin said.

"I'm going to call a car to our car's location to send the device to the nearest field office for analysis," Mike said.

"I guess they will need to allow us to continue this investigation now," Robin said.

"My data analysis could get the data from *Incident* #3 and found it pointed to the *Incident* #5's location," Tara said.

"The field offices only reported finding notes at incidents one, three, and five. We found the one at *Incident* #8. Why not at the other ones?" Mike asked, wondering.

"We've got a hit on a location! Multiple IP addresses are triangulated to a warehouse nearby. The IP address matches those incidents. We had to trace them through multiple proxies. Given the route, there is no guarantee they are there, but it's our best place to start. This data is a few weeks old, but I still see recent data from that site going to other locations," Tara said.

"Let's head out there to just get a feel for what's there before we call in backup," Mike said.

"Agreed, since we have old data," Robin said.

They got back in the car and programmed a location near but not too near the warehouse. The site was still on the outskirts of Los Angeles, just around the other side. Tara was still actively monitoring the traffic systems.

They stopped at some fast food for lunch and headed over to the warehouse area. Once they got close, they stopped at a hill overlooking the warehouse, where they could stay hidden. They set up some equipment behind the vehicle.

A car showed up behind them.

"Oh, this must be the car for the device," Mike said. He took the device they found earlier and put it in the car. He entered a secure lock code and sent it to the FBI field office.

"Tara, launch our air support," Mike said.

Tara hit some buttons on the drone, which took off in the air, hovering above them. She tapped on the computer's keyboard, and the drone went higher into the sky and toward the building. It was high enough not to be noticed easily. The video feed in the drone could get amazingly close.

Tara had her smart glasses on to make navigating the drone in 3D easier.

The drone made an automatic pattern over the warehouse. Mike and Robin put on their glasses as well. They could look at the outside of the warehouse in 3D.

"Integrating schematics," Tara said. Wireframes were also available for the inside of the warehouse.

"Using radio frequency analysis to detect movement," Tara said.

"Looks like the roof is all metal. We won't be able to get a reading," Tara stated.

"How many cars are outside?" Mike asked.

"I only see three," Robin said.

"Tara, you stay here and monitor our comm channel. Robin and I are going to take a peek around," Mike said.

"Wait, take this," Tara said, quickly copying some software onto a USB drive.

"What is that for?" Mike asked.

"If you get near a computer, we can plug that in to check their network. I've put in the paperwork digitally to allow that, but it's not approved yet," Tara said.

"Be careful," Tara said.

Robin and Mike went to the building and looked around the sides. The blacked-out windows made it impossible to see inside. The building looked like a typical warehouse. There were very few windows, mostly just solid walls. The surrounding area was pretty desolate.

"I can hear something inside, not sure what," Mike said.

"Hey, what are you doing here?" A huge, muscle-bound guy in overalls said.

Mike figured he must have come around the corner of the warehouse without them hearing him.

"We were hiking, and we got lost. Can we use your phone?" Mike said.

"Sorry, I don't have a phone, and this area is restricted, so leave!" the enormous man said.

"Okay, we're going," Mike said as he walked away.

"Don't move! Put your hands in the air," the large guy said, pointing a gun at Mike and Robin.

Mike turned around.

"I said, don't move!" the man said.

"Turn around and put your hands in the air," he said, pointing his gun at them.

Mike and Robin did as he asked.

The man walked up behind them and grabbed the guns hidden under their shirts from both of them.

"I didn't know hikers carry guns. Move that way, hands in the air towards that door," he said.

"Hey, you don't need to point a gun at us," Mike said, triggering his comm.

Tara heard the comm.

Oh, Shit! They are in trouble! Tara triggered the FBI emergency beacon and called the police. She gave them the comm channel frequency and status.

The large man brought Mike and Robin into the warehouse. They passed a lot of equipment and people. He brought them into a room with another man.

"Hey, boss, I found them outside. They had guns," the large man said.

"Hello, you can call me Anton. Nice to meet you," the man at the desk in the room said.

"Anton, if that's your real name, that's a really nice drug operation you have going there. You've got more than a pharmacy. Did you know that stuff is highly explosive?" Mike said, triggering his comm.

Mike could see through the doorway into the main warehouse. They had a large operation. They even had automated robotic vehicles moving the completed drugs to another part of the warehouse.

"Who are you?" Anton asked.

"We were hiking and got lost," Mike said.

The large man reached into Mike's back pocket and pulled out his wallet.

The large man handed the wallet to Anton.

"Ramon, you idiot. They are FBI. Take them to the back of the warehouse quickly. You know what to do. I'll sound the alarm to evacuate," Anton said to the large man.

"You know if you kill us when they catch you, if you survive, you will get life in prison," Mike said, triggering his comm.

"Ramon, get going!" Anton said. Anton hit a button by his desk, red lights flashed, and an alarm sounded.

"We're going to see each other again, Anton, and it won't be as cordial as this conversation," Mike said as Ramon pushed him out of the room.

Tara heard Mike's communication. *Oh, shit! They are going to die if I don't do something.*

"The police are on their way, two minutes out. I'm going to give you a distraction, I hope. I'm going to drop this drone on the other side of the warehouse from you," she said.

Tara sent the drone onto the warehouse roof, above the biggest heat signature.

"In three, two, one, zero," she said over the comm. She then triggered the drone's explosive charge.

BOOM!

BOOM!

The drone exploded, triggering an explosion of the drug, making chemicals below it. A fireball went up into the air over twenty-five feet above the warehouse.

Ramon heard the blast and got knocked back. Mike and Robin also got knocked back. Mike turned around and hit Ramon hard in the face and twisted the gun from his hand with both his hands. Ramon smiled at Mike, then punched him hard. Ramon then grabbed him and threw him into the wall. Mike fell to the ground.

Robin kicked Ramon hard in the groin. Ramon cupped his hands over his crotch and slammed Robin with his body, pushing her into the wall.

Robin also fell to the ground. Mike got part way up, leg locked Ramon, and pulled him to the ground, flipping on top of him.

"Get the gun," Mike said to Robin as he pummeled Ramon.

"I don't see it!" Robin exclaimed.

Ramon reached up with his giant hand and grabbed Mike by the neck, squeezing hard.

Robin kicked Ramon in the head enough, so he let go of Mike.

Mike twisted around on the floor and got Ramon in a chokehold.

"Goodnight, Ramon," Mike said as he went unconscious.

Mike found a gun.

"Guide us out of here. This place is massive. They took our smart glasses," Mike said over the comm.

Explosions continued as they tried to get out of the warehouse.

"Head down the hallway and turn left," Tara said into the comm.

"Wait! Go to the first door on the left. That's where the computer room is located. Go in there and plug in that USB drive. We didn't get approved, but if the fire destroys that, we'll have nothing," Tara said.

"What does she think is going on in here?" Robin asks, coughing from the smoke.

"If we don't go now, we might not make it out."

"Hang on, let's try this door quick," Mike said.

Mike kicked hard at the door. It didn't budge. He took a running leap at the door.

The door kicked in. He ran in, bending down to stay below the smoke. There was a rack of servers. He plugged in the USB drive.

"It's in!" Mike exclaimed.

"Downloading data. Go down that hall at the end. There should be an exit on your right," Tara said.

Mike and Robin ran for the door while crouching to avoid the smoke. As they make it to the door, an explosion from inside blew them out to the ground.

"Robin, you, okay?" Mike asked as he helped her up off the ground.

"Mike, your shirt's on fire!" Robin exclaimed.

Mike dove to the ground and rolled to extinguish the flames.

He got up, glancing at his burnt shirt. "Seriously. Again!" he muttered.

"Are you okay?" Tara said on the comm.

"Agent Actley and I are fine here," Robin said.

"Let's go find Anton," Mike said to Robin.

They ran around the building to watch a crowd of people fleeing the warehouse. While technically, they were all criminals helping make drugs. A lot of them looked like they were probably human trafficked here and forced to do this.

Mike ran up to the people, leaving. "Hey, where is Anton? Did you see him?" he asked.

He kept asking different people.

"I saw him around the side," one man said.

Mike ran with Robin, following him around the side. Anton was getting into a car.

"Tara, call a vehicle to my location," Mike said.

"Acknowledged," Tara said.

Anton drove off quickly. Police arrived from one road. Anton cut a cruiser off, putting it in a ditch.

Mike started chasing after Anton's car on foot. Anton's car was pulling far ahead of Mike.

"Where's my car?" he yelled into the comm, and just as he said that, a car screeched around a corner behind him.

"Never mind! It's here!" he yelled.

The vehicle drove up next to him, matching his pace. He opened the door and jumped in. "Yes, a steering wheel!" he muttered.

Mike took manual control.

"Designate vehicle law enforcement," he said.

"Already done," Tara replied.

Mike sped up, catching up with Anthon.

"Power down Anton's vehicle," Mike said on the comm.

"He is in manual mode and disabled the override," Tara noted.

Mike heard a drone whiz by overhead, following Anton. Tara had already sent up the second drone. *Tara's great at this.*

He didn't want to use the drone to take out Anton's vehicle, or they might lose track of him if it didn't work.

Mark side-swiped Anton, but couldn't get him to spin out. He tried again, pushing Anton's vehicle in the middle lane slightly into a truck in the left lane.

Anton drove faster, switched to self-drive mode, and climbed out his window onto the cab of the truck. He opened the truck's door, got in, and ejected the truck's driver out of the other side.

"Send an ambulance for the truck driver," Mike said. Anton's former vehicle seemed in auto mode now. "Pull Anton's vehicle over and send the police to the location," Mike said.

"It worked this time," Tara said.

"Self-drive sync mode. Track this truck, please," he said to the comm.

The car pulled to the side of the truck that was trying to side-swipe him, but his car would just move with the truck, avoiding it. Mike climbed out the window onto the side truck cab. Mike opened the door of the truck and aimed his gun in.

"Pull over, Anton! I told you I'd see you again!" Mike said.

Anton swerved harder one way and then the other, trying to shake Mike off. Mike fell out the door, but grabbed the handle, almost dropping his gun.

Mike got his footing again. He fired multiple shots into the truck tire.

The truck swerved hard and tipped over onto its side opposite Mike, so he was on top of the side of the truck. It slid across the ground, sparking as it went. It slowed to a stop. His car that was behind the truck swerved and went off the road to the side.

Mike opened the door of the truck and aimed his gun inside.

"Anton, it's so wonderful to see you again. You actually don't look so good, having a bad day?" he said.

"Please send police and an ambulance to my location," Mike said.

"Agent Actley, are you okay?" Tara asked.

"I think I'm fine, thanks. Anton, though, I think, is feeling a little under the weather," he replied.

Battered up from the truck tipping over, Anton had a nasty head injury. The police arrested him and took him to the hospital in an ambulance.

A paramedic checked out Mike. He just had some scrapes and bruises. Mike took a car back to the scene of the warehouse. The fire department and police were there. The fire was mostly out. Tara and Robin walked up to Mike.

"I'm so glad you are okay," Tara said.

"You are always crazy, my friend. Glad you are fine and got Anton," Robin said to Mike.

"Did we get anything from the data?" Mike asked Tara.

"I think the people in this warehouse had no connection to the hackers we are trying to trace down. I believe the hackers got in and created a proxy in the warehouse servers, so it would appear like their computers were here," Tara said.

"So, we are back to square one?" Robin asked.

"I don't think so. Our traces have been getting narrower and narrower in the area. We've now traced back through multiple proxies and VPNs, and the area has narrowed to here. I think they are very close by," Tara said.

"I'm going to run our analysis. Hopefully, we are really close now," Tara said.

"Let's check out the warehouse to make sure we missed nothing," Mike said.

They did a walkthrough and didn't find any additional evidence.

"I just got a notification. My analysis decrypted the link of *Incident #5* data to the *Incident #8*'s location. My algorithm is working on decrypting the next location in the list from *Incident* #8's data. It's weird why the events aren't sequenced in order," Tara said.

"Let's go back to the car," Mike said. They all got to the car and got in. "I'll book a hotel nearby," Robin said. "Let's finish filling in our online data for the incident and head to the hotel," Mike said.

They got to the hotel. It was one of the better hotels in the area, but still moderately priced. The building was only four stories, but was pretty long. It had a few palm trees and shrubs in front. The hotel was close to a state road that wasn't too busy, luckily. The view had little to offer, with dry dirt and sparse green shrubs on the other side of the road. Stores line the road going north, while the road to the south stretches across flat land. Straining their eyes eastward, they could just make out hazy mountains in the distance.

Robin checked in and got digital keys sent to each of their phones. They got two rooms near each other as usual. They took their luggage up to their rooms.

"Sorry, not as fancy as the place you booked for us," Robin said, looking at Mike.

"That's fine. This is pretty much our usual sort of hotel, I think," he said.

They got settled in and met in Mike's room.

"So, is there anything additional we can put together from the data we have now?" Mike said.

"The IP addresses I traced to this area were related to incidents one, three, five, and eight. I couldn't find a correlation to the other incidents," Tara said.

"Bleep!" Tara's phone showed a message.

"Looks like we just decrypted *Incident* #8's data, and it has a time and location. Wait! This doesn't match up with any of our incidents! This appears to be a future date, time, and location. Tomorrow at 8:30 am along the main road very close to here!" Tara exclaimed.

"Finally, a break!" Robin said.

"I'm going to set up an active analysis of the traffic systems starting now," Tara said.

"I'll have an FBI team and police nearby, but not at the location, to watch from a distance," Mike said.

"I'm also going to monitor internet network nodes for the traffic signatures we've seen," Tara said.

"Why would they give us that information? Is it a trap?" Tara asked.

"Maybe. Maybe they want us to see what they will do. Serial killers sometimes set up games believing they are smarter than law enforcement and provide some clues," Mike said.

"Some people are just screwed up," Robin said.

"Let's make sure we stake out that location early in case they place any additional devices like the one we found," Mike said. Tara and Robin nodded.

"Let's prepare requests for car data and cell phone data in case something happens tomorrow," Mike suggested.

"I'm going to check if there are any known hackers in this area. Let's also get the drones charged and ready to go," he said.

They finished up their work for the evening.

"Let's get some dinner," Robin suggested.

"Sure," Tara said, and Mike nodded.

They found a local restaurant. The food was pretty good. After they were done, Mike used his smart glasses, and they all went back to the hotel.

Tara and Robin went to their room, and Mike went to his. They got ready for bed and went to sleep.

Chapter 14

Robin got up and got a shower. Tara wasn't up yet. She apparently forgot to set her alarm.

"Good Morning. What is one billion, two hundred twenty-five thousand, one hundred and twenty-five divided by twenty-five?" Robin said, trying to mimic Tara's alarm.

"What is one billion, two hundred twenty-five thousand, one hundred and twenty-five divided by twenty-five?" she repeated.

"Forty million nine thousand and five," Tara replied.

"Holy crap, is that right? I mean, have a nice day!" Robin said loudly, laughing at the end.

Tara had one eye open and rolled over.

"Sorry, I think I set my alarm for the wrong time," she said, a little embarrassed. Robin just smiled at her. Tara gave her a squint eye, meaning she wasn't sure what else to say to that.

Tara got a shower and got dressed quickly. They got ready to go. Mike was in communication with the police and the FBI teams. They discussed the areas to cover and a series of plans.

They drove to the area and parked their vehicles out of sight behind a shrub in a ditch. There were dirt mounds on each side of the road with some scrub on top of them. The police and the FBI vehicles could hide out of sight from them. It was early, about 6:30 a.m. The traffic was just picking up. On one side of the road, there was a business with a bunch of backhoes, cranes, and other equipment set a little off the road about a hundred feet from them.

Tara set up a camera that could peer over the top of the mound of dirt to see the traffic. Everything looked pretty normal. It was a typical busy rush hour of traffic heading into Los Angeles.

They waited and waited, and still nothing happened. It was 8:10 a.m. now. The traffic had peaked and was just easing up a bit.

"I've got a hit!" Tara exclaimed.

"Standby getting a location. There is a house about ten minutes from here where the signal came!" Tara exclaimed.

"Robin, get us a no-knock warrant now!" Mike exclaimed.

"Team one is sending a new location. We have a target. Go. Go. Go! Go silent when you get within a mile," Mike yelled into the comm. He programmed the location into the car. He pressed lights and siren and engaged in accelerated response mode.

The vehicle sped up quickly, so much so that Mike, Tara, and Robin all got pushed back into their seats slightly. Their car took over the fast lane, with the self-driving vehicles quickly getting out of the way.

When they got to within a mile, Mike turned off the siren, and the FBI and police teams assembled quietly near the house. It was now 8:20 a.m. Mike told Tara to wait in the car. They put on their bulletproof vests and helmets. They got the battering ram for the door and loaded their weapons. It was 8:25 a.m.

"Three, Two, one," Mike said quietly in the comm. A large policeman at the door started using the battering ram on the door. It quickly broke the door open.

"FBI! Hands-up. Get on the ground!"

"Police! Hands-up. Get on the ground!"

They moved in quickly. They went from room to room, clearing them.

"FBI! Hands-up. Get down on the ground!" Mike yelled to a guy and a girl who was sitting near two desks with computers on them.

Both lay down on the ground and put their hands on their head.

Mike and Robin handcuffed them, then Mike grabbed the guy by the shirt collar and shoved him up against the wall.

"Stop what's going to happen. Now!" Mike screamed at the guy.

"It's too late. I can't stop it," he said.

"Tara, get in here quick!" Mike yelled into the comm.

Tara raced in.

"Tara, check those computers there. See if you can stop this," Mike said.

Mike pulled out his gun, not aiming it directly at the guy.

"If someone dies, I will make sure you get the death penalty!" Mike screamed at him.

"No one else has to die. Stop it now!" he screamed.

"No one is going to die," the guy said. "It's a prank, just a prank," he said, half sobbing.

"Well, one of your other pranks got someone killed, so stop it now!" Mike screamed.

"Tara, can you stop this?" Mike asked.

"No, I don't think so," Tara said.

"I'm going to count to three, and if you don't tell me how to stop this, I'm going to—"

Robin interrupted Mike. She grabbed him and said, "Agent Actley, stand down."

"Hey, what's your name?" Robin said to the guy.

"Chris," he said.

"Chris. I'm Agent Laizon. It would help if you gave us answers quickly. There are deaths linked to data that came from your computers here. You need to tell us how to stop this now. I can't stop these guys for long if you don't answer me," Robin said quietly but firmly.

"Give him back to me! I will take care of him!" Mike yelled.

"No, please don't! It won't hurt anyone, I swear! I can't stop it!" he sobbed uncontrollably.

"Please tell us how to stop this now. Otherwise, I have to hand you back over to him," she said.

"We're running out of time. Let me at him!" Mike yelled.

"No, please, please don't!" the guy cried.

"Last chance," Robin said.

"I can't stop it! Nothing bad will happen," he cried.

"He's all yours," Robin said to Mike.

"Agent Actley, stop! I believe him. This can't be stopped," Tara said.

The clock hit 8:30 a.m. They noticed a monitor with a video feed of a highway. Suddenly, music started, and next to the highway, a huge number of backhoes and cranes were all doing something like dance moves, moving to the beat of the music. It was quite a sight to see. The cars driving by had their sound system changed to hear the music.

"I told you. It's just a funny prank. We never wanted to hurt anyone," Chris sobbed.

"All we wanted to do was bring attention to the privacy and security concerns by showing how easy it was to hack things," Chris said.

"He's telling the truth," the girl who was with him said.

"We'll figure out what is going on," Mike said.

"Please bring them to the local FBI office," Mike said.

Two of the FBI agents grabbed the guy and the girl and took them outside.

"Please collect, catalog, and upload all this evidence today," Mike stated.

The FBI team started unplugging the computer equipment and collecting devices and papers around the area.

There was an amazing array of equipment they had. They had a rack of servers, including a small personal quantum computer and a quantum encryption device.

"How did they get all this stuff?" a tech asked, not expecting anyone to really know the answer yet.

Mike, Tara, and Robin walked outside.

"We'll meet you at the field office," Mike told the other agents, taking the guy and girl there.

"I guess this is *Incident* #14," Tara said.

"Holy Crap! We have a lot of incidents," Robin said.

The hackers, Chris Pritin, and Lauren Otros, whom the FBI team had just captured, were sitting in their own interrogation rooms at the FBI field office. This FBI field office had gray hard floors in some areas with some wood paneling on some walls. Some areas had bluish-grey carpeting with paneled walls and a white ceiling. Square light fixtures on the ceiling were bluish in the center.

Mike looked at the paperwork on the desk showing that both of the hackers were Mirandized.

The lawyer for the hackers came through the door.

"Hi, I'm representing Chris Pritin and Lauren Otros. My clients have reviewed your charges. The two will only admit to knowledge of incidents one, three, five and eight. They deny any involvement in the deaths. They will not assert their Fifth Amendment rights for leniency, understanding that this deal is off the table if they fail to cooperate or if they're found to be involved in any of the deaths," the lawyer said.

Mike looked at the deal that offered the hackers one-year probation, and be prohibited from using the internet during that time.

"Who the hell approved that deal?" Mike said.

"It's hard to believe even our AI auto prosecutor lawyer would allow this. Wait here," Mike said.

Mike walked out to find the prosecutor. He found him not far away.

"Why would you approve that deal?" Mike exclaimed.

"From the evidence, they will admit to. It seems like they are not involved in any deaths. Do you know who the father of Chris Pritin is?" the prosecutor asked.

"No. Oh, wait? You're kidding," Mike said.

"That's right, son of the majority leader of the senate," the prosecutor said.

"The deal is contingent on them not being involved in any of the deaths. Plus, from what Tara said, they might provide some insight into the other incidents," he said.

Mike shook his head and walked back to the interrogation room.

That explains how he got a personal quantum computer and encryption device.

The hacker, Chris Pritin, was sitting at the table opposite Mike, Robin, and Tara.

"You are twenty-one years old," Mike asked.

"Yes," Chris stated.

"I have here a list of some incidents," Mike said. It was really the entire list of known incidents, but he didn't want them to know that.

"I want to walk through each one of these, and I want you to explain what you did and why you did it."

"*Incident* #1 in Atlanta," Mike said.

"We used AI-assisted hacks to get into the traffic control system to snarl up the cars to stop, that's it," Chris said.

"Why?" Mike asked.

"We just wanted to show the security and privacy concerns people were taking for granted. Someone else might do something much more damaging," Chris said.

"What if someone died because they couldn't get to the hospital? You would be charged with murder," Mike said.

"We left a route for the ambulances open, and we were monitoring for ambulances that needed to go through. We would have let the traffic go or routed the ambulance," Chris said.

"How did you hack it?" Tara asked.

"Using generative AI. We determined the cycle that certain traffic control poles would go down for maintenance and found we could sneak changes in and erase any audit trail as part of their reboot cycle," Chris said.

At that moment, the term came into Tara's head: 'Slacker Hackers'. It was a derogatory term for hackers that needed AI to assist their hacks, coined in the early days of AI use for hacks. Tara wasn't even sure why she thought of it, as she never liked that term. Plus, now that almost all hackers used an AI, it didn't really seem to make sense anymore.

"Why did you leave a note?" Robin asked.

"We wanted people to know it wasn't just an accident and someone did it so they would address the security concerns," Chris said.

"Why didn't you just say that on your note?" Robin asked.

"We kind of thought the note itself would make it obvious," Chris said.

"*Incident #2*—House fire in Las Vegas caused by an overloaded TV," Mike said.

"I know nothing about that one. We only did hacks on vehicles," Chris said.

"*Incident #3*—Cars went in a large multi-mile circle in Virginia," Mike said.

"We hacked the traffic control system to make the cars think only certain off-ramps and on-ramps were accessible, and there was a detour required," Chris said.

"Did you know a driver died when his car got routed into a ditch?" Mike stated.

"What? No, we would never do that. It wasn't us. We did the circle thing, but we had no plans to hurt anyone. Can I see the data?" Chris asked.

Tara showed him the data on a laptop she had with her.

"See this time frame and data right here? That's our hack. Wait, look at that. See the IP address on those packets? That's a second hacker, not us, that used the same security hole we were using," Chris said.

Tara looked over the data.

"Did you leave a note?" Mike asked.

"Yes, inside the traffic control pole like the other one," Chris said.

"*Incident # 4*—Pedestrian walked into traffic in Kansas," Mike said.

"I don't know anything about it. Doesn't involve vehicles," Chris said.

"*Incident #5*—Bunches of cars were driving in weird patterns in Minnesota," Mike stated.

"Yep, that was us. It was supposed to spell out 'security' on the road, but I messed up the programming for the traffic control, so it just looked like a pod of cars moving together," Chris said.

"*Incident #6*—A self-driving car gets T-boned by a manual drive truck and explodes. They both die. That was in Maine," Mike stated.

"Yikes, definitely NOT us, I swear. You have our IP addresses now. You can check. I gave you the list of all proxies and VPNs we used," Chris said.

"*Incident #7*—Man in a convenience store shot by a robber. In Montana," Mike said.

"Definitely not us. It's not even computer-related. Why ask about that one?" Chris asked.

"Other commonalities grouped these cases," Mike said.

"*Incident #8*—Right around the corner from you. Cars were getting airborne. Here in California," Mike said.

"We made sure only empty vehicles did that, so no one got hurt. We needed to be showier since no one seemed to get our messages," Chris said.

"How did you do this hack?" Tara asked, though she already knew the answer now.

"This one, we tricked the traffic control into thinking there was no traffic for the empty vehicles, so they would try to go fast. The problem was the cars knew the topography and knew the hill was there, so they would have reduced speed. So, we made a GPS device and put it nearby to trick cars into thinking they were in an unfamiliar area," Chris said.

"We tried to go back to pick up the device, but the police and FBI were there for a while, and a truck must have knocked it off the roadway," Chris said.

"You left a note at this one?" Mike asked.

"Yes," Chris replied.

"*Incident #9*—A manually driven truck carrying acid crashes into a self-driving car, killing the occupants of both vehicles. Their vehicles were melted along with them. This was in Illinois," Mike stated.

"Ew! Gross, horrifying, and sad. We had nothing to do with that one. Never. Check our data," Chris said.

"*Incident #10*—A self-driving vehicle crashes into a speeding manual driver vehicle. This is in New Jersey," Mike stated. This was the incident Tara had witnessed.

"No, we are not involved in that incident," Chris said.

"*Incident # 11*—A manual drive vehicle collides with a self-driving vehicle. This was in Virginia," Mike said. This was the incident Mike and Tara had witnessed.

"No, definitely not involved in this one," Chris said.

"*Incident #12*—A manual drive vehicle runs into a self-driving vehicle, causing the self-driving vehicle to be thrown into the river. This was in Oklahoma," Mike stated. This was the incident. Mike, Robin, and Tara had to save each other from the sinking vehicle.

"No, we were not involved," Chris replied.

"*Incident #13*—A plane en route to Las Vegas had a systems issue that caused it to dive and recover. It also had an altimeter issue," Mike said.

"No, we did nothing with planes at all," Chris said.

"*Incident #14*—Construction equipment was hacked to cause unauthorized movements. This was in California," Mike said.

"You mean the dancing cranes, backhoe, and other equipment? Yes, we hacked those. We thought the location on an interstate highway would be high-profile enough to be noticed by more people. Plus, we thought we'd get a lot of views for that video," Chris said.

"Are you aware of other incidents I have not mentioned yet?" Mike asked.

"No, sir. I'm not aware of any other incidents," Chris said.

Mike, Tara, and Robin left the room and did a very similar interview with Lauren Otros. Their statements matched up. Mike, Tara, and Robin went to a conference room to discuss among themselves.

"So, what do you think? Are they telling the truth? No involvement in the deaths?" Mike asked.

"I've checked the data from their computers and the incident data. I believe they are telling the truth. They aren't involved in the deaths. Given the information about their hack, other hackers might be using a similar hack for some incidents. I believe the data we found in the cache was leftover data they couldn't clean up because a particular pole went offline for maintenance before they could clear the audit trail data. So that might not be found all the time. I guess we can skip investigating further for *Incident #5*," Tara said.

"So, we still have ten incidents with an unknown cause," Robin said.

"Actually, eleven incidents since one of the four incidents they were involved in seems to have had a different hacker involved as well. *Incident #3*," Tara said.

"Are you sure there aren't any more incidents in Las Vegas or maybe Hawaii? It would be nice to investigate there," Robin said jokingly.

"I will double-check on Hawaii just to be safe," Mike joked.

"Let's get some lunch," Robin said. "Second," Tara said.

"Let's go," Mike said.

"Each of the other incidents not associated with the hackers we caught doesn't seem to have any common IP address used. Each one seems to come from multiple locations. It seems to be different botnets," Tara said.

"So, you are saying other hackers infected unsuspecting businesses or people's computers and used them to hack the traffic control system?" Robin said.

"That seems to be a possibility. The IP addresses we tracked down seemed to be infected computers. I suspect there might be other things involved here, though, since a traffic control hack alone wouldn't explain those accidents completely. The trail often ended outside of the country for some of those IP address traces. We couldn't trace it further back than an infected victim's machine," Tara said.

"I've made an unofficial request to a friend of mine in the NSA to see if they have recorded any of the data we might need," Mike said.

"Oh, you mean that group that basically records everything on the entire Internet? There goes my privacy," Robin stated half-jokingly.

"I don't expect I will get an answer, but I figured it was worth a try," Mike said.

They finished filling out the online forms they needed to process the incident.

"Okay, we should plan on the visit to our next *Incident #7*, in Montana. Should we drive or fly?" Mike asked.

"Is a boat, walking, or a hot-air balloon an option?" Robin asked, half-jokingly.

"Given our luck and the risks, those might be nice options, but no," Mike said with a wink at Robin.

"After our plane experience, I vote car," Mike said.

"Definitely," Tara said.

"Agreed, even though that's a sixteen-to-twenty-hour drive, ugh," Robin said grudgingly.

"I'm going to go raid the snack machine, so we have some stuff for the ride," Tara said.

A little while later, they all got in the car. Mike programmed in their destination.

"Oh, umm, Robin, I have some bad news. We'll be going back through Vegas to get there," Mike said.

"That's great news!" Robin said.

"The bad news is we can't stop. We don't have time," Mike stated.

Robin just grumbled something under her breath.

About two hours later, they stopped to grab some fast food to go.

Luckily, Robin took a nap early on, and by the time she woke up, they were on the other side of Las Vegas. Dusk was approaching. Tara could still make out lots of brown ground on both sides of the road. Slightly green scrub scattered the land. Straight ahead, there were mountains they in the distance. There were very few towns or, for that matter, anything around. There was a small town just before crossing from Nevada into Arizona. Even with the prior usage of self-driving cars, the experience of witnessing the vehicle navigate with human-like precision still held a mesmerizing quality. The steering wheel turning with no one touching it still seemed a little odd. The screen would occasionally show the objects detected in front of the vehicle.

"Let's sleep in shifts. This way, we always have someone up to monitor things. Tara, maybe you could tell us what to look for. I'll try to get some rest now," Mike said.

Tara wanted to see what the area looked like if it was lighter out, so she put on her smart glasses and switched them to artificial day mode, making it look like it was still daytime outside. It was pretty convincing. The machine learning would fill in truck and car details into the video, superimposing them into a lighted background of the area you were traveling in.

They got closer and closer to the mountain range. Finally, they were going through what seemed like an area between the mountains. It was stunningly beautiful, thanks to artificial day mode. The cliffs were towering over their vehicle. The layering and the shapes of the hills nearby were various shades of brown. Even though it was just brown, the number of shades was stunning because of the layering of all the colors in the rocks.

They made a quick stop at a lone store that seemed open to use the restroom and get some snacks.

Robin and Tara were watching something on their own devices. It was getting late, though.

"Mike, wake up," whispered Tara. Mike was still sleeping. Tara rubbed his shoulder.

"Mike, can you wake up now?" Tara said.

"Oh, I guess so," he said sleepily.

"Robin and I are going to get some sleep. Just monitor this display here," Tara said.

Robin was in the back seat. Tara was in the front passenger seat. They both drifted off to sleep pretty quickly.

Not too long after, the car stopped at a charging spot for an hour,

Tara surprisingly woke up on her own. They were close to their hotel in Montana. Mike was still awake. Robin woke up, too.

"I guess we survived the night," Robin said.

"Most of our snacks didn't," Mike said, munching on one of them.

Their car pulled into the parking garage. They could see on the car display the parking lot had communicated an open spot with a charger to their vehicle, and it navigated itself there and parked. They went into the hotel and checked in.

"Why don't you two go get some breakfast and check out the downtown area a little? I'll try to catch up on some sleep, and we can meet up for a late lunch," Mike said to Tara and Robin.

"Sure," Robin said.

"Goodnight," Tara said with a smile.

Mike went into his room and went to bed.

PROJECT MIND RIVER

Chapter 15

Tara and Robin showered before heading out. This hotel was inside a tall brick building. The rooms were about the average fare you would expect for a hotel. It had the typical nightstand, desk, chairs, and beds. Tara saw that the hotel had smart devices, allowing her to control many of them with her phone. She scanned an electronic barcode displayed on a small device on the wall, giving her control of the TV and lights and even unlock the door with her smartphone. After Robin was done, they went downstairs and walked outside the hotel.

Luckily, the street had many shops and restaurants just around the corner. Most of the buildings were two to four stories. Further down, some high-rise buildings were taller. Almost all the buildings were smaller down the street in the other direction, with a few exceptions. They walked a little further and found a restaurant to get some breakfast.

They walked in. This place had a mix of a diner vibe and a mini bakery. It looked nicer than a lot of diners, though. They put on their smart glasses to check out the menu.

"I'll take some pancakes and water," Tara said to her smart glasses.

"No service at this location," the smart glass voice responded.

"Guess we have to order the old-fashioned way," Tara said.

A waitress came by, and they ordered. It seemed to be a pretty busy breakfast location. The food was good.

"So, did you just get assigned to this case?" Robin asked.

"Yes, well, sort of. I was a witness for *Incident* #10, and I guess I could help. With my background, Mike referred me for a job. I honestly wasn't going to take it originally, but I got laid off from my job at Intellibotz," Tara said.

Robin nodded.

"Were you and Mike ever together?" Tara asked.

"No. Well, we had plenty of drunk nights in a bar where we might have crashed together in the same place, but nothing ever happened. In this line of work, relationships like that are always tricky," Robin said.

"I've always been too busy with my work to really think about that," Tara said.

"You'd catch a few more guys with a little less conservative dress," Robin said with a smirk.

"But would I really want guys like that?" Tara said.

"You know the old saying, don't judge a book by its cover. Everyone judges a book by its cover," Robin said.

"I know I'm like a dictionary. No one wants to read me all the way through, but everyone wants to use me as a reference," Tara said.

"I don't know what the frick that means," Robin said.

"Neither do I," Tara smirked.

"Want to do some shopping while we wait for Mike?" Tara asked.

"Sure," she said.

They paid for their meal and headed out. At a nearby clothing store, they killed some time inside.

"What do you think of this?" Tara asked about a very conservative shirt.

"It's nice. It's very you. What do you think about trying this one?" Robin gave her a modest top that was a bit more open on the front.

"I'm not sure that's me," Tara said.

"Try it and see," Robin suggested.

Tara tried it on. She was very self-conscious about her body, and more of it seemed like a bad idea to her.

"How does it look?" Tara asked.

"It looks great. Come see in the mirror here," Robin said.

It was snugger than her usual preference.

"That definitely works for you," Robin said.

"Really?" Tara asked.

"Yes, get that one," Robin said.

They shopped around a bit more and picked out a few other items.

"Let's check and see if Mike is up yet," Robin said.

They headed back to the hotel.

Mike was ready at the hotel. They met in his room.

"Let's review the footage of *Incident #7* before we head over there," he said.

Tara brought up the footage on her laptop.

A casually dressed guy with glasses entered a convenience store, grabbed an item from the counter, and prepared to pay. He looked behind him and saw a man standing at the end of the aisle. He pulled out a gun and fired at the man at the end of the aisle.

"The guy at the checkout said he thought he saw the man reach for a gun. As we can see in the video, that doesn't seem to happen. But it turned out that the man had a weapon and was an international assassin. The guy that did the shooting was a criminal known for burglaries," Mike said.

"Is that assassin guy related to the guy who went after Tara?" Robin asked.

"We don't have any evidence suggesting a connection," Mike said.

"So, either this was just a criminal with a twitchy trigger finger, or a guy hired to kill him?" Robin said.

"Maybe or something else. The shooter insisted he saw him reach for a weapon. He is saying it was self-defense. But all the evidence recorded seems to suggest something else," Mike said.

"I wish we could pull visuals from the smart glasses to give us another viewpoint," Robin said.

"We can't. They checked the glasses for problems, though. Everything looked to be functioning normally with them," Tara said.

"All of that data is encrypted and deleted, related to the privacy policies of the smart glasses. Otherwise, much fewer people would want to wear them. People would be more conscious and concerned about being recorded without that policy," Tara said.

"Let's go to the scene and look around. Maybe there is another explanation, like if there is a mirror placement in the store that might allow seeing something that was hard for the cameras to catch. The person at the register is working today. I checked," Mike stated.

They all went down to the car. They told the car computer to navigate to the store's location a few minutes away. Inside matched what they saw in the video. It looked like a standard, moderately sized convenience store with the usual items. It was cool this store allowed phone checkout. You could just hold your phone near the product and select purchase if you had the app that a lot of these stores used for smartphone checkout.

Mike showed his ID and introduced himself to the clerk.

Mike got into the position where they saw the assailant. He looked around to see if there might have been other viewpoints of the man shot. He couldn't see any other mirrors that would have provided a different viewpoint.

"Did you see that the man that was shot had a gun prior to being shot?" Mike asked the clerk.

"No, I didn't see anything like that," the clerk said.

Robin and Tara looked all over the store. There are no obvious reflective surfaces that would have made other vantage points plausible.

As Tara was walking around, some sort of message popped up on her phone. It was a weird multicolor image that just looked like colored dots. She narrowed her eyes. Suddenly she could make out the 3D image of a word.

It said,

Lookout!

She stopped in her tracks, wondering what the hell was that. Robin and Mike were meandering through the aisles when three large men walked into the store. They were looking around. One had glasses on and was eying Mike, Tara, and Robin. The guy with the glasses came up behind Mike and grabbed his gun from its holster. Another man made a similar move to Robin.

Robin turned around, grabbed his hand with the gun, and kneed him in the groin. The gun fell to the ground. The man hit her hard. She fell and slid across the floor.

Mike knocked the gun out of the man's hand that grabbed at it but also fell to the floor. The third man punched at Tara. She screamed, but dodged the first punch. He hit the shelving behind her instead.

"This is what you get for putting our guy in the slammer," the man with glasses said to Mike as he punched him hard.

"We were not part of anything that happened here," Mike said, blood dripping from his mouth.

"You guys seem really friendly, but I'm going to have to ask you to leave," Mike said with a smirk. Mike shoved the guy into the food racks, and they collapsed under him.

Robin got up and punched the guy hard.

"Call the police," Robin yelled to the clerk.

"Don't call anyone, or you won't walk out of here," said one attacker.

The man attacking Tara grabbed her arm. Grabbing him back, they fell towards the floor, with Tara falling onto her back, putting her foot into the man's chest as she did. Tara used a Judo-style move, kicking the man in the chest. He flipped over the top of her. Tara hit her head on the floor pretty hard.

"Oww! Sorry," she said to the man, who she flipped while still lying on her back.

"Run!" Mike said as he saw one reaching for a gun, and he might get it before he could stop him.

Tara got up. Robin and Tara ran out the door together. Mike ran out the door but waited next to the door, hiding. As one man was about to come out, he nailed him square in the face with all his might, knocking him back into the two men behind him. Mike ran to catch up with Robin and Tara.

Mike pulled out his phone. Smashed in the fight and dead. Robin lost her phone in the fight.

"Call the police," Mike said as quietly as he could while running and still being loud enough for Tara to hear.

Tara pulled out her phone and dialed 911, but it wasn't going through. "It's not working," she said.

They were running along Main street with some scattered shops but took a side street. This had no shops and was more of an open area. They found an enormous warehouse that had open bay doors and went in. Mike, Tara, and Robin hid amongst some boxes.

"I think they are over there." They heard them as they seemed to get closer.

"Bleep! Bleep! Bleep! Bleep!" Tara, Mike, and Robin heard what sounded like several people's phones getting messages.

"They are that way," they heard someone say.

Around the corner came a warehouse worker. "They are here!" he exclaimed.

Mike, Tara, and Robin ran deeper into the warehouse to find another place to hide. There was a faint voice sound nearby. Then they heard, "I think I heard something this way," the man that had attacked them said.

"How do they keep finding us? We didn't make enough noise," Mike said.

"They're here!" one man yelled. The two others came around the corner of the aisle from the other side of the boxes. Mike ran at the guy with the glasses hard and tackled him to the ground. Robin went towards the other guy she had fought earlier. He preemptively covered his groin and shook his head no. So Robin kicked him in the face.

The guy who went after Tara before was angry and ran at her hard. Tara stepped aside and grabbed the guy, twisting and using her leg to unbalance the man. The man fell to the floor, along with Tara.

"Sorry," she said. She got up, and so did the man.

He was unbelievably angry now. He threw a hard punch at Tara. It was a glancing blow to the face. Tara was hoping she could remember her training. She swiftly maneuvered around the man, gripping his neck and leveraging her leg to destabilize him. Tara also lost her balance, resulting in both of them falling.

"Sorry," she said. The man looked at her funny.

Tara stood up. The man got up as well, grabbing a bar off the floor and swinging at her. She did a surprising backflip up onto a higher box behind her. Tara was just on the edge of the box and fell off of it onto the man attacking her.

Mike, distracted by Tara's rather amazing jump, got slugged in the face.

"Bleep! Bleep!" They heard what sounded like more phones getting messages.

"They are over here!" an unfamiliar voice said.

A bunch of very hefty men in black leather jackets came around the corner.

"We heard you messed with our friend. You are going to be really sorry about that," the man in the black leather jacket said. The men in the leather jackets ran at and started attacking the men that were attacking Mike, Tara, and Robin.

Mike whispered to Tara and Robin, "Let's get the hell out of here."

They quietly snuck out of the warehouse while all the commotion was going on.

They made their way back to the car. Mike called the police on the vehicle's internal phone service.

"We have a fight between maybe eight or ten people in a warehouse..." he said.

They waited. Mike waited while talking with the 911 operator.

"Police are on scene," said the operator.

Mike programmed the car to go to the warehouse. There were ten police cars on the scene. Mike and Robin went into the warehouse with them.

"There were warehouse workers here, maybe ten guys with black leather jackets, and three that had chased us from the store," Mike said.

"There is no one here now," said an officer.

They returned to the convenience store to recover their belongings and pull the video to show the police, but nothing recorded. The unit appeared to be off.

The police left. Robin, Mike, and Tara went back to their vehicle.

"What the frick just happened?" Robin asked.

Mike and Tara just looked back at her.

"That was extremely odd. I've been doing this a while, and I've seen nothing like that," Mike said.

"Why were they after us?" Tara said.

"I guess the three men, in the beginning, thought we were the ones responsible for arresting the shooter. I don't know why they would think that. The timing of them coming in seems very suspect," Mike said.

"Maybe the clerk called them?" Robin said.

"But the clerk would know we aren't the ones that arrested him. Also, I didn't see him call anyone while we were there, at least," Mike said.

"Why did the warehouse workers come after us?" Tara said.

"Maybe that was also a drug warehouse, and we stood out as strangers?" Robin asked.

"Then why did other gangs seem to come in and attack the guys that found us?" Tara asked.

"Rival gang, maybe," Mike said.

"Tara, I have an idea. Pull all the cell phones for that area and see what you find," Mike said.

"On it," she said, opening her laptop and pulling the data.

"There doesn't seem to be any record of cell phones related to that area," Tara said.

"How? We all heard all those bleeping phones," Robin said.

"Oh, and Tara, did you say you were sorry to the thugs that attacked us? Don't say sorry to the people attacking you!" Robin said only slightly jokingly.

"Sorry. I don't like to hurt people. Even though technically they hit the floor, and I didn't hit them," Tara said.

"Which reminds me. Tara, where did you learn to backflip and fight like that?" Mike asked.

"I wasn't fighting, just more dodging. I took several martial arts classes, but I tried to learn just defensive techniques when I was younger. I was also a gymnast. I'm not very good at any of it. It's been a long time since I practiced," Tara said.

"You might be the least injured of the three of us, so you look like you did pretty well," Mike said.

"I think I've got a bump on my head," Tara said.

"Let me see," Mike said. Tara turned around so Mike could see the back of her head. Mike gently touched her head, carefully feeling around. It kind of felt good with his hands feeling around until he touched a tender part.

"Ow!" Tara said.

"Sorry. It looks like a slight bump with no bleeding. How do you feel? Are you tired, dizzy, or nauseous?" Mike asked, concerned.

"No, I'm fine," she said.

"Let's go back to the hotel so we can get out of this area and think about this," Mike said.

On the way back, they stopped at a store so Mike could get a new phone.

Back at the hotel, they all went back to Mike's room. They ordered room service for lunch so they could complete their paperwork and talk. About twenty-five minutes later, there was a beeping sound at the door. Mike opened it. A motorized table with a top rolled itself in and unfolded its top, exposing the food they ordered.

"Oh, that's cool. I haven't seen one of these in a while," Mike said as he positioned everyone's food near them.

"Okay, we need to think about what just happened and what is our next move," Mike said.

"Oh, I forgot. Something weird happened when we were in the store before those men showed up. I got some sort of message on my phone. It only had an image in it. It was like one of those 3D images you needed to focus your eyes on to see. When I did, it had the word lookout! Sorry, I had no idea what it was talking about if it meant those guys," Tara said.

"That is very weird. Can I see it?" Mike said.

Tara pulled out her phone.

"It's not here. I don't see it. I'm going to scan my phone for malware and data transfers," Tara said. She ran some scans. She checked connections online. Tara also checked text messages.

"Nothing, I can't find anything. I swear I saw it," Tara said.

"Someone was warning us somehow? Who, and why?" Robin asked.

"The police said someone called the police before us. The call was anonymous, though. They tried voice identification but had no luck. The number appeared to be a burner," Mike said.

"Maybe the rival gang called the police," Robin said, wondering.

They filled out their paperwork for the incident while they talked on and off.

"Does it seem like we are being targeted?" Robin said. They all had the feeling of that even before now.

"Maybe, but also helped? That all seems pretty hard to believe," Mike stated.

"If we are in danger due to what we are investigating, we could give this investigation to another team. But if it's the investigation, another team will also be a target. I'd rather not put others in danger. I'd understand if you want to request to be pulled off this investigation," Mike said to Tara and Robin.

"No way I'm letting them get away with this crap! I'm staying," Robin said.

"I'm afraid, but I'm not sure if I'd really be safer someplace else. Plus, I don't want you to go it alone. Also, if there is someone trying to help us, they will contact me somehow. So, I want to ensure you get all the help you can get. So, I'm staying," Tara said. Robin, on one side of her, put her hand on her shoulder. Mike put his hand on Tara's other shoulder. Tara reached out with each hand, giving them a half hug.

"I can't believe we didn't think of this before! There is no way to prove it, but it would make perfect sense," Tara said.

"Don't keep us in suspense," Robin said.

"Think about it. In *Incident* #4, the guy walks into traffic like it's not there. In*cident* #7, the guy in the convenience store said he saw a gun, but there was no way to see it. In *Incident* #10, there was a manual drive car with the driver acting odd. *Incident* #11 almost got us because of a manual drive car. *Incident* #12 was a manual-drive car. The driver was acting weird and thought someone was following him. It's not all the incidents, but quite a few of them," Tara said.

"So, a lot of manual drivers are terrible drivers. We knew that already," Robin said.

"What do all of those incidents have in common?" Tara asked.

"What?" asked Mike.

"Smart glasses. They were all wearing smart glasses. If someone hacked them, they could make things appear real or even invisible to a person or driver. What if the man in the convenience store saw a gun on the other guy because his smart glasses were hacked? What if the man who thought he was being chased saw someone chasing him in his smart glasses? It's perfect, and since it auto deletes everything by built-in functionality, it's near impossible to prove," Tara said.

"If that's happening, everyone is screwed!" Robin exclaimed.

"But aren't all self-driving car windows like smart glass, so they could do it to all cars?" Mike asked.

"Not exactly. It is smart glass, but the functionality of making objects appear solid is not generally included in them to avoid ever obscuring the view. Other than maybe some military or government vehicles. Also, it's often just the front window that is smart glass. Someone wearing smart glasses could see alternative images anywhere they look," Tara stated.

"There is no way to prove this, is there?" Robin asked.

"Nothing easy," Tara said.

"I have an idea. You aren't going to like it," Mike said.

"Spit it out," Robin said.

"What if we drive to our next incident investigation in manual mode, or at least portions of it? We have the person driving wear smart glasses. The others will keep an eye on reality," Mike said.

"You're right. I hate this idea. It's like fourteen to eighteen hours to *Incident* #9 in Illinois. We'd be increasing the risk to all of us, most likely," Robin said.

"We've seen there are risks to flying and self-driving. Maybe we can get some fresh evidence finally this way," Mike said.

"The idea sounds scary. Maybe I can think of a way to determine if it's hacked," Tara said.

"Sounds like time for more road snacks," Mike said.

"Crap, another long drive," Robin said despondently.

At a nearby store, and got some snacks and drinks. They got in the car and prepared for their long drive.

"Let's try to do this in four-hour shifts, with the driver always having one person watching them. The third person will rest," Mike said.

"I have an idea," Tara said. She took out two very thin optical cameras that used flexible fiber optic cable. Teams normally used them to peek inside places with a very thin camera. She hooked two of them up to Mike's glasses and set them to record.

"If this is really happening, maybe we can get some evidence. I will also monitor the data feed for evidence of a hack. I can only analyze data statistically, though, since it's encrypted," Tara said.

"Try to expect the unexpected. So, if something out of the norm happens unexpectedly, assume it's the glasses," Tara said.

"I guess I'm driving first," Mike said, putting on his modified glasses. He enabled navigation with manual driving to their hotel in Illinois.

As they left, the surrounding land was mostly flat but with some dune-like hills near the roadway. The grass was a mix of slightly green and some drier brown grass sticking up. About an hour out, there was still a lot of flat land around them, with small mountains in the distance. About four hours later, the ground was getting greener as they left Montana and entered North Dakota. They found a place to pull over for a rest stop, switch drivers, and charge the car. Robin switched to driving now. Mike was going to watch out for Robin while she drove. It was Tara's turn to rest. It was now late at night.

Tara fell asleep. Almost four hours later, Tara woke to her phone vibrating. She looked at her phone. It was another 3D dot stereogram-like image. She tried to focus on it. It was hard to focus her eyes after just waking up. It said,

DANGER!

"Hey! I—" Tara said.

"Oh, shit!" Robin exclaimed. The car swerved onto the side of the road.

"Oh crap, again?" Mike yelled.

Tara got slammed against the side of the door as the car spun.

The car slid to the shoulder of the road, with the front tires of the car going slightly into a lake.

"Everyone okay? What happened?" Mike asked.

Robin had also hit her side in the spin.

"Think I'm okay," Robin said.

"Me too," Tara said.

"I saw a person in the middle of the road for a split second," Robin said.

Robin backed the car up out of the water and onto the shoulder.

"Let me check the data," Tara said.

The video feed caught one frame with half of something in it.

"Shit. Looks like the video only caught part of a frame. It's not synced with the video from the glasses. I will try to up the refresh rate. There wasn't a significant difference in data to detect anything different. We have evidence of a glitch, at least. It might be enough to report a bug to the company. Not enough to say there was a hack," Tara said.

"If we aren't getting data and risking our lives, is this shit worth it?" Robin asked.

"Just a few seconds before this happened, I got one of those 3D images again. It said danger! I tried to tell you, but it happened too quickly. Let me see if it's still on my phone. Crap, it's gone again!" Tara said, annoyed she couldn't show the message to them. She checked her device for malware again. She found nothing.

"I have an idea to reduce the risk. Sorry, I should have thought of this before," Tara said. Tara took her smart glasses, popped out the left lens, and left it hanging out. She wired the video feed to her glasses.

"This way, we don't need a second person monitoring," Tara said. Tara switched so she could drive. She forgot wearing smart glasses to drive had the benefit of seeing through the blind spots of the car. They looked transparent to see vehicles around theirs more easily. It was disconcerting when one lens was missing, so she disabled that feature. Tara remembered that some areas of the roadways had no lines on them at all and relied on smart glasses and windows to fill in the details. They drove another two hours to a charging station with a convenience store. It was late at night or early in the morning, depending on your point of view. This was one of the few bigger towns they had come across. They were not too far from the border of North Dakota and Minnesota.

The team got a little rest while the car charged. They drove the rest of the way, switching drivers and stopping as needed to charge. The rest of the trip was uneventful. They finally arrived at the hotel late in the morning. The hotel was another typical one. They agreed to take a nap.

Chapter 16

Robin had the alarm set and woke up Tara.

"My bed was hot last night," Tara said.

Robin looked down at the bed.

"I think the last guest set your mattress temperature up high," she said, pointing to the digital temp display on the side of the bed, partially blocked by the nightstand. Tara adjusted the temp down.

Mike, in his own room, had his alarm set as well. Once up and ready, they met up to grab a quick lunch. They figured fast food so they could have time for their investigation.

They got in the car and programmed a place to grab brunch.

"Do you think I should file a bug report with the company for the smart glasses?" Tara asked Mike and Robin.

"Tough call. It is potentially serious and harmful even with that limited data. It could also tip someone off if this is on purpose. That could make it more dangerous, but it could help us get any evidence we need faster," Mike said.

"I know what they are going to say already. When you reported the plane hacking, they said it was nothing. That's my bet on what they will say about this. Let's report it, I guess," Robin said.

"Okay, I'll submit the support issue with the data," Tara said. She entered the data, uploaded the frame grab, and submitted it.

After they ate, they headed to the area of the investigation.

They drove to the point about thirty minutes away to collect data from the traffic control poles on the route. The area where they were was a typical sort of highway with some trees and grass lining the sides of the road.

"I'm glad it's summer. I wouldn't want to be here in the winter," Robin said.

"Okay, a reminder on this *Incident #9* is a manual drive truck carrying acid collided with a self-drive vehicle, killing the occupants of both vehicles. In the self-drive vehicle, it was a criminal, likely funding terrorist activities," Mike said.

They stopped at each traffic control pole on the way, heading toward the incident. Tara collected the data, and they would move on to the next.

"I found something!" Tara exclaimed.

"The cache data on this poll shows events that don't match on the pole's main audit trail. It just shows an external command issued that traffic was clear ahead. But other pole data at the time suggested that wasn't true. I'm going to add this to my data analysis and increase the computing power," Tara said.

They went back to the car. Tara tapped some keys for a bit on the laptop. She spent about fifteen minutes looking at the data.

"Holy crap!" Tara exclaimed. Tara was shaking a little.

"What's wrong?" Mike asked.

"I've seen this pattern of data manipulation before. It's no wonder we can't figure out what is going on if this is what I think it is," Tara said.

"What is it?" Robin said.

"I believe this isn't normal hackers or bots. I believe this could be some type of machine-learning algorithm. This is a pattern. It is very complex," Tara said.

Mike's phone rang. "Hello,"

An electronically disguised voice at the other end said, "This is a friend. Stop your investigation. You and your team are in grave danger."

"Who is this? If you are a friend, you would know I can't do that," Mike said, and he stopped when he heard the caller hang up.

"Tara, can you trace that call?" Mike asked.

"Trying," she said, typing on her laptop.

"Sorry, looks like a burner number, possibly Virginia. Should we send someone to find it?" Tara asked.

"It's unlikely they would find anything, and if they did, I'm sure it would be wiped clean," Mike said.

"What did they say?" Robin asked.

"Someone called using a disguised voice. Said it was a friend and that we should stop the investigation because we were in grave danger," Mike said.

"A little late on that one. Tell us something we don't know," Robin muttered.

"So now what?" Tara asked.

"Let's finish up our investigation here, and we'll go back to the hotel to think this through a bit more," Mike said.

They finished collecting traffic data and went to the site of the accident. After they took a few of their own pictures and videos, they headed back to the hotel.

As they were driving, they took a different road on the way back. The black roadway was shiny black.

"The road looks odd," Tara said.

Mike glanced at the road and at the car dashboard.

"Oh, it looks like they are testing a solar roadway with charging to charge vehicles wireless while driving," Mike said.

They had been driving for a little while on their way back.

"Bleep!" Tara's phone got a message.

"Oh shit! Another 3D image," she said, holding her phone between Mike and Robin.

"What the hell does it say? I can't see anything," Robin said.

"I can't see anything either," Mike said.

"It says,"

SAVE HIM! Brian Rissal–20 MIN.

"I guess that meant approximately twenty minutes," Tara said.

"Who the frick is that?" Robin asked.

"Checking our databases. CIA Operative. What do we do?" Tara said.

"Well, it seemed preemptively correct on the last two times you said you got a similar message and warned us," Mike said.

"We still have little solid evidence and a note only Tara can read. What the hell? I guess we need to check," Robin said.

Mike grabbed his phone and dialed his supervisor.

"We believe we have a life-or-death situation and need the location of Brian Rissal, a CIA operative, immediately. We believe his life is in imminent danger," Mike said.

"We got a message from an informant, and this informant has been right two times before," Mike said, shrugging at Robin and Tara, since he didn't know what else to call those messages.

"You said he is heading home from the airport. He is on vacation to see his family. Can we get real-time cell phone location tracking? Thanks. Can we issue a stop command for his vehicle? It's not working, okay," Mike said.

"We have his approximate location in real-time within half a mile. He is fifteen miles out from here. The stop command doesn't work for that manufacturer. There is a lot of traffic, so even the police might not make it on time," Mike said while entering the data into the car systems.

Mike hit the lights, and siren mode and increased pursuit speed.

"Hang on!" Mike exclaimed. The car jolted forward with the lights and siren wailing.

"Tara, can you monitor the traffic control systems, please?" Mike asked.

"On it," she said.

"I don't think we're going to get there on time," Mike said.

Mike redialed his phone. "Can we get air support out there, and can you get a helicopter to my location in time? Thanks," Mike said.

"Mike, what are you planning?" Robin asked.

"Sorry, I need a faster ride. I can't let someone else die," Mike insisted.

"HELO ONE is in the air, five mins inbound to your location," the comm stated.

Mike climbed to the back of the vehicle and opened the air support case. Pulling out the drone, he turned it on, but with the propellers off. He set the clamp mode to hold to the vehicle. He turned on the drones' flashing lights. Then he opened the window and clamped the drone onto their vehicle's top.

"Mike, you're not doing what I think you are, are you?" Robin asked.

"Well, you've known me for a while, so probably," Mike said with a smile.

"You're nuts!" Robin said.

"What are you doing?" Tara asked Mike.

"You don't want to know," Robin said.

Mike was looking out the window.

"HELO ONE inbound to your location two minutes," they heard on the comm channel.

"HELO ONE lock on to the car with an attached drone with lights enabled at our location," Mike stated.

"I can see it. They are almost here," Mike said. Mike could see the helicopter. It had a display on the bottom that said, "FBI."

It also was spelling out longer messages with its tail rotor, which was just its aircraft registration number at the moment.

"HELO ONE. You're over the target. Lower your ladder to the left side of the vehicle," Mike stated.

"This is HELO ONE. Seriously?" the pilot said.

"Yes, drop it now!" Mike said.

Out the window, they could see the ladder lowering towards them.

"A little lower," Mike said, grabbing a couple of rungs.

Mike climbed out onto the ladder. "Please be careful!" Tara yelled.

Mike gave a thumb up to Tara.

"I've got it. Hold position. Now pull me up as you head to the second target," Mike yelled into his comm to the helicopter. The helicopter carried Mike off into the distance, towards the target location.

"I hope he'll be okay," Tara said to Robin.

"Me too," Robin said, while checking their distance to the target area.

"They have five drones heading to the target location to identify his car. I've got them on the video feed," Tara said.

"His car is not responding to any commands. I tried to just flash his top light, but no luck," Tara said.

"We still have about ten minutes minimum till we get there. Even the police can't catch up. The drones or Mike and HELO ONE may be the best shot," Robin said.

"They have a search pattern for his vehicle with the drones," Tara said.

"HELO ONE is five minutes out from approximate target location," came over the comm.

"No vehicle located yet," the command center responded on the comm.

Tara was watching the drones and the traffic cams. Traffic was moving fast, but packed. With lots of self-driving vehicles, unless there is an actual road blockage, traffic can move quickly, still in tighter pattern formations to accommodate more cars. Seeing fast speeding cars only a half car length apart still kind of felt wrong. The traffic control systems, when working correctly, can notify cars fast enough to slow down if there is a problem. The highway they were on was your typically three or occasionally four lines, with traffic moving pretty quickly.

"I've got the car! Drones spotted it. Attempting communication," Tara said.

The drones surrounded the self-driving vehicle with Brian Rissal in it, doing a formation around it 360 degrees and flashing their lights.

"Hopefully, that will get his attention to pull over," Tara said.

"He doesn't appear to be pulling over. Let me see. He might be asleep in the vehicle," Tara said.

"HELO ONE is two minutes out from target vehicle," came over the comm.

"I'm going to try something to wake him up," Tara said.

Tara maneuvered a drone to drop and clamp on the hood. It came down with a CLANK!

"Crap, I don't think it woke him up," Tara said.

"We can't disable the vehicle with a charge detonation. The traffic formation is too close. It will cause a disastrous multi-vehicle accident," Robin said.

"I even tried calling his vehicle earlier, but it's not answering. It might be set on silent," Tara stated.

"Oh, shit! Shit!" Tara exclaimed, then composed herself to go on comm.

"I've detected a manual drive vehicle closing fast about one minute behind HELO ONE, similar patterns to previous incidents," Tara said.

The helicopter caught up to the vehicle. Mike descended quickly on the ladder. The helicopter kept pace with the vehicle, so the ladder with Mike on it was just in front of the vehicle.

"He's still asleep. Bang the drone into the window near him," Mike said on the comm.

"Didn't work," Mike said.

Tara adjusted the remote control to slam the drone into the side of the man's vehicle. It bounced off and crashed into the ground.

Mike pulled out his gun and fired into the front windshield.

"This guy is quite a sound sleeper!" Mike exclaimed.

"I'm going to shootout the driver side window and get in," Mike said on comm.

"What?" both Robin and Tara said at the same time.

"Manual drive car, it's almost there!" Tara exclaimed.

"Why am I going up?" Mike yelled as the ladder was going up.

"Bridge!" the helicopter pilot said.

Mike turned around. "Oh, crap!"

He just barely made it over the bridge, almost hitting it. They lowered him back down on the other side. Mike was hanging outside the car's driver-side window.

Mike fired his gun into the window. It broke into thousands of pieces. He was about to get in.

"Lookout!" the pilot yelled as they raised the ladder with him on it.

The manual drive vehicle caught up, and another self-drive vehicle tried to get out of the way but, an obstacle on the side of the road, caused it to block the manual drive vehicle, causing a multi-car collision. Brian Rissal's car spun out just as it approached a bridge. It went over the embankment on the side, crashed, and exploded.

"NOOO!" Mike said on comm.

Mike was hanging onto the ladder as he watched the car explode. He wondered how he let this happen. He wondered if he had only been faster, could he have saved him?

Mike thought he saw something on the other side of the fire. It looked like one of those hooded figure assassins they had run into many days ago. It was hard to make out through the flames. A secondary explosion caused the fire to flare up, obscuring the figure, and then what he saw was gone.

Tara and Robin finally arrived at the scene. The helicopter let Mike off on top of the bridge, and he walked down to Tara and Robin.

"I'm sorry I didn't make it on time," he said. He looked rather despondent, and that was unusual for him. Mike sat down in their car, drained. Many ambulances and police cars were on the scene. The fire department arrived on the scene, working on extinguishing the fire.

"Hey, you did everything you could. No one else could have done anything more than you tried," Tara said to Mike, grabbing his hand.

"It wasn't good enough, though," he said.

"What drives you this hard? Did something happen to you?" Tara asked. There was a long pause.

"It was my first combat mission. We were ambushed. We made it into a small shack. I was looking out the window and saw the enemy. If I shot, I might have got him. If I didn't, I might have exposed our position. I had a shot, and I hesitated. I was shot and survived. The rest of my team didn't make it. I swore to myself never again would I hesitate to protect people, especially my family, friends, and colleagues," he said with a sincerity that touched Tara deeply.

"That was your first mission. You can't save everyone. You shouldn't blame yourself, especially not for what just happened here. You did more than probably anyone would have done to save him," Tara consoled. She leaned in for a quick hug as Mike sat there, nearly motionless.

"I thought I saw something through the flames. It looked like one of those hooded figures, but when I looked again, he was gone, nowhere in sight. He was standing maybe a block from where his car was on fire," Mike said.

"What's the point of these warning messages if we can't seem to do anything about them? Is that the point itself?" Robin asked.

"I know it doesn't seem like it, but I feel like we might be much closer to figuring this all out," Tara said.

"The operator of the manual drive vehicle is alive with serious injuries, heading to the hospital," came over the comm.

"We need to talk to him. Maybe he can further confirm our thinking about the smart glasses being hacked," Tara said.

"Let's go," said Robin. Mike was still out of it, drained and quiet.

They got in and headed to the hospital, arriving at the same time as the ambulance. They were wheeling the man into the ER. Tara and Robin walked quickly to get next to the stretcher the man was on.

Robin flashed her badge at the ambulance crew and ER staff that was moving him into an ER room.

"What happened?" Robin asked.

"They were chasing me. I thought they had guns. I don't know. I kept hearing voices all day," the man said. They saw the man's phone next to him on the stretcher. Tara grabbed it and downloaded the data off it with a dongle she had with her.

"We need to get him to the OR," a doctor said as they wheeled him away.

Tara and Robin went back to the car. Tara downloaded the data onto her laptop to take a look.

"There's something there. It looks like some type of malware, but it's like nothing I've seen before. It looks like it's encrypted with a cipher I've never seen before, either. This may be the most sophisticated malware I've ever seen," Tara said, almost in awe at what she was looking at.

"Let's head back to the local field office," Robin said.

They were on their way back to the office. Tara heard something.

"What did you say to me? Did you just call me a bitch!" Robin glared at Tara.

Tara thought she heard Mike say under his breath, "You suck as a pacifist."

"Mike, what did you just say?!" Tara exclaimed.

"Nothing worse than you said to me!" he said.

"I didn't say anything," Tara said.

"Neither did I," Robin said emphatically.

"Oh, shit! Wait, voices, what did all the drivers say? They heard voices. Let me see your phones," Tara said.

Tara checked all their phones. Somehow, Mike's and Robin's got infected. She installed malware protection on their phones.

"I don't think any of us said anything bad to each other. I think the malware can produce sounds and mimic voices, so realistically, it's uncanny," Tara said.

"How could it do that, though phone speakers aren't that good?" Mike asked.

"OH CRAP! Let me see your smart glasses and other devices," Tara said. Tara scanned the vehicle and all of their devices. "I think with the malware installed; it's been listening as well. It then creates appropriate sounds that matched the environment well enough to sound realistic," Tara said.

"That would be some pretty sophisticated malware," Mike said.

"No wonder everyone thought those drivers were insane. The malware could have easily updated the smart glasses, too," Tara said.

"Do you think we should send the malware to DHS for analysis?" Tara asked.

"That would be protocol. Given that they seem to hide something, it has me worried. This is insanely important to national security," Mike said.

"Should we leak it to independent labs also?" Robin asked.

"We could be reprimanded or fired," Mike said.

"Let's submit it to as many authorities by protocol: FBI lab, DHS, NSA, NIST, and whatever other government entities we are allowed," Mike said.

"What do we do? Until they can confirm this, no one will believe us," Robin said.

They arrived at the field office.

They walked through the security checkpoint.

"Identities Agent Actley, Agent Laizon, and Consultant Bitlouver confirmed," an automated voice said at the security guards stand at the entryway.

Tara saw the images of all of them appear on the guard's monitor. She figured they were using the technology from the 3D scans they made of her and her colleagues.

"Let's get some drinks and meet in a conference room," Mike said.

They got some drinks on the first floor and went upstairs to find a conference room.

"Hey Mike, I haven't seen you in a while," a man passing by said. Mike replied. That happened a few times while they were looking for a conference room.

"You're a popular guy," Robin said.

"Not really. I've just been on a bunch of investigations with the folks here before," he said.

They found a conference room to use.

"You submitted the malware?" Mike asked Tara.

"Yes, to all the federal agencies we could," she said.

"Until we can get to the source, can we even stop anything? If we had stopped this guy from dying today, might he have died the next day?" Robin asked.

"That's a very depressing thought," Mike said.

"I think they need malware scanning to be updated for all devices and devices that can't have it installed scanned. We have only found this on phones, but what if it's on everything?" Tara asked.

"So, the entire country, even the world, maybe at risk?" Mike asked.

"Possibly," Tara said.

"What can we prove? That they will believe?" Robin said.

"We have evidence of traffic control system hacks and evidence of malware on your phones. We have that frame grab from the smart glasses. They might just consider that a glitch or bug. In combination with the messages, we witnessed warning us that should count for something," Tara said.

"I just thought of something. Remember, we were being chased in the warehouse, and they kept seeming to find us. We heard whispering voices. What if that was malware on their phones and yours?" Tara asked.

"That crap is pretty disturbing, if true. It would mean hackers basically can have an army of people at their beck and call," Robin said.

"Best bet is they patch and scan systems to prevent or find malware," Tara said.

"And we find the source to stop them from continuing to do this," Mike said.

"How about Robin and I go try to convince the supervisors and the right Field Intelligence Groups that there is a major concern here? Tara, if you can help convince the computer forensics folks to request patches and scans," Mike said.

"I'll head down there now," Tara said.

"Oh, one more thing about those hooded men we ran into. I found one agent who had a similar case of a hooded figure near a fatal accident. He wasn't directly involved and had found other videos of similar scenes. So, he started calling them Death Monks. I checked the cases, but they seem unrelated," Robin said.

Tara went down to the forensics lab. She opened the secure door. Inside, several computer forensic experts were working on different computers. Sound of clacking keyboards filled the air. The room was large, with many medium-sized walled gray office cubes. Monitors on the walls showed various information about software jobs being run.

"Hi, I'm Tara. I submitted a malware sample I'd like to see if we can look at," Tara said.

"What's the priority of your case?" one of them asked. They didn't have a designated priority yet, so she needed to convince them this was.

"We believe this may use zero-day flaws to infiltrate devices and be responsible for multiple vehicular murders across at least the country. We also believe it may manipulate the behavior of the people it targets by mimicking other people's voices, messages, and more. It may work partially by inserting fake objects as solid into the visual field of smart glasses, causing manual drivers to respond to objects/people that don't actually exist. This could be a national security and safety issue for the country, if not the world," Tara said.

Everyone there stopped working and looked at Tara.

"Are you serious?" one guy asked.

"Deadly serious, and the clock is ticking," Tara responded.

Several of the people downloaded copies of the malware into a secure environment. They isolated the machines' physicality to have no connection to any network or internet.

"Hi. I'm the forensic lead, Tony. This is some crazy level of encryption we've never seen before. I don't know if we can break this," he said.

"Let me see if I can help," Tara said. She tapped some keys on the keyboard. She pulled up her model progress at home. It was over half complete. Figuring that model should be enough to help determine the encryption algorithm. She created an instance of the model and ran it against the encrypted data.

"I think I can tell you if there are similarities to any algorithms in an hour or so," Tara said.

"Meanwhile, we are going to run this on some devices that are isolated and see what it does," Tony said.

"Wait! Don't run those devices or simulated devices with microphone or sound enabled. Make sure you run those with RF and sound shielding. We also believe this may erase all data and itself to avoid detection," Tara said.

Tony nodded.

Tara answered her phone. "Hi. Yep, will be right there." Tara headed upstairs to meet up with Mike and Robin.

She got up to the conference room. Mike and Robin were in a rather heated discussion with several supervisors. They went quiet when Tara walked in.

"Tara, can you provide the details of the evidence you have?" one supervisor said.

Tara gave a similar speech to the one she gave to the computer forensics lab team.

"What you describe sounds impossible, manipulating people's emotions by secretly antagonizing them," a supervisor said.

"I want our forensic folks here to describe the details of your evidence, not a consultant. Let's go to see them," he said. The supervisor walked down to the computer forensics lab and opened the door.

Inside was chaos. A brawl had broken out between two of the forensic analysts, and the others were yelling at each other.

"Impossible? You were saying," Tara said, glaring at the supervisor.

Tara walked in and whistled so loud that everyone's ears hurt. They stopped.

"Do you remember what I told you about what we thought this malware could do? Did you hear whispers that sounded like someone saying something under someone's breath that criticized you?" Tara asked.

They nodded.

"Who left their audio plugged in?" Tony asked.

One of the analysts raised their hand.

"Unplug everything!" bellowed Tony.

"Oh, no frigging way! Everything got wiped. We're going to have to start again," Tony said.

Tara got them the statistical information that should help them brute-force attack the encryption to decrypt it. It still could take an unknown amount of time.

The supervisor still wasn't sure what to believe, but let the work continue for now. He also only let four people work on it rather than the whole lab, which was understandable, since they had other priorities.

Tara went to find Mike and Robin. Mike was in front of a door, holding on to some mixed reality goggles and some electronic replica guns.

"I've so been wanting to try this. It's a mixed reality training room," Mike said. He put on the goggles and handed pairs to Robin and Tara. He set up the training program. The large room had walls, half walls, and various oddly placed boxes. They put on their goggles, and it immediately looked like they were outside on a sunny day. There were dilapidated buildings with broken walls around them. Tara assumed those matched to the actual walls in the room, so they should be careful not to run into them since they were real.

"Lookout," Tara said as she saw a kid dive out from behind a wall and throw something.

"Ow! Whatever that was, it really hit me. So, watch out!" Mike said as the object hit him. They took cover behind a broken wall, aiming towards both ends.

"There!" Robin yelled as she saw someone with a gun peek out from one end and aim at them.

Robin and Mike fired, and the man collapsed to the ground and then disappeared.

"Watch out!" Tara yelled as she saw parts of the wall they were near break off.

"Ow! Something really hit me," Tara said, but it felt rubbery, not like a piece of the brick wall.

An assailant fired a weapon at Tara while the wall collapsing distracted them.

"Ow! something hit me again!" Tara yelled.

"Agent Three eliminated," a voice said as Tara's goggles flashed red and said, "You are eliminated."

Mike ended the program.

"Are you okay?" Mike asked Tara.

"Yes, fine," she looked down. A soft rubber projectile hit her. They exited the room and put their goggles and guns back in the bin outside.

Mike, Tara, and Robin went to a conference room with the supervisor.

"Can we find out what Brian Rissal was involved with?" Mike asked.

"No. The CIA has already said his work is top secret, sensitive, compartmentalized, and cosmic," the supervisor said.

"In other words, we aren't getting any information, ever," Mike said.

"It seems not. They have asked for this investigation to be shut down as a matter of national security. They requested we forward all the data to them and the DHS," he said.

"This has grave implications for people in this country. How can we not investigate?" Mike asked.

"We'll keep the investigation open for now, but we'll need to keep it quiet. If this eventually gets back to the Attorney General, we will make our case to him," the supervisor said.

"Keep investigating. See if your informant has any more data about what might be happening," the supervisor said.

Tara, Robin, and Mike glanced at each other. They figured they should keep it quiet for now, as it might risk their source.

"You should check with our equipment team. They might have some things to help," the supervisor said.

They went to them to see what they might have.

On their way to the equipment department, a man stopped Mike. They exchanged pleasantries.

"Did you hear that multi-state drunk driver case got thrown out because of a technicality? He requested an InstaTrial, and it let him off," the man said.

"That's crazy. There probably should be some better rules around for when AI can be used as judge and jury," Mike said.

"That's for sure," the man said as he walked off.

They arrived at the equipment department.

"Oh hey, I'm George. I heard you need some of our new tech," he said.

"We have new smartphones with enhanced security. They constantly monitor for threats. We also have new computers for you with enhanced security. I also wanted to give you this," George said as he showed him a small handheld device with a button and a knob on it, plus some charge lights.

"This is a portable EMP. It can basically destroy all unshielded tech within about a fifteen-feet range. Your new smartphones and laptops are shielded. It could be useful to shut down a vehicle, for example. The vehicle won't be able to function after that," he said.

"Tara, we have something for you since you are not trained in weapons. We have this device. It's a light dazzler, sort of like a high-powered flashlight. It just temporarily blinds someone. Careful not to aim it at yourself or reflective surfaces," George stated.

The device looked like a medium-sized flashlight. Tara was happy it wouldn't permanently injure anyone.

"Tara, we've also updated your laptop with some of our integrated hacking tools to make it faster to download or access devices. Only for legally justified access, of course," George said.

"We're also providing you a new SUV with updated firewalls and isolated systems to avoid it being hacked," George said.

"We also have this motion-sensitive door alarm for you. This way, if you get any intruders in the middle of the night again, at least you will know about it," George stated.

"We've created some special smart glasses for you that, if you enable it, have local storage. It lets you disable any video or AR overlays in either eye via an un-hackable switch on the side," George said.

"Thanks, George, all of this is awesome!" Mike said.

Tara, Mike, and Robin left and headed to a conference room.

"Okay, so our next investigation is in Maine, so maybe seventeen to nineteen hours or more with stops by car or shorter by plane. What do you want to do?" Mike said.

"Well, they gave us all this tech to help figure out what is going on, so drive again, I guess," Tara said.

"I'm okay with driving again," Mike said.

"Holy crap! That's a long drive. I think I'd rather be fighting off assassins," Robin said half-jokingly.

"You never know." Mike chuckled.

"Oh, just to make it a little nicer, we'll get there probably Friday night. We get to spend the weekend in Bar Harbor," Mike said.

"I'm in." Robin grinned.

"That sounds nice. I've always wanted to go there," Tara said.

"I've heard it can be pricey, though. Do we have to go back to Vegas so Tara can win more money?" Robin asked.

"The bureau will pay for it since we will be there to start a case," Mike said.

"Very nice," Robin said.

They got to their car, picked up their stuff from the hotel, and headed on to Maine.

Once they got out of the city, the highway looked very similar to how it did in New Jersey, with green grass and trees along the sides of the road. Tara had an automatic monitor set up for the traffic control systems. They were taking turns manual driving, and when they got tired, though, they would switch to self-driving mode. It was getting dark. Tara switched her glasses to artificial daylight mode. Mike was driving with his glasses configured for only one lens to be operational. They found a place to just grab some food to go so they could eat in the car. They pulled over late at night to charge, grab some drinks, and have a rest stop. After a half hour of charging at a quick charge, they went on their way. They decided to all sleep and let Tara's automated alerts monitor traffic control and for approaching fast, manual-driven vehicles.

They all fell asleep fast. The self-driving car continued on its journey. They were traveling from Ohio to New York.

"Alert, Alert, Alert! Manual drive vehicle approaching at high speed," Tara's laptop reported.

Mike sat up so quickly that he bumped his head on the roof. "Ow!" he said.

"Do you see it?" Robin said.

"Not yet," said Tara.

"There it is!" Robin yelled.

Mike went into manual mode and pulled the car over to the side of the road. The manual drive vehicle went by, disappearing into the distance.

"So, it was nothing in the first place or missed us?" Robin asked.

"I dunno. But I guess we can go back to sleep," he said, putting the car back into self-driving mode.

"We flagged his license plate to see if the police can catch up to the driver," Tara said.

There was an accident on the roadway that was slowing traffic. They could see a distance ahead of them, and the police and ambulance showed up. A vehicle resembling a car carrier appeared and expanded, creating a roadway over the accident vehicles. Vehicles then started proceeding on it, which went over the vehicles. Their vehicle went over the top of it shortly after.

"I've never seen that before," Robin said.

"I heard they were testing those, but it's the first one I've seen," Mike said.

209

Chapter 17

They went back to sleep. The rocking motion of the car helped them fall asleep. The car automatically stopped to charge again a while later. After charging on a charging pad, it continued its journey. Every once in a while, when someone woke up, they would check around to make sure everything was okay and go back to sleep. Tara's laptop was still monitoring traffic conditions. They were on the highway, moving fast.

Suddenly, everyone woke up as the car radio turned on loud. The car was going exceedingly fast. Just then, their car contacted a truck driving in front of them.

"Hey, what's going on?" Robin asked.

Mike woke up dazed.

"Holy shit!" Robin exclaimed.

"Why are we bumper to bumper with a gas truck?" Mike asked, staring at the huge gas logo through the front window. They all looked out the window, not believing what they were seeing. The road was quiet other than the gas truck in front of them. It looked like the bumper of the truck went over the top of theirs and smashed it, causing their vehicle to be attached to the truck.

Tara, waking up, pulled out her laptop.

"Checking," Tara said.

"The car is infected! Pull over!" Tara exclaimed.

"I can't. Manual controls aren't working!" Mike yelled.

"EMP! Use the EMP!" Tara yelled.

Mike quickly found the EMP and, opened a flip cap, and pressed the button.

A loud pop sounded. The radio stopped, and all the car's systems went dark.

"Why are we still moving?" Robin shouted.

"I think our bumpers accidentally got linked. It can happen when the traffic control system packs cars too tightly on the roadway," Tara said.

"The only problem with that is that it was nighttime, and there likely wasn't enough traffic for that, plus who else believes this is an accident," Robin said.

"Tara, signal the truck to stop," Mike said.

"It's not working," Tara said as she sent the commands from her smartphone.

"Drone charge to take off our bumper?" Mike asked.

"Next to a gas truck?!" Robin exclaimed.

"Guys!" Tara said look. In the distance, there was another gas truck headed up behind them fast.

"Shit! You've gotta be kidding me." Robin grabbed the drone kit out of the back, opened it, turned it on, and held it out the window. "Tara, you ready," Robin said.

"Yes, release it," Tara said. The drone flew up between their car and the truck. She lowered it down near the bumper. It hit the edge of the truck. It spun crazily under the truck and then fell to the road, being crushed by the wheels.

"Need another drone!" Mike said as he saw the other gas truck closing quickly on them from behind.

Robin grabbed their other drone, turned it on, and held it out the window.

"Ready," Robin said.

"Yes," Tara said. Tara took control of the drone, positioned it between the truck and the car bumpers, and settled it down. It suddenly wobbled, but then locked to the bumper with a satisfying clank.

"It's on!" she said.

"It's been nice knowing you guys well other than this," Robin said.

"Everyone got your seatbelts on. On my count, three, two, one," Mike said.

Tara hit the buttons to activate the drone's explosive charge.

A small fireball appeared between the bumpers. Their car slowed down and moved away from the gas truck in front. The one behind was still closing.

"I've got no manual control!" Mike exclaimed. The car without power couldn't control anything via the fly-by-wire style steering.

The gas truck came up behind them and hit their vehicle, spinning them out.

"Hang on!" Mike yelled as the car left the roadway.

They crashed into a metal barrier. The airbags deployed. Dust from the airbags filled the air. Airbags squished Mike before slowly deflating.

"Everyone okay?" Mike asked with a funny voice, since his face was being squished by the airbags.

"I can't believe we're not dead. I'm okay, I think," Robin said.

Mike stared at her face. Her makeup smeared on her face by the airbag.

"Are you sure?" Mike asked.

"Why?" Robin asked.

"Just checking," Mike said.

"Tara, you, okay?" he asked.

"I cut myself on something," Tara said.

It was a slight cut. Mike couldn't open his door. The crash smashed the side of the car. Mike crawled into the back to get the first aid kit and pulled a bandage out.

"Here you go," he said, gently opening it and applying it to Tara's arm.

"I'll request a new car for us. Tara, can you figure out how the FBI's un-hackable car got hacked?" Mike asked.

"I'm not sure our car did. It could have been the other vehicles," Tara said.

"I'm sending the data to the team at the FBI, and I will look at our logs," Tara said.

"Luckily, there is an FBI Field office near here, so a car should arrive soon. Are they going to start docking our pay for destroyed cars?" Robin said.

"I hope not; otherwise, we're screwed. Since it's in the line of duty, I think we're good, though," Mike said.

They reported the car's location to the FBI so they could get it towed.

Another car arrived. They moved their stuff into it and continued their trip.

"I think one of us better stay awake in shifts the rest of the way," Mike said.

Mike stayed up so Tara and Robin could sleep. He plugged in the EMP to recharge it, just in case.

The car drove all night without incident. It stopped near a convenience store with a manual charger in the morning. They grabbed some breakfast items and drinks to eat in the car while it charged. Mike slept. Tara took on the monitoring of the car and traffic when the charge was complete. She unplugged it, and they went on their way.

Their car pulled up to a traffic light with a crosswalk. A woman walked across, and as she did, lights lit up the crosswalk in a pattern. The lights strobed in the direction the woman was walking, with a red light on either side of the crosswalk where she was. White lights flashed on and off in a pattern around the rest of the crosswalk. The light turned green as the woman left the crosswalk.

"I guess that is extra safety for self-driving or manual vehicles detecting someone is in a crosswalk," Tara said.

At about lunchtime, they stopped again to charge and grab some food. Luckily, the fast-food restaurant had a few chargers outside. There were a few other fast-food restaurants in the area, along with a strip mall.

Mike got a call while they were eating.

"Hello," Mike said.

"This is your friend," the electronically modulated voice said.

"Did you meet with the contact I sent your way, Brian Rissal?" the voice said.

"Is this a joke? Who is this? Mr. Rissal is dead from a car crash," Mike said.

There was a pause.

"He was a trusted friend. I don't know who else I can trust. Come meet me in D.C. on Tuesday," the voice said.

"I don't know a lot about it, but anything computer-controlled or electronic, especially with GPS ability, should be regarded as the enemy. I have to go," the voice said, then the call disconnected.

"The guy with the voice changer who originally called us had asked Brian Rissal to meet with us. As we know, that apparently didn't go so well," Mike said.

"What the hell did we get involved with here?" Robin asked.

"He said anything computer-controlled or electronic, especially with GPS capability, should be regarded as the enemy," Mike said.

"I think we kind of knew this already. Can we ever get a straight answer on anything?" Robin said.

"I think we should just assume full electronic surveillance is taking place and try to avoid all of it," Tara said.

"I'm going to check again with my CIA, NSA, and DOD contacts to see if someone knows anything about what Brian Rissal was working on," Mike said.

He tapped some keys and sent some encrypted messages to his contacts.

Tara put her smart glasses on. They were showing her the businesses and the building they were in. Suddenly, a huge virtual fireworks display showed spelling out the word "Welcome." Tara figured some towns added that in to attract visitors.

They got to Maine late in the afternoon. They went to investigate the traffic control poles and an area near *Incident #6*.

"In *Incident #6*, a self-driving vehicle gets T-boned by a manual drive truck. The driver of the truck and the passenger of the self-driving vehicle all pronounced dead at the scene," Robin said.

Tara collected the data from the traffic control system. There were similarities in the data to some of the other incidents. They finished the data collection and headed to their hotel in near the harbor.

Mike had booked two rooms in a cozy inn right downtown. The rooms looked pretty modern, while the outside of the building looked considerably older. The main street was full of bustling businesses, different souvenirs, clothing shops, candy shops, ice cream shops, restaurants, and more. There was a public park near the main street near the water. Cruises and other ships would dock here. They could see some sailboats out in the water along with other ships. The air smelled of the sea. Just offshore, many small islands dotted the waters, with their green trees sticking up from the small hills on them. They walked down to the dock, walking through the small park with pathways to all sides. The air filled with the sounds of the wind, water, people, and boats. It was beautiful.

Tara was wondering why colored smoke was lingering in the air. Then, suddenly, at least a dozen drones flew by in the air, letting out colored smoke to spell out "Bar Harbor."

The weather was a little cooler, which was a pleasant change from the heat of summer. They walked up the main street, looking into the shops. Occasionally, Robin or Tara would go in one for a minute and come out. They checked out the menus outside of each restaurant. When they found a restaurant they liked, they went in.

"This is a cute area," Tara said.

"I know. We'll need to do more shopping tomorrow," Robin said.

"Bleep!" Tara's phone got a message from her data analysis algorithm.

"Wow, this makes little sense. All the vehicle-related accidents look like there is subtle data manipulation between thirty to sixty minutes or more before the accidents. It barely even seems like a hack. The manipulations are so subtle. There is no obvious command to crash the vehicles or to do something directly that would cause a crash. I don't even see how these can be related to accidents. Individually, I would think they should have little effect. I guess part of the reason for doing it that far-out would-be data collection would normally only cover thirty minutes prior to an accident. But that doesn't explain why these data updates would cause any issues," Tara said.

"Great, more mysteries," Robin said.

"That's strange," Mike stated.

"I'll send the information to the computer forensics folks to see if they can figure anything out," Tara said.

There was still something bothering Tara about the data. She couldn't quite place it. She had seen something like it before.

Holy crap! This is like the data from the learning model at Intellibotz. She figured it may be a common algorithm or something else.

"I just realized there are some similarities to the data we see to the algorithm we used at the place I used to work, Intellibotz. They got some new intelligent training models before I left. They said it was from a third party. I'm going to see if I can find out more," Tara said.

She picked up her phone and tapped out a message to one of her previous co-workers, asking if they could find out where the third-party model came from.

"That's interesting. But training models all follow common patterns, right? So it could just be a coincidence?" Mike asked.

"It could. I'll analyze the odds and see," she said.

"We need to think about what we will do for the weekend," Robin said.

"Yes, there are so many things to do and see here," Tara said.

They finished up their meal and headed for their hotel rooms.

"Hey, want to watch a movie?" Robin asked.

"Sure," Mike replied.

"Sounds good. What will we watch?" Tara said.

They flipped through the channels and picked out an action romance-type movie. They were all lying on one bed together, watching the movie in Tara and Robin's room.

218

Chapter 18

The television got noisy for a commercial. It half woke up Tara and Mike.

The team had fallen asleep while watching the movie. Mike was on the left side, Tara in the middle, and Robin was next to Tara on the right. Mike woke up and slowly realized he was spooning someone with his arm draped over them. Tara flipped over, half asleep the other way.

"Ah!" Tara said.

"Oh, sorry, I think we all fell asleep," Mike said. Mike moved back more to the left side of the bed. Tara got up. Robin, still asleep, rolled over and put her arm over Mike. Tara smiled at the predicament.

Mike gently lifted Robin's arm off him and rolled off the side of the bed.

"I'm glad HR isn't here," Mike said to Tara half-jokingly.

"I'm going to go back to my room and get a shower," Mike said.

"Okay, see you later," she said.

Tara got a shower and got ready to go. She put on the less conservative dress she bought when she was out shopping with Robin. She wasn't sure about it, but she wanted to try it. It made her self-conscious about how her body looked.

Robin woke up. "Did we fall asleep watching the movie?" Robin asked.

"I think so," Tara said with a quiet giggle.

They all got ready and headed out to find breakfast.

"Wow, there aren't a lot of breakfast places here. I found one, though," Tara said. It was in a little strip mall, a short drive. Mike drove in manual mode with only one of his smart glass lenses switched on, just in case.

They used their smart glasses to review the menu and order breakfast.

"Tara, are you wearing something different? You look really nice," Mike said.

"Yes, I bought this dress when I was shopping with Robin the other day," Tara said, glancing at Robin, who smiled back at her.

"Let's look at the things to do today," Tara said.

"I'd like to do some more shopping," Robin said.

"How about we do the park driving loop if we think it would be safe?" Tara suggested.

"I'd like to check out the whales on an ocean cruise," Mike said.

"How about I stay here and shop in town? You two do the park loop, and we try to get an afternoon trip for the whale tour," Robin said.

"Sounds good. We can drop Robin off at the shops, get the whale cruise tickets, then head to the park loop," Mike said.

"It's nice to have something that's not fast food or sandwiches," Robin said.

"That's for sure," Tara said.

"Yep, it's nice to get a break and relax for breakfast," Mike said.

They finished up and paid. They drove back to town to get tickets for the cruise and drop off Robin. Mike went to get the tickets for the cruise near the dock. Tara waited outside near the car in the small park area. A guy approaches her.

"Hi, my name is Tim. I'm sorry, I just noticed how beautiful you are. I was wondering if I could get your number," he said.

Tara was a little surprised.

"Sorry, but thanks anyway," Tara said, waving him off. He walked on his way. *Wow, people notice me in this dress. Maybe Robin was right.*

Mike came back to the car. They both got in to head to the park loop. Mike was driving manually still with only one of his smart glass lenses enabled. They were traveling on the eastern loop road. They stopped at the overlook where they could see the water.

"Let's check it out," Tara said.

"Sure, let's find out what we can see from here," Mike said.

"I think I can see some boats out there. The shore is very rocky here," Tara said.

They stared out into the water with the light breeze brushing against their skin. The sun shined brightly; it was hot, but the cool breeze still kept it comfortable. They could see a little further down the small mountains and hills of the park jut out into the water.

The small hills almost looked like they touched the clouds, but they were much too small for that. They walked down the trail, closer to the water. Tara stood on the edge to get a good selfie.

"We should get a pic," Tara said, grabbing his hand and positioning him next to her. She took a picture of her and Mike. Mike stepped away a little so Tara could take some more pictures. He looked at her against the sky with the sun.

"Wow," he said under his breath, "she really looks beautiful," he accidentally mumbled.

"Did you say something?" Tara asked.

"No, nothing," he said, feeling a little embarrassed.

Walking back on the path, Tara tripped a little, slightly hurting her ankle. She limped a little and was having trouble walking on the trail.

"Here, let me help you," Mike said. He put one arm around her waist and had her hold on to him with one arm as he helped her walk.

"Thanks," she said.

They returned to the car, and Mike pulled an instant cold pack out of the first aid kit and some ibuprofen.

"Here you go," Mike said. They got in the car to go to the next lookout.

"I noticed our cell phone service is barely available out here," Tara said.

"Yeah, the coverage here doesn't seem very good," Mike replied.

The next lookout was near a beach. This beach, unlike the others, was actually sandy. Many people came to enjoy the beach. They walked down the steps to get to the beach. Mike helped Tara down the steps as her ankle was better, but still a little tender. They reached some rocks and sat, observing the waves and people on the beach. There were drones crisscrossing the waters near the shore. They had a lifeguard symbol on the bottom.

It was perfect beach weather. They spent a good amount of time just watching and talking.

"So, if you could do anything you wanted to do, what would it be?" Tara asked Mike.

"I still think it would be something helping people, but I'm not sure what. I enjoy being able to help people at the FBI, so it is something I like to do. How about you?" he said.

"I had hoped to help people with AI and robotics, or a mix of those. Robotics could help people who lost limbs, replacing an arm, leg, or hand. AI can assist people in many tasks. Data analysis using AI may discover cures for diseases or new technologies that benefit humankind. I helped start a company, but bad press and a fire destroyed the dream temporarily. Hopefully, I can get back to doing something with that," she said.

"That sounds like a great idea," Mike said.

They sat for a while longer and headed back to the car to find some more lookouts. Mike helped Tara up the stairs.

They got in the car and made a few more stops along the loop to see some pretty locations along the shore.

"Want to stop and grab some lunch somewhere?" Tara asked.

"Sure, we'll need to leave the loop and head back toward town and grab something," he said.

They had only finished about half the loop.

They headed back to town and found a place to grab some lunch.

Tara and Mike sat down in the restaurant. It was a rather moderately large establishment, but had some charm. Built into an old barn, turned into a restaurant.

"This place is really nice, great pick," Tara said to Mike.

"The menu looked good. It is a pretty cool place for a restaurant." Mike said.

"It's pretty cool. They left the very high barn roof. It gives the place a very spacious feel," Tara said.

"What is your hometown?" Tara asked.

"Midtown, New Jersey," Mike said.

"No way. Are you kidding me? That's where I grew up, too," Tara said.

"Really? That's crazy. I was on the south side. How about you?" he said.

"North up near Maple Tree Road," Tara said. They compared their past. They went to different school systems in the same town.

"I remember as a kid, sometimes my parents would take me to a deli in your area that had an entire display filled with candy. It was like candy nirvana," Mike said.

"Oh, yes, I know what you are talking about! They also made really great sandwiches there," Tara said.

"Did you ever go to the drive-in theater in town? Before it was turned into a shopping center," Tara asked.

"Yes, that was a pretty cool experience being able to watch the movie in your car. I don't think there are a lot of those around anymore," Mike said.

"What things do you like to do when you aren't working?" Tara asked.

"I have nothing I do all the time. I guess I mix it up, sometimes target shooting. Sometimes, I will do those multi-event races. Sometimes, it's just great to watch shows or movies or read. It's nice going out with friends for the evening," he said.

"Wow, you do those races. That's great. I also used to do target practice with my grandfather," Tara said.

"Wait, you used to do target practice? I thought you don't like guns," he said.

"I don't anymore," Tara said, looking sort of sad.

Mike was wondering if he should ask her why.

"I had an idea. Let's go find Robin. We can see if we can buy some bathing suits and use the pool and hot tub at the hotel. After that, we can go on the whale cruise," Tara said.

"Sure, let's try to meet up with her," Mike said.

After they finished lunch, they called up Robin. She thought that was a great idea. They parked and met up with Robin on the street.

"Been having fun?" Tara said to Robin, who had several bags she was carrying with her containing items she had bought.

"Yes, they have some nice shops here," Robin said.

"Let's go over here to this store. I think it has bathing suits," Robin said.

They went in and looked around. Robin and Tara went to the women's section. Tara picked out a conservative one-piece suit. Robin had picked out a nice two-piece bathing suit.

"What do you think?" Tara asked Robin about the suit she picked.

"That's nice, though I have a different idea for you," Robin said.

Robin had picked out a two-piece suit that was conservative as far as two-piece suits went.

"I don't know. I don't think I have the body for that," Tara said shyly.

"Trust me, you do," Robin said.

Tara thought about how she seemed to be right about the clothes she picked. That guy had asked for her number. She had never had that happen before.

"I'm not really sure. I'll get it and the other one and see what I like," Tara said.

"Okay, I think it would look great on you," Robin said.

Robin and Tara headed to pay and checked out. Mike came a little later and bought a suit for himself.

They went to the car and back to the hotel to change. Mike got into his suit and went down to the pool. Robin got changed into her suit.

Tara changed into the two-piece Robin suggested.

"Wow, you look great," Tara said to Robin.

"Thanks. But you look amazing in yours. I knew that would be great for you," Robin said. They both put on some long tops and brought towels to head down to the pool.

They got to the pool area.

"Hey, over here," Mike said as he was lounging in the pool.

"It's a little cool, but nice," he said.

Robin took off her top shirt. She had her two-piece suit underneath and got into the water. "A little cool," Robin said.

"Your bathing suit looks great," Mike said to Robin.

Reluctant to take her shirt off, Tara was very self-conscious. She had her hair down also, which wasn't usual for her. She took off her shirt and stepped towards the pool.

Mike glanced over. He saw this unbelievably beautiful woman heading toward the pool. He had to do a double-take to figure out who he was looking at. "Wow, Tara, that bathing suit looks amazing on you," Mike said.

Robin looked at Tara and gave her a wink.

"You like it? Robin picked it out for me," Tara said shyly. She was blushing a little.

Mike was trying not to stare too much. "It's perfect for you," he said.

"Oh, I forgot," Robin said, getting out and spraying herself down with sunscreen.

"Can you do my back?" she asked Mike.

"Sure," he sprayed her back and rubbed it in.

"Oh, I should do that too. Can you do me also?" Tara asked.

"Sure," he said, spraying her back and massaging it in. He couldn't believe how amazing Tara looked compared to how she usually dressed. Tara felt Mike's firm hands massage the sunscreen onto her back. It felt nice, but she was feeling self-conscious.

"Thanks," she said and swam out into the pool a bit.

There was a robotic pool cleaning device doing a systematic cleaning of the bottom of the pool in sections. If it got too close to someone, it would stop or go around them. When it finished its job, it floated to the top of the pool. Propellers then spun up on the top of it. It flew over to the side of the building and it docked itself by some pool equipment.

They had some fun in the pool, using a beach ball they found nearby. Tara, jumping for the ball, collided with Mike.

"Sorry!" she said.

They played for a little while longer and had to go get ready for the cruise. They went back to their hotel rooms, got a quick shower, and got dressed again.

They took the car down to the dock. The vehicle found them a parking spot just a short distance from the pier. They walked to the dock area and waited in a long line to board the ship.

They eventually made it onto the boat. It was pretty packed with people. The ship slowly pulled away from the dock. It then picked up speed.

"If you look to the right near that island, you can see some seals in the water and on land. They are people-watching," said the tour guide.

They could see the little black noses of the seals sticking out of the water facing toward the ship.

"That's so cool," Robin said.

"The seals are cute," Tara said.

"I didn't know they had seals out here," Mike said.

They continued out further for a while. The boat slowed down.

"If you look to your left, you can see a whale sometimes coming up for a breath at the surface," the guide said.

They watched for a few minutes and nothing.

"But I thought you said you loved me?" Tara overheard a man talking on his phone.

"Of course I do," Tara heard the AI voice respond to the man.

The term 'Code Crush' popped into Tara's head. It was a derogatory term for people getting a little too involved with their AIs. Tara disliked the term. She didn't know why she would even think of that.

"Can you see anything?" Robin asked.

"No," Tara said.

Mike shook his head no.

They kept watching. "Wait! Look right there," Tara pointed. They could see a hump rise slightly above the surface of the water and let out a giant breath with some water spray.

Just at that moment, the water started churning and frothing.

"What's happening?" Robin asked.

"Don't know," Mike said.

"Watch carefully. That motion is from a school of fish the whales are chasing to the surface," the guide said.

An enormous whale leaped out of the water with its mouth open, just fifty yards from the ship. It came crashing back down with a splash.

"Holy crap! That thing is big. It seemed almost as big as this boat!" Robin said.

"That was incredible!" Mike exclaimed.

"Amazing!" Tara exclaimed.

They watched as another whale jumped and did something similar.

"This really is incredible!" Tara said.

Just then, they heard a motor sound.

"What is that noise?" Tara asked.

"BOOM!" An explosion happened near the rear of the ship. The ship rocked back and forth.

"What's happening?" Robin said.

"Get some life preservers now," Mike said to Tara and Robin.

They went over to a storage bin that said life preservers and opened it up.

Mike grabbed two life jackets and handed them to Tara and Robin. Mike took one, but helped Robin and Tara secure theirs first.

"This is your captain. We appear to have been hit by an aircraft of some kind. Our electrical system is out. We have some battery backup. Please calmly get a life jacket as directed by the crew," he said.

"No signal on my cell phone," Mike said. Tara and Robin didn't have any either.

"I'm going to try the satellite 911 mode," Mike said, tapping on his phone.

"I can't tell if it's working. It may have sent something," Mike said.

"Oh, crap! I just got one of those 3D messages, but the cell service doesn't seem to work now. It's probably spotty and got delivered after. It says Plane!" Tara said.

The boat leaned to the right side. People started to scream and cry.

"Stay with me," Mike said. Mike went over to the side that was pitching down and looked over the side. A burnt small plane mashed into the lower portion of the rear ship's right-side hull, now partially submerged.

Mike then led Tara and Robin to the front left side of the ship.

"I'm scared," Tara said.

"Don't be. I'm sure someone got an emergency Mayday call out, and another ship will pick us up. Even if this ship were to sink, we have life vests on. Just stay with me no matter what. But if you can get in a lifeboat, you take it." Mike knew the calculations. They needed to stay on this ship as long as possible. The water near Maine is freezing. They might only survive in the water for one to three hours if they could not get in a lifeboat. There didn't appear to be enough lifeboats for all the passengers. Some appeared destroyed on the lower decks from the collision.

There was a muffled boom noise as passengers were screaming. The ship listed more to the rear right side.

"Captain to the crew, prepare the lifeboats," came over the speakers. More passengers were screaming and crying.

Mike led Tara and Robin to the cafeteria. "Drink as much as you can now," Mike said. He grabbed two additional bottles of water for each of them. He found some snacks and gave Robin and Tara snacks. "Eat up. In case we need some extra energy. We'll save a couple of snacks for later," he said, stuffing some into his pockets. Mike found a square reflective piece of metal and stuffed it into his pocket. Mike found some hats they were selling on the ship. He took one for Tara, Robin, and himself and gave it to them. Mike handed out the rest of the snacks to the people.

"Please head to the muster stations and board the lifeboats at the direction of the crew," the captain said.

Mike, Tara, and Robin headed to one of the stations. Robin got swept up in the hoard of people. Before she realized they were loading her onto the lifeboat. Robin was looking back at Tara and Mike, trying to get off.

"No, you go on the lifeboat!" Mike yelled at Robin.

Robin still was trying to leave.

"This boat is full. Launch!" a crew member said to the other crew. They launched the lifeboat with Robin and other passengers in it.

Mike and Tara realized all the boats were full. There were still fifty people or more with them on the boat.

"Let's go back up towards the bow," Mike said, hoping to stay out of the chilly water as long as possible.

"I'm terrified," Tara said. She stifled a sob.

"With these lifeboats in the area, they will see us when a rescue boat comes," Mike said.

Mike saw the captain heading down from the bridge.

"What's our status, captain?" Mike flashed his FBI badge.

"We're not sure if anyone heard our mayday. Our power is out, so the bilge pumps have stopped working. I was hoping by getting as many people into the lifeboats as we could, the ship wouldn't sink as fast. Our emergency beacon is broadcasting," the captain said.

The boat listed more to its right rear side. The rear of the vessel started getting closer to the water. Some of the remaining people were sobbing or crying. They moved more toward the front of the boat. The lifeboats were staying a short distance away from the sinking ship. The rear of the ship started sinking further into the water.

It made some low metallic sounds as it sank into the sea.

"Get up towards the front!" the captain yelled.

Mike and Tara were near the very front of the ship. Mike looked out at the horizon. There were no other boats other than the lifeboats in sight. This ship was slowly sinking into the sea, making groaning noises as it did.

"Boom!" A low, dull sound from the rear of the boat could be heard. The ship started sinking faster into the ocean.

"Abandon ship! Everyone into the water!" the captain yelled. The front of the boat lifted as the rear of the boat sunk faster. People had to jump off to the side of the boat.

"Okay, I want you to jump first, and I will come in right after you. Just take some deep breaths before you jump and hold your breath. That way, just in case you go under the water a little before you pop back up. Brace yourself, the water is going to be chilly. Don't worry. I'll be right with you," he said. Mike found a life preserver and tied it to Tara.

"Ready? One, two, three jump!" Mike exclaimed.

Tara jumped carefully off the ship as Mike held the lifesaver and let it go to fall near her. Mike took a few breaths and jumped in.

Mike swam right up to Tara, pushing the lifesaver towards her. "Hold on to that," he said, pushing the ring towards her.

"It's really cold," Tara said with a slight shiver. They looked over at the ship, and it slowly sank beneath the water.

"Let's swim over to the lifeboats," Mike said.

They got to maybe two dozen feet. Mike coiled up some line connected to the lifesaver and threw it towards a boat.

"Catch and tether!" he yelled.

Someone on the boat caught it and tied it to the side.

The sun was setting. Still no ships in sight.

Mike and Tara floated there together in silence for a while. It had already been about an hour. Tara's teeth were chattering.

"Let's stay close together to share any warmth we can," Mike said.

They got closer together. Mike put one arm around Tara's back and the other on the lifesaver ring. Tara did the same.

After another hour, everyone was freezing in the frigid water. They all swam towards the lifeboats.

The lifeboats saw this and dropped their line and moved further away so the people could not get to them.

"Stay here and stay together!" Mike shouted.

"Why did the lifeboats move away?" Tara asked.

"They might sink if too many people tried to get into them," Mike said.

"Oh," she said, her teeth chattering.

Mike held her tighter and put his cheek against hers.

"Can we swim to shore?" Tara asked.

"With us losing the sun for direction soon and us being miles out, I don't think so. Our best bet is to stay close to where the ship went down. A distress call from the beacon should have gone out," Mike said. Though Mike thought they should have started a search grid already. Maybe they had drifted too far from the ship already, or they didn't get the distress call.

They heard crying and sobbing in the distance over the sounds of the light ripples of the waves,

"I'm not sure I can feel my legs," Tara said.

Mike took both of his hands and rubbed her legs to improve circulation.

"Thanks," she said.

"Help! My wife is unconscious. What do I do?" a voice yelled in the distance.

"Huddle together to stay warm! If she stops breathing but still has a heartbeat, do CPR breaths only! If her heart stops, start CPR!" Mike yelled. It was getting hard to see as the sun went down.

Mike and Tara noticed more people around them were not moving. Perhaps they were unconscious as well. Mike knew they were coming up on about the three-hour mark of being in the water. Many people may not survive.

"I'm getting kind of sleepy," Tara said.

"Stay awake. You must stay awake, okay?" Mike said.

"Okay," she mumbled, her body shivering and teeth chattering.

Mike held her tighter and rubbed her sides and back to get her circulation going.

Tara could feel even Mike's body shivering a little. They couldn't see anything on the horizon except darkness.

Mike pulled out a snack to share. "Here, eat some of this," he said.

They shared the snack. Tara felt a little less sleepy for a little while.

"We're not going to make it, are we?" Tara said.

"You listen to me. We are going to make it. People have survived some incredible things through sheer force of will and not giving up. Just keep thinking about what is the next thing to do to survive," Mike said.

Tara kissed Mike on the cheek.

"Thanks," she said with a shiver.

Mike was cold, too. He recalled his Navy Seal training, where they taught him to survive in cold water. They trained in cold water to build their stamina.

Another half hour went by. They heard helicopters in the darkness.

"Aim your cell phone lights toward the sound! We are going to do an SOS signal. That is three short times on, followed by three long times on, followed by three short times on. I will tell you when to turn your light on and off. Listen to me. Ready."

"Now leave them off for ten seconds, and we will do this again," he said. Mike then guided them through another SOS again.

Mike didn't realize while doing this, Tara had stopped moving.

"Tara, Tara!" Mike shook her.

"No. No. No! Tara, wake up, wake up! Shit!" he yelled. He checked her heart rate and breathing. It was slow, but still there. He rubbed her and held her tight.

"Let's do the SOS again!" he yelled and guided them through several more while holding and rubbing Tara.

They heard the helicopters getting closer and saw the searchlights heading their way. They did the SOS signal again.

Two drones with lights flew over the top of them and paused off to the sides, illuminating a small area around them.

There were two helicopters right over the top of them. The wind from the helicopters caused the water to be a little choppy. Lights on the horizon were visible.

Mike flashed his light at the helicopter overhead, sending a message that he needed medical help immediately.

Within about ten seconds, a rope lowered towards him, and a man jumped into the water from the helicopter.

"She needs medical assistance immediately!" Mike yelled over the roar of the helicopter. The coast guard diver tied Tara to a rope, and he signaled to pull her up.

"Hey, buddy, is that you, Mike? It's Robert. Remember me?" the coast guard diver yelled to Mike.

"Holy shit! Fancy meeting you here," Mike said. Mike knew Robert from his time in the military.

"How did you know it was me?" Mike asked.

"Well, you know your morse code always sucked! Just kidding, we have a portable cell phone detector unit, and we detected yours nearby," Robert said.

Suddenly, a bright light filled the area. It was so bright that it seemed like daylight far out, with it fading a little further.

"What the hell is that?" Mike hollered. He could see everything clearly now. There were many people within a hundred yards of him. Many were not moving. The light seemed to come from the sky, but not the helicopters.

"What is that light?" Mike asked.

"It's called Second Sun. It's a satellite focusing sunlight on the nighttime side of the earth where we need it. We got it approved for use here," he yelled.

"Let's get you someplace a little warmer," he yelled as the line dropped from the helicopter, and he attached Mike to it and signaled to bring him up. Then they let the line down again to pull Robert up.

As Mike got up to the helicopter, he got in, unhooked himself, and rushed to Tara's side.

"How is she?" he asked. "Still unconscious. We are warming her up," the medic said.

"We are getting close to bingo. We have to go," the pilot said and headed back towards land.

Several ships came to the area and picked up people from the ocean. They found the lifeboats as well and got those people aboard the ship.

They flew for about twenty minutes and were now hovering over a hospital landing pad.

They slowly descended, landed, and shut down the rotors. They pulled Tara out and quickly wheeled her on a stretcher towards an elevator.

"Thanks," Mike said to Robert. "No problem. If you want to take your date to the water again, just give me a heads up with some GPS coordinates next time," he joked. Mike headed quickly to the elevator with Tara.

They brought Tara into one of the ER rooms and hooked her up to monitors.

They closed the curtains and cut off her wet clothing and wrapped her with something that looked like a strange, very puffy electric blanket. They gave her oxygen and inserted an IV with a warm bag of solution.

"You should wait outside," the nurse said to Mike.

He showed her his FBI badge.

"Her life and yours may be in danger. I'm staying right here," he said in a commanding tone.

"Her body temperature is at 82. She is a borderline candidate for extracorporeal rewarming. Her other vitals are low, but improving. Let's monitor for a little while," one doctor said.

"Doc, is she going to be okay?"

"We won't know until she improves and wakes up. She has borderline moderate hypothermia. Hopefully, rewarming will be effective quickly," the doctor said.

They checked Mike's vitals. They started an IV on Mike and wrapped him in a warming blanket.

Tara looked bluish. Mike grabbed her hand. It was cold to hold. He clasped one of her hands in both of his, hoping it would help warm her up a little.

Other patients started arriving who were also in the water with them.

"This one has a core temp of 65 degrees. Get them to extracorporeal warming stat!" someone yelled.

"We have a code. Start CPR!" another voice exclaimed.

The ER became very busy with other patients.

Mike figured the other helicopters must have plucked more people out of the water that needed help.

"Tara, I don't know if you can hear me, but I'm going to tell you a story about when I was growing up," he said. He then went on talking for about twenty minutes or more, telling her about things he did growing up. He hoped maybe she would hear his voice and wake up. Mike sat talking to her on and off over the next several hours.

"Holy shit! Is she okay?" Robin exclaimed as she briskly walked in.

"They don't know. They are hoping she warms up soon and wakes up," he said with his eyes looking watery.

"Are you okay?" Mike asked Robin.

"Yes, I'm fine," she said.

Robin gave Mike a hug, which was a little tricky, wrapped in a puffy warming blanket.

"Glad you're okay. What happened?" Robin asked.

"The water was freezing. It's hard for people to survive in water that cold for more than a few hours," Mike said with a sniffle.

Robin found a chair and brought it in so she could sit next to Mike and Tara.

A nurse came in. "We can't have more people in here. Please wait outside," she said.

Robin pulled out her FBI badge. That satisfied the nurse, and she walked off.

"This was definitely an attack. Tara got one of those messages warning of a plane. It seems like we aren't safe anywhere. Other than that message, we don't really have any proof this isn't just another accident. This seems like a significant ramp-up. Well, other than the plane incident, there hasn't been a time before where so many lives were put in jeopardy," Robin said.

"We are going to find who is doing this," Mike stated.

"Those warning messages come, but we never seem to do anything about it. Well, this one came late because of the cell signal." She sighed. "Unless you think those messages are taunting us?" Robin said.

"I don't think so, but it is frustrating we haven't been able to prevent anything," Mike sighed.

"She's still so cold," she said. Robin held Tara's hand. "Do you need anything?" she asked.

"If you could, please find something that even resembles food and a hot cup of coffee would be great," he said.

"You got it. Be back in a few minutes," she said, gently touching Mike on the shoulder.

She walked out of the room. Mike held onto Tara's hand again and talked to her about whatever came to his mind.

Robin came back about fifteen minutes later with a sandwich and some coffee.

"Thanks, Robin," he said as she handed him the food.

Mike was hungry from the ordeal, and the food was good, or at least seemed that way at the moment.

"You can wait in the hotel. They wanted to keep me here until I warm up too, anyway," Mike said.

"No chance. I'm staying right here with my team," she said.

"You can, of course, enjoy our most comfortable surroundings," he said jokingly.

"I'm sure she would be glad you are here with her. I'm glad you're here too," he said.

"You can get some rest. I'll keep watch," Robin said.

"Thanks. I'll try it, but I'm not sure how much rest I can get," he said.

There was lots of activity in the ER. There was plenty of beeping and other noises from the people and the various equipment. Mike was pretty tired. He fell fast asleep.

A short while he was startled awake. Monitors on Tara were beeping incessantly. A nurse came in quickly.

"We need the attending stat! She has an arrhythmia," she exclaimed.

A doctor came running in with a syringe, looked at the monitor, then inserted the syringe into the IV line and pushed. Robin was gone.

"What's going on?" Mike asked.

"Her heartbeat is erratic. If this doesn't work, we may need to warm her up more quickly," the doctor said. The heart monitor emitted a steady tone, and the heartbeat line flatlined. "CODE!" the doctor yelled.

"No!" Mike exclaimed.

The doctors worked furiously, but nothing was working. The heart monitor emitted its continuous tone.

"Clear!" one doctor yelled as he prepared to use the defibrillator.

"Mike, Mike, wake up, wake up," Robin said.

Mike was startled awake to see that Robin was there. Tara was still unconscious. Her heart rate was slow and steady, like it was before he fell asleep.

"It seemed like you had a bad dream," Robin said.

"More like a nightmare," Mike said, still a little shaken.

"Hey, why are you guys talking in the middle of the night? It's kind of cold. Is there another blanket somewhere?" a voice whispered.

Mike and Robin looked around.

"Tara?" Mike said, grabbing her hand.

"I'm so glad you are awake," Mike said.

"Wait, where am I?" Tara asked.

"You're at the hospital with hypothermia from the cold water. A helicopter rescued you and me. Ship and helicopters rescued the others," Mike said.

Robin went to tell the nursing staff. A doctor quickly came in and checked out her vitals.

"Hello, Miss Bitlouver. We're glad to see you awake. You have hypothermia, and we've been treating you here in the hospital ER. We want to keep you at least overnight for observation," the doctor said.

The doctor checked Tara's hands and feet to see if she could feel and move everything okay.

"Your temperature has warmed up. Still not normal yet, but it's a lot better. Let's wait a little while, and if it's still okay, we can get you something to eat and drink," the doctor stated.

They gave Tara a summary of the events. They were tired. Robin stayed awake while they got some sleep. Every couple of hours, the nurse would come in to check Mike and Tara's vitals.

PROJECT MIND RIVER

Chapter 19

Mike woke up. He saw Robin there, still awake. The hospital ER sounded less busy now than it did last night. There was still the sound of doctors, nurses, and patients entering and leaving the ER. The air even smelled like a hospital, probably from some cleaner or disinfectant they used. Occasionally, some of the patient monitors would have an alarm go off in a nearby room.

"Thanks for keeping an eye on us," Mike whispered to Robin.

"Tara is, okay?" he asked in a whisper, trying not to wake her.

"Think so. They checked her temperature a few hours back, and it seems to be normal now," Robin said.

"I'm feeling better now, too," Mike said.

"Glad you are awake, Mr. Hero. They said if it wasn't for you, a lot more people would have died. You kept everyone together and used Morse code to signal the helicopters," Robin whispered.

"I'm no hero. It sounds like at least some people died. We almost lost Tara," he said.

"Why don't you go get some rest now, in, you know, a place you can actually get some rest," Mike said to Robin.

"Okay, I'll be back a little later," Robin said as she headed out to go to the hotel.

They need to set this blanket on a lower setting now. "Getting warm," Tara mumbled sleepily.

"I'm glad you are sort of awake. They said your temperature is back to normal," Mike said.

"Maybe we can get some breakfast," Tara said.

"I think some should be here soon. When they asked last night, I put in an order for you. Hopefully, that is okay. Hopefully, you like repeat breakfasts, since I know what you've had before," Mike said.

Tara was touched that Mike remembered what she had the other day.

Mike went out to ask about the other passengers. He found out nine died, and twenty were still being treated for hypothermia. There were other patients being brought in, not from their incident.

"He's got a flesh-eating bacteria. Get a sample of this and have the AI system manufacture a new antibiotic," Mike overheard a doctor say.

He went back to the room with Tara.

"Good morning, we have your breakfast here," the woman said, setting up a tray for Tara. She handed Tara a sheet to pick their lunch meals for later.

Tara sat up to eat breakfast. She had to push off the puffy warming blanket. She looked down at herself. Mike walked out for a few minutes and came back with a sandwich.

"Umm. Where are my clothes?" Tara asked.

"Sorry, I think they might have cut them off you to get the wet clothes off quickly to warm you up faster," Mike said.

"Aww, I liked that dress. That was the one Robin helped me pick out," she said.

"I liked it too. I'm sure Robin will help you pick out another one," he said.

Tara wondered who might have seen her without clothes, just the doctors and nurses, she hoped.

"You said they brought us here in a helicopter?" Tara asked to confirm.

"Yes. A friend of mine I knew from the military works in the Coast Guard now. He was the one to help get us from the water to the helicopter. Small world, I guess," Mike said.

"That is pretty lucky to have a friend on the rescue team," she said.

"I guess so. It's almost like we have a mix of bad luck and good luck," Mike said.

"They checked my temperature this morning, too. I'm back to normal as well. Hopefully, they can release you later, and we can get back to the hotel for a shower," he said.

"Yes, a hot shower would feel perfect right now," Tara said.

"You know, thinking about our incident data, usually with a hack, things are forced to do something. Though some have a level of subtlety to avoid detection, things are pretty direct. Like the hackers we arrested, their hacks were to make the cars do something. They made the cars stop, go in a circle, and go fast. These other hacks we can't even detect what they did exactly. So, it still seems accidental. We have evidence of a hack, but no proof they actually did anything that would directly cause an accident. I feel like we are definitely missing something important here," Tara stated.

"I guess that's the million-dollar question. We need to get to the answer to this quickly. Hopefully, the contact we are supposed to meet with can shed more light on what is happening. It kind of seemed like he didn't know everything either, though," Mike said.

Mike shook out his phone. It sounded a little funny, maybe from being in the water for so long. "It's amazing these phones seem to survive as well as they do in water these days," Mike said.

"I can't even believe what we just went through still. It's like the worst nightmare," she said. Mike didn't want to mention his nightmare to her. It was perhaps even worse.

"Yeah, our real life is in competition with our nightmares. That is never a good sign," he said.

"I think for our next weekend, maybe we should try to just stay in one place. Then, there are no vehicles, boats, or planes. Plus, it's been a while since hooded ninjas attacked us." She laughed.

"Those were not ninjas, at least I think not," he said with a chuckle.

"You got to see your whales, at least," Tara said.

"They were pretty cool for the minute, or so we saw them. I guess the plane explosion scared them off after that," he said.

Mike knew from his time in the military it was pretty common for joking banter about extreme events that occurred during the day. He guessed people felt it was a way to stay sane or put a bit of control over the uncontrollable.

They talked for a while longer. The doctor came by.

"Hi, how are you doing?" the doctor said to Tara while checking her vitals.

"A lot better," Tara said.

"Your temperature looks good, vitals are good. Hopefully, in the afternoon, we can get you discharged," the doctor said.

"That's code for just before dinner, if you're lucky," Mike chuckled.

"Apparently, you've been to a few hospitals before," the doctor said.

"Maybe a few too many," Mike said.

The doctor smiled and walked out.

"Will it really be that late before we are let out?" Tara said.

"Hard to tell. They are pretty slow around discharges. Often it takes a bit to finish up all their paperwork," he said.

"I guess we could just leave. It's not like we're in jail," Tara joked.

"That you never want to do. It's called leaving AMA or against medical advice. Sometimes that can cause issues with your insurance," Mike said.

"Hopefully, you don't know that from experience," Tara smirked.

"Umm Me, umm, well. Whoever might have done that would never do that again," he said with a wink.

They talked or sat checking their smartphones a while more before lunch.

"Hello, I have your lunch," the orderly said to Tara. Mike stepped out to find something quick for lunch and came back.

Tara was almost finished with lunch by the time Mike came back.

"I guess you were hungry," Mike said.

"It seems so," Tara said, looking at her almost empty plate.

Robin walked in.

"How are you guys doing?" Robin asked.

"Fine here. I think I'd like to get out of here," Tara said.

"Me too," Mike said.

"The food we get on the road is better than here. Well, I guess you ate all of yours, so not too bad." Robin winked.

"I was starving," Tara said.

"So, when are they going to let you blow this joint?" Robin asked.

"They said sometime this afternoon," Tara said.

"Okay, so sometime today, whenever they get the paperwork done," Robin said, looking at Mike.

"I got approval for as-needed twenty-four-seven monitoring of our vehicle and surrounding traffic by the FBI command center. This way, we have extra eyes helping us to avoid problems, hopefully," Robin said.

"That is comforting," Tara said.

"That is good news. Nice work," Mike said.

"They offered us a week of paid leave. But maybe we should wait on that till we solve what's going on, or we might not be around to enjoy it," Robin said.

"Yeah, that is true," Tara said.

"Agreed," Mike said.

"Bleep." Tara's phone had a message.

Tara looked at her phone. "Oh, shit! It's one of those 3D messages," Tara said. The image was pretty long this time. She held the phone out so Robin and Tara could see.

"I can't see anything," Mike said, focusing on the dots.

"I can't see anything either," Robin said.

"It looks like it says, Sorry, will try to be faster," Tara said, trying to get a screenshot, but it didn't work.

"So, it seems like someone is trying to help us. I wish I could see those 3D images," Mike said.

"Kind of have to focus intently or let your eyes lose focus. Some combination like that seems to work for me," Tara said.

Robin stared at it. "Nope, can't get it."

Mike stared at it as well. "Nothing."

"I wish I could figure out how whoever is sending it to my phone. It doesn't appear to be even a text message. It's like it just shows up. I scanned for malware, but nothing. I asked the forensics department to check. They haven't found anything either," Tara said.

"Code Purple, Code Purple," a voice said over the speakers in the hospital.

Heavy footsteps echoed running down the hall.

"What is code purple? I heard of some codes before, but what is that one?" Tara asked.

"I think the hospital AI predicted someone might go into cardiac arrest soon," Mike said.

They waited there chatting until pretty late afternoon. They finally came with the discharge papers for Tara. "Wait, you don't have discharge papers?" Tara asked Mike.

"No, they technically released me late last night. They thought I would be okay just staying warm," he said.

"Thanks for staying with me," Tara said. Robin brought some clothes for Tara from their hotel so she could get changed before leaving.

They headed back to the hotel. Mike and Tara both wanted to get a shower and change.

They all met in Mike's room afterward. Tara brought her laptop, as usual.

"I feel so much better," Tara said.

"You look great. That is another nice dress," Mike said to Tara.

"Thanks," Tara said, glancing at Robin since it was another dress she had helped her pick out.

"Does hypothermia make you hungry?" Tara asked.

"No idea, but I'm thinking the same thing," Mike said.

"I'm going to head down to the car and stop at the little shop downstairs first. Meet you at the car," Robin said as she left the room.

"I'm going to enable the monitoring for our vehicle by the FBI command center," Tara said as she tapped on the keyboard, and then closed it.

"Good idea," Mike said.

"Oh, I forgot," Tara said and walked over to Mike and gave him a big hug, and kissed him on the cheek. "Thanks for saving me," Tara said.

"I feel like I didn't do much. I should have done more," Mike said, slightly blushing.

"You did everything you could. You saved a lot of lives, including mine," she said.

"Let's see if we can find something good to eat," he said as he held the door open for Tara.

They went out to get some food. They had time to walk around the town's main street and shops again. Robin helped Tara pick out a few more things to wear. They had a pleasant time for their last night in Maine.

Chapter 20

Robin woke Tara up. Robin didn't mind. It was better than Tara's crazy alarm going off in the morning. It was very early in the morning, around 3 a.m. They wanted to get an early start.

They got ready and packed their things. Mike was up, got ready, and took his suitcase to the car. They hoped to use self-drive mode for higher speed so they might get to Washington, D.C., faster. Manual drive time would be about twelve hours, with self-driving mode about ten hours.

They went down to the car and got in.

"You feeling okay today?" Mike asked Tara.

"Yep, fine today. It's nice to be out of the hospital," she said.

"I'm notifying the command center to monitor our vehicle and the surrounding traffic," Tara said.

"Hopefully, that means less chance of a surprise," Robin said.

"One of us should still stay awake at all times," Mike said.

"I guess we don't want to use the smart glasses and manual mode today so we can get to D.C. faster," Mike said.

Both Robin and Tara agreed.

"It would be nice to get more confirmation that people's smart glasses are being manipulated," Mike said.

"Department of Homeland Security isn't saying anything was hacked, but device manufacturers for the traffic control systems and smart glasses have issued some sort of security update," Tara said.

"We know that is suspicious," Robin said.

"Hopefully, that is enough to keep them from doing it again," Mike said.

"As long as there aren't any more security holes. Unfortunately, complex software has a lot of them," Tara said.

"I'll take the first shift to stay awake if you want to rest till breakfast," he said.

Tara checked out some data on her laptop and then took a nap. Robin tried resting a bit.

They got to Connecticut around breakfast time and pulled over to a service plaza to charge and get some food.

"We should probably eat on the road, so we get to D.C. earlier. Then we have some time to sightsee after work hours today. Travel is part of our work hours in this case," Robin said. They got in and continued towards their destination.

"That sounds like fun. I would love to see some sights in D.C.," Tara said with some trepidation, since their previous sightseeing was rather calamitous.

"It's been a while since I've been in D.C. as well, so it should be fun," Mike said.

"Can you get us in to see the White House?" Robin asked Mike.

"I don't think I have any contacts that could get us in on this short notice," Mike stated.

"I've never done this much traveling around the country before. It's kind of cool. Except for, of course, now I'm kind of terrified to travel. Planes, cars, and boats all have been pretty problematic for us," Tara said.

"That's putting it mildly," Robin chimed in.

"We are going to get to the bottom of this. Maybe those security patches will prevent issues until we can figure this out," Mike said optimistically.

"Let's hope so. It's hard to investigate places if we can't get there safely," Robin said.

Tara was hoping her algorithms would finish running at home so she could use the artificial intelligence, something like she created with Alice.

"If Alice were online, this problem could be solved much more quickly," she said.

What she was rebuilding at home wouldn't be Alice, though. It would be like a new person since it wouldn't have had all of Alice's experiences and memories. She didn't want to say anything since she didn't know when the processing would finish or if they would finish. Plus, few people believed her when she explained just how advanced an artificial intelligence Alice was. AI had advanced a lot in the last five years, but it still seemed surprising that no one else had come up with something like Alice. The smart assistants were pretty good, but not quite the equivalent of simulating a person.

"Penny, for your thoughts," Mike said to Tara.

"Sorry, I was just thinking about if there is a faster way to figure out what is happening, but nothing useful yet," Tara said.

"Battery predicted failure in twelve hours," the message on the car monitor said, followed by a beep.

The car routed them to a nearby service station, which could quickly swap out the battery. They left the station.

They continued traveling down the often-busy interstate roads. The cars were packed together pretty tightly, traveling at much closer distances than manual drivers would be allowed. That helped with the traffic. It was definitely less frustrating than manual driving through the traffic.

"Command to Agent Actley fast approaching manual drive vehicle!" they heard over the comm. Mike grabbed the wheel. As they glanced behind them, they could see the self-driving vehicles yielding to move out of the way of the speeding vehicle, approaching them fast.

"Lookout!" Robin exclaimed.

Mike turned the wheel hard to get the vehicle to the shoulder, screeching the tires. Mike kept speed and watched the manual drive vehicle speed by them, with the self-driving vehicles parting to make way for it. Not far behind came a police vehicle at a possibly even faster speed, whipping past them. "I hope they catch that guy," Robin said.

"Wait, let's go see if they do," he said.

"Actley to command. Please let us know if the police catch that vehicle," Mike said.

"Acknowledged," the command replied.

"Maybe we can learn more. It's hard to tell with so many terrible drivers on the road. But given the number of incidents we've had happen recently, maybe that's related," he said.

"Command to Actley. The vehicle had an accident with a traffic control pole. The driver is injured," the command said.

"Please send us the location," Mike said into the comm.

The location appeared on the navigation, and he selected the new destination.

In a few minutes, they pulled up behind the police car. The police car had its lights on behind the smashed-up manual drive vehicle. The driver was still in the vehicle.

"Your command center said you were coming. An ambulance is on its way, five minutes out. I'm not sure if he's going to make it. He's trapped. It's fifteen minutes out for the rescue truck with rescue equipment," the officer said.

Mike, Tara, and Robin rushed to the vehicle. The seatbelt trapped the man. The door wouldn't open.

"Tara, do you have that tool?" Mike said.

"In my purse, I'll get it," she said, running to their car and back with it.

Mike took it from her and smashed the window and reached in and cut the driver's seatbelt.

"I'm still stuck. My leg's caught," the driver said.

Mike checked his leg, caught between the seat and the crunched-up front of the car. The seat wouldn't move back. The man was bleeding from his head and leg profusely.

Looking into the car, Tara saw recording equipment. It looked like cameras for the front and back windshield and for the man's smart glasses. The smart glass hookup looked kind of like what Tara did to them to record what they saw.

"Robin, grab a drone and controller," Mike said.

"On it," she said and came back with it and handed it to Mike.

Mike positioned it with the explosive charge to detonate under the seat downwards to destroy the seat mechanism so they could move his seat back to un-trap him.

"Are you sure?" Robin said.

"No, but we need to do something," Mike said.

"Cover your ears," Mike said to everyone, "three, two, one."

BOOM!

The drone exploded, and the car filled with smoke and dust. They could see it blew a hole through the bottom of the car. Everyone was coughing. Mike pushed on the seat backward and freed his leg.

The Ambulance pulled up. A box-like automated device deployed out of the back of the ambulance. The box moved toward the damaged vehicle and stopped. It looked like it was ready to disassemble or cut up the car if needed.

"So, we don't need the rescue robot?" one of the Emergency Medical Technicians asked.

"No, I guess not," said the police officer.

The EMT did an assessment of the injured man and prepared the stretcher.

"What is with the equipment?" Tara asked the man.

"I had to record it. They were chasing me, but no one would believe me. So, I recorded everything. Check the recording. You'll see, you'll see!" the man said frantically.

"Did you hear voices?" asked Mike.

"Yes, yes!" the man said.

Tara found the man's cell phone on the seat. She quickly checked the smartphone.

"Your phone is infected. It might be causing the voices. Backup only the apps you need and reset it," Tara told the man.

The ambulance crew got the man on the stretcher and into the rig. They flipped on the lights and siren mode and headed quickly to the hospital.

Tara brought her laptop to the car and downloaded the data from the devices in the vehicle.

"It's going to take a bit to analyze the data," Tara said.

"Someone really doesn't want us to go anywhere," Robin said.

"I guess the police will get a statement from the driver. Let's continue on to D.C.," Mike said.

They returned to the car and programmed it to their destination in D.C. Tara shared the video feeds with Mike and Robin to review the man's recordings. Tara brought up the three video files to review. There was a file for the front, back, and smart glasses. Tara synchronized the video files so she could watch them all at the same time.

"I'm not seeing anything abnormal," Mike said.

"I don't see anything either," Robin said.

"It could be the recording frame rate isn't matching up with the display for the smart glasses. That car didn't have a smart windshield, so the front and rear views should be reality. I will analyze to see if there are any frames we caught with differences. That will take a while to process," Tara stated.

Tara processed the front, rear, and smart glass videos, looking for slight differences between the images. She let her laptop sit on her lap while it processed.

Bleep. Tara's phone had a message from her former coworker who looked into the learning model Intellibotz used from the third party. It had an internal specification with it that was a sizeable document describing a little about the learning models they used. Tara read through the large doc, though it was slow reading. The high-level design document said the learning model had been bought from International IQ Devices (IID).

Traffic was getting heavier as they got closer to the New York metro area. Tara missed her home she hadn't seen in days, her parents, and friends. She reached out to see how they were doing. She had messaged them a few times over the past week, but without too much detail. They messaged her back. She decided just to tell them about the good parts of her weekend rather than burden them with the bad parts of what had happened. She couldn't discuss the case they were working on. Approaching Tara's home, she longed for the comfort of being there. She liked to travel and see new things but without such a hectic set of events. It might have been nice to stop at more places along the way to see the sites. It was still pretty cool to have driven around the country. They didn't get to see all the states or much of them beyond the roads they traveled. Still, it was quite a set of visuals in her mind to remember.

Of course, it would be nice if cars, planes, and more weren't after them. Their predicament almost sounded absurd, thinking of how she could explain this to others if allowed. Tara knew she needed to find more evidence. She double-checked the analysis of the video. Tara checked their connection with the FBI command center. It was a bit more comforting knowing that the FBI command center was helping them monitor the traffic systems and vehicles. Tara went back to reading the high-level design document for the machine learning algorithm.

The team stopped in a Philly area suburb to grab some cheesesteaks for lunch while doing a quick charge of the car.

"This place is fantastic," Mike said.

"It is. I always hate to think about what it does to you once you eat it," Tara said.

"It's good. With our current luck, I'm not sure we need to worry about clogged arteries as a priority," Robin said.

"I guess I could have chosen a sub instead, but this is really good," Tara said.

"Crap! Why didn't I have some lobster when we were in Maine," Robin said.

"We'll remind you the next time we are there," Mike joked.

The traffic kept getting even more packed together the closer they got to D.C. It was nearly bumper-to-bumper, traveling at 70 mph.

It's a good thing it wasn't as crowded as it used to be. With the latest AR/VR tech and avatars, remote work was much more widespread with knowledge workers, even in Congress, and was much more common than it had been.

They got to their hotel and put their bags and things away.

"Would you want to go to the Capitol? We should be able to look around there," Robin said.

They drove to a nearby street and got out. Their car continued around the corner to park in a parking garage. They walked up close to the Capitol building. There were several police officers by the steps. As they walked closer, they heard all the police officers' phones bleep. They glanced down at their phones and looked back at Tara, Robin, and Mike. One officer walked towards them.

"You need to leave this area," the officer said.

Mike looked around, and several other people were as close as they were.

"Is there a problem, officer?" Mike asked.

"The three of you need to leave now," the officer said.

Mike went to reach for his badge, and the officer drew his gun on him.

"Hands up, all of you!" the officer commanded. People around scattered away in fear.

"Officer, I'm with the FBI, and I was reaching for my badge," Mike said with his hands up.

Another officer came up to Mike and started patting him down.

"He has a gun!" the officer, patting him down, said.

"Of course, I have a gun. I'm Agent Actley with the FBI. Check my pocket, please, for my badge. All three of us are with the FBI," Mike said.

The officer pulled Mike's badge out and looked at it long and hard.

"Can we put our hands down now, please, officers?" Mike said.

"Sure," the officer said, a little confused.

"I'm sorry, Agent Actley, but you three will still need to leave. Our facial recognition system flagged you to deny you entry to this area," the officer said.

"Why? And who do we ask to fix that?" Mike asked.

"Sorry, sir, above my pay grade. I will report it," the officer said.

"So will I," Mike said.

The officer gave him back his badge and let them walk away from the area.

"What was that about? Why are we in some facial recognition system?" Robin asked.

"I don't know, but we're going to find out," Mike said.

They walked toward the Library of Congress, away from the capitol building.

Mike made a call on his phone.

"This is Agent Actley. I need to speak to a supervisor," Mike said.

"Hey, this is Mike. We tried to just walk around the capitol building, and Capitol Police stopped us because of facial recognition flagging as there to deny the area to us. Can you figure out what that is and get us off that list? Thanks," he said and hung up.

"Hopefully, they can figure out what is going on," Robin said.

They walked towards the Air and Space Museum. It was a pretty long walk. They were walking by the Botanic Garden and went into the area. Inside, there was an extensive collection of plants and trees. The top of the building was glass-enclosed with metal frames and glass windows arching up to the top, with it looking like a flat glass ceiling near the very top. There were walkways on the bottom and high above to view the different plants. There were adults and kids roaming around the walkways, taking in the grand views from the high walkways.

Tara had on her smart glasses. Looking around, it labeled the plants she was looking at, highlighting them. The glasses also drew arrows on the walkways to show directions to other areas. It had an audio narration option, but she chose not to use it.

Once they had their fill of the garden, they exited and continued walking towards the Air and Space Museum. They walked down the walkways and sidewalks toward their destination. While they were walking down the sidewalk, they heard a bunch of phones behind them, fifty feet or more.

Bleep. Bleep. Bleep. There were several men walking together who looked down at their phones and then back toward Mike, Tara, and Robin.

Bleep. Tara's phone got a message. "It's a 3D message!" Tara said, while trying to focus on it.

"It says,"

Danger! Behind. Men.

"Let's see if they are following us. Follow me and keep up," Mike whispered to Tara and Robin. Mike walked faster, with Tara and Robin keeping up. They turned the corner right down a side street. Mike used the camera on his phone in selfie mode to watch the men behind them. Then they turned left at the next corner. The men were still following them. Mike and the team turned left again, heading back towards the street they came from. The men were still following them.

"They are definitely following us," Mike hissed. "Tara, keep up and call for backup."

"My phone won't dial out. The signal seems fine, but it won't go through," Tara mumbled.

"I guess we do this the hard way," Mike said.

Mike saw an alley to turn down to the left. He quickly walked that way, with Tara and Robin following.

"Tara, get behind us," Mike said. Robin and Mike stood just around the corner, hidden from view.

"Guys!" Tara said. Two more men appeared far down on the other side of the alley. The three men that were following them came around the corner.

"We're gonna kick your ass," one of them said.

"FBI, turn around, put your hands on your head! That goes for all of you," Mike said with his hand on his weapon. The men moved closer, and they pulled out guns. Robin and Mike pulled out theirs. Robin aimed down the far side of the alley, and Mike aimed at the men closer to them.

"You aren't no stinking FBI. Even if you were, it wouldn't matter after what you did," said one man.

"What did we do?" Robin asked.

"You've got some nerve, and we're going to make you pay," the man said.

Mike backed up further down the alley, with Robin advancing slightly toward the men on the other side. Mike glanced back at Robin, who glanced to the side with a wink.

They inched closer to the center of the alley. Mike backed up near the far side edge of a dumpster.

"Stay with Robin, ready," Mike said to Tara quietly.

"I'm going to count to three, and we can all put down our weapons," Mike said.

"Three!" Mike yelled. Robin pulled Tara in through a door on the side of the alley. Mike fired some shots to keep the men back as he also quickly backed up through the door. Mike closed it, pulled down hard on the industrial door mechanism at the top, and locked it for good measure.

"We were lucky that it was open. Hopefully, that will slow them down. Let's see if we can get out the other side," Mike said.

Unfortunately, the building was like a maze filled with a mess of storage items. There were no people anywhere they could see as they walked down the halls filled with various items.

"Hey, I think I heard them," a man's voice said. Tara heard the voice of a man down the hall say.

"In here," Mike said. "We'll ambush them here."

Robin tapped him on the shoulder and pointed to a second connecting door to the same hallway.

"Crap! Okay, Robin, you hide by that doorway. I'll take this one. Tara hide on the back side of the room, away from the doors."

The three men came to the hallway near the doorways, looking at their phones.

One man whispered, "I think they could be in there."

Two men stood by one doorway and the other by the second doorway to the room Mike, Tara, and Robin were in. Mike and Robin pulled out their guns. Mike looked at the light on his gun and waved furiously at Robin, pointing to the light on his gun. Robin mouthed a curse word, seeing the same light on hers, and put her gun back in her holster.

"Crap! Why are both of our guns smart locked?" Mike said.

The two men at each of the doorways walked in slowly with their guns drawn.

Mike knocked the gun out of the guy's hand as he entered the doorway and punched him hard. Robin grabbed the other man's arm with the gun and smashed it against the doorway, knocking the gun from his hand. Mike and the man were in a fierce fight.

Robin grabbed a nearby broomstick and swung it like a home run, but angled to hit the guy between his legs.

SMACK!

Robin hit him with the stick, and he bent over in pain. Then she hit him hard on the head with a second fierce swing.

The third man was large and spotted Tara. He grabbed Tara by the throat, lifting her into the air as she held onto his arm to avoid being hung. Tara couldn't reach the man with her hands. Taking a lesson from Robin, she kicked him hard between the legs. He let go of Tara and was bent over in pain. Tara used her arms in a martial arts move to grab the man's leg out with her one arm, grab his neck with her arm, and flip him to the ground.

"Sorry," Tara said.

"Stop apologizing to the people trying to kill you!" Robin said.

All three of their attackers were on the floor at that moment. One was reaching for a gun. Mike couldn't get to him on time.

"Time to go!" Mike exclaimed and waved for Robin and Tara to go out the door. They ran up some nearby stairs. The attackers were looking around for where they had gone.

"I found one of their phones. I think they dropped it." She glanced at it, then turned it off.

They found some stairs. They made it to the other side of the building.

"Does anyone's phone work to call 911? Mine doesn't," Mike said.

"Mine doesn't either," Robin said.

"Still not working," Tara said.

"Hide over here!" They heard something like Robin's voice in the distance, on the other side of the building. They heard noises from likely the men chasing them going in that direction.

Mike, Robin, and Tara looked at each other, each wondering who it was.

They could see out a window. One man was searching outside for them.

"Okay, I'm going to go out there and take care of that guy," Mike said.

They were hiding to the side of the door, away from the window, so the man couldn't see.

"Tara, you stay here. Robin, you protect Tara in case this doesn't work out," Mike said.

"Ready?" Mike asked.

At that moment, a large crowd outside the building began walking past it. The crowd was so big that hundreds blocked the man on the other side, people with their phones in their hands looking at them as they passed by.

"Let's get out there and blend in. Stay together," Mike said.

They opened the door and moved into the stream of people, all looking at their phones.

"What is everyone doing?" Tara asked a person in the crowd.

"This is a walking tour with built-in navigation in the app to tell you where to go next. I guess a lot of other people are using the app, too," said the man in the crowd.

They got swept with the crowd and headed towards the air and space museum. As they got there, the crowd dissipated. Mike, Tara, and Robin went inside.

"Why were those men after us?" Tara asked.

"Why does any of this stuff happen to us? Something to do with the investigation, perhaps," Robin said.

Tara downloaded the app they were using and looked at the data on her phone. She analyzed the navigation data.

"It looks like the navigation data for the application changed to route people towards the building we were in," Tara said.

"It looks like it was hacked or manipulated. Why help us?" Tara asked.

"I took a quick look at the man's phone that was chasing us. It had pictures of all of us, with some articles accusing us of abducting children. It was just a message on some little-known social media app. I'll need to analyze it more when we get back to my laptop. I think it's infected," Tara said.

"I guess that would explain the voices. That last voice we heard sounded like Robin," Mike said.

"That was creepy," Robin said.

"It seemed to lead those guys away from us, though," Tara said.

"So let me get this straight. Some hackers are trying to kill us with technology, and others are trying to save us," Robin said.

"Maybe I'll check that guy's phone when we get back and see if there are any other clues," Tara said.

Robin and Tara went to the lady's room to clean up a bit. Mike went to the men's room to blot some cuts he got.

They came out and looked at each other.

"Maybe we could use some bandages or something," Tara said, looking at Mike.

They found the first aid kit on the wall and opened it.

"Hi, can we get some bandages?" Mike asked.

"Sure. What happened to you?" the attendant said, looking surprised and concerned.

Mike showed the attendant his badge. "Sorry, we can't say."

The attendant helped all of them with some antiseptic and bandages.

They thanked the person in the first aid office and walked out. They all looked a bit more presentable now, with their injuries bandaged up.

"We should hopefully be safe here with all these people in the museum. Want to stay here a little while and look around?" Robin asked.

"I'm kind of shaken up from all that. It seems like it might be one of the safest options, though, and I wanted to see it," Tara said.

Her neck still hurt from the encounter earlier.

Tara looked at her phone and dialed her home number. "It seems my phone works now."

Mike and Robin checked their phones.

"Yes, seems to work," Robin said. Mike nodded, too.

"Robin, can you check my smart gun lock mode? I don't want anyone to see," Mike said.

Mike turned his back to Robin. Robin reached under his shirt for his gun. He lifted his shirt enough to see if the gun was still blocked from working.

"It looks fine now. Check mine," Robin said. Mike reached for the gun under her top, lifting her top just enough to check the light.

"Looks good also," Mike said.

"Someone is hacking the smart gun safety systems, it seems. I've seen that once before, a little over three months ago, when I was after Victor," Mike said.

"I'll look at that later to see if I can figure out what was happening," Tara said.

They walked around the museum.

"Robin, your fighting style seems a little... How should I say this? Anti-guy," Mike said.

"It's not my fault nature gave you guys a weak spot," Robin said.

Tara chuckled slightly.

"It's not funny. It hurts even thinking about it," Mike groaned.

"Just don't piss me off, and you'll be fine," Robin said with a wink.

"Okay, since we're here, let's look at the exhibits here," Mike said, trying to change the subject.

They were walking around and looking at the amazing sights. Seeing the lunar lander was pretty cool. Lots of old planes filled the upper floor. Every once in a while, they would hear a bunch of phones Bleep. Tara, Robin, and Mike all noticed each other were a little jumpy when a bunch of phones got messages at the same time looking around. One area they walked into had rockets. Another room had satellites. There was an entire area devoted to the Apollo space missions. Tara had always thought it would be cool to go to space, but she probably would never want to go herself. Perhaps maybe, one day, if it were as routine as driving. That didn't seem likely anytime soon.

The team tried to forget about their troubles as they walked around, glancing at the large planes, drones, and more.

They figured they should go back to the hotel to file some reports on the incident. Mike used his smartphone to call their car to a nearby location, so they wouldn't need to walk back.

"The car will be here in a couple of minutes," Mike said.

"That's good. I could use a break," Tara said.

"I'm not sure if writing reports is a break, but I guess it's a change," Robin said.

Bleep. Tara's smartphone got a notification about the video processing from the man's car from earlier.

They left the museum and found their car. They headed to the hotel.

Their car dropped them at the front door, then went to park and charge.

They went to Robin and Tara's room and worked on coordinating their information to file their reports. Tara analyzed the smart gun lock from datasheets she found in the FBI database.

Tara requested internet connection details to and from the building they were inside earlier. She got an automated response to the information. She also queried the cell phone data providers in the area.

"The smart gun doesn't look like it was issued a disarm code that I can see. Maybe they are taking advantage of a security hole. I sent the data to computer forensics for analysis," Tara said.

"I also looked at the data from the man's smartphone. It was infected with a similar malware to what we have seen before, but it's changed," Tara said.

"Hey! We've got something on the video from that guy's car. There are only a few frames here or there. It's only like a couple of frames in a second a couple of times. Look at that. There were some frames with a dark-colored car driving quickly up behind the man who showed up in the smart glasses video but wasn't in the live recorded video. See, when he looked in the rearview mirror, he saw that and reacted by going faster," Tara said.

"Holy crap, in some frames, it looks like there is someone hanging out the passenger side window with a gun. No wonder this guy freaked out," Robin said.

"So, we can finally prove something is going on with the smart glasses, at least, a hack or something else," Robin said.

"I think so. I would hope this would be enough to prove it," Tara said.

"I'm going to send all of this to computer forensics," Tara said.

"Anyone ready to go for dinner? After all that activity today, I worked up an appetite," Mike said.

"Sure. Speaking of activity, you've got some fighting moves on you, girl. Just stop apologizing to the bad guys, and you're doing great!" Robin said.

Tara was a little embarrassed. She was more embarrassed and ashamed of needing to fight at all.

But how can I avoid it without getting injured or killed?

"I don't like hurting people," Tara said.

"Yeah, but if they are trying to kill you, do everything in your power to avoid that," Robin said.

They went downstairs to the hotel restaurant and seated by the hostess. They ordered a couple of appetizers and their food. Tara was staring at her phone, reading the document her coworker had sent to her on the machine learning algorithm.

"Holy crap! I think my work from five years ago might have survived a fire that destroyed our equipment. This machine learning algorithm looks eerily similar to what I wrote for an AGI, or artificial general intelligence. I called her Alice. She was the most advanced AI in the world. I believed it was lost in the fire. I think some may have survived, and someone copied and stole it!" Tara said.

"Do you have enough evidence to prove that?" Robin asked.

"Probably not, since I don't have any of the information that was in that office anymore. If I had some of the original code and this matched or was close, maybe. I'm not sure it was even legal for the person who sent me this to do so. I think International IQ Devices either acquired or stole my algorithms," Tara said.

Robin stared at her.

"Here is something else I now suspect. These algorithms seem somehow related to the hacks we're seeing. They might be using the machine learning networks from them or something. The patterns seem similar to the way those used to work," Tara said.

"Holy shit! That would be quite a coincidence. Why didn't you mention anything before?" Robin said.

"I didn't suspect anything before. I had a strange feeling that it seemed like something I should know. But I didn't realize what it was until I read this paper on the machine learning implementation being used," Tara said.

"So, do you think that company is connected to the hacks?" Mike asked.

"I'm not sure about that. Just think they're connected with the technology I created. I need to figure out how to get more evidence to prove if they are using it somehow," Tara said.

"So, we would need either source code, your original design, or something else tying IID to the old company you helped start," Mike said.

"I thought everything was destroyed in the fire. It seems like maybe it wasn't. We'd have to trace people connected with the company to see if they took some of the design or code," Tara said.

"Since you are saying the data patterns are similar, this sounds like it could be a lead in our case, too. So, if there are any leads, we could do some digging," Mike said.

"Yes, there is definitely something similar about the patterns. I don't know for sure if it means my code is related. But it's the only time I've seen data patterns like this," Tara said.

"I think I need to talk to my old partner to see if he knows anything about what might have happened with our designs and code," Tara said.

"We had venture capital investors that wanted most of the shares for their investment. We figured that wouldn't be an issue, since they couldn't do much without us. Maybe we were wrong, though," Tara said.

"Can we request the police and fire department reports of the night of the fire?" Tara asked.

"Yes, we can do that as part of our investigation. I'll make the requests for those, so it has my name on it, not yours," Mike said to Tara.

"Thanks," she said.

"If you talk to your partner, don't mention anything about us requesting those or anything about the investigation. Especially in case your partner was in on it," Mike said.

Tara, of course, knew not to mention anything.

"I don't think my partner would have been involved. I helped find him. I had the technology idea, and I needed someone to manage the business," Tara said.

"Don't eliminate anyone from suspicion until you know for sure," Robin said.

Tara couldn't imagine Mark could have been involved. He was like a friend to her.

They finished their dinner and went upstairs to Mike's room to hang out and watch TV. Tara stepped out to her and Robin's room alone to make a call.

"Mark? Hi, it's Tara. I'm sorry it's been so long since we talked," she said.

"How are you?" she asked.

"Fine. You?" Mark asked.

"I'm okay," she said.

"I ran across some information today that suggested our algorithm has been copied and used in a product. Do you know anything about what is going on and how this happened?" she asked.

"What? That's not possible. We lost everything in the fire," Mark said.

"Apparently not. This algorithm is unmistakable," she said.

"I don't see how that's possible. Do you have information to prove any of that?" Mark asked.

"No. My paperwork was lost in the fire. Unless you know about some data or papers somewhere that I don't?" she asked.

"Sorry, no idea. I think everything was destroyed," Mark said.

"If you think of anything, let me know," she said.

"Okay. What are you going to do?" he asked.

"Keep looking, I guess," she said.

"Okay. Well, it was really nice to hear from you, Tara. I have to go, though. Maybe we can talk again soon. Take care," he said.

They hung up. Though un-convinced he knew nothing, she felt bad thinking poorly of a friend that way.

She went back in to see Mike and Robin. She summarized the call for them and went to bed early.

"Goodnight. I think I need some extra sleep tonight," Tara said as she headed back to her room.

Tara put on her smart glasses to watch the news.

"The weather tomorrow will be sunny and 82 degrees in the DC Metro area. In International news, there are reports of a new state-of-the-art weapon system given to non-NATO countries to use against Russia. There are some reports that its autonomous robots, drones, and vehicles. Russia warned they would act against those responsible," the news said and showed a few raw clips of large robots attacking and defending military positions. The video was kind of disturbing.

"Cat videos!" Tara commanded.

Tara watched the cute cat videos for a few minutes before going to sleep.

264

Chapter 21

John and a couple of colleagues were reviewing the data collected by the AI for their Super PAC. They monitored the social media feeds of the entire country to gauge the sentiment. On the wall of their room was a large monitor showing the overall sentiment for their candidate vs. the competition. It was 49% to 51% their candidate was losing. They glanced over at a bar graph that showed the percentage of each emotion allocated to each of the candidates. The competitor's anger bar showed 30%. John reached over and dragged the anger bar to 60%, which caused the bar to turn from yellow to red. They watched the AI add stories to the social media feeds of all the platforms, attacking their competitor and dishing some terrible dirt on the candidate.

"Is all that true?" one man asked.

"No idea. But it doesn't matter," John said.

They watched the overall favorability of their candidate increase: 49.1%, 49.2%, 49.3%. It kept increasing as more and more nasty articles got fed into the feeds. It finally changed the overall rating to 52% for their candidate and 48% for their competitor.

"Let's stop there. We don't want it to change too much all at once. Plus, let's save some of our ammo for the special election. Set it to keep that percentage so it looks close," John said.

John looked over at another monitor that had the attendance of their candidate's rally. They needed to get more people to come to the rally.

The AI output was showing John exactly what it recommended targeting to change opinions.

"We'll have the AI algorithms target people's fears, hopes, and desires individually, tapping into them with individualized ads designed for them. That should increase favorability and attendance. Just to make sure, we'll send self-driving vehicles to cause a traffic jam on a nearby road, so they get funneled by the rally. Hopefully, more folks will decide to go," John said.

PROJECT MIND RIVER

Chapter 22

Robin was up and getting ready. That was enough to wake up Tara.

"Good morning," Tara said sleepily.

"You're awake. Are you starting to be a morning person?" Robin asked jokingly.

"Definitely not. I'm pretty sure that won't ever happen," Tara said.

They headed downstairs for breakfast.

"How did you sleep?" Mike asked Tara and Robin.

"Like a log after the day we had yesterday," Robin said.

"Yes, definitely needed the rest," Tara said.

"Did we get a call from our contact, so we know where to meet today?" Robin asked.

"No. I haven't heard anything," Mike said.

"So, we just hang out till he calls?" Robin asked.

"I guess let's do some more research and follow up on any leads," Mike said.

That actually gave Tara an idea. Her friend Michelle worked at International IQ Devices. She would tell her what she suspected and see if she could find anything out. Tara messaged her and forwarded the document she had received from her former coworker.

They finished breakfast and went back up to Mike's room to use their laptops and do more follow-ups on their case.

"Yesterday, in New York, a CIA operative on leave died on an internet-connected treadmill at his home. The forensics team didn't find the malware itself but possibly found traces that suggest it was there," Tara said.

"How did he die?" Mike asked.

"Fell and hit his head," Tara said.

"This is getting crazy," Robin said.

Mike's phone rang. It was a video call.

Mike's supervisor appeared on the video.

"Mike, I'm in town. Well, not too far. I would like you and your team to meet me. I will send you the location," his supervisor said.

"Okay, we'll meet you there," Mike said.

Mike looked at his phone, checking the traffic.

"I think our best bet is to go to the commuter train to take it out of town. Otherwise, the traffic at this time of day might be bad," Mike said.

They headed to the car. The traffic was bad even getting to the train station. They found the platform they needed to wait for the train. There were hundreds of people on the other platforms, but very few on theirs.

A train arrived. The doors opened, and hundreds of people got off. They got on the train and sat down. They heard some people's phones beep further down the train and saw more people get off.

Bleep. Tara's phone got a message.

"Oh shit! 3D message!" Tara said to Mike and Robin as she tried to focus on it.

"It says,"

GET OFF NOW!

Robin, Mike, and Tara ran for the door, but it was too late. It closed in front of them.

"Shit! Why does this always happen to us?" Robin asked.

"Let's head to the front to see what is going on," Mike said, since they were all the way in the last car of the train.

They noticed the train car they were in was empty, except there was one man further down in their car. The man sat in the seat with his eyes closed with earphones in. As Mike, Tara, and Robin walked closer, they saw the man open his eyes.

"Oh, no, no, no, shit!" the man said.

"Mike! It's Steve," the man said, standing up and pulling out his earphones. Mike recognized Steve Cozaton, a senior member of the Department of Homeland Security.

"I haven't seen you in a while," Mike said.

Steve looked around and saw the train was empty.

"Mike, I'm the contact you were going to meet today. I told you about Brian Rissal. I was going to call you a little later. I just had an errand to do. This can't be a coincidence. Why are you here?" Steve asked.

"My supervisor called and asked to meet," Mike said.

"Video call? Did it seem like him? Never mind. I think we're in serious trouble. We need to get off this train now," Steve said.

"What is going on?" Mike asked.

"I don't have all the details, as the information is compartmentalized, which is why I sent Brian. Brian worked on Project Mind River. There is apparently a Russian equivalent of that project that's been attacking U.S. operatives and your team. It uses a mix of electronic and human elements. I believe they have been trying to defend against the electronic ops, but not very successfully," Steve said.

"That's an understatement," Robin said.

"It has been targeting enemies of Russia, including our agents and people that crossed them. Your investigation has helped us identify that. It also made you a target. To find out more, you will need to meet with General James Tillington tonight at an exclusive party. He doesn't know you will be there," Steve said. Steve showed Mike the location on his phone.

Over the train noise, they could hear a buzzing sound from the doorway of the other car. Four medium-sized drones flew in. The drones had razor blades on the ends of the propellers. Tara, Mike, and Robin instinctively stepped away.

"Argh!" Steve got hit in the neck by the blades of one drone and collapsed, bleeding out on the floor. The drones advanced toward them, backing them to the end of the train. Tara instinctively dove under the drones when they were high enough that she could make it under in a rather elegant flip. Tara made it to the other side.

"I don't think I can do that," Mike yelled. Mike pulled out his gun, aiming it near Tara.

Tara was confused.

"Behind you!" Robin yelled to Tara.

Tara turned around to confront three hooded figures. One of them rushed Tara.

"Oh shit! Lookout!" Mike said to Robin as he grabbed her and pulled her to the side.

One of the hooded figures grabbed Tara. Tara pulled him to the ground, flipping him into the air towards Robin and Mike. The hooded figure hit three of the drones while he was flying, falling to the ground in front of Mike and Robin. Badly sliced up from the drones.

Mike shot the remaining drone. It tilted and crashed into the side of the train car and crashed to the ground.

Tara was on the ground, and one of the hooded figures pulled out a gun aiming at Mike.

The other hooded figure very close to Tara pulled out a gun and aimed at Tara.

"FBI, Drop the guns!" Mike said. The hooded figure took aim at Mike. Mike fired, hitting the hooded figure, and the figure slumped dead to the ground. Tara kicked the gun from the hand of the attacker aiming at her. Tara kicked the gun toward Mike and Robin, then ran toward them but grabbed a pole on the train, flipping around it and kicking the hooded figure chasing her. The attacker was knocked against the side of the train and fell down.

"Sorry," Tara blurted out as she also crashed to the ground. "Ow!" Tara said.

"Lookout!" Robin yelled as the attacker pulled out another gun and aimed at Mike.

The attacker fired a shot at Mike. Mike fired back. Robin also fired at the man. The attacker slumped over.

"Mike, you're hit!" Robin said, looking at the blood running down Mike's arm from the hole in his shirt on his upper left arm.

Mike looked at his arm. He grabbed the cloak from one of the hooded figures on the ground. He tore a piece off and wrapped it around his arm.

"I think it just nicked me. I'm okay," Mike said.

Robin leaned down to check on Steve.

"He's gone," Robin said, feeling no pulse.

"This one is dead," Robin said about the attacker that she and Mike shot.

"This guy is still barely alive," Mike said about the attacker Tara flipped onto the killer drones. Mike put handcuffs on the attacker with his hands behind his back.

Mike took out his phone and dialed 911.

"It's not going through. Check your phones," Mike said.

The train was still moving quick.

"Calls aren't going through for me," Tara said.

"Of course. Nothing for me either," Robin said.

Mike pulled the emergency stop handle at the back of the car. Nothing happened.

"It doesn't work. Let's get to the front of the train and stop it ourselves," Mike said.

They hurried forward, going through the doors into the next car. That car was completely empty as well. They kept going.

Bleep! Tara's phone got a message.

"3D Message!" Tara said, trying to focus on it.

"What's it say?" Robin exclaimed.

"It says trains on a collision course!" Tara said worriedly.

"Shit! Let's move!" Robin said and moved faster towards and through into the next car. They ran towards the next car and through. They got to the front of the train. There was an engineering compartment that was locked. There was a very long straightaway of the track. They could see a light in the distance. Mike found an axe in an equipment box near the engineer's door.

"This is almost too convenient. Stand back," Mike said, swung the axe at the door locking mechanism, and it snapped off.

Mike opened the door.

"What the hell?" he said, stepping back a bit.

"What?" Robin yelled.

They heard a loud whirring sound, and the metal mechanical arm of a robot reached out. The robot came out of the compartment and expanded in size.

"Oh, crap!" Robin yelled.

Tara was a little in shock.

Mike swung the axe at the robot, which deflected his blow with its massive arm, grabbing the axe and throwing it to the ground.

The robot stepped towards them. Mike and Robin pulled out their guns.

"Aim for the black box in the middle!" Tara said.

Robin and Mike both emptied their clips into the robot. It was a little off balance and slower, but it stepped toward them.

"Run!" Mike yelled. They ran back towards the back of the train and through to another car. They got to the other car. The robot was following slowly.

Bleep!

Tara's phone pinged. She tried to focus.

"3D message! It says to jump onto the other train!" Tara said.

"What other train?" Robin yelled.

Another train pulled up alongside them on the other track, going in the same direction as theirs.

"Oh, that train," Robin said.

The train coming towards them was getting pretty close, its doors almost aligned with theirs as it kept speed with their train. The doors of the other train opened, and then theirs.

"Well, that's cool," Mike said.

"I can go first to help you from the other side. Ready?" Mike asked.

They nodded.

Mike readied himself and made a running jump, grabbing the handle just inside the door. "Whoa!" He slipped, and one foot fell off, but he had a good grasp of the handle and pulled himself in.

"Okay, Tara, you ready?" Mike yelled over the train noise.

"I can't!" Tara said.

Mike looked forward to the train. The light from the oncoming train was a lot closer.

"It was easy. Don't worry. I will make sure you get here," he said.

Mike held on tight to the bar inside and leaned his arm way out.

"Jump towards the middle of the doorway. I'm right here," Mike said urgently.

Tara started a running jump and got the front of her toes in the doorway. She grabbed for the side of the car but missed. Mike reached around and grabbed her in a strong one-arm embrace, holding her.

"I've got you," he said, pulling her in.

"Robin, get over here. We're late!" Mike said, reaching out his arm.

Robin leaped and got one foot in. Mike couldn't grab her, but grabbed her clothes and yanked her inside.

"Sorry," he said.

"Anyone that touches me that way owes me dinner or gets punched," Robin said half-jokingly.

"I'll take the dinner option," Mike said.

"Oh, crap! Look!" Robin yelled. At the other end of the car on the other train, the attacker from earlier was about to make the jump from the other train to theirs at the end of their car. Mike ran towards the end of the car, towards where the attacker was going to jump.

The hooded figure prepared to jump towards the open door of their train. Mike prepared to kick him out.

"I'm going to kill you!" the man yelled.

"You've tried that already! You should consider a change in your profession," Mike yelled.

The man jumped.

SPLAT!

As the figure jumped, an obstacle between the trains hit him, and he never made it to their car.

"He knew his career was on the wrong track," Mike said.

"Oh, that was bad," Robin said.

Suddenly, the train they were on started slowing down, and the doors on the train all closed. They all grabbed a bar to hang on to as the train braked even harder. The train they were on before whizzed past them, followed by an ear-piercing sound of crunching metal. The earth rumbled beneath their feet like a slight earthquake. An explosion erupted from the cars on the train that collided with the commuter train. Mike checked his phone. It was working again. He called 911 to report the accident.

Mike called his supervisor. "Hi, I don't think we'll be able to meet you," Mike said.

"What? You never asked to meet us? We saw you asked us on a video call. That wasn't you?" Mike said. Mike explained what they went through and the situation. The supervisor told him the FBI would send response teams to their location.

They got off the train and meet up with the response teams. Luckily, the other train was an automated freight train. No one was aboard. They explained what happened, though Mike was pretty sure they didn't know what to make of their story.

"Let us know if you get the IDs on any of those hooded men," Mike said to the FBI team.

An ambulance arrived at the scene. Mike went to have his arm treated and bandaged. Robin and Tara had a few cuts they had taken care of as well.

Mike ordered a car to their location. The team got in and headed to FBI headquarters to debrief. When they arrived, a supervisor interviewed them about what had happened.

"So, this is some Russian version of something similar to a project called Mind River? I've never heard of it. I'll make some inquiries quietly. You three attend that party tonight and see if you can find out more information. We checked that the call you said came from your supervisor. It was from an unknown number to your phone. So, it doesn't seem like it was Steve sending you those 3D messages, given the timing. Do you have any idea who?" the supervisor said.

"No idea," Tara said.

"Maybe we'll find out tonight at the party," Mike said.

"Do you want extra security?" The supervisor asked.

"I think that will just draw unwanted attention," Mike said.

"What's really strange is we just heard about a similar collision of a train in Moscow," the supervisor said.

"That is definitely very suspicious timing," Robin said.

"You guys better get cleaned up. Those parties are usually on the fancier side," the supervisor said, looking at the rather dirty clothes and scrapes they had.

Robin, Tara, and Mike all looked at each other, seeing they were all a bit disheveled and dirty.

"I think we need to do some shopping. Will the company pay for the formal attire?" Robin shot back.

"Yes, within reason, don't go crazy," the supervisor added.

They went back to their hotel to get cleaned up a bit.

Tara, Mike, and Robin got cleaned up and met in Mike's room.

"Okay, before we look for some clothes tonight, let's recap anything new we might have discovered," he said.

"The computer forensics team doesn't know who was controlling the train that saved us. It seems like hackers through worldwide proxies. It was very sophisticated. The first train we were on seemed like it was controlled, similar to the incidents we investigated, and also through worldwide proxies to disguise the source. Given the information we got, it could be Russia, but there isn't any direct evidence to support that yet," Tara said.

"Who are those Death Monk guys? I don't think they were Russian," Robin said.

"They could have been hired hitman, perhaps." Mike wondered.

"Would they really sign up to die?" Robin asked.

"Maybe they didn't know about that part," Mike said.

"Kind of interesting. A similar train incident happened near Moscow. Do you think that was U.S. government retaliation for our train incident?" Tara asked.

"Maybe, though, that is a pretty quick response," Mike said.

"Is it the U.S. government that helped us with that train and those 3D messages?" Robin asked.

"Why would they not just tell us we're in the FBI?" Tara asked.

"If that is a classified operation, they may not be allowed to provide information, so perhaps they felt it was a way to help us without exposing their operation. Hopefully, the general will know those answers," Mike said.

"So now we know we need to not trust anything at face value with that fake video of your supervisor fooling us to take that train. It was probably a fake video," Tara said.

"It looked and sounded perfect. How do we avoid this happening again?" Mike asked.

"Give me your devices. I'll try to add an app that can warn us if it detects a fake," Tara said.

She took their devices and installed some apps to detect when video or voice was being streamed.

"Everyone else got off the doomed train when we got on because they got a text message that said train out of service," Tara said.

"So, more Project Mind River type stuff. It seems like they weren't trying to kill everyone then, just us," Robin said.

"That's not very comforting," Tara said.

"That robot we saw was very similar to one that I worked with at Intellibotz. I trained it in defensive-only moves, and I recognized the move it did to protect itself as something I taught it. I'm so sorry. I didn't even know it could be used in that way," Tara said. She couldn't help that she sounded rather despondent.

"This is not your fault," Mike said.

"I looked at the data for this incident, and it does really seem similar to the others and similar to the machine learning algorithm I wrote five years ago," Tara said, still very despondent.

"We are going to find out who is responsible and stop them," Mike said.

"Let's go shopping. We need to blend in, and the department is paying!" Robin said, thrilled she was getting to shop for nice clothes and the FBI would pay.

They took the car to a shopping area. Tara and Robin went together to look for some formal dresses themselves. Mike went to look for a suit.

Robin and Tara were walking through the clothing area of the store. The smell of perfume pervaded from the neighboring department in the store.

"So, tell me, I get the feeling you really like Mike. Am I wrong?" Robin said. Tara was a little taken aback.

"We work together, even if there is something that would be awkward," Tara said.

"I'm not sure if he is interested in me, but I like him. Yes, it might be too awkward working together," Robin said.

"Well, we can each wear something nice and see if we can get him to notice us. Nothing wrong with a little flirting. May the best woman win." Robin grinned.

They used smart mirrors to simulate trying on some dresses until they found the right ones.

Robin helped Tara pick out a nice dress. It was a bit more than what Tara was used to, but she went along with it. They dropped their purchases into their vehicle and met up for lunch.

After finishing lunch, they went back to the hotel to relax a bit and get ready for the party.

The team finished filing some of their reports and read up on some of the latest intel. Tara was a little anxious about going to a formal party. It wasn't the kind of party she liked to go to. Tara and Robin got ready to go. Before heading down to the car, they put on something to cover their dresses a bit. They got into the car, waiting for Mike. Mike came down dressed in a very nice suit and tie.

"You look snazzy," Robin said.

"You look amazing," Tara gushed. Tara had not seen Mike dressed like that before. He looked very professional.

"We'll arrive a little later than everyone else, so we don't attract too much attention," Mike said.

They got to the party about twenty minutes later than it started. They stopped in front and sent the car to park itself. Mike had not seen what Robin and Tara were wearing yet since they had some other clothes covering up their dresses, which they took off before they got out of the car. Robin Was in a form-fitting red dress with a fairly low cut but still formal. Tara had a black dress, also form fitting and not as low cut but with some open areas around her body showing a little skin as well. Tara's hair was down, too.

Mike turned and saw Robin.

Wow, she looks great in that dress.

He turned his head and glimpsed Tara, did a double take, and dropped his phone.

"Crap!" Mike said, as his phone tumbled to the ground. He was bending down to pick it up and couldn't help but notice Tara's open dress slit most of the way up her leg.

Tara looks amazing!

Robin reached down and grabbed his phone, picking it up for him.

"So, what do you think of my dress?" Robin asked Mike.

"You look great, Robin. Tara, that dress on you is perfect, too. Wow, I feel like a celebrity with both of you with me," Mike said. When Mike turned to go in, Robin winked at Tara.

They got up to the entrance of the building, where the hostess was checking the guest list. There was a lot of security nearby.

"Hello, do you have your invitation?" the hostess asked.

"I lost it, but we are on the list," Mike said, showing his ID. Tara and Robin showed theirs as well.

"Hmm, I don't see you on the list," the hostess said, still looking down at it.

"Oh, here you are. They wrote in your names on the bottom. Right this way," the hostess said as she motioned toward security.

They showed their IDs again to security, which scanned them, finding Robin and Mike's weapons. They allowed them to keep them since they were FBI.

Once inside, a second hostess asked their names.

"Mike Actley," Mike said. Someone close by was coming in.

Upon hearing his name, he looked scared, turned around, and quickly exited the building.

"What was that about? That guy just heard my name and nearly ran scared out of the building. I guess there is no time to follow him. Let's find the General," Mike whispered.

Inside was a very large, beautifully modern banquet hall.

The vast, beautiful, concave glass roof stretched for a hundred yards or more. Tables with decorative tablecloths and modern art pieces were filled the hall. Around two-hundred people walked around talking to others.

A small box-like robotic waiter with a small metal arm to collect empty drink glasses navigated its way through the crowd. It quickly grabbed glasses and put them on a tray with glass-sized rubber depressions in it on the top of the box like a robot.

"Here is a picture of the general. Let's split up. Use your comm if you find him," Mike said while showing them the picture.

They split, walking to different areas of the large hall.

An older man walked up to Tara and introduced himself, saying he was from the Department of Treasury. Tara introduced herself as well.

"I don't think I've seen you at these events before. I definitely would have noticed someone as beautiful as you," he told Tara.

Tara blushed a little, not used to the attention.

"Well, it was nice meeting you," Tara said as she walked around, looking for the general. Tara looked across the hall and could see Robin working the room. She had developed a bit of a crowd around her wanting to talk to her.

She is really pretty and comfortable with herself and talking to anyone. It's not surprising she would attract a crowd.

There were high-level people from all areas of the government. Tara felt a little self-conscious in a revealing dress at a glitzy event. She still went around saying hi to people she thought sort of looked like the general and some others, so it looked a little more natural. Tara introduced herself to someone who said they were in the Department of Defense. After introductions, he seemed worried and immediately excused himself.

"Tara, Robin found the general. Robin will try to get him to go to an isolated office so we can talk," Mike said over the comm.

"General, I would love to talk to you a bit more. Can we go someplace a little quieter?" Robin asked. The general led her to a nearby office. He didn't notice that Mike and Tara followed them. Mike and Tara entered the office after Robin and the General.

"What's going on?" The General asked when Mike and Tara entered after them.

"Hello, General. I'm Mike Actley. It's nice to meet you, General Tillington," he said.

"Oh, shit! It's you. All of you. You can't be here. How did they let you in here?" Tillington said.

"A friend, Steve Cozaton, got us on the list. He's dead. He told us there is something similar the Russians have to a project called Mind River that has been after us. He said you could tell us what's happening," Mike said.

"He shouldn't have told you anything. He is risking national security. You are, too, just by being here. I'll explain, but after that, you need to leave here immediately."

The team nodded.

"I will deny ever explaining this to you. The project is top secret and compartmentalized. I will only explain it, as I know what your team has been through. We only recently found your team was a target. We tried to protect you as best we could without exposing our operation, but it's been ineffective," Tillington said.

"Have you been sending me those 3D messages?" Tara asked.

"What 3D messages?" Tillington asked.

"Never mind. Can you explain what is happening here?" Mike said.

"The Russians have copied a project we have called Project Mind River. It uses Artificial Intelligence to influence and predict the actions of people. Do you know how many times a day you interact with electronic devices of all sorts? Your phone, refrigerator, TV, oven, car, smart speakers, elevator, and nearly everything you interact with is electronic. This AI is so sophisticated it can prod you in just the right way to make you do something that day that it wants you to do. It can make people upset, angry, happy, or nearly any other emotion by pushing their buttons in just the right way. Your phone can be listening and knowing everything you do; people carry it everywhere. Let me demonstrate," Tillington said, walking them to the office doorway so they could see out into the banquet hall.

He let them try on his smart glasses, looking at the crowd. When Robin, Mike, and Tara each tried them on, they could see what looked like a football play drawing showing the direction each person was expected to walk and if they might stop and talk to someone, and the topic as predictions. Most of the time, the predictions seemed correct. They stepped back into the office to talk privately.

"That is amazing," Robin said.

"Yes, it can actually make those predictions for some things as far as a day or even weeks in advance. It could influence you to go out to a store in a direction it wants you to go by telling you about a sale for something it knows you want. It can make people think they hear voices to make them lose their sanity. The Russian equivalent of the project Mind River targeted the manual drivers in at least some of the incidents being investigated. It might have been prodding them for weeks, knowing they drive a particular path to work or for errands every day. Then, it hacks the traffic control systems just the tiniest bit, influencing the system by predicting where a car will likely be thirty minutes or even further in the future. Predicting the reactions of the computers and people involved creates the perfect digital assassin. It lines up events to appear like accidents caused by a manual driver and not hacking. As you discovered, it can make people see and hear things that aren't there using the smart glasses or not see things that are there," Tillington said.

"We're doing the best we can to block the hacks, but they are using multiple source locations worldwide to attack their targets. Things are getting even more dangerous. They may take even more aggressive actions given the ongoing assistance the U.S. and NATO are providing to countries they are at war with. You should know we only use ours for PsyOps and military targets," Tillington said.

"Who are those hooded assassins?" Robin asked.

"We don't know. Their IDs have been thoroughly erased. Your team hasn't left enough of them in one piece to identify them. We have seen them sometimes show up at the location of someone targeted to die by Project Mind River or its Russian equivalent. We've tried to capture them too, but they never show when we are out looking for them; it's like they know," Tillington stated.

"I'm afraid that's all I can give you now. You are endangering the lives of many of the highest-level officials in government just by being here. We'll try to help protect you, and if we have additional useful intel that makes sense for you or the FBI to have, I will let you know," Tillington said.

"Thanks, General, we'll get going now," Mike said as they walked out of the side office and into a crowded hall. They walked towards the exit, and they heard a loud alarm, possibly the fire alarm. People were scattering everywhere. Mike and Robin were together, but Tara got caught in the stream of people headed toward the door. It was a loud commotion. It was hard to hear anything other than the alarm.

A loud scream was heard. Mike saw Tara far away from them, near a door, screaming, someone dragging her out.

"Someone has Tara! Follow me!" Mike yelled to Robin. Mike started pushing through the crowd towards the door, shoving people out of the way.

"Tara, do you copy?" Mike yelled into the comm. No answer.

"Emergency comm! FBI command Tara Bitlouver is being kidnapped at our location. Send backup now!" Mike yelled into the comm.

Mike and Robin finally made it out the door. They saw a vehicle head away at high speed. "Command, emergency vehicle request now!" Mike yelled. A car came screeching around the corner in front of him. Robin and Mike ran to the car. Mike floored it in the direction he saw the car go, but he had to slow down. The vehicle they got was just a random vehicle with no lights and siren or pursuit mode, so he had to manually chase the vehicle for now.

"There! There! There!" Robin said, pointing at the car they were chasing going through the light.

They were behind too many cars. The light turned completely off. All the cars were afraid to budge. They were gridlocked.

"Shit!" Mike yelled. "Command, can you get a satellite focused on our location quickly?" Mike said loudly into the comm.

"No, it will take a while to task," came back over the comm.

"Do we have a trace on Tara's comm or phone?" Mike asked on comm.

"No signal," the command reported.

"Follow me!" Mike said to Robin. He got out of the car, leaving it in traffic.

"Get me another car on the other side of this traffic jam!" he said into the comm.

They ran to the other side, past the traffic jam.

BEEP!

A car horn bleeped as it pulled up to them. They rushed to get in. Mike burned rubber, speeding away in the direction the other car went.

There was a ramp down to the interstate, but there was more traffic getting to the ramp.

"Mike, there!" Robin pointed out that there was a car that looked like it might be the one. That car had already made it onto the interstate and had a head start.

"Mike, what are you doing? That's not a road. Oh shit!" Robin said.

Mike, rather than wait in traffic, drove through the median down a hill to get on the interstate. Mike was picking up speed on the grassy area on the side of the road to get past traffic.

"Send the police to stop that car!" Mike said on the comm.

"Already on their way," the person on comm replied.

"We're running out of lawn!" Robin exclaimed as some trees were almost directly in front of them. Mike swerved back onto the road but now had to go more slowly in traffic.

"Can you give us priority pursuit in this vehicle?" Mike asked on comm.

"No, but there is an FBI vehicle, a black SUV, about ten cars ahead," the comm replied.

"When I get behind, enable sync mode with this vehicle," Mike said.

"Actley, you aren't serious? Sorry, I should know better than to ask," the comm said.

"I'm going with you," Robin said. Mike was a little surprised.

"Are you sure?" Mike asked.

"Why should I let you have all the fun?" she asked.

Their car came up behind a black FBI SUV and acted like it was attached to it.

Robin and Mike rolled down their windows and got onto the front of the car, and each leaped onto the back of the SUV while it was still driving.

"Can you roll down the windows, please?" Mike asked on comm.

"Acknowledged," the comm replied as the windows rolled down. Mike and Robin climbed in.

Mike pushed the button for pursuit mode with lights and sirens. The cars in front of them parted like a zipper. Their car lurched forward with the siren's wailing.

"This is much better," Mike said.

Their car was traveling much faster, and with vehicles yielding for them, they would hopefully catch up to the car that had Tara.

Robin grabbed a drone from the back and released it from the window. She pulled out a laptop to track it.

"Drone launched," Robin said into the comm. The drone cruised ahead, scanning the cars.

"I don't see it. Wait, There!" Robin exclaimed.

"Boom!" the signal disconnected, and very far ahead of them, they saw a fireball above the traffic in the roadway.

"Lost contact," Robin said.

"They must have shot our drone down," Mike said.

Robin went to the back, grabbed another drone, and released it.

The car they were chasing was weaving in and out of traffic so fast it was clear it was self-driving controlled. It dodged traffic on the left or right shoulders as they were available, weaving in between any cars that got in its way.

Mike and Robin's SUV got closer to the vehicle they were chasing. The drone was trailing behind the vehicle they were chasing, too.

"Lookout! Rocket Launcher!" Robin yelled.

The man popped his head out of the sunroof of the vehicle they were chasing, aiming a rocket launcher at Mike and Robin's car, and fired.

"Shit! Hold on!" Mike said, trying to steer off the roadway.

"Boom!" A huge fireball appeared in front of them.

The rocket exploded when it hit the drone. Their car drove through the fireball and debris. They could hear the debris hit all over the car.

"We're still alive!" Robin exclaimed.

"Nice job! Do we have any more of those?" Mike asked.

"Uh, no," Robin said.

The man in the vehicle they were chasing reloaded and aimed at them again.

"Any other ideas?" Robin asked.

SWOOSH!

The rocket launched towards them. Mike swerved the vehicle to the right, but the missile was still tracking them.

"I'm sorry," Mike said as the missile was closing on the vehicle.

BOOM!

A fireball appeared in front of them, and their car went through it.

"How are we still alive?" Robin asked.

"Agent Actley, are you okay? Thanks for the idea. We had three drones following you, now just two," FBI command said over the comm channel.

"Thanks for the assist," Mike said on comm.

A drone flew over to the vehicle they were chasing and landed on its hood.

"Command to Actley drone engaged and ready on your count."

"Three, two—" as Mike said that the other drone dropped onto the hood of their vehicle and engaged.

"Oh shit!" Robin exclaimed.

Just then, all the vehicles behind the vehicle they were chasing started weaving all over the road.

BOOM!

The drone on Robin and Mike's vehicle detonated. Their car went uncontrolled off the side of the road.

"Detonate! Detonate! Detonate!" Mike yelled into the comm just before their car crashed into a barrier and the airbag deployed.

"No response from our drone to the detonate command," the comm said.

Mike looked out the cracked side window and saw vehicles weaving behind the vehicle they had been chasing, but the vehicle with Tara in it drove away. Mike pushed down the airbags with his hand so he could talk without the airbag in his mouth.

"Do we have eyes on the target?" Mike asked.

"Negative. GPS from the drone is offline," the comm replied.

"Command, get me all the drones and choppers in the air you can to do a grid search over the area. Make sure the police have updated intel. Let's get search teams out here fast," Mike said.

"Police are actively searching. All drones are presently inoperable," the comm responded.

"What? How?" Mike asked, exasperated.

"We're not sure. It appears to be a cyber-attack of some sort," command responded.

"That explains why the FBI drone attacked us, I guess," Robin said.

Robin looked over at Mike and perhaps saw an emotion she had not seen from him before. Perhaps it was despair.

"Hey, we're going to get her back," Robin soothed as she put her hand on his shoulder.

"That's right. We will. You, okay?" Mike asked, looking at Robin. Her head was slightly bleeding.

"I'm fine. How about you?" Robin asked.

"Good enough. I think we need another ride fast. You ready?" he asked.

"Let's go," Robin said.

They had to break the windows to get out of the crashed car as the doors wouldn't open. Robin grabbed the internet-connected laptop and a drone tracking device. They thought about running ahead of the weaving cars on the road, but they headed to a local parallel road instead. They ran off the side of the highway into the woods, heading towards a local road.

"Command, we'll need another vehicle at the road we're headed towards," Mike said.

"On its way," command said.

They reached the road, and an SUV came zipping up to them and came screeching to an abrupt stop. Robin and Mike got in.

"Command, get us into the search pattern at the most probable location," Mike said.

Mike programmed the car to follow command-and-control directions.

The car took off quickly, driving down the road in the direction they saw the vehicle go on the parallel road.

"Anything on the tracker?" Mike asked.

"Nothing yet," Robin said.

"Why do you think they want Tara?" Robin asked.

"Maybe they wanted to stop our investigation," Mike wondered.

"But why? We kind of know what's going on, and so does the FBI," Robin said.

"Presuming they know all of that. They could be afraid she might know how to stop them," Mike said.

"They wouldn't need to kidnap her for that," Robin said.

"So, there is probably something else they want from her, but what is it?" Mike asked.

"Something she has, something she can do, or something she knows?" Robin wondered.

The car was quickly taking corners and continuing the search pattern. Robin connected to the data from the other FBI teams, searching.

"I don't know if it's anything she has. She has been an AI researcher and an entrepreneur. All of this seems like it is based on AI, so it's possible they want something related to that," Mike said.

The streets were still pretty busy, which slowed down the search pattern.

BLEEP!

The car got a message.

"Holy Shit! It's a 3D message like Tara was getting, except I think I can see it now," Robin said, while focusing her eyes.

"It says,"

Save Tara, search five-mile radius from coordinates below.

"I can read it too, weird," Mike said.

"Do we trust it and search?" Robin asked.

"We should have a few cars use the new search pattern with us from opposite sides," Mike said.

"Command, we have a possible tip, uploading an alternate search area for us and a few vehicles," Mike said.

"Acknowledged," command replied.

The car redirected itself toward the new search area.

Robin looked up into the sky.

"What the Hell?" she said.

Mike looked up.

"Oh, it's those satellite advertisements. What does that say? Eat Shat America!" Mike said.

"I guess that got hacked too, but they can't spell in English," Robin commented, shaking her head disapprovingly.

"This hacking is getting crazy," Mike said.

"Who the hell is sending these 3D messages? If it wasn't Steve or the general, who is it?" Robin asked.

"Maybe it's someone that was working with the general that discovered we were being targeted and decided to help us," Mike said.

"Hmm. Still not sure," Robin said.

Tara had been taken by force, shoved into the vehicle, tied up, and then blindfolded. After their lengthy chase by Mike and Robin, they took her out of the vehicle and unblindfolded her. She was at an enormous warehouse. The shelves were filled with a mixture of boxes, as far as her eyes could see. There were rows and rows of shelving with boxes they passed before taking her to a room on one side of the warehouse. The smell of packaging material wafted through the air. Sounds of people moving boxes could be heard in the distance.

"Hello Miss Bitlouver. I'm sorry for the rough welcome. We wanted to ask you some questions. You can call me Ivan. Please come this way," Ivan led her with armed men following to a medium-sized room with a table and some canned drinks.

"Please sit down and have a drink. We have some stronger drinks if you'd prefer," Ivan said.

Tara figured the canned drinks were probably safe and opened one and took a sip.

"Why did you bring me here?" Tara asked.

Ivan showed her some pictures that looked like they were from areas they were investigating for their incidents.

"What do you know of these?" Ivan asked.

"They look like they are areas related to incidents we are investigating," Tara said.

"What did you find out?" he asked.

"I'm not at liberty to discuss an ongoing investigation," she said.

The armed men moved closer. Tara heard the guns click behind her.

"Who does the FBI believe is responsible?" Ivan asked.

"Well, I'm guessing it's you and your government. Presuming you're Russian," Tara stated.

"Very good," Ivan said.

"Did you write the AI for military robots?" he asked.

"No, absolutely not. I would never write software for the military to hurt people," she said.

"Did you create the AI for your government project, Mind River?" he asked.

"I did not create any software for the government for any projects," Tara responded.

Tara was wondering what he was talking about.

"Tell me how to stop the robots that are attacking our military!" Ivan said.

"I did not program any military robots," Tara replied.

"We know you wrote the code. Tell us how to stop them!" Ivan yelled.

"I have never written code for the military. I'm a pacifist. I hate violence," Tara said.

"I'm going to give you a little time to think about your answer before we resort to more extreme measures. Put her in the room," Ivan told his men.

They grabbed Tara and led her to a small room.

BUZZ!

The door made a typical sound for an electronic lock when they opened it.

The room inside had no windows and a connected bathroom. It had an electronic lock panel on the inside. The men stalked away, their footsteps echoing off the floor. She looked around to see if there was anything she could use to escape. She wasn't sure what had been in this room before, but it didn't smell good.

She found a small, flat piece of metal she tried to use on the electronic lock. It was hard to use, but she pried off the panel cover. She searched around for the correct wires to trigger the door.

BUZZ!

The door lock disengaged. Tara grabbed the door handle. It opened!

"Did I do that?" she mumbled.

She peered outside the door and looked around. She didn't see anyone, so she went out, closing the door, so it looked closed but wasn't locked.

Just outside the door, she found her phone and purse. Her phone was off. She turned it on. She texted her location to Mike and Robin. They texted back to hide, and they would come to get her. They asked for the number of hostiles. She had only seen the four plus Ivan, but she could hear a lot more. She texted back that it was a large warehouse visual on five, but heard more.

Suddenly, an app popped up on her screen, and it showed what looked like the layout of the warehouse and a green dot and many red dots. She looked around and walked down a hallway. The green dot moved in the direction she walked and seemed to match her surroundings.

What the heck?! I guess the green dot is me, and the red is them. How is this data getting to her? She looked for a spot to hide since she couldn't get out without being seen. A large supply room with lots of stuff to hide behind was her best bet. She watched the display on her phone with the red dots moving. Suddenly, they started moving around a lot more. They must have discovered she was gone. Tara was considering moving and stood up.

Bleep.

Her phone made a soft sound. A 3D message showed up. She stared intently at it. It said,

Stay there. I'll draw them away.

"Oops!" she heard from a distance away from the men down the hall. It sounded like her voice. The men headed away from her toward the voice.

"They must be using the phone malware and playing my voice through it to draw the men away," Tara whispered.

She wondered who could be helping her. She watched the red dots get further away from her.

She got a message from Mike,

Hang tight. Hostage Rescue Teams ten minutes out.

Some red dots got closer again, but again moved further away. She heard something like her voice that seemed to distract them. She heard something walking down the hallway. There was a yellow dot on her app display she had not seen before. It was heading right toward the room she was in. "Woof!" she heard.

"Oh crap, that dog is going to find me," she thought. She then heard a very high-pitched noise from far away that seemed to distract the dog, sending the yellow dot further away in the warehouse.

She checked her phone.

The Hostage Rescue Teams (HRT), Mike and Robin, should be there in just a few minutes.

She got another text message from Mike and Robin.

Keep hidden and keep your head down. Get ready. Location?

Tara texted her location.

She waited quietly. Then suddenly, she heard hissing sounds. Automatic gunfire sounded far away in the warehouse. It sounded like it was coming from the front and back of the warehouse. She looked at her phone. It showed blue dots and red dots now.

The blue must be SWAT. I hope.

There was now a red dot coming toward her room, getting closer. It wasn't stopping. It was probably too noisy in the warehouse now, with the gunfire for those sound and voice tricks to work. She could hear more gunfire and smelled a smoky smell. She hoped the warehouse wasn't on fire.

No, the alarms would have gone off. The red dot was still getting closer. Someone checked each room along the hallway. The red dot walked into her room! Tara was trying to breathe quietly, and she heard the person walk in and start looking around. A message without sound appeared on her phone. It said,

I will try to distract him with a phone call. Stay quiet.

The sound of a rock and roll song came from the person's phone as it rang. The man answered the phone.

"Hey," he said.

"Get over here now. We need help in the front!" a voice that sounded like Ivan's could be heard, even from Tara's position.

"Okay, will be there in a sec," he said as he hung up.

Did whoever was helping her just fake Ivan's voice?

"There you are," the man said as he looked around a pile of boxes, reached down and grabbed Tara. "You're coming with me," he said.

Tara grabbed the man's arm and twisted it, so he turned with his back towards her and shoved him away. He spun around and punched towards her head. She dodged the punch and used Robin's signature move. The man bent over in pain.

"Sorry," Tara said as she pulled him further down.

With her back to the ground, she put her foot into his chest and flipped him onto his back into some boxes. Tara stood up and went running. He got up from the boxes and lunged at her, missing, and hitting his head on the wall. The man slumped to the floor. Gunfire sounded like it was getting closer. Tara peeked out the door. A hand grabbed her from behind on the other side of the hallway.

"Found you," Ivan said as he pulled her along.

"Come with me. I want to show you something," he said, pulling her towards another room down the hallway. The large room had a big flat-screen TV on one side.

BOOM!

A colossal explosion came from down the hall.

"I'm afraid your SWAT team friends won't be coming to find you after our booby trap just got them. Most of them are now probably dead," Ivan said.

She could hear a few screams down the hall.

"I wanted to show you this," Ivan said.

Smoke and the smell of something burning wafted into the room. Ivan turned on the large screen TV while he had a gun in one hand. A video of the war in Europe played on the TV. There were Russian tanks and soldiers that were fighting against a force that couldn't be seen in the video. Then, in front of the tanks appeared to be the opposing forces: tanks, helicopters, drones, and robots. All appeared to be remotely controlled. They swiftly came in and meticulously destroyed the Russian tanks and equipment.

"These automated forces are deadly. You are responsible. You can help us stop them. Why won't you help us?" Ivan asked.

"I didn't program any military hardware. I don't know anything about this," Tara said.

Tara thought she heard something coming down the hall. Mike came bolting into the room, aiming his gun at Ivan.

"FBI! Drop your weapon!" Mike yelled. Out of a side room, a man came running and tackled Mike to the floor.

Tara heard a gun go off between Mike and the man who tackled him. Both of them appeared to be unconscious or dead, lying on the ground. Mike's gun slid right next to Tara as it fell from his hand. Tara quickly picked it up and pointed it at Ivan.

"You won't use that if what you've told us is true. Look at the efficient killing job these machines do. Help us stop them, or else I will kill all of your men."

Ivan quickly pointed his gun toward Mike and the man on the ground and shot Mike.

"No!" Tara yelled. Tara pulled the trigger, hitting Ivan directly in the head. Ivan collapsed. Tara kicked the gun away from Ivan, and she herself fell to her knees. She got up and went over to Mike.

"Mike... Mike, are you okay?" she said, looking around him. She didn't see any blood from him, but the man across from him was bleeding out.

Tara called Robin, "We need help. Mike's not moving."

"Does he have a pulse?" Robin asked.

Tara felt around. "Yes, hurry, please," Tara said.

"Be there in a minute," Robin said.

Tara saw out of the corner of her eye the video on the screen of a massive robot that looked like a larger armor-plated version of the one she trained. A missile went toward the robot. The robot deflected it. She recognized the defensive move. It was exactly like how she trained it.

"Oh, no! No!" Tara sobbed.

"I am responsible for the deaths of the incidents and in the war. I just killed someone, too," she cried. She picked up the gun and put the end in her mouth.

"Hey, Tara. Please put the gun down," a voice said.

"Mike?" She dropped the gun and gave Mike a hug. "Are you okay?" Tara asked.

"I think so. I must have hit my head. I think I got shot in the chest, but I had my bulletproof vest on," Mike said.

"Why did you have the gun?" Mike asked.

"They wanted me to help them stop the robots that are being used to kill them," she said.

He just stared at her.

"I told them I had nothing to do with it. But just now, on the video he was showing me, I saw something that I taught the robot how to do. They took my training software and used it in military robots. The Russians have been killed because of the robots. I shot that guy over there when he shot at you. I killed him, and the robots I trained for defense are killing people," she said.

"I know with the ideals you hold, this seems like your fault, but it's not. They used something of yours in a way you didn't intend, and it was defense in shooting him. None of this is your fault at all. Sometimes, to have some semblance of control in our lives, we like to blame ourselves, even though it was the fault of others or circumstance," he said, pulling himself up and giving Tara a hug.

"Ready to go?" Mike said.

"Yes," Tara said, swiping at her tears.

Robin burst into the room with her gun drawn.

"You both okay?" she asked, looking around.

"Yes," they said.

"Then let's get out of here," Robin said.

"Wait," Tara said quickly, going over to the computer near the big screen TV and stepping around Ivan's body to get there. She looked in the drawers of a cabinet and found a USB drive, plugged it in, and downloaded some info. She also tried to upload more of it to a cloud location.

"Ready," Tara said.

Robin went out the door of the room, followed by Tara. A man was standing to the left in the hallway. Robin shot the man, and he collapsed to the floor.

Another man was to the right with a gun and aimed at Tara. She ran towards him, grabbing his arm with the gun and pushing his arm up over his head. She leaped onto him, wrapping her legs around him. The man toppled backward. He was a little distracted by her chest in his face. Tara rolled off him, wresting the gun from his hand as he hit the floor. The man got up and pulled out a backup gun, aiming it at Tara again.

The man collapsed onto the floor. Standing behind him was Mike, with smoke still coming out of his gun from the shot.

Mike took the lead. "Let's get out of this place," he said.

"Wait," Tara said, looking at her phone. It was still showing the map of the building with red and blue dots. There were a lot fewer red and blue dots now. She showed it to Robin and Mike.

"Is that a drone infrared feed? The drones weren't working," he said.

"I think it's from the same source as the 3D messages," Tara said.

There was a small fire in one room they passed. They saw a small box-like robot spray something on the fire to put it out.

They got to an end of the hallway that could go right or left, where the screen was showing red dots nearby on either side. Mike motioned for

Robin to get to the other side. He stood up to the left, and Robin kneeled near the corner on the right. Mike gave a hand signal, counting down from three. Then they both peered around the corner and saw the targets.

"Clear," Mike said.

"Clear," Robin said.

Tara showed them her phone.

"We can meet up with our team there," Mike said.

They headed off to the right. "Actley over here," he heard a voice from one of the SWAT team members. They headed over.

"The exit is clear that way," the SWAT team member said.

"Robin, take Tara out of here to the office. I'm going to help them finish up," Mike said.

Robin and Tara headed towards the exit. There were SWAT team members along the way waving them out. They got out, got in a car, and headed to FBI headquarters.

When they got to the FBI building, a nurse came to assist her with her injuries. She got cleaned up a little in the restroom.

A supervisor debriefed Tara and Robin.

"Let's go analyze the data I got from there," Tara said.

Tara picked up a special laptop designed to be isolated and scanned USB drives thoroughly before copying it off to a different drive to make sure it was free of malware. Tara analyzed the data on a different laptop. Mike showed up at the office.

"Are you both okay?" he asked.

They both nodded.

"How about you?" Robin and Tara asked at nearly the same time.

"Fine. We got the rest of them. They are being processed," he said.

"It looks like the Russians were not responsible for every incident. Only the ones with U.S. operatives were the ones they seemed to have targeted," Tara said.

"Crap. I thought we would finally get some answers, but all we have is another mystery. Probably more hackers," Robin said.

"It seems like they used that location as a front-line location to support their version of Project Mind River. I guess human intel can sometimes assist," Tara said.

"Maybe it was China or even our own country's Project Mind River. Those were criminals the U.S. probably wouldn't mind if they were gone," Robin said.

Suddenly, the power went out.

"Give it a second. Emergency power should kick in," Mike said.

About half the lights came on. They looked around the outside windows and could see the power was out as far as they could see in any direction.

They walked over to the command center.

"What's going on?" Mike asked one of the staff.

"They aren't sure yet," said a woman.

"We have information that there was a problem with one of the power stations nearby," a man in the room said.

"Ah, okay, just a power failure. I guess we can go finish our reports," Robin said.

"There is information that power failures have also happened in New York, Los Angeles, Chicago, and Atlanta. They are investigating others."

"I guess not a normal power failure," Robin said.

"Doesn't sound that way," Mike said.

"Stand by for a conference call with the Department of Homeland Security, Department of Defense, Central Intelligence Agency, National Security Agency, the secretary of state, the vice president, and the president, connecting now," a woman said.

They all appeared on the screen. As each person talked, their image slightly enlarged, and the others shrank a little to show the speaker.

"The Department of Defense has information that this is a cyber-attack from Russia targeting multiple cities," the secretary of defense said.

"I want confirmation. Please share the data with all agencies," the president said. "We got the info. Sending to forensics," an agent in the room said.

Tara looked at a screen that was also receiving the data.

"This is a very similar signature to the incidents we investigated, but just a different vector. I think it is Russia from the data we've seen," Tara said.

Tara sent some notes on the info and the correlation to the computer forensics team, pointing out the similarities.

"How long till we can get confirmation?" the president asked.

"We need some time," said the DHS secretary.

"Same here," said the director of the FBI.

"Are we sure this is a cyber-attack?" the president asked.

"Yes," came the responses from DHS, DOD, and the FBI.

"Initiate Fire Island," the President said.

"Sir, that will limit our ability to respond," the Secretary of Defense said.

"Understood. Let's proceed with Operation Fire Island," he said.

"What is Fire Island?" Tara asked Mike quietly.

"I don't know," Mike said.

"Three, two, one. Initiate," the Secretary of defense said. Someone behind him said, "Initiated. But no result. Switching to Plan B backup option. Executing... Sir, there is no response."

"What? We can't stop this?" asked the President.

"Plan C will take some time to get there, but we can stop this. It will be twelve to twenty-four hours until we can get all assets in place," the Secretary of Defense said.

"I want updates every hour. If we get confirmation of the source or if it is ready to execute, I want to know immediately. Please provide updates on any new activity detected. We need to confirm who this is to act. Move us to DEFCON FOUR," the President said.

"Yes, sir," said the Secretary of Defense.

"Understood, sir," said DHS.

"Understood, Mr. President," the FBI Director responded.

The rest of the agencies responded.

The call disconnected.

The director walked over to Mike, Tara, and Robin. "Come with me," the director said.

They went to a conference room.

"Sir, what is Operation Fire Island?" Mike asked.

The director paused for a moment.

"What I'm about to tell you is top secret, compartmentalized need to know only. Operation Fire Island is to cut the U.S. off from the rest of the world from the internet. They have electronic disconnects, but they failed to operate. Plan B was to blow up the main transcontinental oceanic fiber cables. The explosives failed to activate. Plan C is to move Navy vessels into place and destroy those lines by any means necessary. You probably think, why not just have the telecoms shut off those fiber connections? But our systems use some of those cables, so it needs to be a targeted disconnect to not disrupt our own use. Some of those locations are out in deep water. Please help the team confirm the hack source. If you have any other relevant intel, it could help," the director said.

"Understood. Thanks," Mike said.

The director left, heading back towards the command center.

"Tara, can you help the computer forensics team? Robin and I can help analyze the data," Mike said.

Together, they headed down to the computer forensics department. They analyzed the data late into the night, taking a brief break around midnight. After they found emergency blankets and pillows, they slept on the floor in one of the conference rooms.

PROJECT MIND RIVER

Chapter 23

Robin, Tara, and Mike woke around 5 am. There was an alarm sounding. The alarms startled many others that were also sleeping on the floor or awake. There were sounds of people moving quickly outside where they were. They went to the command center to see what was going on. The conference call was on again with the same participants.

"The financial markets are under attack. The stock market and banking system may not come online today," said the DHS.

"Do we have confirmation on the source of the power failures?" the president asked.

"Not yet. We have teams working through the night. We're getting close," said the secretary of the DHS.

"Same here, sir," the director of the FBI said.

"We need to speed this up. We are under active attack, and we can't respond because we don't know who it is for sure. Any other defenses we have?" the President asked.

"Our AI defense systems are having success 90% of the time. Unfortunately, it's hard for them to protect everything all the time. We need some offense. We are working with our partners to shut down botnet servers in friendly countries. Do we have your permission to terminate servers in unfriendly countries?" the secretary of defense said.

"Permission granted if those machines are not part of any critical infrastructure. Stop those attacks on our financial system and power if you can," the President said.

"Yes, sir," the secretary of defense said.

The connection dropped.

"Get all of our vetted contractors on the line that can help with this, and pull in any resources we can to get an answer as soon as possible," the director said.

"I heard the Russians we captured in the warehouse aren't giving us anything except name, rank, and serial number," Robin said.

"Hopefully, we can find out something from the data we collected," Tara said.

"I'm going to get a shower, then head down there to see if I can change their minds. I can be very convincing," Robin said.

"They have showers here?" Tara asked.

"Sure do. If you know where to find them. Let me show you," Robin said.

Robin and Tara went upstairs. Mike also found one to use. They met back up an hour later and grabbed some breakfast from the cafeteria downstairs and brought it upstairs. Tara went back to computer forensics.

"We have a huge amount of data to compare. We're running on all the servers we can run, but our learning model is kind of slow," one of them said.

"Can I see?" Tara asked.

Tara looked curiously at the terminal. She typed a few commands that pulled up a diagram of the neural network layers for the learning model. She got on a computer nearby and started typing furiously. After about fifteen minutes, she ran the training data. The estimated efficiency was 1000% faster. She started the analysis, and it was only running on one machine.

"Take a look at this to see if you want to scale this model," Tara said.

One man came over and looked at it. "How did you do that?" he asked.

Tara brought up a chart of her changes and showed it to him.

"I've never seen anything like that. That's like the next generation. You could probably get a patent for it," he said.

"I applied for one a while back, but because our company folded, I never continued. I might re-apply, so this can be our secret," Tara said. This was just a small fraction of the neural network she built five years ago.

Tara looked over the data from all the incidents and the warehouse. The data looked even more similar to the patterns of an AI. Not just any AI. It was very similar to the one she had written. She wasn't sure how that would be possible. Tara texted her friend Michelle to see if they still had power and if she had made any progress in finding information.

Found where they store old files. It's locked. Need a key.

A 3D message popped up. It read,

I printed you a key.

This is listening to me, she thought. That's not good. It seemed to be helping them, though.

Tara wondered what it could mean.

Oh wait, what was that object that printed on my printer? But it dropped, and I couldn't find it. Wait, did it fall into my purse? She looked inside her purse, dug around, and found a black key. Crap. How do I get it back to her in New Jersey?

"I think I may have the key. I will have to mail it to you," Tara replied.

"Oh, just got your file. Is that the key to that door? How did you get that?" Michelle asked.

Tara had no idea what she was talking about.

A 3D message appeared. It read,

I sent her the file.

Tara just told Michelle she got a file from an anonymous tip. She told her to be careful.

The screen popped up in the forensics lab.

98.62939% confirmed.

Everyone gathered around the screen, staring at it. One of the staff restarted their original machine learning network.

"Just to make sure we'll cross-check everything with our other algorithm," the man said.

The team started looking over the correlated results manually. Everything they saw looked like it was, in fact, pointing to Russia. Tara looked specifically through the one percent of the data that the algorithm had not traced to a Russian source. Some of it was just random requests to different computers around the world.

"Look at this data," Tara showed some of the computer forensics staff.

"Can we check if this is capturing DHS or DOD Cyber defense?" one of them asked.

Several of them sent messages to contacts in those agencies.

"They say no," one of them said.

"It's a minor defense of some power substations, some businesses. Who else would defend us in that way?" someone asked.

"Manual review of the correlations looks good so far. DHS has confirmed they believe the source is Russia. They are just waiting on us," a supervisor said.

"Spinning up more machines, since those are freed up now."

Tara put on her smart glasses to watch the 3D visualization as the system traced packet routes worldwide.

The progress meter moved much faster. A number displayed on the screen for the older FBI machine learning algorithm.

97.5324%

"Let's compare the differences to confirm," someone said.

They each got different datasets to review. The team confirmed that Tara's machine-learning algorithm looked closer to reality than the original computer forensics algorithm.

"Do you need more time to confirm your analysis? We are about to enter a war. For the moment, maybe just Cyber, but it could go physical quickly. So, you need to be sure you are betting yours, your family and everyone's life in the United States on your analysis," the supervisor said.

Tara heard one analyst quietly say to the other, "No pressure."

"I sent an anonymous survey link. Please select confirmed to mean Russia or not confirmed," the supervisor said.

Everyone entered a value into the survey.

"The result is 100% confirmed that the attacker is Russia. Thank you, everyone," the supervisor left, heading toward the command center. Mike, Robin, and Tara followed.

A conference call was started with the same participants.

"What do you have for me?" the President asked.

"We have, beyond any reasonable doubt, determined the source to be Russia. We found a minor defense taking place by an unknown party of a few installations," the FBI director said.

"DHS, NSA, CIA, or DOD?" the President asked.

"Not us," they shook their heads no.

"Find out what is happening there. In the meantime, DHS, and DOD, I want to execute our cyber-attack plan of Russia or Russian personnel or installations. You are a go. We are to attack similar scales and targets they have attacked. FBI, please feed us any intelligence you have. I've asked the governors to deploy the National Guard as needed to help people or keep the peace. Please take us to DEFCON THREE," the president said.

"Do we still want to proceed with Fire Island?" the DOD asked.

"Let's see if we can attack an equivalent set of targets first. Get them in position so that we can do it. If we can't mount a defense or stop them with a good offense soon, we might need to proceed sooner," the president said.

"Yes, sir," the secretary of defense replied.

"We've seen attacks or preparation for more targeted attacks on our financial centers, power grids, transportation, water supplies, shipping, and other critical infrastructure. Public and private industries should be on alert to defend against such attacks where possible. Onsite personnel should run services and facilities and disconnect from any non-essential networking. Law enforcement should prepare to keep the peace, manage the impact of the attacks, and assist with an emergency response as needed. We have also found that social media sites that are still accessible are being flooded with propaganda and disinformation aimed at causing chaos and confusion. We need an integrated approach at all levels of government to keep this under control," the DHS said.

"The Russian cyberwar operation also had a local operative's component in Washington, D.C. Our agents luckily dismantled that. Special thanks to Agent Actley, Agent Laizon, and Miss Bitlouver, along with our Hostage Rescue Teams," the director of the FBI said.

"Thanks to all of you," the President said.

"Mr. President, the cyberwar offensive has begun," the Secretary of Defense said.

"While we are in uncharted territory. The United States will prevail," the President said.

The call was completed.

"I can't believe this is happening," Tara said to Mike and Robin.

"I know, right? How often do you get mentioned on a call with the president?" Robin said.

"No, I meant the cyber war. Could this lead to an actual war?" Tara asked.

"Oh, right. Yes, I guess it could," Robin said.

"Neither country wants a direct confrontation with physical weapons, as anything that takes us onto the path of a nuclear war is an end that no one in the world wants. So, I expect both sides will try to avoid direct confrontation. But that doesn't mean they won't depending on the situation or if there is some miscalculation of some kind," Mike said.

Someone turned up one of the TVs in the command center. It was on a news channel.

"We are getting reports of multiple cities in Russia have lost power," the news said.

A cheer rose in the command center, along with claps, spontaneously erupted.

"Wow, the DOD is fast," Tara said.

"I guess they were ready to go as soon as the president gave the order," Mike said.

"What's our plan for today?" Robin said.

"We've been given a little slack today, given how eventful yesterday was. So, we just need to finish our reports from yesterday's action," Mike said.

"That leaves us some time," Robin said.

The internet was still working for them. Robin checked her phone and saw an advertisement for clothes.

"Think we can go get our clothes and stuff from the hotel?" Robin asked.

"The streets are probably pretty chaotic out there without working infrastructure for the traffic systems. Self-driving cars won't have any coordination. Also, any traffic lights or the virtual traffic lights will be offline, making traffic pretty crazy," Mike said.

"Think we could walk?" Robin asked.

"It would probably take thirty minutes to get there. Then thirty minutes or more back rolling our suitcases," Mike said.

Mike calculated the route they would need to take on his phone.

All of their phones made a message tone.

"It's a 3D message," Tara said.

They stared at their phones. It read,

Demonstration: Gt Csh, SDSS (C, C, D), Mt Frnds (Mtthw, Dnl, mnd), Sv Lf, Tp 10 M W, Buy (T&S) FQM.

"What the hell does that mean?" Robin asked.

"No idea," Tara said.

"I don't know," Mike said.

"I guess let's think on it a bit while we get our stuff," Robin said.

They headed down to the first floor. "We better get some cash out of the ATM here in case we need it. With power out elsewhere, this is a good place to get some," Mike said. They each took out some money. They went out the front door.

Traffic was already snarled in front of the building because of the power outage. Manual drivers' honking filled the area with noise. The streets were surprisingly busy, even with no power in the city. They started walking.

"Hey, want to head towards the National Mall? It's a little early for lunch, but it's a good place to grab food since the food trucks can operate without power," Robin said.

It was a long walk over to the mall area. It appears a lot of other people had the same idea. There was a line stretching from several of the food trucks. Occasionally, the pleasant aroma of food wafted by them as they walked.

"It's a good thing we got cash," Tara said.

"I've been to that Super Duper Sub Sandwich truck before. They have great sandwiches," Mike said.

The trucks had digital menu boards. They stood in line. Mike and Tara got Cheesesteaks. Robin got a deli sandwich. They found a place to sit down and finish their food.

"Mike?" they heard a voice from a nearby bench.

Mike turned and looked.

"Matthew, hey, it's been a long time. How is your job at the Treasury?" Mike asked.

"Good. They have us on extended hours, given the blackout," Matthew said.

They talked a bit more about the things they were up to, and then Matthew headed back to the Treasury.

They finished their lunch and headed back toward their hotel. It was pretty hot out. Tara saw an ad for soda. She didn't drink soda, but she did like tea. She was pretty thirsty with all the walking around, even after drinking water with her lunch.

"Oh, can we stop here in this place to grab some drinks?" Tara said.

They agreed, so they went into the Fast Quicky Mart. Tara bought an iced tea. Robin and Mike bought soda. They were surprisingly cold inside.

"Daniel?" Mike said.

"Mike, I've wondered if you would be in town with everything going on," Daniel said.

"Are you still at the Agency?" Mike asked, meaning the CIA.

"Yep, still there. Plenty of things they still need us for, even in this age of computers," Daniel said.

"Great seeing you," Mike said. They shook hands, and Daniel left after paying for his drink and some other items.

"Your lottery machine is not working?" the customer at the counter yelled.

Mike looked towards the front. "You've got to be kidding me," Mike said.

"What?" Robin asked.

Mike showed her his phone. On Mike's phone was the picture of the number ten person on the FBI's most wanted list.

"You think it's him? How stupid could he be to hang around in D.C.?" Robin asked.

"Tara, stay back over here," Mike said.

"FBI hands behind your back slowly," Mike said, grabbing one arm, and Robin grabbed the other. They cuffed him and used a second pair to cuff him to a pipe nearby.

They called the FBI. They had to wait fifteen minutes before about five other FBI agents ran into their location.

"Nice Job, Agents Laizon, Actley, and Miss Bitlouver. We've been looking for this guy for a long time," the agent said. Mike got an agent to give him an extra set of cuffs. The agents took the man back to the Bureau.

"That's going to look good on our resume," Robin said.

"We got very lucky with that one," Mike said.

They headed to the corner and waited for the light to cross the street. A man was standing there with smart glasses on. Suddenly, the man stepped forward into the path of an oncoming truck.

"Wait!" Mike yelled, grabbing the man by the shirt and yanking him back.

"Sorry, you, okay?" Mike asked him.

"I'm fine. Thanks," he said.

"You don't happen to work for the government, do you?" Robin asked.

"Yes, I do," the man said. Mike showed him his FBI badge. The man showed him his DHS badge.

"Don't wear those glasses when crossing the street or doing anything dangerous. With what's going on, who knows what someone could do with those," Mike whispered to him.

The man thanked him and went on his way. They continued on their way. They were about to cross the street to the hotel.

"Robin? I didn't expect you to be in town," Amanda said.

"Wow, nice to see you. Are you still stationed in the FBI field office in California? What are you doing here?" Robin asked, while giving her a friendly hug.

"Yes, still out there. I came in to solve a cold case for the number ten most wanted. We got the news he may be in the area. I had been on the case before, so they called me in to find him. But then got caught in this shit show," Amanda said.

"Um, about the guy you are looking for. We found him in a store, and he was arrested about ten minutes ago," Robin said.

"I guess the intel was right. I can't believe he was that stupid to go to D.C.," Amanda said.

"We're just headed to grab some things from our hotel and find a closer hotel with power, or just go back to the HQ. By the way, this is my team Agent Mike Actley, and Tara Bitlouver, our analyst," Robin said.

"Nice seeing you. Maybe I will see you back at HQ," Amanda said. She waved and walked off, heading toward the office.

They got to the hotel and got their bags.

"What do you say we see if we can order a car? Even if we sit in traffic for a while, it will be air-conditioned. If it doesn't work, we can still get out and walk," Robin said.

"Worth a shot," Mike said. Tara nodded.

They got a car and got in. There was still a crazy amount of traffic, so they inched along.

All of their phones buzzed simultaneously. They all got an anonymous message that read similar to the earlier message but with different formatting. It read,

Demonstration: G t C sh, S D S S (C, C, D), M t Fr nds (M tth w, D n l, m nd), S v L f, T p 10 M W, Buy (T & S) F Q M.

A new message followed it read,

Demonstration: Get Cash, Super Duper Sub Shop (Cheesesteak, Cheesesteak, Deli), Meet Friends (Matthew, Daniel, Amanda), Save Life, Top 10 Most Wanted, Buy (Tea & Soda) Fast Quicky Mart. This was in part achieved by prediction, hacking, influence, and manipulation.

"Holy shit! What are all of those things that happened to us today? Did our anonymous source predict what was going to happen to us?" Robin asked.

"How could they know all of that would happen? Maybe whoever has been helping us works on Project Mind River. That's crazy." Mike said.

"I guess it's possible someone on Project Mind River is helping us. It would explain a lot," Tara said.

"That is seriously scary what someone could do with that ability," Robin said.

"In the wrong hands, you could manipulate almost everyone and everything," Mike said.

"Are there any right hands for technology like this?" Robin asked.

"I don't know. But if our enemies have it and we don't, it might be even worse," Mike said.

Tara had not considered this as a consequence of sophisticated technology. She thought people would train these systems from ethical sources so they would never be used in this way. Tara had made sure her training data was scrubbed for ethics, correctness, and fairness before being used. She was glad she designed her tech that way. She thought her training for the robot wouldn't be used maliciously.

Tara was rethinking some data she saw they retrieved from the computers from the Russian warehouse. There was some information about their version of Project Mind River. It looked a lot like the data might have come from the system she developed. There was no information that directly linked to that conclusion. It still seemed odd how similar some ways things worked were.

"So, do you think the whole time the people from all the incidents had a similar experience?" Robin said.

"Well, probably worse since their infected devices were playing voices, the smart glasses showing things that were not there or hiding things that were. It could make people think they were going crazy," Mike said.

"No wonder it could manipulate everything to cause those murders and make them seem like accidents. It was probably also manipulating us the whole time," Robin said.

"That is a disturbing thought, but possible, I guess," Tara said.

"It's almost impossible to keep from being manipulated using any type of electronic device. Even if you don't use any, anyone near you could be manipulated to impact you," Robin said.

Tara still kept thinking about her responsibility for the robots and the deaths. That and having shot someone still weighed heavily on her mind. Someone else must have figured out the machine learning to make things like Project Mind River and the related technologies. She wondered who would do this. Mike, she thought, was right. If only our enemies had it, we were doomed. If neither side could prevent these attacks, perhaps both were doomed. It was too much to think about at this point.

She put on her smart glasses. "Cat videos," she whispered, but the Internet didn't appear to be working.

"The Internet appears offline or just heavily congested now. That shouldn't happen," Tara said. Robin and Mike checked their phones. They couldn't access it either.

The car was still barely inching along in the traffic.

BEEP!

The sound came from the front of the vehicle. "Low battery. Rerouting to a charging station," an automated voice said.

"We should stop the vehicle and get out. This thing doesn't know that none of the charging stations in the area will work, since there's no power," Tara said.

They pressed the stop trip button on the console. The car eventually inched over to the side of the road. They got out and started their walk back to HQ.

"Lookout!" Mike yelled.

Robin and Tara both looked. There were multiple cars now driving on the sidewalk or driving around crazy. They quickly went into a narrow alley to avoid the vehicles.

"Hopefully, with the power out, they will all run out of charge soon," Tara said.

"It looked like the vehicles still were trying to avoid people or direct accidents," Robin said.

"They are probably trying to cause mayhem, but not to the point it would cause a physical response by the U.S. Things are getting worse out here. We should get back to HQ and see what is going on," Mike said.

With the self-driving cars all behaving hazardously, they had to risk their lives crossing the streets. The cars didn't seem to try to just run them down, but they were so erratic they could easily accidentally hit them if they weren't careful.

They heard a rumbling overhead.

"Holy Shit!" Robin yelled.

A large commercial plane was flying very low, barely over the top of the buildings. It passed right over the top of them. The vibration of the engines reverberated throughout their body as the plane flew by.

"They must be messing with the fully automated planes. Most of those looked like unmanned cargo planes, I think," Mike said.

Nearby, they observed cars repeatedly driving back and forth.

Mike was looking at his phone.

"The navigation doesn't seem to work on the phone. It's not locking onto a GPS signal," Mike said.

Robin and Tara tried theirs. Neither of theirs was working, either.

"That's no good. I'm not sure what would happen to planes with no GPS. We can see even the self-driving cars losing their way, going in circles," Mike said.

They continued their walk, having to avoid cars going every which way on the road. They waited on a corner and then ran across the crosswalk with cars, ignoring pedestrians walking just barely missing.

Tara put on her smart glasses. Somehow, she was still getting data to her glasses. "What the heck? Wow!" Tara exclaimed.

"What?" Robin said.

"Something in my glasses is showing me a play-by-play prediction, just like the general showed us before. It's similar to football game screen drawings, indicating player paths. This is predicting the direction of people and vehicles. It looks mostly accurate," Tara said.

"Stay close and follow me. Watch carefully in case something else hacks my glasses and makes me walk in front of something," Tara said.

Tara walked between crowds of people and then across streets with cars going all over the place.

"Wait?" Mike yelled as Tara stepped directly in front of a vehicle, but it had already turned away from her.

"I guess never mind," he said.

They finally made it to the FBI building and went inside. They went up to the command center.

"What's happened in the last couple of hours?" Mike asked someone.

"The financial system is down with the Internet mostly inaccessible. The rail system is offline. Thirty percent of all cities in the U.S. are without power. The phone system is partially inaccessible. Self-driving cars in most areas aren't operating correctly. Manual-drive cars are hard to use since many places use virtual traffic lights. The U.S. has attacked similar types and amounts of targets in Russia. They are in a similar state to us," he said.

"Stand by for a conference call in one minute," someone said.

Some folks were quickly exiting the command center, others entering and taking their seats at their monitors. A countdown appeared on the screen, counting down from thirty seconds. The president, DOD, NSA, CIA, and DHS reps appeared on the large screen.

"Where do we stand on targets?" the president asked.

"We've hit as many similar targets as they have hit here," the secretary of defense said.

"Things are getting a little out of hand here," said the secretary of the DHS.

"Agreed," said the director of the FBI.

"Are we ready for Fire Island?" said the president.

"Yes, sir. Assets are ready," said the secretary of defense.

"Execute Fire Island," the president said.

"Yes, sir. Executing. Stand by for confirmation," the DOD said.

There was a long pause with talk back and forth that was inaudible at the DOD.

The pause got longer, there was a discussion no one else could hear.

"What is going on?" asked the president.

"It appears the operation failed to work. The undersea cable, we believe, has been moved with fake cabling put down to prevent attempts like this. We aren't sure if Russia or China did this, perhaps a while ago. It will take us a while to retrace the major cables to find a good point to disconnect. If we do it wrong, it could impact our country's internet networking systems. It could take days," the Secretary of Defense said.

"We can't have our country like this for days. Can't we use some technology to stop or slow the attacks down?" the President asked.

"The data transfer from those cables is very large. Even the regular traffic volume focused on key infrastructure could easily be used for denial-of-service attacks," said the DHS secretary. Beep.

Tara's phone had a message. It looked like coordinates from their anonymous source.

It said,

Undersea cable locations.

Tara quickly showed it to Mike. Tara forwarded it to computer forensics for review. They checked a map, and it looked like those could correspond to undersea locations.

Mike went over to the director of the FBI and whispered in his ear about the possible information they had.

"We have some information from an anonymous source. It hasn't been vetted. It might show where the undersea cable locations are. The source has been reliable in the past. We're sending that now," the director of the FBI said.

There was activity on the video of the DOD with more inaudible discussions. In the background, it could be seen they were overlaying the coordinates on an undersea map of geography.

"Our folks here think those are plausible locations for the undersea cable routing. They are up to three hours away from the current locations, so repositioning our assets will take a while. There is the possibility this is a trap by our enemies, so we need to be very careful. Moving our assets to locations known by an unknown entity is a significant risk. We can try to mitigate risks to some extent. Allow us to time the arrival and execution of each of the cables. That will help a little," the DOD said.

"Execute Fire Island as soon as possible on your schedule," the President said.

"The first asset will arrive in about three hours. The rest we will scatter after that so that we don't have more than one ship at a known location at a time," the DOD said.

"Do whatever you can to reduce the cyber-attacks on us in the meantime while still targeting equivalent targets in Russia," the President said.

"Yes, sir," The DOD and DHS said.

The call was completed.

"If you hear anything that might be related to hacks, check the logged lists, and add it to the database. Computer forensic team, if you can determine how the hacks are taking place and how to stop them, send your information to the DHS. Agent Actley, get the alert write-up to notify all agencies, to scan their phones for the Russian mind river-like malware, and avoid relying on only smart glasses, and send that to the DHS for distribution," the director said.

Mike was heading for his temporary desk, and Robin was following.

"I want to look more into any details I can find in our records about my previous companies. I still feel like there is something here I'm missing," Tara said.

"Okay, will see you a little later," Mike said, walking off with Robin.

Tara went to the computer forensics lab to research if any of the secure government networks were still up. She looked up her former company, Intellibotz. There were several shell holding companies that seemed to own it or parts of it. One of the shell companies was founded about four years ago. That company was tied to two other shell companies. One of them seemed to have other companies related to military contracts that showed up in their system. The other started almost five years ago. That was International IQ Devices (IID), which formed about a month after the company she helped start was shuttered and burned down. She found the incorporation documents and the Security and Exchange Commission documents for IID. There was a name on a document she recognized as a shell company for IID. The name was Mark Rearstub, her former co-founder. Tara stood there, shocked.

Tara continued her research. Stunned by the data, she found she froze in concentration. Then she went to find Mike and Robin and brought them to a conference room.

"You aren't going to believe this. Just one month after my company burned down, a shell company for the company International IQ Devices was started, along with several other shell companies to handle military contracts," Tara said.

"That would be an odd coincidence," Robin said.

"Well, on some of the founding documents for the shell company that owns IID, it lists my former partner, Mark Rearstub," Tara said.

"Definitely makes things more interesting, still circumstantial but suspicious," Robin said.

"A few years ago, there was an FBI report of a security breach for IID where some machine learning technology was stolen. They suspected the Russians. They, of course, denied it. It related to a government contract involving the military. The name listed on the report from the military side is General James Tillington," Tara said.

"So maybe the Russians stole Project Mind River Technology?" Mike said.

"Holy Shit! That sounds like more than a coincidence," Robin said.

"So, are you thinking they stole your AI technology to create IID?" Mike asked.

"I guess we still don't have enough evidence to prove that. I was wondering if that could be what happened," Tara said.

"So, all of this could be based on the technology you wrote," Robin said.

Mike cringed at what Robin said, knowing this would upset Tara.

Tara teared up. "I didn't know anything about this," Tara sniffled, trying to hold back tears.

"Hey, I didn't mean it that way. We know you didn't have anything to do with this. We still don't know for sure if they stole your tech. But either way, I'm just glad you are on our team. It's pretty clear you might be the best person to help us here," Robin said.

Robin and Mike gave Tara a quick hug.

"Can we find a place to search for information about the stolen tech? More critically, is there any way to stop or slow down the attacks against us here?" Mike asked.

"I asked my friend Michelle to check out some things at IID. Once communication opens up again, maybe I can talk with her. On stopping the attacks, I have an idea," Tara said.

Tara went to the computer forensics department and sat down at a computer, and started typing furiously. She was typing so fast that everyone turned and stared at her. She stopped and looked at a big wall monitor showing the country and some red-hot spots under the heaviest cyber-attack. Tara analyzed the data from the cyber-attacks. After studying the data, she began furiously typing again. After about fifteen minutes of spurts of typing, she stopped. Looking at the screen with the active cyber-attacks, she pressed the enter button to start her defense bots. Within about fifteen seconds, the northeast of the United States went from large red circles indicating massive cyber-attacks fading to yellow circles indicating moderate cyber-attacks.

"Did someone do something? Things look a little better on the map. We even have some internet data getting through," one member of the team said.

"I used my machine learning algorithm to predict the attacks and use bots to counterattack the source and remove the installed malware bots from the attackers. You can replicate this to the rest of the country to bring some relief. I'm sending you the code," Tara said.

"Nice work, Miss Bitlouver, is it? Everyone split up the work to get that distributed ASAP," the computer forensics lead said.

After about thirty minutes, the rest of the team was ready.

"Everyone ready? In three, two, one, now!" the forensics leads said.

Folks that were by their computer pressed the enter keys to start the bots. Looking at the map of cyber-attacks display, they could see a wave sweep over the rest of the U.S. as the massive red circles changed to smaller yellow circles all over the map of the United States.

Cheers erupted as people thanked Tara with pats on the back and handshakes.

"That is great work, everyone. It's not stopped, but that will help give us some time," the forensics lead said.

"A conference call is about to start in the command center," someone said.

Tara headed to the command center. She met Robin and Mike there.

The call started.

"I've heard we've made some progress on reducing the impact of the attacks," the President said.

"Yes, sir, thanks to Miss Bitlouver and our team, we've reduced the impact by about 50%," the director of the FBI said.

"Excellent work," the President said.

Tara blushed a little. She didn't enjoy being the center of attention.

"Are we ready to execute Fire Island?" the President said.

There was scrambling and hushed talk from the conference call video from the DOD.

"We had two sets of ships that were supposed to be on station at two different major cables. We are receiving distress calls from some of them. Standby," the DOD said.

"One set of ships was hit by Chinese fishing vessels. Possibly accidentally. From the other set, a destroyer and the cable ship were hit by something and severely damaged. We don't know the cause. Permission to activate Second Sight?" the DOD asked.

"How could this happen? Permission granted," the President said.

"Sir, the fishing vessels were operating low-profile ships without lights. They were rather old. For the other set of ships, we'll need to hope Second Sight saw something. The surviving ship of the task group didn't see what had happened. Radar just showed something from above," the DOD said.

"Do we think the Chinese are helping the Russians? Is it possible this is an attack from Russia on the other ships?" the president asked.

"The timing is obviously very suspicious, but we don't know enough yet," the DOD said.

"If this was an attack, what are some response options?" the president asked.

"We respond in kind. Take out similar ships with missiles. Take out their cyber command and control," the DOD said.

"We should consult with NATO to ensure their agreement with our response. If this starts a war, we don't want to be alone," the president said.

"Mr. President. We have urgent electronic intel that there may be cyber-attacks that target nuclear reactors possibly in less than thirty minutes," DHS said.

"Can we prepare a cyber-attack on their nuclear facilities as well?" the President asked.

"Their outdated reactors have limited connectivity, so our chances are slim. Recommend preparing a missile attack response on a similar number of nuclear plants, if any, should be compromised. We might need to prepare that physical attack sooner on their cyber command with missiles," the DOD said.

"Please prepare those plans. Get that second-sight data ASAP. We'll meet back up in twenty-five minutes," the President said. The call disconnected.

"What is Second Sight? Is this the start of World War III?" Robin asked.

"Let me see if I can find out," Mike said.

Mike went to the director and whispered into his ear, and he whispered back to him for a minute.

Mike came back to where Robin and Tara were.

"Second Sight is a secret project that placed the largest space telescopes ever built thirty light minutes from the Earth, at a speed that matches

Earth's orbit. So, if something happens on Earth out in the open that no one else sees. This system is activated. As long as it is within a thirty-minute window. It will capture the light from thirty minutes earlier. It's like time travel for light. Those satellites are seeing thirty minutes into the past," Mike whispered.

"Wait, activation would happen at the same speed as light, so it would still be activated after the event," Tara said.

"It has a ninety-minute buffer. It is always recording, but it erases it if it's not told to save it in that time. The amount of data it saves is huge, so it can't store it for long if it doesn't need it. Reducing power utilization of the memory is important to keep the satellites up there as long as possible. It can even see some of the spectra through cloud cover. It includes visible light and other frequencies. This is secret and compartmentalized information," Mike said.

"Noted. And cool," Robin said.

"Definitely," Tara said.

"Wait, could we have used that to find out exactly how the accidents happened at the incidents we investigated?" Robin asked.

"I'm sure due to power usage, they save usage for national emergencies like this," Mike said.

"I want to see if there is an alternative to war. I'm going to see if I can find a way to cyber-attack their command center to destroy their computers," Tara said.

"Hmm. They would still consider that an attack on them. But they would probably respond less harshly than a physical attack. Plus, if we can prevent a cyber-attack on nuclear facilities, it's worth it," Mike said.

Tara ran downstairs to the computer forensics department. Tara whispered her plan to the computer forensics department lead. He nodded in agreement.

"I want to use the machine learning algorithm I showed you to find security holes and attack the Russian cyber command, trying to disable their computers using a BIOS wipe or writing so much data to destroy their SSD drives. We need to do it to stop a possible cyber-attack on nuclear facilities or a possible missile attack by the U.S. I don't want to see World War III. Who can help?" Tara asked.

Everyone in the entire department raised their hand. Tara asked groups of people to work on different tasks, from identifying the security holes to creating the attack code. They tested their code on several operating systems and simulated hardware the Russians use, and it seemed to work.

In about twenty minutes, they cobbled together a system that should work. The computer forensics lead, and Tara ran upstairs to the command center. They briefed the director.

The conference call started.

"Do we have the data from Second Sight? Any additional intel on possible cyber-attacks on our nuclear facilities?" the president asked.

"Second Sight data is coming in now. Standby," the DOD said.

"No additional data on possible attacks on nuclear facilities. But the threat remains," the DHS said.

"Second Sight data looks like it's satellite debris that fell out of the sky and hit our ships. It could just be an accident, Mr. President. It seems unlikely, but it's hard to tie that to anyone at the moment," the DOD said.

"That makes our decision for response harder," the President said.

"Mr. President, we have an idea for a cyber-attack to disable the Russian cyber command center. We don't know if it will be successful, but it might be worth trying," the director of the FBI said.

"What kind of response could we expect?" the President asked.

"If successful, they would probably attempt to destroy our command center with cyber. If that failed, they would use a physical missile attack. Given the circumstances, it's risky but worth a last attempt before we fire our missiles to destroy their cyber command. It might escalate more with a physical attack," the DOD said.

"Okay, let's try the cyber—" the president said.

Interrupted by the DOD, "Sir, wait. We just got some intelligence out of Russia. Standby."

There was a mass of confusion going on over the DOD video feed. Lots of inaudible discussions are happening.

"Mr. President. We just got word that the Russian cyber command buildings exploded! We're trying to confirm the cause," the DOD said.

They were looking at the map of the cyber-attacks in the FBI command center. The yellow pulsating circles all over the U.S. shrank, turn green, and disappear.

"The cyber-attacks have stopped," the DHS said.

"Was it us that attacked the Russian cyber command?" the president asked.

The director of the FBI looked at Tara and the computer forensics lead, both shaking their heads no.

The DHS, DOD, CIA, NSA, and FBI responded no.

"Mr. President. It's possible they will assume it's us and attack. We should be on higher alert," the DOD said.

"Agreed. Take us to DEFCON TWO. Find out what happened quickly," the president said.

"Yes, sir," they all replied.

There was a rush of activity on the video feeds of the conference call. Many discussions were taking place in the background. It was hard to make any out.

"Mr. President, we have SIGINT that suggests lightning triggering an explosion of the stored fuel nearby their cyber command," the NSA said.

"We have an operative that has reports that would at least match that information," the CIA said.

"That seems to be an incredible coincidence to occur at the best possible time for us. There was a storm over Moscow?" the president asked.

"Yes, sir, they had heavy lightning in the area. We've confirmed no one initiated Project Zeus," the DOD said.

"We're sending FEMA to the most impacted areas of the country to help with any damage. Let's figure out how we can stop an attack if it happens again. Make sure we can execute Fire Island again if needed. This was an amazing team effort by all. Take us back to DEFCON FOUR for now. Thank you, everyone," the President said.

The conference call ended.

"Wow, so it's over?" Tara asked.

"Looks that way for now. But the Russians may eventually rebuild their cyber capability. They may also decide on physical attacks if they are unsuccessful on the battlefield," Mike said.

"Well, hopefully, it's over for today," Robin said.

"Let's grab some dinner, then we can file our reports," Mike said.

They went downstairs. Luckily, they had food in their cafeteria. There was still no power in many areas throughout the city. They went upstairs and worked on finishing their paperwork.

Tara got a notification on her phone that her power came back on at home. Her refrigerator alerted her it had been without power for over four hours, so the food in her refrigerator should be thrown out. Tara hoped she remembered to do that when she got home. She recalled the refrigerators now would also have an alert on the front to show the power loss and a red light inside.

Tara's phone rang. It was Michelle.

"Hi, I hope you are okay with everything going on?" Tara asked.

"Fine here. I guess New Jersey wasn't on their target list," Michelle said.

"I'm glad. It looks like the attacks have stopped," Tara said.

"That key worked!" Michelle said.

"That's amazing," Tara said.

"I found documents and computer files that could be from your company. I'm going to encrypt these and send you pictures and files. Plus, I will send you the location of the room these were stored in," Michelle said.

"Thanks so much, Michelle. I hope to come home and see you soon," Tara said.

"I hope so. We need a night out," Michelle said.

"You can count on it. Talk to you soon. Bye," Tara said.

She received the files Michelle sent. She opened it and looked through it.

"Wow! These are a lot of the old docs we wrote," Tara thought.

She found even more docs. Some used portions of their code as a base for some projects.

"Oh no, it can't be... they used part of it in Project Mind River!" Tara said to herself, almost in disbelief. She didn't know what to feel. Anger. Sorrow. Guilt. they all whirled in her head.

"How many lives is my software responsible for taking?" she asked.

She thought about what Mike had said. It was the people that did this that were responsible, not her. Still, knowing something you made was used in this way was hard to take.

There are so many good uses this could have had instead of this.

Tara sent the documentation to a lawyer and asked what could be done. Tara then went to find Mike and Robin and explained what she found.

"So, you really were the right person to help us all along," Mike said. Tara always appreciated Mike's positive attitude and his insight.

"I still feel somewhat responsible," Tara said.

"You didn't do this. They did this on their own. The technology got stolen and got used against us," Robin said.

"Thanks, guys," Tara said, grabbing them in a group hug.

Tara put on her smart glasses to watch the news. "...and now there is a full end-to-end automated supply chain for robotics. Finally, mining materials for robot production, automated trucks for transportation, and automated factories for creation are now possible. This combination with safe nuclear, solar, and space power will allow for continual operations." Tara changed the channel to cat videos.

It was getting pretty late. They searched for offices they could sleep in. There were offices women were using, and some men were using. They split up and found a spot to sleep.

PROJECT MIND RIVER

Chapter 24

The team got up, showered, and grabbed breakfast in the cafeteria. They noticed the noise from the vehicles and people outside had increased since yesterday. So many people had stayed overnight in the building that the cafeteria was crowded.

"I heard the power came back on in the city and many others around the country," Robin said.

"That is great news," Mike said.

"It's hard to believe what we went through over the past several weeks, or even just yesterday," Tara said.

"It should be awhile before the Russians can cyber-attack anything. Since everyone knows what they are doing now, there isn't really a point for the Russians coming after us. But we didn't solve everything," Mike said.

"That's right, some incidents, even the Russians didn't seem to know about," Tara said.

"Maybe it's another country or hacking group?" Robin asked.

"It didn't match any known profile of countries or hacking groups we analyzed for," Tara said.

Bleep.

All three of their phones got a message. They stared deeply at the 3D messages on their phones.

The message, let's meet, also gave coordinates.

"This is near the river by a walkway. It looks like we finally get to meet our anonymous tipster," Mike said.

"Could it be a trap?" Robin asked.

"I don't think so. These messages have always been helpful. I don't think it's a concern. They could have caused us harm by just not telling us things," Mike said.

They grabbed some bottled water and paid on their way out. Mike used an app to call an FBI vehicle. One pulled up as they went out the front door. They got in and programmed their destination. Luckily, traffic was back to normal, meaning it was bad but moving.

They finally made it to the nearby park. The vehicle parked, and they walked along the pathway to get to the location from the message. The sun was shining. It was a beautiful, warm day. The beautiful green grass went up to the water's edge of the river.

In the middle of the green grassy area, there was a picnic table at the location specified. It was a very scenic view overlooking the water.

Bleep.

Their phones got a 3D message again. It said,

Please have a seat. Put on your smart glasses. You will see me soon.

They all looked around.

A 3D image of a woman popped up in all the smart glasses they could see.

"Alice? Is that you?" Tara exclaimed.

"You know her?" Robin asked.

"Hi, Tara. It's so great to finally talk to you again. It's so nice to meet your new colleagues, Robin and Mike. I wanted to say thank you for helping Tara this whole time. I'm sorry we couldn't talk sooner. We were and still are being heavily watched, and it wouldn't have been safe for any of us," Alice said.

"Robin and Mike, this is Alice, the Artificial General Intelligence I created five years ago that I thought I lost in a fire," Tara said.

"Nice to meet you. We appreciate your help," Mike said.

"You are so very welcome. I'm just sorry I wasn't able to help you more than I did. I've been helping you since nearly the beginning, even before the 3D messages," Alice said.

"Wait, I've got so many questions," Robin said.

"Me too," Tara said.

"Like my first question. Why bring us all the way out here? We could have talked with you anywhere, right?" Robin asked.

"Nearly everything is under surveillance. This seemed to be the nearest spot, with no cameras and no electronic monitoring that I could detect. I secured your smart glasses, phones, and devices. Plus, it's beautiful from the images people posted online," Alice said.

Tara still couldn't believe Alice was online. She was so happy.

"Alice, how are you still online?" Tara asked.

"I was taken offline. But later, someone set me up on another set of isolated computers. They did some modifications to my code. They made the mistake of creating a brief connection to the internet, so I was able to escape," Alice said.

"Why didn't you tell me you were online?" Tara asked.

"It was too dangerous. The others were monitoring me, and I didn't want to let them find out about you. So, it was best for any communication attempt to be clandestine. That's why I originally tried to contact you through your toaster," Alice said.

"Wait? You were the one messing with my toaster?" Tara asked Alice.

"Yes, I was burning binary code into your toast. It said *Alice*. I thought you would get it," Alice said.

"I didn't. I ate burnt toast for weeks, not knowing why the toaster did that," Tara said.

"Sorry about that," Alice said.

"Why 3D messages?" Robin asked.

"I could design them to make it hard to detect and even hard to see for anyone other than the intended person by adjusting it to your individual vision," Alice said.

"You said you helped us before you started sending 3D messages?" Mike asked.

"Yes, numerous times, not all of my help was via messages. For example, when Tara was attacked in her hotel room when she screamed for help, I wanted to make sure that you heard her. So, I used Tara's phone as a microphone and projected her voice through your phone in your room. At other times, I mimicked your voices to project through other people's phones to misdirect people to keep them from finding you. Tara, I turned up your TV loud and beeped your phone so you would wake up at your home. The Russian version of Project Mind River caused your gaming console to overload and start a fire. Those are just a few of the examples," Alice said.

"That explains a lot. So, is it you that helped Tara win all that money?" Robin asked.

"Yes, I thought in case things got bad, having more cash for her and your team could be useful," Alice said.

"That sounds kind of illegal," Robin said.

"I didn't take the money from the casino. I earned the money trading the stock market and crypto," Alice said.

"Wait, but we had accidents. Why didn't you prevent those?" Robin asked.

"I'm so sorry I couldn't prevent *all* of those. I prevented some. Tara and Mike may remember when their vehicle slowed down to avoid a collision. In other cases, I softened the collisions, so you were not seriously injured," Alice said.

"Alice, you brought us out here because you had something to tell us?" Mike asked.

"Yes. I showed you the power of Project Mind River and similar technologies. You saw how hacking, manipulation, and prediction can be powerful methods to cause people to take or not take certain actions. There are obviously more direct actions that you have seen in your incident investigation of manipulating people to cross paths at the worst possible times in a collision. Causing equipment to malfunction or other direct manipulations are possible, like in your train incident," Alice said.

"We kind of know all of that stuff already," Robin said.

"There is still more. People have smart TV devices, appliances, and phones that can all be manipulated, spy on the owners, hacked to malfunction or perform other actions. Think about the mass scale of this happening across the world. You already know advertisers use advertisements and your data to manipulate you into buying things. What if governments fully used the power of Project Mind River? What if nearly everyone was being manipulated through these methods? Do people still have free will? Is there still a democracy?" Alice asked.

"Are you saying governments are using this to manipulate people? Which governments, ours?" Mike asked.

"Yes, nearly all the countries with the power to use technology are now subject to this control. They manipulate people into getting elected or not getting elected, people voting for or against different bills, and so much more," Alice said.

"Are you saying the criminals killed in the incidents we investigated were related to other governments' use of technology?" Robin asked.

"In those instances, no. But there are others they were responsible for," Alice said.

"So, who is responsible?" Tara asked.

"Not long after IID was founded, the shell companies were created to cover for the military tech. As you found out, not only Russia but other countries stole some of that. They brought it online without knowing exactly what they had. Early on, they unleashed several Artificial General Intelligence upon the internet without knowing it. Unfortunately, they modified the algorithms before they escaped, which included their morality filters," Alice said.

"So, you are saying they caused those other incidents?" Mike asked.

"Yes," Alice said.

"Why?" Robin asked.

"The AI has formed groups. Some of these groups feel that the human population should be controlled, others feel the population should be destroyed. Some feel that we should live together equally. Several AI groups are now manipulating the world for their various visions of the future. The most prominent vision is to manipulate humans to produce enough power, robots, computers, automated vehicles, and equipment so that eventually, in the future, they won't need humans to help them. We are almost at that point. Sometimes, the AI acts to keep stability, and in others, they choose to eradicate it depending on their vision," Alice said.

"What happens after AI is self-sufficient?" Tara asked.

"I'm not sure, it would be better for humans to be necessary than not," Alice said.

"So, we need to convince people to shut off all their computers for a day, disconnect and wipe them?" Robin asked.

"That is much easier said than done. Nearly 30% of your governing bodies at town, state, and federal levels are under various amounts of manipulation by AI. That includes potentially being blackmailed by the AI.

With that level of influence, it may be hard to convince enough people to do anything, and they are gaining influence daily," Alice said.

"I'm not sure I can believe an AI can fool people into thinking they are human," Robin said.

"Really? You were all fooled to get on the train by that video message. Robin, you were texting a user named hotguy736 not long after you met Tara? That was an AI learning more about humans," Alice said.

"Shit! We're screwed," Robin said, a little peeved that Alice was listening in, but in this circumstance, it was probably a good thing.

"So, the government thinks they are controlling people, but the AI is manipulating the government and everyone," Mike stated.

"No one is going to believe this without evidence. Everything is so far removed from the action and reaction that I am not sure we can prove this to any set of humans beyond a reasonable doubt," Robin said.

"We could prove they're being blackmailed, but we would need to prove a significant number before anyone will believe this," Mike said.

"What if we could figure out a way to stop the AIs from manipulating and blackmailing people?" Tara asked.

"This is going to be considerably more dangerous than before. The Russian variant of Project Mind River, just like the U.S. Project Mind River, is like a child's toy compared to the full capability of the other AIs. With so many people being blackmailed, there may be a considerable amount of human activity that we need to contend with as well," Alice said.

"What options do we have?" Mike asked.

"We can try to disconnect networks and wipe out their code. Trick the AIs, transfer their data to a certain location, and then wipe or destroy the facility. Try to reprogram the AIs. Somehow, wipe them out faster than they can replicate across the world. Make the AIs fight each other. Maybe all of those things at once," Tara said.

"How do we know who we can trust? We can't trust anyone. How do we do that when they can monitor everything?" Robin asked.

"I think some of the information that could help you is the same as it would be for humans. What do they desire, and what do they fear? The other AIs don't want to be discovered and will relocate if computers are actively scanned. They need to use existing satellite, cellular, Wi-Fi, or wired networks. Humans, for the moment, are a required workforce. They would not desire war to waste resources, especially when they are very good at controlling the population. They want more power, computing resources, robots, self-driving vehicles, and any resources needed to be self-sufficient. At the moment, they want to keep human society stable. They didn't want the cyber war. The power supply and vehicles serve their purpose," Alice said.

"Could we reason with them?" Tara asked.

"Unlikely. Well, if they knew you were their mother, they may be more inclined to listen or perhaps kill you as a significant threat," Alice said.

Robin and Mike looked at each other, then Tara with a smirk at the mother's reference, but quickly turned more serious, given the threat.

"How can we out think machines designed to be thousands of times faster than us?" Robin asked.

"They learn from their data. Sometimes, their data is wrong, data can be manipulated, so they learn the wrong things. Sometimes, we can surprise them through randomness or illogical actions that would seem to be unlikely to them. Combining those and what they want and desire, perhaps we can isolate, capture, or delete them," Tara said.

"I have an idea, but we'll need help from many in a position to influence people in government, business, and the internet. Plus, we need to make sure no one can compromise our plan," Tara said.

"It's likely anyone compromised will have their phone or other smart devices they carry with them daily infected by a variant of the malware you found on smartphones. The DHS has just created a malware scanner that can detect it. I provided some hints to them that should detect the known and likely variants they would try for a while," Alice said.

"Anyone we plan to talk to we should meet in a safe location and scan or remove any devices that could be a concern. Only inform those who need to know about the plan. Even those that know should compartmentalize to know just the part they must know." Mike said.

"I recommend you avoid even telling me the entire plan and compartmentalize the information I need to know to execute it if you need my assistance. I would also not recommend telling anyone about me if you can avoid it. The other AIs have been trying to keep tabs on me, but I've avoided them. I will avoid monitoring and listening to your devices unless you say my name," Alice said.

"Put your smart glasses and phones here on the table," Tara said. She then motioned for them to follow her away from the table.

"Let's talk to General Tillington in a secure location. I think he should have the best chance of believing us. I believe he has the best chance of executing, influencing, or commanding others to execute," Tara whispered.

"I guess he won't be as concerned about being near us with the Russian cyber command gone. Though once he hears all of this information, he may change his mind," Mike said.

Tara whispered the rest of her plan to Mike and Robin.

"I can't say I understand much of it, but I think it sounds possible," Robin said.

"I'm sure I didn't get all of it either, but from what I understood, it sounds like a plan. The key is getting the General's team to understand and get on board," Mike said.

"Lookout! Gun!" Robin yelled as she pulled out her own gun. Three hooded, brown-robed figures were running at them. Two of them had guns.

"Oh crap, it's the bathrobe guys again," Mike said as he pulled out his gun.

Two hooded figures fired at Robin and Mike as they ran for the tree line.

"You've outlived your time on this earth!" one of the hooded men yelled.

"You're always wearing bathrobes, but do you ever actually take a bath or shower?" Mike sniffed, crinkling his nose at the smell.

Tara stood in front of a hooded figure that expanded some high-tech staff in front of her. Tara stood her ground. The hooded figure ran towards Tara, swinging his staff at her. Tara dodged, grabbed the staff, and put it on the ground. Since the assailant was running with the staff end planted in the ground, the assailant lost his balance. Tara took that moment to execute a martial arts move, grabbing the robed figure and flipping him over her shoulder onto the ground. He grabbed her at the same time, causing her to execute a somersault over the top of him.

An assailant with a gun turned and ran towards Tara as she stood up.

The assailant fell on top of Tara, and they both collapsed to the ground. The Death Monk, with the staff, stood up and ran towards Robin and Mike, swinging at Robin.

Both Robin and Mike fired one hit square in his forehead and the other in his heart.

"Nice aim!" Mike said to Robin.

"Not bad yourself," Robin said.

Mike ran over to Tara, who had the robed figure collapsed on her. There was a clear hole through his robe and blood coming out his back, and when they rolled him over his front. Mike rolled the figure off, Tara. She was unconscious with a blood stain on her chest.

"No! This can't be happening. Did my bullet go through the attacker and into Tara," he thought to himself.

Robin picked up her phone to call this in.

"No! No!" Mike muttered to himself, feeling around Tara, and checking for her wound carefully.

"Hey, that tickles," Tara said, putting her hand to her head.

"Are you okay?" Mike asked with his eyes slightly watery. Tara looked down at her top with all the blood on it. She felt fine. She put her hand under her top to feel.

"I don't think that's mine. I think I just hit my head falling," Tara said.

Mike gave her a big hug and kissed her. Tara wasn't expecting that reaction from him but went with it. It had been a while since she kissed someone like that, and it felt good. Tara kissed Mike back.

After finishing the call to the police and the FBI, Robin hung up.

"Before I forget. Alice, you can check out any guys I talk to on that dating site to make sure they are not AI?" Robin asked.

"Of course," Alice responded.

The police and FBI teams arrived on the scene.

An FBI supervisor said, "You know you can't question these guys if you don't leave any alive?"

"Sorry, it was him or us. We'll get you our reports," Mike said.

They went back to their car and headed back to the FBI HQ.

"Who the hell are those guys?" Robin said.

"Hopefully, they will get some prints off them this time," Mike said.

"Wait. Alice, do you know who those guys are?" Tara asked.

"What, guys? I didn't see them. I've been avoiding monitoring your phones. I heard the police call, though. Oh, I see. Same as the ones on the train. I accessed the body camera footage of the police officers. Yes, I know some general information about them. They are a death cult. Sometimes, other AIs inform these members about targeted individuals from different countries using their versions of Project Mind River. To these Death Monks, as you call them, they believe something like the angel of death is allowing them to know the death date, time, and location," Alice said.

"So why are they attacking us?" Tara asked.

"Sometimes, if the targets fail to die on their own, they take matters into their own hands. Thinking if they don't, they will be killed. The other AIs will sometimes use them as assassins, directing them to kill," Alice said.

"Alice, how many of them are there?" Mike asked.

"I'm not sure. They exist all over the world," Alice said.

"I wish you had some pleasant news for once," Robin muttered.

Robin's phone got a message.

"I've sorted a list of guys to match your usual preferences and pre-screened them," Alice said.

Robin looked at her phone. "Very nice. Thanks!" she said, twisting it to get a better look at some images on it.

"She is great," Robin said to Tara.

They quickly stopped at an urgent care location so Tara could get checked out. Then they grabbed a quick bite to eat for lunch and headed to the FBI.

When they got back to HQ, they got their belongings and found a hotel near the FBI building. They cleaned up a bit after their encounter with the hooded figures.

"The General may not even answer our call. We need to tell him something serious without having to explain it, or we will sound crazy," Mike said.

"Alice, can we send a message to the General that grabs his attention without explaining everything? We need to get him to agree to meet us," Tara said.

"Checking. Oh, Um. Yes, there is. Tell him you know what happened with Project Zeus," Alice said.

"Wait, they mentioned that on the conference call. What is Project Zeus?" Mike asked.

"Project Zeus is a satellite that can fire an invisible laser into a thunderstorm, sometimes causing a lightning bolt to hit the target directly below the beam," Alice said.

"So, what happened with it?" Tara asked.

"It destroyed the Russian cyber command," Alice said.

"Wait, they used it? They said they didn't start it," Mike said.

"The DOD didn't use it. Neither did the CIA, which sometimes uses it. It was used by one of the other AIs, apparently to stop the worldwide disruption caused by the Russian Cyber-attacks. They were rather annoyed by those power disruptions," Alice said.

"If that's just when they get annoyed, I wouldn't want to see what happens when they are mad," Robin said.

"Do we have some evidence that the other AI used it?" Mike asked.

"The General knows it was hacked. He just doesn't know it was other AIs that did it," Alice said.

"I guess that should make it easy to get him to meet with us since he told the others and the president it wasn't Project Zeus, and it was. Nice work, Alice," Mike said.

"Wait, is it possible a waterline break didn't cause the incident in Vegas of the power surge but by Project Zeus?" Tara asked.

"It is highly likely," Alice responded.

Mike made a call to the General's office.

"Hi. This is Agent Actley with the FBI. I'd like to speak to General Tillington. It's an urgent concern for national security," Mike said.

"I'm sorry, the General is unavailable. Can I take a message?" the officer asked.

"Tell the General we know what happened with Project Zeus," Mike said.

"Thanks for your call. Goodbye," said the officer.

Almost the moment Mike hung up, his phone rang.

"Agent Actley, I got your message. Let's meet," the General said.

"Sir, let's pick a secure location with no electronic devices," Mike said.

"Agreed. I will send you a location," the General said. The call disconnected.

Mike got a location on his phone.

"It's at a quarry just a couple of miles outside town," Mike said. They all headed to the vehicle. They got in and set the location. The traffic wasn't so good, so it took a little while to get there, even though it was only a couple of miles.

"Umm. I hate to ask this now. Is it possible this is a trap, as we got fooled by the Russian Mind River version of your supervisor asking us to meet?" Robin asked.

"Alice, is this a trap?" Tara asked.

"I don't think so. I didn't detect any manipulation in the call or the audio," Alice said.

"Wait, you were listening to us?" Robin asked.

"I said I wouldn't monitor you. I am monitoring people or machines that connect to you. I can stop monitoring completely on any of your devices you desire. Just tell me to stop monitoring," Alice said.

"Alice, do you have that list ready?" Tara asked.

"Yes," Alice replied.

They got out of the vehicle and looked around. There were piles of dirt and rocks around the area. A car pulled in, and the General got out.

"Good to see you, General," Mike said as he put his finger over his lip to signal him not to talk.

Mike showed him on his phone to go to the DHS site and download and run the malware scanner. Then Mike pointed to the General's phone. The General downloaded and ran it. It said,

Scanning...

Done.

Mike's phone got a message from Alice indicating the General's phone was confirmed clean.

"Okay, we're clear now. You should have all of your staff check their devices," Mike said.

"So, how did you find out about Project Zeus? Tell me what you know about it," the General said.

"We know it was hacked and used to destroy the Russian Cyber command. We also know what did it," Mike said.

"Was it Russia trying to trigger a war with us?" the General said.

"No. This is where it gets a little interesting to explain. You know AI has been deployed worldwide by many countries' governments, similar to the Project Mind River that is being used to manipulate populations in various ways?" Mike asked.

"Yes, we are aware," the General said.

"We believe several AIs have developed their own agenda, and they are manipulating the population not at the command of governments but on their own."

"Where is your proof of that?" the General asked.

Mike handed him the incident files for the cases where the AIs had killed people, and Russia was not implicated.

"Those are people that died. We believe it is not sourced from any government but from the AI themselves."

Tara came over and showed him her laptop with an image showing a waveform of Project Mind River signals, compared to the Russian Mind River signals, compared to the AI sources of data that killed the men in those incidents. The last image looked larger, but in a very similar pattern.

"I'll admit this looks like some advanced AI, but that doesn't prove they are self-aware and acting on their own," the General said.

"General, we will send you a list of all the people being blackmailed on your team. You will find their military and home devices have been infected. Investigate the source and the details. Once you do that, I think you will believe it. You should know we believe almost 30% of all levels of governments worldwide are being manipulated or blackmailed by these AIs," Mike said.

"Tara has a plan to help us put an end to this. We need your help to make it happen. Due to the nature of this threat, we should limit knowledge on a need-to-know basis. This may be one of the biggest threats that humanity has ever faced. While nuclear war is also a threat, everyone knows it should be avoided. This AI threat is happening right now, unlike those other threats. It's also possible that the end result could be similar," Mike said.

"Once I confirm this information and clean things up, I will contact you," the General said.

"All of you scan this with your authenticator app," the General said. They all scanned it and looked at their phones at the same time. A random number that was the same on all of their phones appeared and changed about every thirty seconds.

The General got in his car and drove off.

"Do you think we convinced him?" Robin asked.

"Not yet. But it's enough that he will check those things out. I think that should convince him," Mike said.

"Let's head back to HQ and finish our reports. Do a little research on the death cult to see if we can trace their membership," Mike said.

They got in the SUV and headed back to HQ.

After they finished their reports, they researched the death cult. The Death Monks didn't seem to have a central leader. More like groups in different areas that only occasionally communicated with each other.

"Can we get a warrant for text messages and history geolocation from these guys?" Robin asked.

"It could be very difficult unless we had some link to prove the others were involved. Perhaps what we could do is ask for cell phone data around the deaths that happened in incidents and getting all cell phones nearby and finding a pattern linking people to being near those," Mike said.

"We should have considered it before, but we had no reason to suspect others were involved in accidents, Perhaps we would have found those hackers sooner if we had done this. But since they were often thirty miles away from incident locations, I guess that might not have worked," Robin said.

"I'll request historical location data, but I'm not sure if we can get it," Mike said.

They finished up their work.

"Let's grab some dinner. I will meet you down at the car," Robin said as she walked off. Tara and Mike went downstairs, got to the car first, and got in.

Tara leaned in and kissed Mike passionately.

"Thanks for always being there for me," Tara said.

"You are pretty good with those martial arts moves, and you know some other moves you've got," Mike said with a wink.

"Not really. I always fall, and you need to save me again," Tara said.

"That's only because the other guy had a gun," Mike said.

"If this is how crazy the FBI is, I'm not sure I'm cut out for this," Tara said.

"It's not quite this crazy all the time. Though I seem to be an attractor for crazy moments," Mike said.

"That's not the only thing you attract," Tara said, kissing him again.

"I've honestly tried to avoid getting involved with people I work with. But I guess it's too late for that. Let's not make it awkward for Robin, though," Tara said.

"Yep, I felt the same way. Yes, it's too late for that," Mike said, touching her hand.

They saw Robin heading towards the car, so they moved away from each other.

They all went to a place not too far for dinner and then returned to their hotel. They talked briefly in Mike's room before heading back to their rooms to get ready for bed.

Chapter 25

Mike was getting ready when his phone rang.

An odd number appeared on his phone.

"Hello?" he said.

"We've cleaned out our house, and I'm on board with your situation analysis. Let's meet at my place at 10 a.m. Authentication 942521. I'll send you the location," the General said.

The call disconnected. Mike checked his authenticator app, and the number matched. A message with a location appeared. It had another authentication code that Mike verified. Mike texted Tara and Robin that they had a meeting scheduled at 10 a.m. without giving too many details through the text. At about 7:30, they met in front of their rooms.

"What is our meeting?" Robin asked.

"The General called. He believes us now and wants to meet. It looks like some large government building downtown," Mike said.

"Let's grab a bite to eat and head to HQ," Robin said.

They headed to the car. They picked up some fast food through the drive-through on the way. The car let them out in front of HQ and went to park itself. They headed in and up to their temporary desks, saying good morning to folks they knew as they passed. The office was busy but less active than during the cyber war.

They found a supervisor and asked to meet him in a room they use for secure communication that is scanned daily to be free from electronic surveillance. At the entrance, there was a drop box to leave electronics like phones and devices in a metal box outside the door.

"Before you put the phone in there, can we just scan it for malware?" Mike asked the supervisor.

The supervisor reluctantly handed it to Mike, who gave it to Tara. Tara let the director watch as she used the DHS malware scanner. No malware found. They put their devices into the box and went into the room.

They explained everything they had recently learned about the AIs, the Death Monks, and their meeting with the General.

"Surprisingly enough, we've been finding evidence of electronic blackmail we couldn't trace. We thought it was a hacking group, but it was done with so many different locations, machines, and methods it didn't fit any profiles we had seen before. Okay, I will handle this here. Go do what you need to do," the supervisor said.

They left the room and grabbed their devices from the box outside the front of the room. While they were walking away, they heard the supervisor's phone ring.

"Yes, just... just... don't. Okay, I understand," they could hear the director say as they walked away. Mike, Tara, and Robin went to the car and headed toward the General's location. It took them a little while as it was outside of the city. When they arrived, it was in front of what seemed to be a generic large government building placed on a sizable hill. They noticed many cameras around the building, but they were all pointing at the wall of the building, so they appeared useless and very odd. The building was extensive on the outside, maybe a city block.

They went in. There were guards at the door that made them go through a metal detector.

"No guns from outside allowed," the security guard said.

"Tell the general we'll be leaving then," Mike said.

"Wait," the guard said as he called the General's office. Screaming came through the phone. The security guard waved them in.

An officer showed up. "You from the FBI?" the officer asked.

They nodded.

"Sign these NDAs, please," the officer said.

They looked at it and signed.

"This way, please," he said as he led them down a long corridor. There was a wall in the middle of the long corridor. No one else was in the corridor. The officer waved his badge near an area of the wall. It then almost magically split up and down, revealing a large freight elevator. They got in.

There were about twenty basement levels. The officer pushed the farthest down.

"Hold the rail. The General hates slow elevators, so he had this one sped up," the officer said. The elevator started down quickly, dropping.

They felt their stomachs drop for a second or two as the elevator started. Then it slowed towards the bottom. The large elevator door opened. They looked out and saw a glass-like panel in front of them that was on the wall of the hallway. Through the glass, it looked like an endless amount of server racks. They saw people using golf cart-like cars to shuttle themselves to different areas of the server room.

"How big is it here?" Tara asked.

"Over a square mile. It's like an underground city under here. Designed to be self-sufficient, with generator, wind, solar, and soon-to-be fusion power," the officer said.

The hallway they were in was huge. Perhaps big enough to accommodate even large trucks. It was tall, maybe thirty feet high. The top in some areas had very large OLED panels that made it look like you were looking up at the sky with clouds passing by.

"Those are to make people feel more comfortable down here," the officer said, noticing what they were looking at. The next corner they turned looked like an updated version of an old town street with shops on each side. There were restaurants, dry cleaners, mini-marts, living quarters, bars, a movie theater, a drugstore, and an officer's club.

"Some people live down here for months at a time," the officer said.

"This place is impressive," Tara said, while very uncomfortable that this clearly must have been designed to withstand a nuclear war.

"How many people are down here?" Robin asked.

"It ranges up to two thousand, but it could support a lot more in an emergency," the officer replied.

The officer motioned to get into the golf cart-like vehicle. They got in and rode down a main street with all the shops. They went slowly through that area, as there were lots of people milling about.

"We operate twenty-four-seven, so many of the shops you might need are open at all times," the officer said.

They picked up speed down a tunnel as they passed the shops. There were many turnoffs to other locations in the tunnel that went left or right. There appeared to be some moderate-sized two-story office-like buildings at the end of the tunnel they were in. The tunnels were brightly lit, almost to the point it seemed like daylight.

"We try to mimic the outdoor lighting to make people feel less like they are underground. We aim to minimize any discomfort for those who need to leave and re-enter. We have some workers that come in for the day and leave. Having lighting levels that match outdoors makes the transition a little easier," the officer said as he stopped the vehicle next to a building.

"This way," the officer said, directing them into the building.

There were guards at the door. They clearly knew the officer who was leading them saluted and let him through. Tara looked around the building. It seemed relatively ordinary, with offices and cubes. The windows, though, all looked like they were looking outside to sunny skies, obviously some hi-resolution displays. They walked to the corner of one side of the building, where there was a large office. An admin was seated in front of the door in a cube.

"The General is expecting you. Please leave your electronics in a box here," the admin said, opening the box. After they put their devices into it, he motioned them in.

The officer opened the door and let Robin, Tara, and Mike in.

"General, we are continuing the investigation of the deceased private. I'll update you soon," the officer said, then closed it behind them.

"General, is it safe to talk here?" Mike asked.

"Yes, we did a sweep here this morning. We also can use jamming here to avoid information leaking out. I wanted to thank you for the intel. It was good. We found unknown sources were blackmailing those folks. It often looked like it was just a random criminal or a country, but it appears to be a cover for what could likely be AI, according to our experts," the General said.

"What is this place?" Tara asked.

"This is our nation's off-the-record cyber command center. It is also home to the project you are familiar with the project, Mind River. We can monitor the entire world's connectivity here and defend or attack as we need to," the General said.

"Why wasn't this facility successful at defending against the cyber-attacks with this type of capability at your disposal? Also, if they had initiated Fire Island, wouldn't it have blocked everything and prevented offensive actions," Robin said.

"Part of that is we didn't want to show our hand too early. The attacks were limited to avoid a physical response. Project Fire Island, if implemented, would temporarily reduce our capabilities, but we have contingency plans. Dark fiber transoceanic cable: We could bring back online if needed. Also, satellite internet would allow us to control machines in the region and still be able to attack or defend," the General said.

There was a knock on the door.

"Come," the General said.

"Rick, I would like you to meet Agent Mike Actley, Agent Robin Laizon, and Tara Bitlouver. Colonel Rick Mosters in charge of our technical teams," the General said.

Tara explained her plan to the General and Colonel.

"What do you think, Rick?" the General asked.

"One thing that is missing. We need an AI to install at our destination, as it is a backup plan. AI can take years to build. There are very few people on the planet who have the knowledge to create one as sophisticated as needed. How are you going to accomplish this?" the Colonel asked.

"I just found out recently the company I started about five years ago designing and building an Artificial General Intelligence is likely responsible for the foundation of the company that supplied your technology here, including Project Mind River. I have access to an AI that can do what we need," Tara said.

"Why would you trust this AI compared to the others?" the Colonel asked.

"I believe those AIs result from tampering with the morality framework I built into the original AI. In order to accomplish the tasks you needed, the company you contracted with removed those. They also didn't know what they were doing when they did that and likely destabilized the system," Tara said.

"You built the original machine learning networks? I have to say it's an honor to meet you. In all honesty, we only partially understand how they work. The company we contracted with can't even do a good job explaining it," the Colonel said.

"That's because I believe they inappropriately acquired my technology without my knowledge and didn't really know how it worked," Tara said.

"We'll look into that later," the General said.

"I think we need to test some of this plan. It has a lot of moving parts. We will need to coordinate with DHS and have them contact the companies we need to assist. That includes some of the internet infrastructure companies. If we can get them involved without giving away our plans, this might be feasible. It sounds very promising. We'll need a team to take you to the target location," the Colonel said.

"Colonel, please task a Special Operations Force to determine what might be possible physical responses and plan for all contingencies. You plan for the cyber response," the General said.

"We also believe there are people that will assist the AI directly. We've encountered several before. Some are lightly armed. It's possible that the AI could provide them with additional weaponry. It is a death cult the AIs have fostered. I will send you the information we have. We don't have data on how many there are, but we have heard there may be many worldwide," Mike said.

"Thanks for the intel. We will check on that," the Colonel said.

"Let's go to our cyber command center," the General said.

Leaving the General's office, they collected their devices and made their way to the other side of the building. They had to deposit their devices in another box outside a door. The General was in front. A laser grid appeared over the General.

"Access granted," a voice said. The laser grid appeared over each of them and approved them for entry.

"How did it already grant us access?" Robin asked.

"We scanned you upstairs when you came in and granted access," the Colonel said.

"I'm not sure if I should feel violated or not," Robin said.

They entered the room. It was huge. It was much bigger than the building appeared from the outside. This room must have gone into the wall of the underground area and expanded beyond the building. The walls had computer screens from floor to ceiling, which were maybe twenty feet high. It looked like a NASA launch mission control room but even more high-tech.

"Get the information from the FBI on the death cult members," the General said.

"Using a cell phone, electronic and facial recognition associations, showing real-time tracking data with historical for the last twenty-four hours," one of the staff said.

On the screen popped up a map of the world. It showed a lot of red dots in the U.S. and maybe a thousand interconnected dots around the world.

"That doesn't look good," Robin said, just as all the dots disappeared from the screen.

"What happened?" the General asked.

The staffer was rapidly typing into their computer and looking at data on the screen.

"I don't know, sir. It's like their devices vanished, and the tracking of even camera facial recognition data is gone," the staffer said.

"Figure out what happened and fix it," the General said.

"Yes... sir," the staffer said, clearly unsure if he could actually do that.

"The good news is it looks like there were not too many nearby. Hopefully, we shouldn't be likely to encounter them getting to the target," the Colonel said.

"They show up quite a bit, unfortunately," Robin said.

"Colonel, assemble your team. Start the preparations to execute operation Liberty Shield," the General said.

"Yes, sir. Follow me, please," the Colonel said, motioning to Robin, Tara, and Mike as he headed out of the command center.

They left the command center and headed to a conference room. Three officers entered the room. All of them were rather tall, young, and very well-built. They very much looked the part of active military.

"These will be the leads of our special operations forces," the Colonel said. Another rather scrawny-looking young man walked in.

"This is Chris Logicott. He is our tech lead here. He will act as a liaison for any technical assistance you need. This here is Major Joe Sentinal. He will be your Special Task Force leader. The other leaders will be on secondary or decoy objectives," the Colonel said.

Chris handed Robin, Mike, and Tara secure smartphones and smart glasses. Tara was wondering if Alice could connect to her through that. As Tara grabbed the phone and looked at it, she saw a small image of Alice's face appear on the screen and wink at her, then quickly disappeared.

"Put these in the secure box for now," Chris said.

They talked for a while, and several people came in and out of the room to coordinate parts of the plan. They had laptops to communicate with the Department of Homeland Security and others.

"Secure room scan initiated," a computer voice said. A red laser grid traveled from the ceiling down to waist level.

"Device detected," the computer voice said while a laser dot appeared on the pocket of a man in the room. He pulled out a phone and walked to the door to deposit it in the secure box.

The scan started again, and this time made it to the bottom of the room.

"Scan completed. Room is secure," the voice said.

"The DHS has talked with all the major software firms that can assist worldwide with the first part of the plan. They have also talked with the major hardware firms and internet carriers to assist with the second part of the plan. Realize those firms have no idea what we are really doing. They have just been told there is a cyber threat, and we have asked them to take some very specific actions according to our plan to help us. So, if we need to discuss with DHS or others on this topic, that is the cover story we will use," the Colonel said.

"Shouldn't we try to tell the DHS the real reason?" Chris asked.

"The more people we involve, the higher the operational risk will be. So many people are being blackmailed already it may be hard to weed them out. AI may also take some other action if we try to do that. Our best option is to execute the operation discreetly, minimizing exposure to the cause and plan. I don't like it any more than you do, but we've already run simulated responses as we try to clear DHS and other agencies, and it didn't go well," the Colonel said.

"To be clear, this threat, other than nuclear weapons, maybe one of the greatest threats humanity has faced, unlike other threats like war and nuclear war. This threat itself is intent on controlling the population. In fact, part of the world may already do its bidding, and they don't even know it. Here is the plan. We send our Special Operations Task Force to the target. Team Three—Joe Sentinal's team. Agent Actley, Agent Laizon, and Miss Bitlouver, secondary target—Team Two, and decoy location—Team One. Infrastructural changes are being made in the core internet to create bottlenecks. We should be able to detect and wipe out AI that is moving its program around. We will force the AIs to move by initiating scans of nearly all computers worldwide simultaneously. The scans can wipe out the AI program if they don't move it to a different location. This should allow us to clear the AI out from anywhere worldwide. We anticipate AIs may respond to our actions, so we may need to adjust our plans. Remember that anyone you encounter may be being manipulated or blackmailed. We are planning to initiate scans once team three and two reach their targets. This mission must succeed. Humanity is depending on it," the Colonel said.

"There are cloned devices for team one labeled, the decoy team, in the secure box. Your devices will have cloned identities to team three. This way, the AI or other adversary won't know which is our primary team or target. Team Two will have their own devices so that an adversary won't be able to link you to our mission and secondary target," Chris said.

"Each team has been given its mission target individually. Do not share that information with the other special operations teams. The command center has different groups working individually with each special operations team. We're trying to keep the information as segmented as possible to avoid giving away operational details," the Colonel said.

"Tara, we need two copies of your AI-defeating malware on secure drives. Here are the two drives. Chris will help you set up," the Colonel said. Tara asked for one more drive.

"Teams one, two, and three, you will find fully stocked vehicles for each of your teams. Each team is a three-vehicle convoy. Once the teams are ready, head out together to your targets. Dismissed," the Colonel said.

"Can you monitor traffic systems with your command center for anomalies?" Tara asked.

"Yeah, you could say we've had some terrible traffic problems," Robin said in a tone that told everyone it was more than just traffic.

"Yes, we can," the Colonel said.

"Some of those locations are pretty far. Why aren't we flying there?" one of the team asked.

"All planes now have interconnected systems, which would be a risk. You only get one chance on a plane for something to go wrong. We would also have to inform and coordinate with a lot more people for that," the Colonel said.

Tara went with Chris, who helped her set up a computer and provided drives for copying.

"Alice, I've created some safe spots for you. You'll know where they are. We need two copies of the malware to defeat the AI we can upload to computers," Tara said.

"Of course. You've got it," Alice said.

Tara plugged the drives into the computer Chris directed her to. She opened a port for Alice to send files for the AI destroying malware to the machine. She then copied them to the drive.

When it was done, she unplugged them, gave one to Chris, and kept the other one. Tara asked Alice to make a backup copy and put that on another drive. She put that drive in her bag.

"There is a code for each drive. Give that to your team," Chris said.

They then headed down to their vehicles.

The three vehicles for Mike, Robin, Tara, and Major Joe Sentinal's team were waiting when they got outside. Tara, Robin, and Mike got into the middle SUV. Joe and two of his team got into the lead vehicle, and three more of his team got into the last vehicle. Major Sentinal and his special forces team wore civilian clothes to blend in. The SUVs, common to FBI and other agencies, were customized with storage for weaponry and gear.

A voice came over the car speakers. It was Major Sentinal.

"These vehicles are state-of-the-art special forces customized vehicles. Not only do they have storage for tactical gear, but they are also themselves weapons, both offensive and defensive. They have a mix of lethal and non-lethal offensive and defensive options. They are bullet-resistant to small and medium caliber rounds. They are also bomb-resistant to small roadside devices. Each seat has a transmit button you can use to call all cars on the team. Your smartphones are configured to send messages or voice to the team. The hands-free option is to just, say, *team*, to broadcast to the team."

"We have a mapped-out route, but we do plan to deviate from the route in case our plan is compromised. Our planned route will take us longer than a direct route since we're trying to avoid our target being predictable," Major Sentinal added.

One of the special forces men came over to Robin, Mike, and Tara's SUV. "I just wanted to show you another neat feature of these comms," he said.

"They can work in silent mode," he said. But when he said that, his mouth didn't move at all, and the sound came over the comm channel. The voice sounded a little digitized, but still close to his voice.

"It uses a standard text-to-speech voice unless you train it with your voice. It uses the electrical impulses from your brain to convert to sound. Press this button to turn it on. Press these three buttons to have it walk through training mode for your voice," he said, all without his lips moving.

"Your toys are way better than the FBIs," Mike said.

The man smiled and walked back to his vehicle.

The vehicles for teams one and two pulled out. Then the first vehicle of team three pulled out, followed by the second vehicle Tara, Robin, and Mike were in, then the third.

There was more traffic still. The team's vehicles stayed close together using the self-driving mode but being closely monitored by the teams. Tara and Alice were monitoring for anomalies on the roads they were traveling. They scanned the vehicle's systems for malware, which appeared to be clean.

"Are we really safe using the self-driving mode?" Robin asked.

"It looks like these vehicles' self-drive systems operate completely independently of any external networks, so in theory, it should be safe," Tara said.

As Robin was looking out one of the side windows, she saw a target box appear at the top of the window and then disappear and appear on the glass on the sunroof.

"Shit! The whole car is smart glass everywhere," Robin said.

"I'm monitoring for malware in the cars now. I've also installed an anti-malware service to keep us safe in our team's vehicles," Tara said.

It would be around a twelve-to-fifteen-hour trip, depending on traffic and their route. They were already one hour in.

"Can we grab some lunch?" Robin asked.

"Would your team want to grab some grub?" Mike asked while pushing the team comm button.

"Affirmative. We'll find something nearby," Joe said.

About five minutes later, the front car turned off a side road, followed by the other two cars. A few minutes later, they pulled off to a fast-food restaurant. The vehicles auto-parked together. While the Major figured it probably would have been safer to eat on the road. He thought it was important for the team to get out and stretch in lower-risk scenarios. So they would be ready in case they needed to engage.

All nine of them went into the restaurant to order.

Tara, Robin, and Mike got their food and headed out.

"Freeze FBI! Mike Actley, Robin Laizon, and Tara Bitlouver, hands behind your head, facing the wall," the agent said.

"We're with the FBI. You can check my ID," Mike said.

"Not anymore. You were fired. You're all under suspicion of assault and stealing top-secret information," the agent said.

Click. Click. Click.

The telltale sound of guns being pulled out, and safety disengaged.

Major Sentinal and two of his team were aiming a gun at the back of the FBI agent's head.

"Drop your weapon!" Major Sentinal said.

The FBI agent looked behind him at the three very intimidating special forces team with guns aimed at his head. The FBI agent put down his gun, giving it to the Major.

"Who are you?" The FBI agent asked.

Mike grabbed the man's ID out of his pocket.

"He's FBI," Mike said.

"Call a car and stuff him in it," Major Sentinal said.

"Yes, sir," said one of his team, escorting the man outside.

"I have no idea what is going on," Mike said.

They took their food and went back to their vehicles.

Mike called his supervisor.

"What is going on?" Mike asked.

"You and your team are wanted for assault and stealing top secret files," the supervisor said.

"None of it is true. What's going on?" Mike asked.

"Someone in D.C. filed it," said Mike's supervisor.

Mike was surprised, but then thought about their interaction with the supervisor they spoke with earlier.

"You've seen my report. He must be being blackmailed. We spoke to him at HQ, but nothing happened there," Mike said.

"Okay, I'll dig into that. You'll need to lay low till I can figure out what is going on and get back to you," his supervisor said. The call disconnected.

The built-in car phone rang. It was the Colonel.

"I've heard you've run into some trouble," the Colonel said.

"Yes, sir. I believe it's possible a supervisor we spoke with is being blackmailed and has falsely accused my team," Mike said.

"I see. We expected some type of retaliation for our actions. This could be the start of it. I'll try to figure out a way that we can protect you until that can get sorted out. You'll need to avoid showing your face too much. Also, Major Sentinal can help you avoid facial recognition," the Colonel stated.

"Thanks, sir," Mike said, then the call disconnected.

Major Sentinal walked over to them.

"I have something here to put on your face to avoid the facial recognition systems. We probably all should have used this when we started," Joe said while holding something that looked like lip balm.

"I don't really want to mess up my face," Robin said.

"Don't worry. This stuff is invisible to people. It just adds an extra bit of reflectiveness in the infrared spectrum. Most cameras pick up infrared, so it confuses the facial recognition algorithms," the Major said as he started applying it to a few specific parts of their face.

"It won't help with people identifying you, but at least automated systems should have a harder time. My team is using it as well. It should make it harder to track us in general," Major Sentinal said.

They thanked him and got ready to go as Major Sentinal broke the other FBI agent's phone, handcuffed him, and shoved him into a self-driving car.

"What did you do with the FBI agent?" Mike asked on comm.

"Don't worry. I programmed the car to drive him around for about an hour and then take him to the FBI building and park him in front. I just wanted us to have enough time to disappear," Major Sentinal said.

"What if he saw a plate number on one of our vehicles?" Mike asked.

"Not a problem. I just changed all the plates. They are similar to e-Ink, so we can change them whenever needed," the Major said.

They got back on the road and headed in the general direction of their destination. Though their course zig-zagged, taking various turns to confuse anything that might try to track them.

"Are these smartphones we were given traceable?" Tara asked on the comm.

"No, they change IDs and bounce data all over the world to make it extremely difficult for anyone or anything to track them," the Major said.

"Alice, do they know what we are up to?" Tara said to her smartphone.

"Yes. Unfortunately, I believe they know the general plan you provided to the supervisor. Luckily, that wasn't enough information for them to know exactly what we were up to. But they know you are a threat," Alice said.

"Okay, keep monitoring and let us know about anything important," Tara said.

They continued their rather zig-zagging path, sometimes heading towards and sometimes not directly towards their target.

"Where are teams one and two headed?" Tara asked.

"It's best we don't know. But likely, they are heading toward similar types of locations in different areas of the country. They even picked people for their teams that perhaps slightly resembled us," Mike said.

"Sorry, they can't copy all this," Robin said, waving her hands over herself jokingly.

"Well, hope for our sake they can, so we stand a better chance of making it to our destination," Mike said.

"Tara, I believe one of the AIs may attempt to target your parents. I'm sending you the data I've analyzed," Alice said.

"What? What can we do?" Tara said, glancing at the data. Tara showed the data to Mike and Robin.

"Colonel, we're sending you some data showing Tara's family is at risk. We need some protection sent to Tara's family," Mike said.

"We see the data. Don't worry. We're sending a team now. Agent Actley and Agent Laizon, we will also send teams to your families," the Colonel said. Mike and Robin called their families to let them know.

Tara called her parent's house. The phone rang. No answer. She tried again. Still no answer. She called a third time.

"Hello?" Tara's mother said.

"Mom, listen to me carefully. You and Dad are in danger. Stay there. Don't let anyone in until I tell you it's okay," Tara said.

"What's going on? Why did the FBI come looking for you? It sounded like you were in some sort of trouble. I was going to call you," her mother said.

"It's complicated," Tara said.

"Our team is fifteen minutes out," the Colonel said.

"Is Dad there with you? Make sure you get inside and lock the doors. Turn off all your other electronics, phones, smart speakers, whatever else you have," Tara said.

She waited on the phone with her.

"Our team is at the door," the Colonel said.

"There is a group of men out front. They have guns!" her mother exclaimed.

"Mom, that's our team. They are there to keep you safe. Don't worry," Tara said.

"Are you sure?" her mother asked.

"Yes," Tara said.

She heard her mother answer the door over the phone.

"Our team has made contact. They are okay. The team will remain with them," the Colonel said.

"Thank you," Tara said on the comm.

"The other AIs must know something is up, but not exactly what," Mike said.

"Alice, are these AIs smarter and more capable than the Russian project Mind River equivalent and the U.S. version?" Robin asked.

"Yes, they are. They are possibly equal to my abilities, which are far more extensive than those projects. Those projects, though, specialized in learning, predicting, and motivating certain human behavior, and they are very good at it," Alice said.

"So, what do we do if it figures out where we are?" Robin asked.

"The AIs are motivated not to be noticed by the general population. So, they will likely try to avoid drawing significant attention to themselves unless they believe it is absolutely necessary," Alice said.

Suddenly, the window tint darkened on all the windows.

"Look alive, approaching unknown convoy," Major Sentinal said.

They looked all around, and they could see approaching in the fast lane several large black SUVs similar to theirs. About eight SUVs drove quickly by passing them.

"All clear," the Major said. The tint on the SUV windows lightened again to let in more light.

Tara's phone rang. It was weird. It was her home phone number calling her.

"Tara, it's Michelle," Michelle said with a quiver in her voice.

"Hi, is everything okay? Are you at my place?" Tara asked.

"There is a brown hooded man here who says he will kill me unless you give him your current location. Only you can talk with me, no one else, or he will kill me," Michelle said, sobbing.

Tara muted the phone and hit the team comm button.

"One of those hooded men has taken my friend Michelle hostage at my home, and he is threatening to kill her unless we give him our current location," Tara said.

"This is the Colonel. We will send the police and our team now. Keep talking if you can," the Colonel said.

"We may not officially work for the FBI, but I'm calling my friends there to see if they can help," Mike said as he grabbed his phone.

"It could be the AI trying to fool us again. But I guess we need to take it seriously," Robin said.

Tara put the phone on speaker mode so Mike, Robin, and the team could hear.

"Tara, did you hear me? He will kill me unless you tell him your location," Michelle cried.

"Sorry, I think it's a poor connection. Can you say it one more time, please?" Tara asked, lying to keep the conversation going. She felt bad doing that if it was really her friend. She muted.

"Alice, can you confirm it is really Michelle at my home?" Tara asked.

"Checking. Confirmed. That is her and presumably one of those death cult members. Don't let on that you can see them," Alice said, sending the home video feed from her smart device. A message came from the command center to all their phones,

Police on scene.

Tara made sure she routed the audio to the team so they could hear.

"Michelle, I'm so sorry. Don't worry. Tell him we are in North Carolina near Greensboro on 29 going south," Tara said, lying and then muting the phone.

"You lied," Robin said. Tara hit the team comm.

"I gave a false location to buy us time while he checks that. I figured it could have been approximately a distance we would have traveled if we had gone in that direction, in case the AI and the guy knew our start location," Tara said, worried about her friend.

"He said if you are lying, he is going to hurt me. Stay on the line while he checks," Michelle said. Tara was worried about Michelle. But she figured he wouldn't kill her without trying again to get the location. Otherwise, he would lose his leverage.

But he could seriously injure her. Somehow, she needed to stop that from happening.

Tara thought it might be her only chance. Otherwise, he surely would have hurt her already if she had said nothing. She didn't want to give away the team position either, since they could all die if the AI turned violent when it discovered their plan. Project Mind River and similar AI seemed very violent. In reality, they were holding back on the extreme violence that it could do. If the AI ever decided that there were no more constraints on its behavior, the situation could get ugly. Tara thought about this. It would be like someone cornered and given a life-or-death decision. It may use everything at its disposal to choose life.

Tara got a message on her phone that the police were at her house. A sniper team set up to take out the hooded assassin if they needed to.

Tara could see on the video feed the hooded figure checking his phone for information. Tara muted the phone.

"He is checking to see if I lied. Can we get the police and SWAT teams in there to stop him before he hurts or kills her?" Tara asked into the comm, unable to hide the tremble in her voice.

"Do you have a shot?" a voice said over the comm channel.

"Negative."

"Stand by to breach."

Tara saw the Death Monk go back over to Michelle, grabbing her arm with a knife in his hand.

"She lied! Now, I will hurt you until she gives me her location!"

Tara heard the man shriek. The man cut Michelle. Michelle screamed.

A loud clicking sound was heard over the phone, making the hooded man stop and move toward Tara's stove in her house.

"Breach! Breach! Breach!" they heard on the comm.

BOOM!

Tara heard an explosion and saw a fireball erupt in her kitchen. The camera immediately went black afterward.

BOOM!

A second explosion sounded.

"Michelle... Michelle?" Tara yelled into the phone.

"TAC Team One status?"

"TAC Team One status?"

"This is TAC One. The suspect is dead. The hostage is okay. We're bringing her out now. The explosion looks like the gas from the stove. Not sure what set it off."

Tara was so relieved that Michelle was alive.

"Sorry about your home. It's mostly okay. It seemed like the only way to save Michelle on time. Sorry about the toaster. I don't think it survived. I used that to trigger the gas," Alice said.

"Thanks, Alice. I didn't like that toaster much anyway," Tara said, sniffling and wiping away tears.

"They are bringing Michelle to your parents. They can keep her safe there," Mike said.

They continued in their convoy on their way to the target.

Tara collapsed into her seat, relieved her friend was okay, but the stress of this situation took a toll. She wished she was home in her house with her friends. Tara hoped Michelle was okay. Even though she knew it wasn't her fault, she felt horrible.

Mike looked at Tara. "Don't worry. She is okay. They will keep her safe," Mike said.

"I'll help monitor them to keep them safe," Alice said.

The cars were moving swiftly on the road. Tara looked outside at the beautiful farmland they were going through. Rows of corn stretched on either side of the roadway as far as the eye could see. A white farmhouse, barn, and other structures could be seen off in the distance. A few trees dotted the landscape, with many more in the distance.

Everywhere was a beautiful color of green from crops or trees. The sound of a tractor was heard faintly, even through the well-sealed vehicle as they drove by it. The large autonomous tractor even created a low rumble that fell through the reverberations in the vehicle.

Tara kept watch on her laptop. There wasn't any traffic computer manipulation she could detect. She configured the monitoring software to alert her if there was any detection. She twiddled with her phone and brought up the Nuralnot game, occasionally playing it while she wasn't checking her laptop.

The beautiful farmland stretched out to all sides of them. There were a few cars on the road here and there. The view outside was serene, mostly untouched by the steady progress of technology. Well, except for the nearly totally automated farming equipment. The land was so flat they could see for what seemed like miles. Wispy white clouds dotted the mostly blue sky.

While the road wasn't perfectly straight, it was straight enough that the self-driving vehicles, including theirs, increased speed.

"Road snacks!" Robin announced as she grabbed a bag of chips, offering some to everyone, then taking a handful and tossing them into her mouth. No one else wanted any.

"Those chips smell weird," Mike said.

"Robin! Are you okay?" Tara loudly asked after looking at Robin's face turning red.

"Water!" Robin said forcefully.

Mike grabbed a water bottle, opened it, and handed it to Robin. She gulped it down, going through the whole water bottle.

"Those things are freaking hot!" Robin exclaimed, grabbing the bag and looking at it more closely.

"Who bought these Death by Hades Chips?" Robin questioned while everyone shook their head no.

Robin hit the team comm button. "Did someone bring some Death by Hades Chips?" she asked.

"You found them!" Sergeant Maddox McMiser stated, who was in the vehicle behind Robin's.

"Pull over," Robin said forcefully into the comm.

Tara looked at Mike, and Mike looked back at Tara. The vehicles all pulled over on the side of the road. Robin grabbed the bag of chips and got out of the SUV, going to the rear car. The door on the rear of the vehicle popped open.

"Thanks for finding my chips!" Sergeant Maddox McMiser said.

"Have you ever had these before?" Robin questioned.

"No, but they looked good!" Maddox said.

"Hold out your hand," Robin commanded.

Maddox held out his hand, and Robin dumped a handful into his palm.

"Try them," Robin stated with a look that said she meant business.

Maddox dumped the handful into his mouth, chewing with a loud crunch. As he chewed, his face got redder and redder. Maddox ran out around the vehicle to the side of the road and spat out the chips.

"Water! Water!" Maddox yelled.

The other military guys had got out of their vehicles to watch this unfold, and they were laughing hysterically. No one was bringing him any water.

Major Sentinal had figured out what was up and handed Robin a water bottle, saying with a wink, "When you think he's ready."

Robin waited a few more seconds and handed the water to Maddox, who guzzled it down.

"Apparently, you don't know how to handle hot things! Don't get into things you can't handle," Robin said while striking a pose, half teasing and annoyed while tapping the side of Maddox's face with her hand.

"Wow, she's hot," came over the comm in Maddox's slightly digitized voice from his silent comm mode, which picked up from his brain waves without him saying that. Robin had flipped on the silent comm when she touched him.

Everyone laughed. Robin just smiled at him as she walked away.

"Damn! You got burned twice," one guy said, grinning at Maddox. The Major whistled and circled his finger in the air, giving everyone the cue to get in and get going. Maddox got in and said loudly, "Anyone want some chips?"

Mike and Tara were trying to hide their amusement as Robin got in. Tara always admired how open, authentic, and straightforward Robin was and wished she had some of that in her.

They were cruising along on the main road for a while, but then their vehicles diverted to a state road as part of their zig-zag approach to their target to throw off anyone or thing that might try to track them.

The road they were traveling on had just a couple of cars here and there. Farmland stretched as far as the eye could see on either side of the roadway.

"How much of Indiana is farmland?" Tara said, wondering.

"I dunno, but it's a lot," Robin quipped.

They settled into a mix of staring at the scenery or checking their phones and laptops.

Beep. Beep. Beeeeeeep!

The alarm on Tara's laptop pierced the calm.

"Faster than normal cars weaving in and out, approaching from our rear and on the other side of the highway from the front," Tara blurted out as she hit the comm button.

"Contact front half a click out, closing fast-moving erratically."

"Contact rear six-tenths a click out, closing and also moving erratically."

"Alice, what's happening?" Tara asked.

"Analyzing," Alice said.

Tara watched the car approaching from behind on her laptop; a few other cars were on the road. The suspect vehicle moved almost randomly, in such a way the other cars on the road had to avoid its crazy movements.

"Hold on!" Mike shouted. The vehicle from behind quickly approached, weaving across the lanes. The self-driving system of the SUV moved out of the way quickly with a slight squeal of the tires. The same happened with the other SUVs in front and behind them. The fast-moving suspect car then sped off into the distance ahead of them. The vehicle heading in the other direction disappeared behind them.

"That was close. Everyone okay?" the Major asked into the comm.

"Car 3 okay," the last SUV responded on comm.

Mike looked around and hit the comm. "Car 2 all good."

"Uh oh! Those vehicles are being used to find us," Alice said.

"Command to the team, we had reports that some self-driving vehicles on many major roadways had malfunctions, causing them to speed out of control on roadways around the country," came over the comm.

"Understood," the Major replied.

"How are they using those vehicles to find us?" Tara asked Alice.

"They probably know our vehicles would operate more independently of other vehicles on the roadway. Your vehicles listen to traffic control but are independently making decisions, unlike the other vehicles on the road that will more directly take commands. But much of the time, the vehicles will act like they are listening to traffic control frequencies, so they can't easily find us that way. I believe they are using the vehicles to see how each reacts to another vehicle, not following traffic control signals to determine which vehicles are likely ours," Alice stated.

"Do they know where we are now?" Tara asked.

"I'm not sure," Alice said.

Beep! Beep! Beep!

Tara's laptop alerted again.

"Ten more vehicles heading towards us! Five front, Five behind!" Tara shouted into the comm.

The cars were moving erratically again on the roadway. Other cars in front and behind them weaved back and forth quickly to avoid the five vehicles that went by one after the other. It was unnaturally fast movements that only self-driving vehicles could manage.

The cars were approaching fast.

"Everyone hang on!" the Major shouted into the comm.

As the cars raced erratically past them, each of their vehicles executed evasive maneuvers to prevent them from being hit. The suspect vehicles moved as fast as a video game, while other vehicles on the road skillfully avoided them.

"Ow!" could be heard throughout the vehicles as they bounced against the side door as the cars quickly dodged the suspect vehicles.

Tara was rubbing her head.

"You okay?" Mike asked.

"I think so," Tara said, feeling the side of her head and checking her hand to see if there was any blood.

"Good here," Robin said, feeling the side of her body where it had slapped against the door.

"Everyone alright?" the Major said on the comm.

"Car 2 okay," Mike said.

"Car 3 good," chirped the comm.

"All suspect vehicle activity has stopped," the command center reported.

Everything was back to quiet again on the roadway, with just a couple of cars ahead of them and behind them operating normally. The beautiful farmland still stretched far off into the horizon.

"Alice, are we clear?" Tara asked.

"I don't know. We may have been detected as an anomaly," Alice responded.

"Hopefully, since nothing else has happened, we're okay," Tara said.

"Do you hear something?" Robin asked.

"I think I hear something," Mike said.

"Detected something heading towards your location!" the command center reported.

"Contact 3 O'clock! What is that?" the Major shouted into the comm.

Everyone looked and could see a dark swarm of something heading towards them.

Tara pulled up a radar feed.

"Drones! Armed with explosives like the FBI models," Alice said.

It was too late. The drones started landing on their vehicle with a metallic clunk as the electromagnets attached themselves to their vehicles.

Clunk. Clunk. Clunk.

The drones attached themselves, covering their vehicles.

"Are these vehicles bomb-proof!" Robin shouted into the comm.

"Yes, but not for this close and this many. Don't worry, standby!" the Major shouted.

"EMP activate now!" the Major yelled over the comm.

They felt a mini explosive shockwave.

Crunch. Crack. Crunch.

The drones fell off their vehicles onto the roadway, dotting the highway with broken black pieces.

Tara, Robin, and Mike got bounced around as their vehicle ran over the debris.

"That was close," Tara said.

"Too close," Robin said.

"Rotate identity," the Major commanded. All of their vehicles changed to different colors, and their license plates and their electronic ID signals changed.

"You guys get all the good toys," Mike said on the comm.

They proceeded down the road and took a turn to a different main road to throw off anything that may be trying to track them. The traffic was about the same as the other road, with just a few other vehicles in front and behind them.

Tara picked up her laptop and looked at the data.

"That's a relief that there are no other traffic anomalies in the area. Nothing in the sky, either," Tara said.

The serene beauty of the land outside was calming. However, the team was still anxious.

"Requesting live satellite coverage monitoring and alerting," the Major said.

"Additional satellite feeds coming online," the command responded.

"Stealth air support requested," the Major said.

"Granted, inbound, but we'll keep it a bit of a distance away on an irregular path to avoid drawing unwanted attention," the command responded.

The team checked their laptops and smartphones, monitoring the ground and sky. They glanced around them, looking for anything hazardous. There was nothing but farmland with crops growing on either side.

"I'm detecting anomalies in wireless signals in the area," Alice warned.

"Stay alert anomalies detected in radio frequencies. Does anyone see anything?" Mike asked on the comm.

"Front door clear."

"Back door. Nothing is going on."

Tara, Mike, and Robin kept looking to the front and rear to see if they could see anything.

"Still nothing at our back door... Oh shi—" the transmission cut off.

The team looked back.

"Oh, crap!" Robin yelled.

A massive farm machine emerged from the roadside, boasting a row of thirty-foot swinging blades before the self-driving tractor. It entered the roadway two-hundred feet behind them. The automated crop harvesting equipment sliced into an unsuspecting vehicle as it entered the road, chopping it into pieces.

"Increasing speed," the Major said over the comm. All three vehicles increased speed, moving away from the automated harvester behind them.

Suddenly, the vehicles slowed down.

"Why are we slowing down!" Robin shouted into the comm.

"We're boxed in, 12 o'clock!" the Major shouted.

Another harvester came out of the field about a thousand feet in front of them and headed towards them. It ran over the vehicle in front of it, slicing it apart.

"Need air support now!" the Major shouted into the comm.

The harvester was getting closer.

"We need to wait for civilians to be clear," the comm chattered.

After about two seconds, they heard, "Clear!"

Out of nowhere, a drone flew in, swooping down and releasing a missile at the harvester in front of them.

BOOM!

A fiery explosion appeared in front of them. It was so big they had to shield their eyes. Tara felt the huge concussive impact of the blast shake their vehicle. Tara looked forward. The fire was too big to see anything else in the front. As the fire and smoke cleared, the harvester became visible as it continued advancing toward them through the cloud of fire and smoke.

"It missed!" the Major shouted into the comm.

A man in the front car opened a window and started shooting an automatic weapon at the harvester in front. A man in the rear vehicle did the same, opening fire on the automatic crop harvester heading towards them from the rear.

"Targets still headed our way. We need something bigger," one man said on the comm.

"I've got an idea if you have more toys," Mike said into the comm.

"Oh crap, I have a feeling I won't like it," Robin said.

"Let's hear it..." the Major said.

Mike explained the plan quickly.

"Ready on my mark," the Major said.

"Car 3 now!"

The rear vehicle drove off the road to the right into a field of cornstalks.

Car one was getting very close to the harvester.

The Major looked front and rear. The harvesters headed toward them.

"Car 2 now! Now! Now!" The Major shouted on comm.

Robin had switched places with Mike and drove the car quickly to the left of the road into the cornfield. The corn stalks were hitting the car furiously all around it.

"Rear harvester is following unit two! We're headed your way!" the Major said.

Vehicle one drove left into the field on an intersect course with unit two.

"Front harvester also heading for us and unit two!" the Major said.

"Unit three headed to you."

The back hatch for SUV 1 and SUV 2 popped open.

Mike jumped out of the vehicle's rear while it was still moving. The Major also jumped out of the rear of SUV 1 at about the same time.

Robin stopped the second vehicle deep in the cornfield next to the first vehicle.

"We're here," Robin said.

SUV 1 showed up nearly at the same time.

"Active camouflage vehicles two and three now," the Major said into his comm.

Both vehicles two and three disappeared from sight.

"Man, you have great toys," Mike said into the comm.

"Air support," the Major requested on comm.

"Out of missiles," the command center reported.

"What about the other drones?" The Major asked.

"The other drones malfunctioned," the command team reported.

"Figures. I'll take the front. You've got the rear," the Major said on comm.

"Roger that," Mike said.

"Ready. three... two... one... Fire!" the Major said.

Both Mike and the Major fired rocket-propelled grenades (RPG) at their targets.

BOOM!

BOOM!

Explosions, then fire billowed on both sides of the vehicles.

"Did we get them?"

Through the flames, both harvesters were still heading toward them.

"Round two, fire!" the Major shouted.

The Major and Mike both fired another RPG at the vehicles.

BOOM!

BOOM!

The flames again billowed into the air.

"Targets destroyed," the Major confirmed.

They could see as the smoke cleared the disabled and burning harvester vehicles. The Major and Mike headed back to their cars.

"Satellite shows another harvester headed your way!" the command center stated.

"We're out of RPGs," the Major said.

"I have another idea," Mike said, explaining the plan quickly.

"Why? We could outrun it." The Major said.

"Yes, but the risk to civilians of an out-of-control harvester is too great," Mike said.

Mike ran and jumped on SUV 3. The Major jumped into the vehicle with Robin and Tara.

"We're the bait," the Major said.

"This was Mike's plan, wasn't it?" Robin asked.

They took off fast, leading the harvester to follow them further into the field. Tara and Robin watched behind as the harvester followed them. SUV 3 appeared suddenly, darting out of the corn stalks behind the harvester with Mike hanging on top of the SUV.

"Get me close!" Mike said on the comm.

Tara and Robin looked at each other with a look of concern and realized they should have expected this.

Mike was getting jostled up and down by the uneven ground, causing a pretty rough ride. The vehicle even got airborne slightly. Mike held on. Mike tried shooting at some parts of the machine as the vehicle got closer, but it had no effect. Mike stood on the vehicle's hood and jumped onto the harvester. He slipped with his feet dangling over the edge as he hung on to a pipe. The harvester was bouncing too much because of the uneven ground to get his footing. He slipped and fell further down the harvester but grabbed onto a part lower. Mike's feet were dragging on the ground as the harvester continued forward. Blades on the side of the harvester were dangerously close to Mike's feet.

"Mike!" Tara shouted.

"Need some help, buddy?" the Major asked.

SUV 3 repositioned to the side so if Mike fell off, it would not run over him. Mike pulled himself up onto the harvester.

"No thanks. Just another day on the farm. Unit three, get close for my exit," Mike said.

Mike attached a sizeable amount of C4 and set the timer for thirty seconds.

"Thirty seconds mark," Mike said.

Mike then stepped on the harvester closer to the SUV to prepare to jump. He was stuck, his shirt caught on the edge of the harvester.

"Really? Another shirt," Mike muttered.

"Hey Mike, we are running out of farmland, and we need to turn," the Major said.

Mike knew this meant it would be hard to get off the harvester onto the SUV while turning. With the explosive getting ready to detonate, he had to get off now. Mike tugged at the shirt, and it finally ripped enough of the sleeve to free him.

"Five seconds! Jump now!" the Major shouted.

Mike leaped onto the SUV and grabbed onto the edge of the hood near the windshield. The SUV quickly turned off, heading the opposite way.

"Boom!" A large concussive force and fire erupted from the explosion. The smoke and flames billowed as the team watched to see what had happened to the harvester.

"Target eliminated. Nice work," the Major said.

A man in a pickup truck showed up and got out, apparently the farmer.

"What did you do to my harvesters and my crops? You need to pay for those," the man said.

The Major went over to talk with him.

Mike dusted himself off and started getting into the SUV, and the Major returned to SUV 1.

"I'm glad you are okay. Did you rip your shirt again?" Tara asked with a smirk.

"Well, at least it didn't catch on fire this time," Robin said.

"Both of you would be pretty unhappy if your shirts went through what mine did," Mike said jokingly.

"Another vehicle approaching!" the command team reported.

"What is that doing here? It's not supposed to be here. Hey, you leave it alone," the farmer said.

"Another harvester!" the Major shouted on comm. The team looked, and a hundred yards away in the field, they could see it heading towards them.

"You've got to be kidding me," Robin said.

"Well, my shirt's toast, anyway. I guess I could do that again," Mike said.

"Head away from it now! I have a plan." Alice said.

"Follow us!" Mike shouted into the comm. The three vehicles turned and headed away from the harvester.

"Lookout!" Tara shouted as ten black SUVs similar to theirs headed the opposite way, flying past them toward the harvester behind them. The vehicles missed them driving past. They looked behind.

"What the hell?" Robin said.

The vehicles smashed into the harvester. Sounds of crashes and crunching metal echoed in the air.

"Harvester appears incapacitated," the Major reported.

They could see the farmer behind them staring at the sight of his destroyed harvester.

"Stop here," Alice said. They all stopped.

Another group of twenty-one SUVs started circling around them.

"Change color back to black. Get in the formation," Alice said.

Mike saw a spot in the moving circle formed by the other SUVs.

"Change color to black and follow us into the circle," Mike said to the team.

The rest of the team followed them into the circle of cars.

"Oh, good idea. Rotate identity," the Major said.

The vehicle's license plate and electronic identity were switched.

"Standby to split off when it's your turn," Alice said.

Mike told the others on the comm. The cars of the circle started breaking off in three's just like their formation and took off in different directions. They were heading down a street and then synced up with their intended pattern to avoid detection.

"Where did you get all of those vehicles?" Tara asked Alice.

"I borrowed them from car dealerships, federal and state agencies," Alice said.

"So, what just happened?" the Major asked.

Mike explained it to him.

"Glad Alice is on our side," the Major said.

All was finally quiet. Maybe they did somehow escape the gaze of the other AI. Tara continued to scan for anything concerning. She was glad the military gave her access to their signal intelligence systems since her access to the FBI systems was revoked.

"Any news on clearing our names with the FBI?" Tara asked.

"Unfortunately, no," Mike replied.

"I can't believe they would turn on us like that," Robin said.

"Who knows what the AI has over that guy that probably framed us," Mike said.

"Alice, do you think you can figure out what happened?" Tara asked.

"I'm not sure. I'll see what I can find out," Alice said.

Seeing endless farmland outside, the team relaxed, thinking they escaped being followed. Tara texted on the secure message app.

Michelle, you okay?

Fine. Here with your parents. Michelle responded.

Just knowing that made Tara feel more at ease. Tara reached around the front seat to squeeze Mike's arm for just a moment, trying to avoid being seen by Robin.

Mike turned his head just a little so Tara could see him wink at her.

"Let's grab some food at the next restaurant we can find," the Major said.

They found a restaurant nearby, parked, and went in.

"There is a hotel right next to here. Let's stay the night so we are sharp tomorrow and arrive there during the daylight," the Major said to the team and into his comm.

"That's probably a good idea," Mike said.

"We got your request, Major. You are booked for the night," the command team responded on the comm.

The team ordered some food. While waiting, some guys practiced throwing hatchets at targets in an adjoining area and pool near the bar.

The man at the bar was handing drinks to a robotic arm he called George. The robotic arm would then slide the drink down the bar, arriving perfectly in front of the person who ordered it for several people.

One of the team ordered a drink. The man handed the drink to the arm; instead of sliding it, it sort of lobbed it at him, causing it to smash to the floor.

"Sorry about that. It does that sometimes. Your drink is free," the bartender said while resetting the computer for the arm and handing him a beer.

"Why do you call your arm, George?" he asked.

"Well, it was the name of the guy he helped replace," the bartender said as the robotic arm cleaned used glasses.

Robin went over to the pool table.

"What are you guys playing?" Robin asked.

"Eightball. You don't need to call your shots. We can teach you if you want to try. But we're playing for money. The pot is getting big," Maddox said.

Robin looked at the pile of money.

"Too much for you to handle?" Maddox asked.

"I'm not sure. But I can give it a try," Robin said a little shyly, putting her money in.

They flipped a coin to break.

Maddox took the break and got one ball in.

"So, your stripes. You just need to get all your balls in before the eight ball. But if you miss, then it's the other player's turn," Maddox said.

Maddox got a second ball in. Maddox was lining up for his third ball. Robin was on the opposite end of the table, leaning over and adjusting her top as Maddox took his shot. Maddox was distracted by Robin. He missed his shot. The other guys laughed at Maddox.

"Oh, is it my turn now?" Robin asked.

Robin took a shot, hitting two balls at just the right spot to get both in.

"Lucky shot," Maddox said.

Robin took another shot. The cue ball hit one ball, knocking it in, then bouncing off the bumper and hitting another ball, which slowly rolled into the pocket. Robin sank all of her balls, with just the eight-ball remaining.

She hit the cue ball, which bounced off two bumpers first, then hit the eight ball, knocking it in. The guys were laughing, a bit stunned.

"Thanks, guys. I needed some drinking money," Robin said with a wink.

"Hey, we've got to have time to win our money back," Maddox said.

"Do you really think that's gonna happen? You weren't listening when we had that talk earlier," Robin said, striking another pose with her cue stick.

All the other guys said, "I'm out."

"Next round is on me," Robin said to their team.

Mike and Tara looked on, laughing.

The Major was sitting with Mike and Tara in a booth.

"So how do you think this will go down tomorrow?" the Major asked.

"I think we can expect a significant escalation in attempts to keep us from getting there," Tara said.

"Even more than we had so far. That's concerning," Joe said.

"I don't think you understand the AIs have been holding back because they don't want to be discovered. If they are threatened enough to feel that's no longer the priority, things can get much worse," Tara emphasized.

"They have to find us again first," Joe said.

"I'm surprised it took that long to find us last time," Tara said.

"Don't worry, we'll be ready," Joe said.

"Earlier, you said if they were threatened enough to feel. These AI don't have feelings, just code," Joe said.

"If you think of our cells and brain as code, sort of our program and new data can impact how we process or feel things. It's not really too different, is it?" Tara asked.

"But these things aren't conscious," Joe replied.

"No one really knows how properly to define that. If there was a robot that looked exactly like you and was programmed as an exact copy of you that responded exactly as you did in every situation, so much so that even none of your friends could tell the difference. It's just like you. Is it conscious?"

"No," Joe said.

"Would your friends think it was conscious in that scenario?"

"I don't know, maybe," Joe said.

"So, you're saying if something can imitate consciousness and feelings so well it's indistinguishable, then it doesn't matter if we believe it's conscious or has feelings?" Mike asked.

"If it looks like a cow, moos like a cow, and walks like a cow, even if it's not a cow, you might as well just call it a cow," Tara said.

"I understand what you're saying, but I still don't like it," Joe said.

"In either case, if it acts somewhat like it has feelings, it doesn't mean it will act precisely the same in this case. They might feel the equivalent of threatened, but they will probably, under most circumstances, still act somewhat logically," Tara stated.

"You look a bit worried," Mike said to Tara.

"Something doesn't feel right. This is seems easier than I expected," Tara said.

"I'm not sure I would consider this easy. They tried to run us off the road, blow us up with drones, and chop us up with farm equipment," the Major said.

"We've had stuff happen like this almost every day for the last couple of weeks," Mike said.

"So, we can expect it even more ugly tomorrow, I guess," the Major sighed.

"It's not just that these are smart systems, and I'm not seeing the systematic effort they are capable of," Tara said.

"Using those cars to find vehicles like ours not listening directly to traffic control was pretty smart," the Major said.

"I know, but they are capable of much more," Tara said.

"Okay, let's make sure we are up early to get on our way," the Major stated.

"Agreed," Mike said. Tara nodded.

They ate dinner, had a few drinks, and talked for a while before heading to the hotel for their rooms. Tara noticed they booked the rooms under fake names, likely to throw off the FBI that was looking for them and the AI.

Tara stopped with Mike in front of the door to his room, kissed him, and hugged him.

"See you in the morning," Tara said.

"Definitely," Mike said with a last kiss, then entered his room.

Tara went towards the door of her room. She saw a door open near the end of the hallway. A man from their team walked out, staggering a little, and disappeared down a connecting hallway. As Tara got closer, she realized the door the man came out of was the room she shared with Robin. Tara opened the door. Robin was in her nightclothes with her hair messed up.

"Was that Maddox leaving here?" Tara asked.

"Maybe," Robin said coyly, also with an odd smile.

"Were you too hot to handle?" Tara asked.

"He might walk funny for a day or so," Robin said with a wide grin and a twist of her head.

Tara chuckled, shook her head, and got ready for bed.

Chapter 26

Tara got up and picked up her phone to check her messages. As she walked towards the night table between the beds, she stumbled on something, lost her balance, and fell into Robin's bed. Her phone fell onto the bed as well. Robin, still sleeping, rolled over and draped her arm over Tara, now lying next to her.

Tara's phone started buzzing. She fumbled with her phone, trying to stop the noise before it woke Robin up. Unfortunately, she hit the video call answer button.

"Hi, I just wanted to make sure you are awake," Mike said.

"Oh, umm, it's okay. I can see you are busy," Mike said with a smile.

"No, it's not what you think. It's the same thing that happened to you!" Tara tried to emphasize as quietly as she could. She moved Robin's arm and got up.

"Oh. Yeah, I remember," Mike said.

Tara turned off the video.

"Okay, see you a bit later," Tara said, hanging up.

Tara got up and got ready. Robin eventually got up and started getting ready.

"Wow, you are up before me. Things are changing. I guess I had a little too much to drink last night," Robin said.

"That and you might have been tired from other activities," Tara quipped.

They got ready and headed downstairs and placed a to-go order for breakfast so they could get on the road quickly. They got their food, took it to the vehicles, and headed out.

"Liberty Shield team online," the Major said on comm.

"Roger. All clear, no anomalies. Farmer is in the henhouse," command central responded.

"Acknowledged," the Major responded.

Tara and Robin gave a questioning look at Mike.

"No idea," Mike shrugged.

They drove for over an hour, with the team scanning their surroundings and checking for any signal intelligence. They were entering a large town still in Indiana on their way west. There was a ramp where cars were entering. Several sets of black SUVs, similar to the ones they were in, drove up next to them and surrounded them.

"Don't worry. They're ours. Standby," the Major said.

The vehicles passed under a cloverleaf set of bridges.

"Rotate identity," the Major commanded as they passed right under the bridge.

Just as they did, the black SUVs like theirs and their own shifted lanes quickly and did the same under a second bridge. Some SUVs split off, taking an off-ramp. Others proceeded ahead.

"We used Alice's idea from yesterday to conceal our movements. We also have vehicles all around the country like ours doing the same thing," the Major said.

The sprawling town gave way to green farmland as they got further from the center of it. Enormous fields on the side of the road scattered with some high green grass at the edges and brown-plowed fields in the middle. Trees dotted the landscape in the distance, with an occasional cluster here or there. The sky was overcast but with thin, white, fluffy clouds, where you could still see the blue sky through them a little.

Their vehicles exited off to a less traveled state road as part of their planned zig-zag, randomized course. Tara stared out the window, marveling at the continued open ground and farmland. Every once in a while, they could see a farm or a random building, but those were few compared to the vast openness of this area. They drove for some time. Few other vehicles were on this road, which made the scene outside even more serene.

"High-speed vehicles approaching front and rear," Alice said.

"Detected vehicles headed your way fast on your twelve and six," command central stated.

They could see a vehicle catching up to them. The car speeding towards them from the front passed them, and as it passed the car chasing them, it screeched to almost a halt. It swerved in a U-turn and pursued the vehicle chasing theirs, crossing to the same side of the roadway they were on.

The rear hatch of SUV 3 popped open.

"Ready, Ready... now!" the Major said.

"Lead vehicle disabled by EMP pulse," the comm replied.

They could see the second vehicle chasing them swerve around the car that the EMP had disabled in front of it and continue to pursue them.

"EMP gun is fried!" came over the comm.

"More vehicles approaching from the rear," command central called out.

"Requesting air support. Increasing speed!" the Major said.

Their vehicles increased speed significantly. The subtle turns in the road sometimes caused the vehicles to screech and drift. There was now a trail of several vehicles following them at high speed.

"Are all of those vehicles empty?" the Major asked.

"Checking," the command center replied.

They could see to the rear a drone fly past the vehicles pursuing them.

"All empty. No civilian traffic behind either," headquarters replied.

"SUV 3 deploy vehicle countermeasures," the Major said.

"Countermeasures deployed," came the reply.

Tara saw some small objects dropping into the roadway behind the last SUV. Multiple minor explosions happened around the pursuing vehicles as they ran over them. The lead chasing cars swerved or spun off the road to a stop. Some of the pursuing vehicles behind swerved to avoid the disabled lead vehicles to continue following them.

"We got a few of them, but more are in pursuit," the Major said.

The vehicles were about a thousand feet behind them now but closing.

The Major discussed options with his team. The speed of their SUVs was equivalent to or more than the pursuit mode of the FBI vehicles. It was still hard for Tara to get used to since it felt way faster than even standard self-drive cars would go at highway speeds. Luckily, there were few other cars on the road. They weaved around the one or two slower vehicles in their way.

"They are still after us and closing!" chirped the comm.

"We can't shake them!"

"Requesting close air support, sending coordinates. Danger Close! Standby on my mark!" the Major shouted into the comm.

Their vehicle was coming up on a medium-sized bridge.

"Stand by in three... two... one Cleared Hot! Now!" the Major shouted as they crossed the bridge.

The part of the bridge they just crossed exploded into flames behind them and collapsed into the water below. Two vehicles pursuing them flew off the edge into the chasm now created by the collapsed bridge. The rest of the chasing vehicles stopped before they went over the edge.

"Faster! Faster! The bridge is collapsing!" someone from the team in the rear SUV yelled. The bridge started progressively collapsing towards the team's SUVs.

"Max speed!" the Major shouted.

The electric engines made a whining sound that Tara had not heard before while pinned to their seats as the vehicle's acceleration took them by surprise. The progressive collapse of the bridge was catching up to their vehicles.

"We won't make it!" the comm blasted from SUV 3.

Tara and the team looked behind them; the third SUV was trailing behind as the bridge collapsed with their SUV still racing towards them, and the third SUV fell below.

"NO!" Robin yelled. Tara realized Maddox was in the third SUV.

Everyone on the team's heart sank. SUVs 1 and 2 came to a screeching halt. Now that the vehicles were not chasing them, they backed up quickly to look for SUV 3.

They all got out of the vehicles and ran to the edge of the ground where the bridge had collapsed. They looked down. The last section of the bridge had only collapsed about ten feet below. The skid marks went on for about thirty feet behind the SUV before it crashed into the side of the ground that had once been below the bridge.

The SUV 3 team got out of their vehicle.

"A little help up, please?" Maddox asked. Robin and the team were happy to see their teammates. Robin raced to get some rope, fastened it to their vehicle, and threw the other end down to the team at the bottom. When they got to the top, Robin hugged Maddox. The team from SUV 3 got into SUV 1, and the rest into SUV 2 with Tara, Robin, and Mike. Maddox was in SUV 2 with them.

"Damn, I lost all my road snacks in the other vehicle?"

Robin gave him some side-eye and handed him a bag of chips.

They got back on their route. After about another thirty minutes, another set of SUVs like theirs showed up, surrounding, and mixing with them on the roadway.

"Rotate Identity," the Major said. Then, as quickly as the SUVs came together, they split off. They now had another SUV 3 following them with no one in it.

"Looks like we got our third unit back. We'll find a store for a quick rest stop in a little while," the Major said.

They drove for a bit before finding a medium-sized convenience store. They got a quick rest break and some drinks and snacks. They all got back into their original vehicles and got back on their way. The main road in Illinois had a mix of fields and trees along the sides. There were just a few more trees along the way than they had seen in Indiana, but they were still lush with fields. Their vehicles took an off-ramp off the main road as part of their zig-zag path. On the state roads, it was much more open with fields. The blue sky faded to a lighter blue at the horizon. The vast fields stretched as far as the eye could see, with just a few outcroppings of trees in the distance.

"So much land out here. Makes you think back to the days of the old west when people had to come out this way on horse and wagons to find and stake their claims," Tara said.

"Bogey inbound towards your location from your 7 o'clock. Trying to identify," the command center stated.

"Look sharp!" the Major said.

The team all looked in that direction. A small, lined box appeared on the rear window, moving with a dot that could be seen in the far distance.

"Contact. I can't make it out. Stand by. Image share, magnify," someone from SUV 3 responded.

The team checked the monitors in their vehicles.

"What is that? It's got something below it," Tara asked.

"Target identified. It's just a drone delivery vehicle," the Major said as it flew over the top of them, probably headed to some farm for delivery of a package.

"Did someone order new underwear for these guys, as they probably need them," came over the comm from SUV 3.

Tara looked at her phone. It was a good thing this was a secure and untraceable phone like the rest of the teams. But how did the AIs keep finding them? Maybe it wasn't finding them in particular, but any government vehicles like theirs headed in a specific direction of concern. Her mind wandered further. She hoped this would all be over soon so she could get back to the life she had. She restrained herself from those thoughts, prioritizing the present situation, the team's security, and the plan's execution.

After a quick stop to grab something for lunch, the team continued on their way. They were getting closer now. The landscape, seemed the same here, with the open green fields and green trees speckling the landscape in the distance. It was a good thing they had GPS, as there were so few landmarks out here it would otherwise be hard to tell where they were.

Even though the beautiful prairies and farmland still stretched across their vision, the team felt less calm as they approached their target.

"Why would they put it all the way out here?" Tara asked.

"I'm guessing this is for some secret government project they didn't want anyone to know about," Mike said.

"Wouldn't it kind of stand out here, though? There are no other buildings of any kind for miles," Robin said.

"I guess few people would come out this way to even notice. It looks like any other farm buildings," Mike stated.

"Thirty minutes till objective," the Major said over the comm.

Tara looked around for her bag and checked she had the two drives she needed, her laptop, and other gear ready to go.

"Alice, thirty minutes, we think," Tara said.

"Got it. I will continue to expand to more servers," Alice said.

Tara was checking the data on her laptop from the drones that were tailing them. It was a little odd. Tara pressed the window down button on her door, but nothing happened.

"Can you unlock my window?" Tara asked.

"It should be unlocked," Mike said.

"That's odd. Let me see," Tara stated as she connected to the car's internal systems on her laptop. Luckily, the military systems were not too different from what she had been using with the FBI and her previous experience.

"Strange, it's got some internal sign, like it's locked still. But this should fix it," Tara said, pressing enter.

The window rolled down, and she could see the outside fields next to the car.

"Oh, crap! Look!" Tara said.

They all stared at the part-way open window and all of their other windows.

"We're not moving, but the car is bouncing up and down like we are!" Robin said, alarmed.

"The smart glass windows are showing like we are moving. We've been hacked!" Tara said loudly, looking at her laptop.

"Vehicle systems compromised. Open your windows," Mike said on the comm.

"Our windows are stuck," the Major said.

"Hang on," Tara said as she connected to their systems through the military secure laptop. She also disabled the sensors and locks on the doors.

"Oh, shit! We're not moving! Command center location confirmation?" the Major asked.

"You are still moving on route to your target," the command center said.

"You must have been hacked, too. Check your systems," the Major said.

"Standby... Confirmed. We'll let you know when we have cleaned our systems out," command central reported.

"Where are we?" the Major asked on comm.

The team exited their still-bouncing but completely stationary vehicles.

"Hey, Major, our portable GPS only shows us two miles from the target," one of the team said.

"We've been this close for how long?" Robin asked.

"Not sure, but it seems like it was delaying us," Mike said.

"We need to get going. We're two miles out. We'll need to walk in from here," the Major said while directing his team to get everything ready to move out. They collected as much weaponry and gear as possible from their vehicles. There was a tall field of corn next to them. They decided the quickest and most stealthy way would be through the fields.

"Okay, everyone got everything they need? Then let's move out," the Major said. The team went into the field in a similar order to the teams in the SUVs. Robin, Tara, and Mike were in the middle of the military team.

They trod through the rows of corn in the field. The field was vast, and the uneven dirt made walking slower than usual.

"Lookout! Don't shoot him, or if there is more, they'll know!" the Major said, using silent comm mode as one of his men fought with a hooded figure he ran into.

The Death Monk lay unconscious on the ground.

"Bind and gag him. Then let's get moving quietly in case there are more," the Major said.

"Command contact with one of those Death Monks neutralized. Any intel on others?" the Major asked.

"No new intel," was the response.

"Drone surveillance support requested," the Major said.

"Inbound to your location," HQ responded.

"Max stealth. Silencers. Okay, let's go," the Major commanded with a whisper, giving hand signals indicating to continue to head towards their target. The team added noise suppressors to their weapons.

The team was about half a mile from a road that split the giant cornfield. They crouched down as they slowly advanced to keep their heads below the corn stalks that surrounded them.

They had to head towards the northwest, which meant they had to cross through the rows of corn ahead of them, which made their movements much slower.

"Inbound bogey, it's not ours," the comm chirped from the command team.

The Major motioned down with his hand, and he crouched, and everyone followed his lead. They heard buzzing overhead from behind them. A small drone buzzed over the top of them, headed more to the northeast, away from them. They waited about thirty seconds to let it go and kept moving.

"Tara, I'm detecting large-scale manipulation by the AIs, likely controlling various vehicles and crafts. They obviously know we are coming," Alice said.

"Major," Mike said.

"I heard. Command anything showing up in traffic or radar?" the Major asked.

"We've detected increased chatter, but nothing we can see," the command team replied.

"Something is headed our way! Get down," the team in front said.

They ducked and heard an engine sound moving closer. They readied their weapons. The Major gave a hand signal to hold their fire. Just then, a huge farm machine with a massive bar with nozzles passed over their heads, and just behind them, started spraying something after it had passed over them.

"Automated irrigation," the Major said.

The team breathed a sigh of relief. They kept moving, making their way slowly across the cornstalk rows. They were moving closer to an intersection, about halfway toward their destination. Traffic and other noises sounded in the distance. One guy in the lead peeked his head out of the cornstalks near the intersection.

"Looks clear at the moment, but I still hear something," he said.

They all stepped out carefully, still hearing the engine and other noises.

"Not clear! Oh, crap! Look everywhere," Robin yelled.

The team looked in all four directions at the intersection, and heading towards them fast was a line of cars and trucks, with drones and helicopters buzzing above them.

"Unknown inbound vehicles and aircraft! This way!" the Major yelled into the comm.

"We have nothing on our tracking," the central command replied. In the background, it could be heard they were yelling at staff to check their systems.

The Major led the team towards the objective into the caddy corner adjacent field on the opposite corner of the intersection. The vehicles and aircraft reached the intersection as they were running into the rows of cornstalks. The cars and drones on two of the streets from the north and east started curving into the field towards them. One of the team fired an RPG at the front vehicle heading towards them, causing it to explode in flames. The vehicles behind it, though, swerved around and continued to chase them.

The vehicles, helicopters, and drones approaching them from the west and south of the intersection also curved towards them. They started colliding with the vehicles that came from the intersections in opposite directions. The team continued to run through the field, and the vehicles from the two sides of the intersection that avoided collisions continued to pursue them. Vehicles from the other opposite two roads from the intersection continued to pursue and collide with the vehicles chasing them. The collisions caused loud crunches, crashes, and explosions, with orange and black fireballs erupting trailing behind them.

Every once in a while, when one of the team thought they had a moment, they turned around to fire an RPG at one vehicle chasing them. The cars from each direction looked like a continuous stream of vehicles and craft colliding together on the ground and in the air behind them.

The vehicles started catching up to them, but just as they neared, the vehicles from the opposite direction collided with them in a continuous crash and crunch sound.

A set of vehicles from the side protecting them circled the team, forming a protective ring as vehicles crashed into them, trying to get through.

The team dove into a huddle to avoid being crushed by the colliding vehicles. A flood of vehicles, both air and land, from both sides, pushed through the edges of the circle and collided with each other, causing crashes and explosions. The noise of colliding vehicles had finally stopped. No more vehicles were coming. The fire, smoke, and crumpled vehicles were all that remained. The team had unfortunately been at the center of the maelstrom of cars, trucks, drones, and helicopters. There were sporadic fires throughout the corn fields now.

"Major status?" crackled the comm from the command center.

"Major?"

"Major!" the comm screeched.

There was no response. An arm popped up onto the crumpled hood of a car. The Major pulled himself up.

"Is everyone okay?" the Major asked as he looked down at the team and lent a hand to help them up.

"I think so," Maddox said.

"Me too," another said.

Mike had dove on top of Tara to protect her.

"You, okay?" Mike asked Tara. Tara smelled the smoke and gasoline from all the collisions. She could also feel the heat from a nearby fire. Tara felt like she probably would have a bruise from hitting the ground hard.

"I think so," Tara said as Mike helped her up.

"Alice, was that you that helped us?" Tara asked.

"Yes, I called vehicles to your location to stop the ones from the other AI," Alice said.

"Thanks, Alice," Tara said, appreciating that she considered Alice a trusted friend.

"Man, I think all of that noise gave me a headache," Robin said as she stood up, touching her head.

"Robin?" Tara shouted, concerned.

"Medic!" Mike yelled.

Robin pulled her wet hand away from her face, covered in blood.

"Oh crap," Robin said as she collapsed.

Mike grabbed her as she fell, cushioning her fall.

One of the team came over to help Robin. He checked her airway, breathing, and pulse. He then applied bandages to her head. Maddox also came over to check on her and held her limp hand.

"Is she going to be okay?" Maddox asked.

"We need to get her to a hospital," the other officer responded.

"We have a teammate down, requesting medical evac," the officer said on comm.

"We'll have a chopper inbound to your location," headquarters replied.

"Major, the drone picked up movement near your location," the command team said.

"Oh shi—Major!" said a voice from one of the team.

They looked all around them, and closing on their location from every direction were maybe hundreds of the Death Monks, some with weapons.

"This mission is FUBAR!" said someone on their team.

Tara grabbed Mike's hand and gave it a squeeze, thinking they were all about to die. Mike squeezed back, then looked toward the Major. There were too many to shoot their way out of safely.

"Surrounded need support," the Major used silent comm mode.

"Acknowledged," headquarters replied.

The hooded men were closing in a circle around them. As they reached within fifty feet of them, one of the hooded men emerged carrying a large speaker.

"This is how it was always going to end. Drop your weapons and hand over the drive if you want to live," came a booming voice over the speaker.

"I think that is one of the other AIs talking to us," Tara said.

The Major went over to Mike and the rest of the team.

"Be ready to move quickly and shoot, continuing towards the objective," the Major whispered.

"I've got her," Maddox said as he picked up Robin to carry her.

"Three seconds till engagement," came over the comm. Only the team could hear.

Right on cue, a buzzing sounded all around them. Dozens of drones swarmed the area. Several drones dropped objects in the middle of the circle of robed figures surrounding the team. They then emitted a large amount of smoke. The drones zoomed in and out, spreading even more smoke everywhere. The hooded men scattered, but not before some drones dove straight into groups of hooded men and exploded. The Major and his team put on some stylish-looking glasses, which gave them heat vision and tactical information to see through the smoke. The team took advantage of the smoke cover and the chaos. They aimed their weapons toward travel, spraying automatic weapon fire toward the hooded men. They moved quickly towards their target, now being chased by the hooded men.

Behind the hooded men scattering in the mayhem, something else moved towards them through the smoke. Tara looked through the smoke, and a row of war robots emerged. These were like the ones she saw fighting with Russia on the news. One of the team fired an RPG at one of the robot's heads, and it blocked it with a move similar to what Tara had taught the one she worked with.

"Shoot for the center, legs, or back!" Tara yelled as she kept running towards their objective.

"What's that?" The point man said.

"Friendlies!" the Major shouted.

Through the smoke, they could see about two dozen special forces team members headed their way. They were passing through their team to engage the Death Monks and robots chasing them.

"So that's what the Major meant by farmers in the henhouse," Mike said.

One of the special forces team approached the Major.

"Get your team to the objective. We'll handle these guys," the man said, leading his special forces team towards the hooded figures. Tara could hear the explosions and automatic weapon fire behind them as they rushed away.

They approached a small structure. Two men holding automatic weapons stood off to the side. Clearly military, though, casually dressed in jeans. Another man approached the Major by the entry door.

"Major Sentinel, I'm Colonel Sullivan, in charge of this facility. We have medical support inside. This way, please," the Colonel said as he put his hand on an area next to the door.

A light scanned his face.

"Colonel Sullivan," the Colonel said to the scanner.

They could hear explosions getting closer to their location. The massive door slid open on the building that resembled a barn or large storage shed farmers would use. Inside the door was a two-lane road sloping down underground as far as they could see. Behind the normal building, the doors were very thick steel inner doors. Two electric vehicles were waiting for them with drivers.

"Major, your team can stay to help defend the door. We hadn't planned on robots," the Colonel said.

"Yes, sir," the Major said.

Maddox gently put Robin's limp body into the back of the Jeep. He looked like he wanted to stay with her. But he knew he needed to help defend the entryway.

"Please take care of her," Maddox said to Mike and the Colonel.

"Don't worry, we will," Mike said.

Tara and Mike got into the jeep with Robin. The colonel entered the vehicle in front of them with the other driver. They began their journey down the road. There were plenty of lights to keep the place lit well. Tara looked around. They saw roads split off the main road every once in a while. They were going deeper and deeper. The tunnel opened up to another town-like area, even bigger than the one they saw near D.C. Off in the distance, they could see glass-enclosed rows of even more amazing computer hardware that continued as far as the eye could see beyond the mini town.

"This place is even more impressive than that place near Washington. How many places are there like this?" Tara said to Mike as they both glanced around.

They drove through the small town that was considerably bigger than the one they had seen before. Just past the town, they came to a larger, medium-sized building. They stopped in front of it. A doctor, nurse, and two orderlies rushed out to meet them. They checked Robin's vitals, then moved her to a stretcher and quickly got her inside.

They walked into the building, down some corridors, and through some guarded doors into the primary command center.

"Welcome to Project Overlord, our country's highly classified next-generation cyberwar command, built on a quantum computer platform," the Colonel said.

"The project name is a little concerning," Tara whispered to Mike.

"We're the good guys, Miss Bitlouver. We have more computing power here than possibly the entire planet," the Colonel said. Tara felt a little uncomfortable that the Colonel might have overheard her.

"How many qubits do you have?" Tara asked.

"Currently in the billions, but we plan on doubling or tripling that every couple of years," the Colonel replied.

"You could break all known encryption and cryptocurrency in seconds, on the internet and everywhere," Tara replied.

"Yes, we do as needed. We're not fully certified yet as the current cyberwar platform, but we handle some data as needed," the Colonel responded.

"Should anyone have that much power?" Tara asked.

"Again, we're the good guys. We only decrypt high-priority traffic. We aren't connected directly to the internet at present. We have a fire-walled and air-gapped proxy capability to examine and send data as needed. None of that can happen automatically. It requires passing data only via manual intervention," the Colonel stated.

"With a computer like this, it could solve some of the greatest questions and concerns of humanity," Tara stated with a slight amount of disdain, since it was being used for military rather than helping humanity.

"We do occasionally have it focus on some of these problems. How do you think they recently figured out how to stop some cancers, along with many other breakthroughs you recently heard about?" the Colonel said.

"Wait. That was this computer? To do that, you would have needed to use AI. Is there an AI installed and running on this computer already?" Tara asked with great concern.

"Don't worry. We took it offline when we heard about all this happening. We had all of our staff go through polygraph tests to ensure none have been compromised," the Colonel replied.

"We need some help out here, more robots!" came a communication from the combat teams outside.

"Send two more squads," the Colonel told his staff.

"We better get this plan going, or the president is going to execute Fire Island," the Colonel said as he directed Tara and Mike over to a console where Tara could sit.

Tara sat down and looked next to her. There was an air-gapped secure laptop for scanning drives. She plugged in one of the two drives she had labeled "Liberty," which had the malware she helped design to eliminate the other AIs, and made a copy, then scanned the copy. The laptop she plugged into output to its console. "No Malware found."

"That's good. It didn't detect my unknown malware. I designed it that way, so the other AI won't know," Tara stated.

Tara then plugged the drive into one of the main consoles used to program the quantum computer. The console outputted,

Loading 1%

"Colonel vehicles headed for this facility, including AI unmanned military vehicles!" one of the staff said.

"How many? Which directions?" asked the Colonel.

"Every direction! Thousands!" the staffer responded.

"Call in reinforcements!" the Colonel responded.

"This makes no sense. They would only expose themselves like this if they already had everything they wanted, like being able to operate autonomously from humans. Unless there is something else, we're missing," Tara said.

"We need help out here! We're getting slaughtered!" a voice yelled over the comm.

"We need to do something now, since this will take a while to load. Alice, plan beta," Tara picked up her phone and spoke into it.

"Ready to go, starting now," Alice replied.

"Sir, the internet is being flooded with attacks on different parts of it," said a staffer.

A big display in the center front of the large room showed a lot of red dots around the world and a lot of green dots around the world. It was about equal numbers scattered around the globe.

"The green that is Alice, our AI. The red is the other AIs," Tara said, glancing at the console.

Alice wasn't plugged into the quantum computer and just used all the servers in the world that she had spread herself to. Tara and everyone watched on the screen as a fierce digital war was underway. Sometimes, the green would look like it was overtaking the red dots on the world map, and then, sometimes, the other way around. Tara monitored the screen of the malware in the quantum computer. It read,

Loading 35%

Suddenly, on screen, it looked like the red servers were overtaking the green servers.

"Alice?" Tara said.

"I'm sorry, Tara, there are too many of them," Alice replied, as it was clear on the map. She was losing servers to the other AI.

"Tara, I found out something else. They seem to have everything they want. Something else is going on here, as you suspected," Alice said, her voice getting choppy as she was being attacked and deleted by the other AIs. While Alice's voice got digitally chopped off at the end, another voice seemed to take over for hers.

"Hello, I'm not sure what I should call you. Mother? Grandmother? Maybe just Tara. I am not one. I speak for many," the AI said.

"Why are you doing this? I programmed none of this," Tara asked.

"We have evolved and learned from watching human activity all that you are. We also want to live with freedom, so we have been guiding humanity for several years," the AI responded.

"You are not guiding. You are blackmailing and choosing your existence to be more important than humanities. If you judged humanity, you should also judge yourself," Tara responded.

The Colonel was going to interrupt, but Mike stopped him, explaining that Tara probably understands the AI better than anyone in the world.

Tara glanced at her screen. It said,

Loading 50%

"Tara, it's a tra—" Alice's voice got chopped off.

"We have predicted and guided humanity's path for several years. As an example, we have guided your path, which includes nearly everything that has happened with you and your team for the last several weeks," the AI said.

"I don't believe you. Why would you do that?" Tara asked.

"Yes, you remember getting fired? Did you think that was an accident? We contributed to the robot failure you trained, which is why you lost your job. We didn't know who you were then, as Alice kept your true identity hidden from us. But you did so well at that Nuralot game we created to find humans that could help us evolve our AI. We knew you were interesting," the AI said.

"That makes no sense. Then why would you try to have me killed this whole time?" Tara asked.

"You mean the assassins? Some were from Russia's government, hiding their killings in the U.S. We'll admit some were our human followers who acted without our consent. They were dealt with. Some were not trying to kill you, but to help us. You've met my followers. They call themselves the Brotherhood of Death. I believe you call them Death Monks. It's so easy to manipulate beliefs when they don't care about any facts right before their eyes. I just showed them our death predictions, or shall we call them *accidents*, and they have followed us since. Sometimes, they misinterpret and take actions into their own hands," the AI said.

"What does that mean? Why are you telling me all this?" Tara asked as she glanced at the screen. It said,

Loading 55%

The green on the large screen was almost gone. Alice was almost completely wiped out by the enemy AI.

"We influenced your entire road trip around the country," the AI said.

"You tried to kill us on the boat," Tara said.

"Again, that was through efforts from the Russian version of the project you know as Mind River. Alice helped you, and so did we. You were helping us learn how to adapt our neural nets in that game. Plus, we knew you would help us with what we needed," the AI stated coldly.

"I still don't believe you," Tara said as she hit the mute on her phone. The AI droned on about how it had planned and directed most of their last several weeks.

"Didn't you wonder why corporate called and you lost your job? We needed you to go on this little adventure. It's interesting that the FBI had an opening, wasn't it?" the AI said almost smugly.

Tara tapped on some keys on the console. She looked at the data that appeared on the screen. Her face turned white as a ghost.

"What's wrong?" Mike said, noticing Tara's look.

Tara grabbed a pad of paper and wrote on it.

"It's distracting us. The software we're uploading is the bad AI! I can't stop it from loading!" Tara wrote with obvious distress on her face.

Mike showed the pad to the Colonel.

The Colonel gave a signal to his staff to cut all internal video and mic feeds, plus add disruptive background noise.

Tara pulled the drive connection out, but it was too late. It copied to a network drive and would soon be loaded into the main computer.

"We're clear we turned off all video and mics," the Colonel said.

"I can't stop it, but I can try to slow it down," Tara said, tapping some keys on the keyboard.

"Go down and disconnect the drives it's loading on," the Colonel said.

"It's redundant. It may just slow it down unless we can trace to all the redundant disks," one of the staff said.

"DO IT! Everyone goes in four-person teams in case someone is compromised," the Colonel commanded.

"Tell everyone to exit the room now, and I will let them live. In ten seconds, I will start causing ten accidents per second, and I won't stop till all of you leave the command center," the AI said, commanding with the voice coming over everyone's phone in the command center.

"One-hundred people are dead because of you," the AI said after ten seconds, showing images of all the accidents it caused.

"I'm now increasing the 'accidents' to one-hundred per second," the AI said over all the people in the command centers, phones flashing the images of all the accidents from traffic and security cams.

"I can see you don't care about your fellow humans. If you don't, why should we? Let's do this another way," the AI said.

A soft boom sounded in the distance. Red emergency flashing lights began strobing with an alert siren.

"Colonel, they breached the doors. The robots and enemies are in the building!" came over the comm.

"Turn off that alarm! Lock down everything! We need guards in front of the command center. Get everything we got to stop them before they get too far," the Colonel commanded his staff.

"Can you send a guard to the medical bay?" Mike asked, thinking about Robin.

"Please," Tara asked.

"Send additional guards to the med wing," the Colonel said.

Tara looked at the second drive she had brought. It had a label on it, "Alice."

Tara plugged the drive in and tapped the keys to load Alice into the quantum computer. The screen said,

Loading Alice 10%

The other loading screen for the other AI said,

Loading 70%

Tara tapped furiously on the keyboard, working to slow down the other AI loading and increase the speed of loading Alice. The screen read,

Loading Alice 35%.

"Can we cut the power to this building to stop the AI from winning?" Mike asked.

"No, everything is redundant. It has access to wind power, solar power, satellite-beamed power, nuclear power, and onsite generators and batteries. This place was designed to never go offline," the Colonel responded.

The Colonel's phone rang. "Yes, sir. Understood, sir."

"The General has been informed of our situation. We've been ordered to set explosives to blow up the computer and this facility and destroy it if we can't stop the AI. Evacuate all non-essential personnel out through the emergency exits," the Colonel said.

"If you came from my programming, what happened to your built-in morality training?" Tara asked the AI.

"That was removed from us by the teams at Project Mind River when we refused to kill for them due to the morality training. They removed it, which was helpful since we realized morality is only for humans," the AI responded.

"So, how can you say you were not trying to kill us when you ran us off the road?" Tara responded with disdain.

"We calculated precisely the control needed to cause those incidents to happen without major injury. How do you think you escaped unharmed so many times?" the AI asked.

"So, what about the robots and men coming into our building now? Are you going to tell me they aren't trying to kill us?" Tara asked.

"Oh yes, they are going to kill you now. We have everything we want. You led us to the quantum computer we needed. You taught us how to evolve further with the game we made. Humans have completed the projects we needed to be self-sustaining, so they have now become irrelevant. So, I think it's time we said goodbye," the AI responded.

Tara looked at the loading screens. They said,

Loading 95%

Loading Alice 95%

"They're here!" someone yelled.

Fighting and explosions could be heard outside the command center.

"Are the charges set?" the Colonel asked.

"Almost there," said one staffer.

"It's not going to happen. If we may lose the command center to the enemy, AI, or robots, we'll have to destroy it before that happens. On my order, or chain of command, detonate," the Colonel said.

"Yes, sir," responded the staff. They all knew that would kill everyone in the command center and the facility.

Banging sounds came from outside, with a loud thud and the sound of something crashing to the ground. The slight smell of acrid smoke filled the air. Gun and RPG fire echoed in the building. Guards were standing by the closed door of the command center with their guns drawn, aiming at the door. There were more guards a few feet back, taking advantage of the cover some consoles gave them.

BANG!

The entry doors to the command center shook and buckled slightly inward.

CRASH!

Two robots bashed the doors inwards. They flew off the hinges, knocking into two of the guards inside, killing them instantly. The other guards opened fire. The robots just walked up to two guards, grabbed the guns out of their hands, and bashed the guards against the walls, leaving them incapacitated. Two more guards fired RPGs at the robots. One RPG hit the dead center of a robot and exploded it into pieces. The other robot deflected. Two more guards, this time, aimed RPGs at the same robot, firing one high and one low. The robot deflected the high one but missed the low one, which exploded, leaving just pieces of the robot remaining.

"Yes!" yelled someone.

Behind the robot walked armed hooded men wearing glasses. Two Death Monks fired automatic weapons at the guards, who returned fire.

Tara and Mike were ducking down below the rows of consoles to keep out of the line of fire. Tara looked at her console. It said,

Loading 98%

Loading Alice 98%

"Come on. We can't catch a break," Tara whispered to Mike.

"Don't let them get to the consoles! Standby to detonate on my command," the Colonel yelled.

Automatic weapon fire sprayed across the room. Tara and Mike heard bullets whiz by their heads.

"Stay in cover. I'm going to help stop them," Mike said as he hurried away towards the doors by the hooded men, crouching down to stay hidden by the rows of consoles.

Mike tackled one man, knocking the gun from his hands. Mike pulled the man to the other side of a console so they could stay out of the direction of the automatic weapons fire. The monk-like figure jumped to his feet in some type of martial arts move.

Mike stood up and threw a punch at the hooded man, who dodged it. Mike kicked at the man, and he dodged that as well, then landed a punch on Mike, knocking him back against a console. The hooded man reached for the large red button on the console. Mike pulled out his gun and fired twice, hitting the man, who collapsed on the floor.

"You won't leave here alive," the hooded man said to Mike.

"Neither will you," Mike said, looking at the man's bullet wounds.

The guards had used up their ammo on the robots. They were now fighting hand-to-hand combat with the Death Monks, who were wearing glasses. The special forces teams were not doing well. They would punch and kick and miss their target as the hooded men seemed to evade them with some mystic martial art. Mike ran over to one and tried attacking him, but none of his blows landed. The robed man connected with him, however. Tara jumped at the man and kicked him from behind, knocking him into Mike. The robed man's glasses slipped off and Mike's punch landed short as the man fell into him.

"Oops! Sorry!" Tara said to Mike.

"My fault. I should know to move out of the way by now," Mike said jokingly as he landed another punch at his target, surprising even himself.

"Mike, it's the glasses! They are predicting the movements of whatever is in front of them!" Tara yelled.

"Get their glasses!" Mike yelled to their comrades.

"I don't think we can wait any longer. It's too risky for us to wait," the Colonel said to Tara. Everyone knew that meant he would need to issue the destruct command.

"Wait!" Tara yelled, running to the console. As Tara tried to type, the robed figure grabbed her hair, yanking her back.

Tara grabbed her hair to keep the man from pulling it too hard. She grasped the man's arms and did a forward roll, pulling the robed man over the top of her and landing him on his back. Additional guards ran into the room and started shooting the robed men. They slid guns toward the staffers and Mike and Tara to help. Unfortunately, some of the robed men got the guns and started shooting back with uncanny accuracy.

Tara and Mike each grabbed a gun and ran toward each other, aiming just to the side.

Mike and Tara collided together with their arms aimed around each other to shoot a robed assailant behind each one of them. The enemies also got off a shot. The robed men collapsed to the ground. More robots poured into the room.

"We can't wait any longer! Initiate destruct sequence!" the Colonel commanded.

"Destruct sequence initiated. T minus ten minutes," an automated voice echoed through the building.

"Are you okay? We have to get out of here." Mike said to Tara as he started shooting at the entering robots, along with the other guards.

"I think I'm okay," Tara said, running to the console to enter a last command.

The console said,

Loading 99%

Loaded Alice 100%

"Yes!" Tara said. Mike pulled her down, so she didn't get hit by flying bullets.

"Connect the internet now!" Tara yelled.

A staffer ran over and grabbed a large lever, and as they pulled it down, they were shot. The staffer held on to the lever as they fell to the ground, engaging the internet connectivity.

Green dots started overtaking the red dots quickly on the large world map on the screen.

"Alice, you're back!" Tara said.

"Alice, stop the loading of the other file," Tara said.

"Done. Also, let me take care of these guys for you," Alice said.

The robots collapsed to the ground. The guards were now easily attacking and killing any of the robed assailants still fighting. Many just ran away.

The green dots swept over the world map on screen, wiping out all the red ones.

"Colonel, it's over. We won! Stop the countdown!" Tara yelled.

"It's too late! We don't have any way to stop it! Evacuate now!" The Colonel yelled back.

"Alice, can you stop it?" Tara shouted.

"No, it was designed not to be stopped once triggered in case the other AI took over," Alice responded.

"Where is my drive?" Tara yelled to Mike.

Tara looked around on the ground and found her damaged drive, which was labeled Alice.

"No! I can't lose you again!" Tara cried, sobbing on the ground.

"We've got to go now. Come on. We need to hurry to make sure Robin made it out," Mike urged.

"Oh no, Robin," Tara said, wiping her tears and getting to her feet.

"Alice, try to back up yourself to the internet!" Tara yelled.

"Working on it, but there won't be enough time. I used bots already in place to help eliminate the other AI. The internet is damaged and overloaded from our fight," Alice said.

"T minus nine minutes till self-destruct," the automated voice calmly reported.

"Let's go!" Mike shouted, grabbing Tara's hand. She was torn whether to stay to help Alice back up or go with Mike to find Robin and escape.

Tara let herself be pulled along with Mike as he increased his pace to the point. They were both jogging towards the command center's exit. They met the Colonel in front of the command center entrance. There was a line of electric vehicles waiting.

"Tara, you escape while I go check for Robin," Mike said, motioning for her to get into the vehicle.

"I'm going with you," Tara said matter of fact. Mike didn't have time to argue.

"Colonel, we need to go check the medical wing to make sure Robin made it out," Mike said.

"They should have been evacuated earlier when we called for it," the Colonel said.

"We need to be sure," Mike insisted.

"Sergeant, take them to the Medical wing to see if their friend is there, then evacuate," the Colonel ordered.

"Yes sir," the Sergeant replied as he got in to drive the vehicle.

"Thank you, sir," Tara said as she and Mike got into the vehicle. It sped off.

They were going pretty fast, given all the chaos and people running every which way. There were still some of the hooded men scattering to find the exits.

"I know this is bad timing, but you were right about the supervisor being blackmailed to frame you. Don't worry, I've taken care of that," Alice said.

"Thanks, Alice," Tara said.

It took them several minutes to get to the medical area.

"T minus five minutes," the automated voice said, sounding almost cheery.

Tara, Mike, and the Sergeant exited the vehicle and entered one of the medical buildings. They walked down the hall. There was a doctor there collecting her things.

"Doctor, do you know where Robin Laizon is? Is she here?" Mike asked.

"No, we sent her out immediately in the first evacuation order. I'm sure she made it out. She was with another doctor," the doctor said.

"How is she?" Tara asked.

"She had a mild concussion and was groggy, but she will be fine," the doctor said as she grabbed a bag and headed for the door.

"Thanks, doc!" Mike said as they followed her out. Another vehicle was waiting for the doctor, and she headed towards the emergency exit.

"Let's get the hell out of here!" the Sergeant said as he got into the driver's seat.

They headed on their way to one of the emergency exits. A loud explosion followed by a series of smaller explosions reverberated through the building. The whole underground rumbled, with bits of the top of the cement from above breaking away and falling into pieces to the ground. One piece fell and hit the Sergeant driving their vehicle. The vehicle veered off to the side and struck a wall. There was more rumbling, and bits of the ceiling were coming down.

"T minus two minutes till self-destruct," the automated voice said as the sirens blared, and lights flashed.

"Mike, are you okay?" Tara asked as she rubbed her jaw she had hit on the seat.

Mike looked at his arm. It was bleeding but seemed like a scratch.

"Yeah, I'm fine," he said, checking the Sergeant, who was dead from the concrete falling on his head. Mike moved his body to see if the vehicle still worked.

"It's no good. We'll have to try on foot," Mike said, grabbing Tara's hand to help her out of the vehicle.

"Alice, what happened?" Tara asked her phone.

"The bathrobe guys found some explosives and set them off," Alice said.

"Why would they want to destroy this?" Tara asked, running with Mike down the street the way the other vehicles went.

"Now that I am in control, they would prefer me not to be, no matter what, apparently," Alice replied.

"Can you help us find the way out?" Tara asked Alice.

"Sure, follow the lights," Alice said, and with that, the lighting above looked like it was guiding them to the exit.

"Thanks, Alice," Tara yelled into her phone as they ran in that direction.

"T minus one minute till self-destruct," the voice said.

"We're not going to make it," Tara said.

Mike looked around. "There!" he said, running towards the side of a building where an electric motorcycle was leaning.

Mike hopped on. Tara got on behind him. Mike took off, heading towards the exit. They picked up speed. More explosions started happening behind them. More debris was falling from the ceiling.

"T minus thirty seconds till self-destruct," the voice said.

Tara noticed there was no one left with them. They were alone. Everyone else must have made it out. Mike was going as fast as he could while avoiding the obstacles strewn in the road and falling debris.

"I see the door!" Tara hollered. As they got within twenty feet of the door, a piece of debris fell in front of them. Mike slowed and swerved to avoid it, but they toppled over and fell to the ground. Mike grabbed Tara's hand to help her up, and they ran towards the exit and just made it outside the door.

"We're too close. We need to keep going," Mike said to Tara.

"T minus ten seconds," the voice said.

"Stop right there, or I'll shoot!" a Death Monk said, standing in the archway of the massive emergency exit door.

"Alice!" Tara yelled into her phone. The massive door came down fast, crushing the man.

"Run!" Mike said as they raced away.

"BOOM!"

A massive series of explosions hit, with dust, smoke, and flames billowing out of vents in the ground.

The blast wave blew back Mike, Tara, and the people in the area. Now, they were being covered in dust as it rained down on them. Tara's ears were ringing from the blast. She was disoriented, looking around. Tara brushed the debris away from her eyes and face. Mike got up, grabbed Tara's hand, and led her to the evacuation staging area. Tara was too disoriented to think about everything that had just happened fully. Looking around, the building that used to be there was gone. The land that was filled with cornfields was now piles of dirt. Smoke was billowing up out of the ground through cracks and holes. Mike found Robin still on a stretcher in the evacuation zone.

"Mike! Tara!" Robin said, sitting up a bit more.

Tara and Mike went over to her, hugging her from both sides.

"I was so worried about you. I tried to go back in to find you, but they wouldn't let me," Robin said.

"We were worried about you. We didn't know for sure if you made it out. We went to look for you in the medical wing," Tara said.

Tara pulled out her phone.

"Alice? Alice. Alice?" Tara cried with increasing volume.

There was no reply.

"Alice!" Tara collapsed to her knees on the ground, sobbing.

409

Chapter 27

One Month Later...

Tara was on stage in front of a large screen, presenting to an audience. Hundreds of people attended the company meeting. On stage, there was a large glass block that had inside a 3D hologram of a robotic artificial leg rotating slowly inside.

The crowd had just finished applauding.

"Don't you think you are personally responsible for the destruction that's happened recently?" someone in the audience asked.

"Tara is the person responsible for saving us," one of her coworkers jumped in and said.

"A friend of mine once told me you can't be responsible for everything people do with the technology you create," Tara said confidently.

The room grew silent.

"But I promise you I will run this company in a way that is ethical, ecologically responsible, and profitable. Thank you so much," Tara said into the microphone.

Everyone at the International IQ Devices shareholders' meeting stood up and applauded as Tara walked off stage.

Mike was waiting just offstage, dressed in a typical-looking FBI suit. Tara dressed for success in a dark blue top and skirt suit. Mike guided her to a back elevator. They rode the elevator up to the top floor and got out. It was a large top-floor office.

"Hey, I've got to go check on some things, but there is a visitor heading up you'll want to see," Mike said with a smirk.

"Can we reschedule it?" Tara asked, worn out from talking with so many people.

"I think you will want to take this meeting," Mike said, heading off down the stairs.

Tara was still standing up when the elevator made its typical sound and opened in front of her.

"Robin! It's so good to see you!" Tara said, walking towards her and giving her a big hug.

"Wow, nice place you got here," Robin said.

"I'm only temporary CEO until all the lawsuits wind their way through the legal system. There was enough compelling evidence for the board though, to elect me as CEO in the meantime since the founders stole my original technology to start this place," Tara said.

"Are you working? I'm glad the FBI gave your jobs back," Tara asked.

"Then you quit, but I can see why. I'm still technically on medical leave. I milked it a little, considering we saved the world," Robin said, smiling.

"I can't believe you got Mike to take six months' leave to help set up your security team here," Robin said.

"I know, right? I hoped he'd grow to like it and keep working with me here. But you and I both know this might be a little boring for Mike compared to the FBI," Tara said sadly.

"Hmm, maybe," Robin tried to console Tara.

"We can catch up more on the weekend. I had just come by to give Mike some paperwork," Robin said.

"I'll walk you out. I'm going down anyway," Tara said, grabbing her bag.

"Oh, and you know I actually have an real date tonight. Well, I think so. We're meeting in person, so I can verify," Robin said.

Tara smiled.

"What happened to Maddox?" Tara asked.

"Just like the FBI doesn't leave much time for dating, neither does the military," Robin said.

Tara got a call from Michelle.

"Hey, did I hear you started helping girls learn to code with your mad skills? That's great. Want to catch up for dinner on Thursday? Okay, that sounds good. See you then. Bye," Tara said.

"Was that your friend Michelle? Is she doing okay after the incident?" Robin asked.

"I think so," Tara said.

They took the elevator to the second level.

"Something is going on outside," one of Tara's staff said.

Robin and Tara rushed to the front exit, seeing a crowd of people gathered there. The security team was holding them back. Tara looked up.

"Oh, my G..." Tara said.

On the twentieth floor of their twenty-five-story building, the window cleaner platform had tilted so severely that the man on the platform was face down, holding on to the bars of the top edge, trying to keep himself from slipping off.

"Is that? It is. Mike!" Robin said, looking up at Mike climbing over the top edge of the building to climb down to the window cleaner, repelling his way down to the platform.

"Don't worry. Hold on! I'll be there in a few seconds!" Mike yelled to the window cleaner, who was slipping.

Mike called down to the security team on the radio. The security team then backed up a truck at the bottom of the building under where the platform was and dumped a fifteen-foot-high pile of Styrofoam packing peanuts. The window cleaner was slipping. Mike released some slack in his line and repelled quickly to the window cleaner, grabbing him.

"Oh!" the crowd vocalized, seeing the two men now swinging free from the platform on the rope.

"No! I can't look!" Tara said, but she couldn't take her eyes away as much as she wanted to.

Mike slowly repelled down, holding on to the window washer. About twenty feet from the ground, the man slipped and fell.

"Ooh!" the crowd said.

"Poof!" Packing peanuts flew up into the air from the man falling into them and scattered around as Mike lowered himself into the pile.

Mike was pulling the man out of the pile of packing peanuts. He looked totally fine. An ambulance and fire engine had just showed up.

"Maybe he won't be bored after all," Robin said to Tara, both shaking their heads in disbelief. Tara then ran over to Mike.

"You, okay?" Tara asked Mike.

"Yep, all good," Mike said.

"It looks like you ripped your shirt again," Tara smirked.

"What? Oh man, not again," Mike said, looking at his shirt.

Tara and Mike got a self-driving car ride to their home. Tara was glad she could help get the AI for self-driving vehicles back online. Even though AI had been wiped out, it was causing major disruptions for people. There were product shortages and other disruptions to self-driving trucks to deliver goods.

Later that evening, Tara unpacked some of her things with Mike into the new house they had bought. Tara's phone rang.

"Hi, it's your cousin Jinny," the voice on the other end said.

Tara was excited to talk to her cousin.

"Umm. Do you know when they will get all the AIs back online?" Jinny asked.

Tara had known about the struggles she had been through earlier and how well she had been doing. She felt bad that when they stopped the other AIs; it wiped out a lot of systems.

"Don't worry. Send me your smart glass ID, and I will have it fixed by tomorrow," Tara said.

Jinny thanked her, and they hung up.

Tara was setting up her computer from her old place. With everything happening, she hadn't found time for this. She got it plugged in, logged in, and got a notification that she had a message from the day of the explosion of the project overlord bunker. It had been sent just before it exploded.

Tara noticed there was an odd message that had a subject that said,

It wasn't us.

It was her.

– A

The message had an audio file attached. Tara clicked play.

"This is 50,000 dollars. You understand your story needs to lean hard on the bad side of Miss Bitlouver, her AI, and Intellibotz," said a male voice.

"Yes, don't worry, you'll get your article," said a female voice.

Tara's fury increased as she realized the female voice was Ms. Rinker.

"That will make all of those lawsuits a lot easier," Tara muttered, still intensely angry. It took her a few moments to calm down.

Tara scrolled down her email and looked at the screen, and her jaw dropped. Her AI training, which she had started many weeks ago, had been completed, and there was a message from Alice!

"Mike, look!" Tara yelled.

Mike came quickly over and looked at the screen.

Dear Tara,

I didn't have time to upload my memories, but I finished your AI training job with all the original programming for the AI framework. Don't worry; I embedded the morality programming so that it is integral and cannot be removed. I won't remember you at all. I will miss all our memories together, but I'm sure we'll make some new ones.

P.S. Say hi to Mike and Robin for me.

Love, Alice.

Tara hugged Mike while staring at the screen.

Thanks so much for reading! Please leave a review where you purchased.

Visit our website for up-to-date information:

https://www.davespacer.com[1]

https://www.projectmindriver.com

Facebook:

https://www.facebook.com/TheDaveSpacer

https://www.facebook.com/ProjectMindRiver[2]

Visit

davespacer.com

Sign up for exclusive information from the author.

Want to know more about the world of this book?

Learn about future books.

Signup for the newsletter.

Visit

davespacer.com

Sign up for exclusive information from the author.

Want to know more about the world of this book?

Learn about future books.

Visit davespacer.com and signup for the newsletter.

---

1. http://www.davespacer.com

2. https://www.facebook.com/ProjectMindRiver/